W9-BEP-970

## High Praise for
## MARINE ONE

"Riveting." —*Dallas Morning News*

"An outstanding thriller."
—*Publishers Weekly* (starred review)

"Gripping." —*Booklist*

"[An] intelligent political thriller that's full of surprises and insider knowledge." —*National Review*

"*Marine One* has good lawyers, evil lawyers, a fascinating premise, and an inside look at the down and dirty world of litigation where billions are at stake. Add in a dead president and shadowy assassins and you have a very good read." —Phillip Margolin, author of *Fugitive*

"A mystery with political intrigue, courtroom drama, and international controversy. Huston is a solid storyteller and brings it all to bear."
—*School Library Journal*

"This novel will have you reading on the edge of your chair, and maybe beyond. [It's] almost impossible to read it fast enough." —Bookreporter.com

Also by
**JAMES W. HUSTON**

*Marine One*

*Secret Justice*

*The Shadows of Power*

*Fallout*

*Flash Point*

*The Price of Power*

*Balance of Power*

# FALCON SEVEN

*James W. Huston*

St. Martin's Paperbacks

This is a work of fiction. All of the characters, organizations, and events portrayed in this novel are either products of the author's imagination or are used fictitiously.

FALCON SEVEN

Copyright © 2010 by James W. Huston.

For information address St. Martin's Press, 175 Fifth Avenue, New York, NY 10010.

ISBN: 978-0-312-54413-3

Printed in the United States of America

St. Martin's Press hardcover edition / May 2010
St. Martin's Paperbacks edition / July 2011

St. Martin's Paperbacks are published by St. Martin's Press, 175 Fifth Avenue, New York, NY 10010.

10  9  8  7  6  5  4  3  2  1

*For Shannon Marie Huston*

The President is authorized to use all means necessary and appropriate to bring about the release of any US or allied personnel being detained or imprisoned by, on behalf of, or at the request of the International Criminal Court.

American Servicemembers' Protection Act,
22 U.S.C. § 7427 (2002)

# PROLOGUE

"What the hell was that?" Rawlings asked as he threw the stick of the F/A-18F Super Hornet to the left and pulled the jet around hard.

Dunk looked up from his radar in the back seat and braced against the building G-force. "Small arms," Dunk grunted as he watched muzzle flashes below in the dark.

"Obviously," Rawlings said. He pushed the throttles up full to military power.

Duncan glanced at the flashes far below them, barely visible in the distance. They were definitely shooting. He glanced at the altimeter. "We're way out of their range."

"They don't know that."

Dunk rolled his eyes. "Actually, they probably do."

"Then why? Wasting fifty of the ninety bullets each of those shitheads has for fun?"

"Beats me. They're just not—"

*"Call Fireplug. Ask 'em if they're expecting anything around there."*

*Dunk considered. Fireplug was the E-3 AWACS controlling all the air traffic over the mountains of Afghanistan and in particular where they were, the border with Pakistan near Waziristan, as it was called, which had declared itself to be part of the FATA in Pakistan—the Federally Administered Tribal Areas. Dunk and the other aviators thought it should be called the Non-Federal, Non-Administered, Non-Tribal Area. It was mountainous and full of al Qaeda and Taliban.*

*Dunk checked their fuel. They had a long way to go to get back to the carrier. "Let's head home. We're almost bingo."*

*Raw dipped the right wing of the Hornet violently and transmitted to his wingman,* "Bronco—you see that small arms fire?"

*Bronco, the pilot of the other F/A-18 in the two-plane flight was also a lieutenant, senior to Rawlings but junior to Duncan. Bronco replied over the encrypted channel,* "No threat. They're near the border."

*Rawlings said to Dunk again,* "Call Fireplug."

*"I'll call them when I feel like it. You just fly the plane."*

*"Call them! Get us cleared in there!"*

*Dunk gritted his teeth.* "Fireplug Control, Whiskey Hotel 09, over."

*The E-3 answered quickly.* "Whiskey Hotel 09, Fireplug Control, go ahead."

"We're picking up some small arm—"

*Rawlings interrupted and transmitted over Duncan,* "—substantial small arms—"

*Duncan continued,* "—about four miles from us, on a radial of 044. Do you want us to investigate? Otherwise we're RTB."

"Stand by."

*Rawlings continued his jerky left turn around the distant shooting, which continued. "Get ready to roll in on these assholes," Rawlings said.*

*"Forget about—"*

"Whiskey Hotel 09, we have reports of small arms fire from many sources across the border; not considered a threat to any coalition forces. You are instructed to RTB." *Return to base.*

*"Unbelievable," Rawlings said on the ICS that only Dunk could hear.*

*Dunk transmitted,* "Roger, Fireplug. Wilco." *Then to Rawlings, "Take heading of 205, set three hundred knots."*

"Whiskey Hotel 09, Fireplug Control, over."

*Dunk was surprised and answered quickly.* "Go ahead, Fireplug."

"Are you able to accept a fifteen-minute diversion for a new target for your JDAM, over?"

*Dunk looked at their fuel remaining, then his fuel ladder on his kneeboard.* "Will we be able to maintain our current altitude?"

"Affirmative."

*"Tell them we'll take it!" Raw insisted over the ICS. "I'm going to blow something up tonight, damn it."*

"Fireplug, Whiskey Hotel 09, affirmative. What's the vector?"

"Whiskey Hotel 09, vector to your target 125 for forty miles, over."

"09, Roger. Send me the coordinates."

*Raw whipped the Hornet around to a heading of 125 as Dunk grunted against the Gs and watched the target icon appear on his screen. He rolled his cursor over it and read the coordinates and the vector. It was the same bearing and distance as the vector Fireplug had given them over the radio.*

*Dunk slaved his radar around in the direction of their turn and searched for buildings in ground mode. "I've got good coordinates and good Predator uplink,"* he reported. *He looked at the chart superimposed on his display.* "Fireplug, this target is over the border."

"Concur, 09."

"We cleared?"

"We'll give you final clearance when you have the target image and can identify it. We have intel on several high-value targets in a building. You should be getting a Predator uplink to confirm."

"I'm getting it."

*Raw glanced at the HSI and steadied out on their heading. He increased speed to four hundred knots.*

"Five minutes to our drop point." *Dunk transmitted to Paco—the WSO wingman—on their encrypted discrete squadron frequency,* "You getting that Predator feed?"

"Yep. Sweet. You got a good radar confirmation yet?" Paco responded.

"No final ID yet . . . wait . . ." *He saw the target in-*

*formation flash up on his screen. He said to Raw, "We've got good info from the Predator. Transferring lat/long." He watched his indications from the JDAM, the GPS-guided bomb, that it had received and confirmed the targeting information. He saw the target indication on his radar fixed over what appeared to be a large flat building in a village. "We're ready." He ran through the challenge-and-response checklist, and finished with, "Master arm on."*

*Raw was more than ready. "Master arm coming on."*

*Dunk saw the indication.* "Fireplug, Whiskey Hotel 09, ready to drop."

"Whiskey Hotel 09, Fireplug, good data link, target confirmed, cleared to drop."

*Dunk checked his weapons panel, confirmed everything was correct, and hit the lighted bomb release button by his left knee.* "Bomb's away," *Dunk said to Raw as they could feel the airplane leap as the two-thousand-pound bomb came free and plunged earthward, accelerating in the darkness.*

*"Shit hot," Raw said gleefully as he turned hard left toward Afghanistan to go all the way around to a heading of 185 to the carrier. "Let's get back to the ship."*

*Dunk looked over his shoulder to watch the bomb hit. They were at 25,000 feet, but the target was in a high valley maybe fifteen thousand feet below them. He strained to keep looking between the tails, waiting for the impact, and suddenly saw the unmistakable flash and plumes of several missiles racing up at them.*

"Shit! Flares!" *he yelled to Raw.*

"What?"

*"Flares! Break left! Come to idle! Missiles guiding on us!"*

*Raw was confused but complied immediately. He hit the button on his stick to fire the flares that would draw heat-seeking missiles away. But it was too late. The American-made Stinger missile hit the tailpipe of the left engine. Three other Stingers followed it home and exploded inside the disintegrating engine. The F/A-18F Super Hornet's engine afterburner section exploded, ripping the tail off the fighter.*

*"What the hell?" Raw screamed as he fought to keep control of the jet.*

*Dunk reached between his legs, put his head back, and pulled the handle firing the rocket motors that threw their ejection seats into the air and opened their parachutes in the night sky. Dunk looked down between his feet at the dark Pakistan countryside below.*

# ONE

I stopped in at the deli next to my apartment building to get my usual bagel with egg and black coffee. But unlike other mornings, the *Today* show wasn't on the television in the corner. The images on the screen were graphic and disturbing. A group of men were dragging two Americans in flight suits through the dirt streets of a dark, menacing city. A graphic on the bottom of the screen read "Peshawar, Pakistan." I strained to hear the commentary on the television over the conversations around me in the deli. Most people weren't paying attention, assuming it was just the next story in an unending series of stories on the wars in the Middle East. I could hear some of what the reporter was saying. The footage showed a city that was dark, but numerous small lights illuminated the two Americans from odd angles, flashlights, cigarette lighters, car headlights, whatever they could find. They all illuminated the Americans in this midnight parade of humiliation. I grew angry.

I paid for my breakfast, stepped to the side of the cash register, and stared at the screen. As I bit into the bagel I held by the brown bag, I noticed the Americans had their hands bound behind them and leather dog collars around their necks. Their faces were unmasked and their eyes were wide open with confused courage.

The growing crowd chanted and screamed at them. Occasionally something would fly from the side of the screen and hit one of them in the face or the chest. They had nicks and cuts all over their faces.

They looked around, like they thought they were being led to the place where they would be beheaded. A reporter came on the screen as the image of the two Americans was frozen behind her.

She said, "These images are from earlier today when two American navy pilots were captured after their F-18 Hornet was shot down in a strike in the western mountains of Pakistan. They parachuted out of their plane and landed near a village where they were immediately attacked. The tribal leaders were able to restrain their people, but the two Americans were turned over to others and taken to Peshawar.

"It is unclear what happened, but apparently the navy jet was on a mission and dropped a large bomb on what it thought was an al Qaeda headquarters. The tribal leaders claim it was a building being used for medical treatment for the refugees from the war in Afghanistan. The reports are filtering out—though we have had no access to the site—that forty Afghan refugees and medical workers have been killed, mostly women and children. It is a disaster according to the Pakistanis, and the protesters believe it was done intentionally. They believe it was a message to the people in Pakistan to stop sheltering al Qaeda. Tribal leaders are furious and have stated that they cannot control their people. They will be making claims for payment from the United States government, and want the Americans out of the skies of Pakistan. A spokesman for the United States Navy has said they are investigating the incident, that they cannot independently confirm that the target that was struck was an error, but they will be looking into it. They also call for the immediate release of the navy pilots so they can be returned to their ship. The navy said they had no information on how the F-18 had crashed, or whether it had been shot down as the Pakistanis claim. Right now there are as many questions as there are answers. But one thing is for sure, the Pakistanis are very angry, and this is not going away."

CNN then returned to rerunning the loop they had been showing when I had come in to the sandwich shop. Damn. Targeting was hard, but it wasn't that hard. You sure as hell ought to be able to avoid a refugee medical facility. I couldn't imagine how that happened, nor could I imagine how they'd shot down an F-18. It's not easy. I couldn't remember the last time it had happened, if ever.

It wasn't going to be easy on the pilots either. The people of Waziristan aren't easy to befriend. I'd been there, and had no interest in going back. I sure wouldn't want to be there on the ground with a dog collar around my neck being pilloried by every angry man in Peshawar. I also knew, without a shadow of a doubt, that, somewhere, several people with a very high level of capability were planning to extricate those naval aircrew from wherever it was they were being held. But I also thought that the likelihood of them being found was low. The video I saw was taken at night. Probably from the nighttime that had just passed. But it could have been from the night before. In all likelihood the videotape had simply been delivered, like a prepackaged propaganda kit. It wasn't CNN film, and it wasn't the BBC. It was somebody with a digital camcorder. So even though it claimed to be Peshawar, it could've been taken anywhere and nearly any night. They were going to be very hard to find.

I wrapped up my bagel and headed to my office a block away. I picked up a copy of the *Post* on the way out the door to see if they had anything on it.

The images pulled at me. I had been in the navy for several years. I wasn't a pilot, but I'd been around. I knew a lot of pilots. I'd even pulled a couple of their asses out of pretty big fires. But seeing those two about to be subjected to whatever was coming was horrifying.

I looked at my watch. It was 8:30 A.M., 6:30 P.M. in Pakistan. I had a court appearance for one of my clients in a criminal case in a half hour. It would take most of the morning, then I was supposed to have lunch with Rick Fielding, an old friend of mine who still worked in the criminal division at the Department of Justice where I used to work. We had lunch together probably once a month. I liked to catch up on what they were doing. I was mostly on the other side now, though I rarely went against my former DOJ colleagues. I do

criminal defense work and am therefore considered irrational, or a turncoat, by most of the other prosecutors.
Unless you went over to doing big-time white-collar
defense for big money at a big firm, you were considered a loser. Anybody who went into general criminal
defense work and took run-of-the-mill cases was thought
to be unable to get good work. That wasn't my experience, and Rick understood that, but others didn't get it.
Neither of us had much time for lunch so we usually
met at Casey's on K Street.

My hearing went fine, and I got out in time to meet
Rick. He was there when I arrived. We ordered and
Rick immediately mentioned the F-18. Everyone was
talking about it. Most stories about the ongoing war in
the Middle East didn't get much attention. Somebody
else got blown up, another wedding that got bombed by
an American jet, or even better, an unmanned Predator, and the U.S. was sorry for killing a bunch of people,
or some suicide bomber in some market somewhere, or
an attack on an Afghan army outpost, whatever. But this
was different. American officers had been captured and
nobody knew where they were.

"You believe those guys got captured?" Rick asked.

"No. But I wouldn't want to be holding them right now
because some tough men with bad attitudes will be
looking for them."

"Your friends."

"Yep. They may not succeed, but I wouldn't want to
be the ones hiding them."

"How could they find them? They got GPS transmit-
ters on them or something?"

"No comment."

"So how do two Americans end up in dog collars in Peshawar being stoned by a mob?"

I shook my head. "No idea. Must've had a midair, or got shot down. Obviously they got out of their plane intact, but now they've got big problems."

"You hear the latest rumors? What the bloggers are saying?"

"Must be true if someone's saying it on a blog."

"Point taken. But get this. You know Flight Track? I can't remember the name of the site. Anyway, they're saying that a charter jet has been tracked. A high-end business jet. Nonstop, all the way from Pakistan to Holland."

I sat back and frowned. "What does that mean?"

"Beats the hell out of me. That's just what they've seen."

"Why Holland?" Then it hit me. Oh shit. "The Hague?"

"Yeah. How'd you know?"

"You know what's in The Hague?"

"The dope smokers who can't fit into Amsterdam?"

"Seriously. Know what's there?"

"What?"

"The International Criminal Court. I'll bet you these Pakistanis have arranged with the International Criminal Court to transport these two guys there and put them on trial for war crimes. Holy shit." I looked around. "This could run completely out of control. The European public will cheer, the Middle East will celebrate, the Muslims who make up about twenty percent of Holland will be weeping for joy, and the American public will demand blood."

"Shit, Jack. You really think that's where they're going?"

"If your blogger is right, I guarantee it. And the shit will really hit the fan. This is really going to put our president in a fix."

"Why?"

"He's long implied he wants to cooperate with the ICC. The first speech his new U.N. ambassador gave endorsed the then current investigation of the ICC. We'd never endorsed anything they had done. Big sea change. So he can't oppose the ICC now. I think he eventually wants to sign the ICC treaty and get the Senate to ratify it."

"Clinton didn't want it ratified."

"And Bush hated it. It was a joke. But almost everyone else signed it. We're out there in the distinguished company of Iran, and Israel, and North Korea."

"Didn't you work on some study group while you were at Justice?"

"Yeah. Led it. The attorney general wanted a report to update Congress on our opinion of the International Criminal Court. I was the only one around with military experience."

"What did your report say?"

"The court still claims to have worldwide jurisdiction even over countries that haven't signed the treaty. They don't have any of the fairness guarantees that we take for granted, and the definitions of war crimes and aggression are wide open. It still looks like an anti-American tract since we're the one doing all the global enforcement."

"And we *still* never signed it. Right?"

"Well Clinton signed it, but then told Congress not to ratify it. And Bush unsigned it. We probably never will unless they put in some guarantees. But these assholes have gone after American servicemen, and they're going to have a fight on their hands."

He smiled. "I bet you'd love to be part of that fight."

I shook my head. "You think there's any chance they won't get a conviction? If they were on their way to The Hague before the night was out, that means this whole thing has been planned. Someone was waiting for them."

"There you go with your defense attorney conspiracy mentality."

"Yeah. That's me." I glanced at my watch. "I've got to get back to the office. Another slam-dunk habeas petition to argue this afternoon."

"You making any money yet?"

"I get by."

"Shit, man. I figured those two felony cases you tried back-to-back last year would make you the man."

"Got me on the front page of the *Post*."

"Twice. And what about those Marines you defended out in California? Where was that?"

"Camp Pendleton."

"That was *huge*. Didn't you get some guys off who got crosswise with some villagers somewhere? That even made CNN."

"Yeah."

"Didn't you get some award?"

"That was for the two felonies here."

"What was it?"

"Criminal Defense Lawyer of the Year."

"That's got to get you some big cases. At least some notoriety. And *maybe* even some people who can pay."

"Maybe. We'll see. I gotta go."


I walked back down K Street to my office, which is in one of the oldest buildings on the block. My secretary handed me a stack of phone messages.

"On top. That guy is really trying to get ahold of you."

I looked at the phone slips. Three of them were from the same person. I didn't recognize the name or the number. "Who is he?"

"Wouldn't say." She looked at me with a inquisitive look. "You recognize his number?"

I looked again. "No. You give him my cell?"

"No sir. You told me never to give it to anybody. I believe you told me I could exercise good judgment, but so far that's meant never giving it out."

"He say what he wanted?"

"No." The phone rang and she looked at her caller ID. "Here he is again. Want to talk to him?"

I nodded and headed toward my office. I took off my jacket, put it over the back of my chair, and looked at the phone. She had put him on hold. I closed the door, sat down at the desk, picked up the phone, hit the button, and said, "Jack Caskey."

"Jack, Chris Marshall."

I didn't recognize the name or the voice. "Do I know you?"

"We have friends in common. I need to talk to you."

"What about? You in trouble?"

"No. Recent events."

"Who are you exactly?"

"I'd rather not talk on the phone. Can I come to your office?"

"I have a hearing in thirty minutes."

"Where?"

"District Court. Courtroom three."

"I'll see you there."

"How will I know you?"

"I'll know you. I'll talk to you after the hearing." He hung up. I glanced at the clock, picked up the file for the hearing, stuffed it in my briefcase, grabbed my suit coat, and headed for court.

In my former life in the navy I learned to spot people who are physically dangerous. By the way they carry themselves, their build, the way they hide their athleticism in their clothing, and by a certain look in their eyes. A complete lack of fear and a complete belief in their ability to do whatever they want. I didn't encounter that look very often practicing law in Washington. I run into a lot of men who think they're tough, who think because they can talk big or baffle you with a bunch of bullshit that they're somehow better than you; some—most who had never been in an actual fight—think they can kick your ass. Probably because they had taken a couple of years of kung fu when their kids were in training. But it's a vast leap between that kind of person and the kind who can truly do it. And I spotted him immediately.

He was waiting for me at the back of the courtroom until the hearing was over. He was clearly the one who had called. He probably now did what I used to do. I walked right by him like I hadn't seen him. But I knew he had seen me noticing, and I knew that he knew that I had chosen to walk right by. Outside the courtroom I stood in the hallway. I put down my briefcase and waited for him to approach while I checked my e-mail on my iPhone. He walked up to me slowly. He was about my size, maybe an inch shorter, and stockier. I'm six feet, and he was probably five feet eleven. Where I weigh 185, he probably weighed 190. My hair used to be closely cut, but now had that sort of slightly too long look to it that a lot of criminal defense attorneys wear as a constant symbol of their general rebellion, and to distinguish themselves from the cookie-cutter government prosecutors. But now I was just a plain old criminal defense lawyer in Washington, D.C., and loved what I did. But whoever he was, he wasn't the usual kind of person who came looking for me. I waited for him to speak first. "You're Jack."

"Chris Marshall."

"That's me."

We shook hands. He had a firm grip but was careful not to try to show how strong he was. I studied his face. He wasn't in trouble, and from what I could tell he didn't have a friend or a wife or a nephew who was in trouble.

This was something else entirely. "So you haven't been charged with anything, and I would guess based on the look on your face that nobody you know has either. What can I do for you?"

"I need to talk to you in private. Is there somewhere that we can go?"

"Depends how private you need to be. We can go to the cafeteria, which is pretty loud. Good place to talk. You couldn't record there unless you had a boom mike. Or we can go back to my office."

"I've got a better idea. Can you spare a couple of hours this afternoon?"

"I don't know, I've got some meetings."

"Cancel them. It's important."

"Where do you want to go?"

He reached into his pocket and pulled out a leather business card holder. He opened it, pulled out a card, handed it to me. I looked at it. Deputy Director, Counter-Terrorism, National Security Council. I looked at him and he said, "The White House. Or more specifically, the Old Executive Office Building."

# TWO

He didn't say a word the entire way. I assumed he was going to try to lure me back into the government, either as a Navy SEAL like I had been before, or maybe on his staff. Neither interested me. I was done with that. It had been ten years since I'd been in the navy. Three years of law school, and now seven years of law practice. I was past government life. And while I had developed something of a reputation in the SEALs, I had decided long before that wasn't where my future lay. I had to do something else. It was addicting, intoxicating, and an amazing existence, but I knew I had to head in a different direction, and did. I wasn't about to go back. The longer I sat in the silent car, the sillier I felt for falling for the old "secret government . . . we need you" bit that might make me feel important again. It made me mad at myself.

He drove into the guarded parking lot and pulled into a reserved spot. We parked and walked into the office building. He showed his badge to the security guards and got a visitor's badge for me. The guards searched my briefcase and walked me through a metal detector. We took the elevator to the fourth floor and walked down the marble hallway. The building was in excellent shape. It had that austere yet impressive look that well-kept government office buildings can have. We turned down a second hallway and into his office. His secretary stood up when he entered the outer office. I'm not sure I'd ever seen that before. She said, "Good afternoon, sir."

It suddenly struck me that she was in uniform. She was a navy yeoman first class. So he had brought a navy clerk with him to his job on the National Security Council. That meant almost certainly that he was still on active duty, even though now wearing a suit instead of a uniform. No dress blues, no SEAL insignia, no medals or impressive display of anything. Just a good-fitting inexpensive suit like any other government bureaucrat but with a military haircut.

His secretary looked at me with a clear point of evaluating me. She was extremely pretty, which caught my eye. She checked me out as I checked her out, just a little longer than was comfortable, but neither of us looked away. I wasn't used to that. I was always the one looking. I wasn't married and never had been. Always wanted to be, though. She probably had spent a lot of time with Navy SEAL teams as a yeoman, and had the top secret clearance required to review the documents necessary to hold that job. She was perfect for his current position, and knew how to keep her mouth shut. And no ring.

"Come on in. Have a seat." We walked into his office, he closed the door behind me, and crossed over to a coffeepot that was on a burner in the corner. "Coffee?"

"Sure. Black." He took two porcelain mugs and handed me one. It had a SEAL Budweiser emblem on the side. Nice touch.

"So. You're probably wondering what all this is about."

"You might say that. You going to try to recruit me back into the navy for something *really* important? Or your staff?"

"Not even close. But that's what I would have assumed too."

"So who are you exactly?"

He smiled slightly. "Like you I went through the teams, couple staff jobs, but unlike you I didn't get out. I stayed in. I went on to DEVGRU—like you—and then on to command one of the teams. West Coast. This job happened out of the blue." So he'd been a part of the navy's elite counter-terrorism team too. I listened carefully as he went on. "They were looking for somebody to fill the new position. The National Security Council decided that they needed to know more about counter-terrorism operations, and they needed a snake-eater to be in charge. They asked me. Not sure why, maybe because I'm not quite as controversial as some, and I'm not so senior that anybody would have to listen to me. So here I am. And I already know all about you. You went to the DOJ after law school. Right?"

"Yeah. I got out, went right to law school here at Georgetown, then went to the DOJ. Because that's what good people do. Right? They prosecute bad guys. They put them away forever. Right?"

Marshall smiled.

"Only when you start doing it, you find out that some of the bad guys aren't guilty, and that some of the prosecutors are vindictive and mean, and some, even worse—although few—are politically driven. Shocking, I know. Go prosecute Congressmen So-and-So because he voted against my bill. He has cash in his refrigerator. So then you see the dark side, the corrupt side, and you realize sometimes you're just a tool, and it's complete and total bullshit. That's when I traded in my government paycheck for the life of a poor criminal defense lawyer."

"Where there's nothing but sweetness and light."

I didn't respond.

"And you're not so poor. You've been responsible for some of the biggest criminal defense trials—successful, I might add—in the last three years."

"Well, in my world, if you get anybody off it's nearly a miracle, and if you get somebody off who has made it to the newspapers, you're a genius. But being in the papers doesn't pay the bills."

Marshall nodded and looked at the door. He was making sure it was closed. He said, "You've been following the events in Pakistan, I'm sure. Nobody who has ever chased al Qaeda into that godforsaken land would ever forget it. You tend to notice other things that are going on there."

"You've been reading my file."

"Had to. So unless you've changed a lot, I think I know who I'm dealing with."

"You never know."

He nodded and sat up slightly. "You saw the two F-18 guys that got nabbed."

I nodded as I drank from my coffee.

"How do you think that happened?"

"How would I know?"

"Let me hear you think about it."

I thought for a minute. "Well, it sounds like they were attacking a target which was inside Pakistan—which I suspect is unusual—most of the attacks I've heard of recently have been by Predators to prevent this very kind of thing. Anyway, I don't know, they got a target, hit it, and got shot down, or had a mechanical failure."

"Okay. You think they had a mechanical failure that happened to cause them to come down inside Pakistan?"

"No."

"Correct."

"So they were shot down?"

"Correct."

"How do you know?"

"Because their wingman saw it. They said there had to be six shoulder-fired missiles launched at them at the same time. They dumped flares, but their countermeasures were overwhelmed. The missiles may have been Stingers. They're tuned to ignore flares."

"Why are we going through this? Why are you asking me questions you already know the answer to?"

"Because I want you to think this through very

carefully. It's likely to blow up and get shit all over a bunch of people, and I want to make sure we do this right. So they got shot down."

"Okay."

"And then we see them being led through Peshawar. The standard parade."

"Right. The Somalia bit."

"Exactly. Black Hawk Down. We don't want another one of those."

"Clearly."

"So why the parade?" he asked.

"So we know they have them."

"And that they were able to get them to Peshawar within hours. They're all over this."

"Who is?"

"Whoever."

"Okay."

"So then what?"

I said, "Don't know. I assumed they were being led off to some basement where they'd videotape cutting off their heads with a carpet knife."

"No no. They're much too valuable for that. Maybe a finger, but they won't kill them. *Think* of the leverage."

"But someone like you or me could be coming through the window any minute."

"Ah." He smiled. "Did you notice their flight suits?"

"Just that they were wearing them."

"No patches, no wings, no insignia. Stuff in the wrong places. Those weren't their suits. They've been stripped, and everything they're currently wearing was probably bought on the black market in Pakistan, which is quite robust, as you know. Probably where whoever got the Stingers got them."

I nodded.

"So no glint patch, no transponder, nothing. Impossible to find without HUMINT, which we don't have."

I waited.

"So now what? A video?"

"Nope," I said. "Off to the airport, aboard a plane and off to Holland."

He looked completely shocked. "Where'd you get that?"

"At lunch."

"That on the news?"

"Nope. Friend from DOJ, obsesses about stuff like this. Read on some blog that someone had traced a private jet flight from Peshawar to Den Haag—The Hague."

"Well I'll be a son of a bitch. Why do we have intelligence services? Why don't we just use bloggers?"

"Because most of them are full of shit."

"True, but sometimes they get things right. Ask Dan Rather." Marshall opened a file on his desk. He handed me a small chart that traced a flight path from Peshawar to France. "This is as of about an hour ago. Their clearance is to The Hague. Falcon 7X. Very nice jet. Top end. So why there?"

"The ICC."

He stood up, walked beside his desk to the window, and looked out. He gazed at the White House and the lawn in front of it and all the way to Pennsylvania Avenue. Everything looked calm and quiet. He turned and leaned on the sill and folded his arms. "See? You're exactly the right guy. You've got this all figured out." He pulled two photos from the file. They were navy file photos of two officers in dress blues. "These are the two aviators. The first one, Rawlings, is the pilot. The one underneath him is the WSO, Lieutenant Duncan. He's actually senior to Rawlings. Both good guys, but Raw, as he is known, is . . . temperamental. He's a hothead. Great natural pilot, best landing grades in the squadron, which is unheard of for a nugget. But very volatile. Duncan is the intellectual. ROTC guy from Notre Dame. Best WSO in the squadron. These guys don't screw up a mission. They always hit what they're aiming at. Lots of missions. Never a problem."

"So how'd they end up on the ground with dog collars around their necks?"

He nodded vigorously. "Exactly. How the hell did this happen?"

"They were waiting for them."

"No doubt. Where did these shitheads in the mountain get six Stingers and know how to fire them all at once at an F-18 in the dark?"

"Planning."

"Yep."

I asked, "So *did* they hit some refugee medical facility?"

"We don't know. We're tracing back the targeting. All we know right now is they hit what they were told to hit. And we know they hit it. We've got IR images of bodies all over the place. What we don't know is exactly what it was, and where the targeteers got the information that there were al Qaeda leaders there. We'll track it down, but right now, we don't know."

"So what do you want from me?"

"This is going to really get ugly. Politically. I think these boys are in big trouble. And I think the United States is going to come completely unglued when they learn that the Europeans are prosecuting two American pilots for the accidental bombing of a refugee facility while pursuing al Qaeda based on a treaty that we never signed."

"This is going to be a complete firestorm. But it's the moral fight a lot of Europeans have been itching to have since Bush went into Iraq."

"And we're going to give them that fight."

"How?"

"You've got to get over there."

"I'm sorry? Get over where?"

"The Hague. Somebody's got to represent them at the International Criminal Court."

"No, you need some English barrister with a dusty wig."

"I read the memo you wrote for the DOJ on the ICC. As you know—"

"That was six years ago."

"Still, you were the AG's darling on the ICC. Your memo became the internal bible on the ICC."

"It wasn't anything special."

"Well, I appreciate your humility. But you're wrong. And you're just the guy. You're the most well known criminal defense lawyer in D.C. right now. There are the usual old lions who don't really try cases anymore, but you're the new, young stud. DOJ is scared of you."

"Oh, right."

"I've already talked to them. I'm not making this up."

"I don't know. I can help out, I can give you some suggestions on the side, but I'm not the guy to go over there and represent them. It's out of my league. You need somebody who's world-famous. Get someone from the DOJ. The 2002 act says you can use government lawyers to defend somebody held by the ICC."

"You'll get help from them. All you need. They're already setting up a team. But they'll report to you. Quietly. They'll be support. You'll be the guy."

I thought about it, and he said, "I want you to leave tonight. Maybe we'll send others, maybe we'll supplement your team, maybe we'll call in F. Lee Bailey."

"He's a little past his prime; but at least he's colorful." I replied.

"Maybe we'll send someone like that, but maybe we won't. We'll see how this plays out. But the critical thing is you're on your way tonight."

I thought of the implications. "Is this an official government deal? Am I to say that the United States government asked me to come over here and represent these two guys? Or is this one of those semi-shady gray area deals where I talk to you, I report sort of to you but really to them and their wives, and you fund it through some untraceable account?"

"You'll get paid, and you will be retained by their wives. We'll work out the details later. You and I will be in constant communication." He pulled out a card that had nothing but a phone number on it. "That's my cell. Get to The Hague tonight. By the time you get back to your office they should be parading your clients through The Hague. Probably no dog collars, at least not literal ones. So get over there. Start banging on doors, and desks, and whatever else you criminal lawyers like to bang on. Then we'll decide which way to go with this once we know what they have in mind."

# THREE

I went straight to my apartment in the northwest section of Washington, turned on the television, and watched every piece of news I could find. The first thing I saw was a feed from European television, actually a replay of what had been on European television earlier that night. It showed the two navy officers being led off the Falcon jet at The Hague in leg chains, with their hands tied behind them. Their heads were uncovered, and their faces were flooded by the journalists' lights. They squinted and turned their heads, which made them look defensive and uncertain. European reporters yelled at them in English, and then demanded to know why they had killed refugees, and women and children. The Americans looked angry and baffled. They probably weren't even sure where they were. My guess was that they hadn't been told where they were going, and assumed it would be somewhere hostile. They were right, but not in the way they thought.

The European media frenzy was shocking. They had clearly been notified long before the plane landed. They knew what the allegations were, they had seen the parading of the Americans in Peshawar, and now they were ready to put them in prison until they were convicted of war crimes, then put away for life.

The American reaction was just starting to form. People who knew anything about the International Criminal Court were being called on to comment on the fly. One of the first people interviewed on Fox News was a gentleman whose name I didn't catch from Human Rights Watch. He was commenting that the charges that have been leveled against the American aviators, if in fact there have been charges—which wasn't yet clear— were appropriate under the treaty. The fact that the United States had not signed it did not mean that we were not subject to its terms.

What an ass. He was on his horse, shining with righteousness. He went on. It was appropriate and correct that anyone accused of war crimes, especially by a body as serious and respected as the International Criminal Court, answer those charges in the appropriate forum, which was at trial in The Hague. If the Americans had targeted a refugee medical facility in order to "send a message" that was a war crime, and they *should* be put on trial. In fact he said that he was surprised more war crimes charges had not been entered against Americans relating to the Iraq war and the Afghanistan war, and said that it was his belief that under the treaty even those in the chain of command above the two navy fliers could be charged. America was not exempt. He commented that

America had entered into separate Article 98 agreements with several countries in which they agreed they would not refer charges to the ICC that arose out of our peacekeeping or other defense support missions or they would lose military aid.

But he noted, somewhat smugly, it appeared that Pakistan had not referred the charges, but that they had come directly from the ICC itself. Right out of the office of the prosecutor, who had so-called *proprio motu* powers. He could bring the charges by himself with the agreement of two judges of the ICC.

He knew his stuff. Not many people in the American legal community had read the Treaty of Rome that closely.

In short, he was an enthusiastic supporter of the idea of charging American aviators for "collateral damage" if proved to be intentional. He did not automatically assume it was accidental as the military was claiming. He agreed reluctantly that if it was truly an accident, then they should get off; but he wanted to also say that there was a lot of this so-called collateral damage that was supposedly unintentional; but at some point the very scope of it showed it wasn't accidental.

The news accounts went on. The surprise and anger built as the news media were able to interview more and more people. Various politicians and nongovernment organizations were taking sides. No one had yet heard from the president, or the secretary of defense, or the secretary of state. No doubt they were huddled at the White House deciding how to handle this.

If they weren't careful they would end up sounding

like the president of Sudan, who was charged with war crimes and responded by saying he didn't acknowledge the existence of the International Criminal Court, that the treaty wasn't worth the paper it was written on. The last thing the new president wanted to be was someone who disregarded international law and treaties. He was going to be in a very difficult position.

I opened my computer, downloaded the ICC treaty from the ICC's Web site, as well as all the regulations, evidentiary rules, and commentary I could find. I found several articles on the few trials the ICC had actually conducted. Notably, no one had gotten off. As I downloaded another PDF from a Web site, my iPhone dinged on the counter with a text message. It was from Chris. It had one word. "Go."

The first flight I could get from Dulles left at 10:00 P.M. I drove to the airport, and on the way called a classmate of mine from Georgetown Law School, Kristen Chambers. She and I hadn't agreed on much, but were good friends. She shared the background of many law students in our class at Georgetown. They'd grown up in the Northeast where they had gone to college; some had Ivy League educations. They came from good families, they had no real work experience, and now had a law degree. She, like most of the others from that group, were politically liberal, had never served in the military, and thought they had all the answers. And like most of the others, she went to work for a very large D.C. firm's New York office where she made very good money. Nothing wrong with that. I'm all for making money and living the big life. I was more on the conservative side of the political spectrum, not fully conservative—depends on the issue—but she was hard left.

I called her cell phone. It was almost 8:30. She was probably just finishing her takeout meal at her desk. She picked up. "This is Kristen."

"Jack Caskey."

"Well, well. How are you? Long time no hear. It's been what, a month?"

"Since that last article I sent you proving you're wrong again."

"You never prove anything. You don't get it."

"I know. I just stumble along. Look, I have a proposal for you."

"Can't. I'm dating somebody who would think it was forward of you to propose right now."

"Aren't you hilarious."

"That's what you always said. What's up?"

"You still at the office?"

"Is it ten yet?"

"Nope."

"Then of *course*, I'm still at the office."

I swerved around some traffic as I approached the long-term parking at Dulles. I signaled to turn into the parking lot. "You been watching the news? Those two navy pilots that were shot down or crashed, and captured in Pakistan and have now been flown to Holland?"

"No, sorry."

"You haven't been watching the news?"

"No. I never watch the news. What's going on?"

"An F-18 off the USS *Ronald Reagan* was shot down

in Pakistan, and the pilots were captured, they were paraded through Peshawar, Pakistan, with dog collars
around their necks while people basically stoned them.
Now they've been flown to The Hague in the Netherlands to be put on trial for war crimes."

"For what? Are you kidding me?"

"Not kidding. Supposedly they dropped a bomb on a
refugee medical facility and killed a bunch of refugees
and women and children."

Kristen paused. She said, "Then maybe they should
be put on trial for war crimes."

"Well, I guess that remains to be seen. What if it
was accidental?"

"Well, as you know, you can be charged even if killing somebody was negligent. It's called negligent hom-
icide, or manslaughter. But shit, Jack, what were they
thinking?"

"Well I'm on my way to Holland to defend them before the International Criminal Court. So why don't
you hold your tongue?"

"You're going to defend them?"

"That's what I do. I'm a criminal defense lawyer."

"Good luck."

"I'd like you to help me."

"I've got a job, Jack."

"You'd be perfect. You're bright, energetic, you work
for one of the biggest and best law firms in the country
that does fantastic work. And you hate injustice."

"I don't think they'd be able to afford us, and I don't
think they'd want me to help. But thanks for the offer."

"You're right about them not being able to afford

you. I'm sure they can't, which is why I want you to do it for free."

"Are you doing it for free?"

"No. I'm going to get paid."

"Then why should I help for free?"

"Your law firm was widely featured in an article in *American Lawyer.* They sang the praises of your firm, holding it up as a paragon of virtue, for the hundreds and *thousands* of pro bono hours that were donated to the terrorists—sorry, detainees—who are being held at Guantánamo to challenge the United States government."

"We did a lot of work for the Guantánamo detainees. It was important work. We achieved a lot."

"Understood. So how about you now do some pro bono work and help out some Americans instead of some terrorists? Find one of your litigation partners who has some military experience. I'll talk to them if you want. But put in a request. Let's see your firm do something in support of the military for a change."

"Tempting, but no thanks."

I pulled into a parking spot and turned off the engine. I jumped out of the car with my Bluetooth headset still on. "Kristen, let me be real clear here. I think you would be a big help. You firm has the smartest lawyers in the country. You've got to do it."

"I don't think so—"

"—and if you don't ask your pro bono committee to take this on, if your firm doesn't approve it, I will personally make sure—and believe me I can do it—that there's an article in every newspaper you can imagine

that says your firm works for free for terrorists but refuses to help out American servicemen. Think about
it." I hung up, and put my phone in my briefcase as I
headed to the terminal.

My flight landed in The Hague at 6:00 A.M. Thankfully
I wasn't met by the European journalists who were so
interested in the two navy fliers. If they knew who I
was, and why I was there, they would probably have
met me with equal enthusiasm. They probably would
have liked to have seen me led off the jet in chains as
well, particularly if they knew some of the things I'd
been involved in during my time in Afghanistan and
Iraq. But that morning I looked like any other American landing in Holland.

I took a cab to my hotel and tried to check in. It was
far too early so they wouldn't let me. I had to buy the
room for the night just ending so I could take a shower.
I turned on the television and watched the news in Dutch.
I couldn't understand a word, but they were playing
over and over again the footage of the two Americans
in Peshawar, then of them being led off the beautiful
Falcon 7X as it landed in Holland. They also had some
additional footage I hadn't seen before, of the Americans being interrogated, but not answering any questions. It was a brief clip, and was clearly intended to
show that they were being uncooperative. The interro-
gators seemed to be Pakistanis. The tone of the news-
caster was one of outrage. The piece ended with a long
lingering shot of the building in which the International
Criminal Court was housed. I looked at the building

carefully, and tried to imagine what it was like inside, who was in charge, who I would meet, and how difficult the day was going to be.

I unpacked, put my clothes in the closet, got my suit out and my shirt ready for ironing, and jumped in the shower.

At nine o'clock I went downstairs, found a café, and ordered American coffee and a croissant. I dialed Kristen's cell phone. She picked it up immediately. "Jack, are you kidding me? It's three o'clock in the morning!"

"Did you submit it?"

"No! You called me at what, nine o'clock last night? And now it's four o'clock in the morning? So, no. And I really don't know if I'm going to. I can't really get enthused about helping some American war criminal."

"So your firm's representation of war criminals is limited to known terrorists."

"Cut the bullshit, Jack. That's a really tired argument. Are you bitter because my firm didn't give you an offer or something out of law school?"

"No. Never applied."

"Well get off your horse. And leave me alone. I don't want to do this."

"Well I'm going to keep hammering on you until you agree to help me. And I mean you personally. I don't want your firm assigning some first-year to this. I want the same level of dedication that you gave to the detainees. What was it the *American Lawyer* said? Your firm dedicated over ten thousand attorney hours to helping the detainees? Sounds about right to me. I'd like ten thousand attorney hours from your firm dedicated to helping these two Americans get off these bogus charges based on a treaty the United States refused to sign. What do you think?"

"You're a real pain in the ass. I think you're threatening us. If we don't help you with your little endeavor then you're going to try to humiliate us. That it?"

"Exactly. I will try to make your firm look stupid and unpatriotic. So have you submitted the request?"

"I said no. It hasn't even been twelve hours since we talked."

"Long enough for me to fly to The Hague. And I'm sitting over here in my suit at a café, about to walk over to the International Criminal Court; right into the lion's den. They don't even know who I am, or that I'm here, or what I'm going to do. So the sooner we can get some people working on this, the sooner you can help me with research challenging their jurisdiction, the sooner we can go public with our representation, and the happier I'm going to be. So get that request in today. Agree?"

"I'll see what I can do. I'll talk to somebody on the pro bono committee."

"I want your guarantee, Kristen. I want it to be you and me doing this. Not me and some committee. If your firm approves can I have your word you will personally help?"

"I don't know. I'll have to think about it. Usually when our firm takes on a pro bono matter, we're in charge. If I do find someone who has military experience, and who wants to do this, he'll want to be in charge."

"Well, he can't be, sorry. He can be in charge of

your side of it, but I'm the one who's going to do the trial for these guys if it goes that far. So you have to submit it with that understanding. And if that means that they don't do anything, and it's just you and me and a few other associates, it's okay with me."

"I'll see what I can do."

I looked around the café at the people preparing to go to work. I glanced down at the two engagement letters signed by the wives of the two pilots. Chris Marshall had faxed them to my hotel. I don't know how he even knew where I was staying. I put a knife on the two letters so they wouldn't blow away. "Seriously Kristen, These Americans are being railroaded. We need to get them off."

"No. We don't need to get them off. The system will take care of itself, and if they're guilty of war crimes, they ought to go to prison."

"All I ask is that you keep an open mind. Let's get into this and find out where the truth is."

"I'll call you." She hung up.

I folded the two letters and put them in my suit coat pocket. I hadn't slept all night and was starting to feel the effect. I ordered an espresso, and drank it quickly. I left a pile of euros on the table under the knife, and headed for the International Criminal Court.

It was a six-block walk from the café. I used the time to clear my head and let the caffeine do its work. It was a beautiful sunny day, the kind that makes you glad to be alive, to hang glide off a cliff in San Diego or windsurf in Virginia Beach, both of which were among my favorite things. But that day I had to go to work to protect two men in an international firestorm.

The buildings—the ICC's temporary headquarters—looked exactly like they had on the video clip from last evening's news, and the photos I'd pulled up on the Internet. The future building, which would be on the outside of The Hague at Alexanderkazerne, would be even more elaborate and ornate but hadn't even been started yet. Nonetheless, even these headquarters were impressive.

There were two buildings, each different from but complementary to the other. They were attached by an architectural novelty, a two-story crossbeam of offices that appeared to sit on top of the other two sixteen-story buildings. I had read everything I could get my hands on about how the court was structured, how many courtrooms it had, prosecutors, administrators, all their procedures, and had stayed bleary-eyed through most of my flight trying to remember it all. All that was about to come to a head.

I opened the door in the lobby, walked across the marble floor to the receptionist, who had a large seal of the International Criminal Court behind her, and said, "Good morning. Do you speak English?"

"Yes," she said quickly.

I nodded and reached for my wallet. "My name is Jack Caskey." I handed her my business card. "I'm an attorney from Washington, D.C., and I'm here to represent two American pilots who were brought to the International Criminal Court yesterday."

She looked up startled. "Excuse me?"

"I'm here to represent the two Americans who have been arrested and were brought to the International Criminal Court yesterday. Did you not see the news shows?"

"Yes, of course. I did not expect anyone so soon."

"Yes. Well, here I am. I'd like to see the two Americans. Please put me in touch with whoever I need to speak with about seeing my clients."

She seemed puzzled. Finally she picked up the telephone, dialed a number, spoke in what was probably Dutch, and hung up the phone. "Mr. Magnette, our court administrator, will be with you shortly."

"Thank you."

I put my briefcase on the floor in the corner and stood waiting for Magnette to arrive. Through the lobby windows I watched people passing by the building; I wondered what they thought as they passed. Were the Americans being held here? Were people already forming opinions? Was the crisis passing, and apathy setting in, or was this one of those crises that were going to build and fester and have a life of its own?

I heard a door open behind me and turned to see who it was. A man headed straight to me and introduced himself.

"Good morning," he said cheerfully. He turned and walked back the direction he had come, clearly expecting me to follow. We passed through the security where they checked my briefcase and I walked through the metal detector. I followed him through two heavy ornate doors and down a lush carpeted hallway to his office. He went around to the other side of his desk, sat down, and directed me to the chair across from him. He leaned on the desk and folded his hands. He was perhaps sixty years old, refined, and small. He had wavy gray hair and bright blue eyes. He seemed very happy. His eyes examined me as if I were on display. He spoke in good but accented English. Probably French or Belgian. "Yes, sir. I have your card. Mr. John Caskey. An attorney from America. What may I do for you?"

As if he didn't know. "You're the court administrator. What exactly does that entail?"

He smiled at me. "I don't usually discuss my job description or my responsibilities with someone that I don't know. And we don't know each other yet. Please tell me why you're here."

"You know why I'm here," I said, looking directly at him. "I told the receptionist. Is it possible she didn't tell you that I am the attorney representing the two Americans that you're holding? Because if she didn't tell you that, then you should probably talk to her about her job."

He nodded, no doubt thinking inside that I was one of *those* kind of Americans. "Yes, she did tell me that. But frankly I did not believe her. I thought you were probably an American journalist who had someone else's business card that he had gotten at a cocktail party."

I held his gaze. "But while you made me wait, you checked my name on the Internet. You found out that I'm a criminal defense attorney from Washington, D.C., you saw the cases that I have won, and you saw that my reputation, while not perfect, is pretty good, and you saw my picture. A journalist may have phonied up a Web site, or claimed to be me, but you searched newspapers too, and noted the photographs, and found that I am who I say that I am."

He sat back slightly and put his arms on the armrests of his leather chair. "You have caught me." He smiled. "I was checking on you, as you Americans say. And it does seem that you are an attorney. But that is all I know. Please tell me more."

I nodded slightly. "I have been retained by the wives of the two Americans you are holding. I will be representing them in whatever charges are brought against them in this court."

"I see. Well, I don't know that we can really have that."

I waited. He wasn't going to say anything else. "You don't allow defendants to be represented by counsel?"

"Yes, of course. But they must be admitted before the International Criminal Court. Not just anyone who is an attorney in his home country can come to the International Criminal Court. We must have only those who . . . like barristers in England . . . only the best representatives, highly skilled, people that we know will take the processes seriously, and are of good ethical reputation."

"And who is it that gets to make this determination?"

He smiled again. "I do."

"Based on what criteria?"

"The criteria I just outlined." He swept his hand across in front of him dismissively. "You must apply. You must submit your curriculum vitae. You must submit rec-

ommendations, and you must submit a certification from
the bar wherever you are admitted in the world that you
are in good standing and are not under any charges aris-
ing out of ethical violations. Would you like to have a set
of the rules? I would be happy to give them to you. You
could then go home, put your paperwork together, submit your application through the appropriate channels,
have the appropriate recommendations sent on your behalf, submit the ethical certification from all the bars in
which you've been admitted—in America that means
*each* court before which you are or were licensed to
practice—and then we will *consider* your application."

"I'll take a look at that information, submit whatever
is required. I certainly want to comply with the requirements of the court. Because I will be representing these
two Americans in whatever trial comes out of this."

"We will see." He reached into his drawer, pulled out
a booklet, and handed it to me. It was printed on the European paper, which is slightly larger than the American standard eight and a half by eleven. "All of the
requirements are listed. The formats are specified.
Please comply with them. And also please submit three
copies when you do submit your application. We'll no-
tify you of whether you have been accepted within a
reasonable time."

"I will do so." I put the application into my briefcase
on the floor, and looked at Magnette. "But the reason
that I'm here today is to see the American prisoners.
Could you tell me where they are being held?"

"Well you certainly may not see anybody being held

by the International Criminal Court until you are licensed to practice before it, so you are subject to the ethical rules in our administrative rule book."

I looked around his office for the first time. It was large and comfortable. He had apparently practiced law before various courts around Europe as he had numerous legal certificates or documents in Latin hanging on the wall. There were many photographs of him in various courtrooms and robes. Based on his age, he probably semiretired to take this job. He was not to be taken lightly, in spite of his geniality. He knew the game. I said, "I came over here to see the Americans that have been captured illegally, transported illegally, and are being held illegally. I know you disagree, and that you intend to put them on trial for something—war crimes of some kind I'm sure—even though they are from a country that has not signed the treaty which gives you your supposed authority. We'll have those debates later, at the right time. The question now is whether I am able to see my clients. Your rules do not define my attorney-client relationship. They are my clients. I have been retained by their wives, and I'm entitled to see them." I reached into my suit coat pocket and extracted the two letters of engagement. I handed them to him.

He took the letters, examined them, and handed them back to me. "Those are very interesting, but have nothing to do with access to those being held by this court. Access to such prisoners is determined by me, and it is based in part on whether you have been admitted to the court. Only then can we even consider giving you access to the Americans." He sat back.

I wasn't about to leave without seeing my clients. It wasn't negotiable. "I don't think you appreciate how this is going to be perceived in the United States. The current state of mind of the American public is shock and confusion. It's been barely twenty-four hours, and people are just now starting to understand what has happened. Two navy pilots on a routine mission, with a routine target given to them by their targeting people, complete the mission, and somehow get shot down in the process or otherwise crash. I'm still not sure what happened. They're captured, paraded, humiliated, and then somehow, magically, flown to this city, and brought to this court. What an amazing set of circumstances. That will, over the next few days, cause absolute fury within the United States. I promise you that. And with fury comes acute interest.

"They will follow this case every single hour of every single day it's pending. It will become their new favorite reality show. They will keep calendars of how many days this hostage crisis has continued. They will build signs and send letters to 'Free the American pilots!' The crazy right-wingers in particular, who are all over the country clinging to their religion and guns, will hate you more each day you keep 'their boys' in your prison. They will write to you every day, they will find your e-mail account and threaten you.

"And an army of American journalists will be here nonstop. I was surprised there weren't any journalists banging on the door when I arrived this morning. But I suspect they are now. The first step in this new process is up to you. If you refuse to let me see my clients I am going to walk out on the sidewalk in front of this building, and get on my cell phone. And I'm going to call CNN, and Fox News, and MSNBC, and Reuters, and tell them to bring their cameras and meet me here, because I am the attorney representing the Americans, and I'm going to hold a press conference. And I will stand there until I have a whole shitpile of journalists waiting to hear what I have to say. They'll probably build some kind of a microphone stand like they do—they're very good at that with very little notice—that will have dozens of microphones on it waiting for me to say whatever it is I'm going to say. And you know what it is I'm going to say?"

I waited for him to respond, but he didn't. "I'm going to say that Americans are very suspicious of the International Criminal Court. That's why the United States Senate never ratified the treaty, even when Clinton was president. Not even close. We have *never* agreed to the jurisdiction of this court. Yet this court, on its own, decided to arrest, charge, and imprison two Americans who were doing their jobs as navy pilots in the war on terror. And they are now being held in a First World country, one of our European *allies*, the Netherlands. A fellow NATO member. And even though they are going to be charged with terrible crimes, unlike in America where the most basic right is the right to counsel, they are being denied even the opportunity to meet with an American lawyer who has been retained by their fami-

lies to represent them, because an *administrator* has
said he can't. *That's* what I'm going to say. So would you
like to come out there with me and stand on the sidewalk and answer for the court why it is that an attorney
who flew all night to get here at the request of the families of the American pilots is not able to meet with his
clients and talk to them?"

He smiled again. "Of course. The American threat
of going to the press. Of course."

"It's not a threat. It's an absolute fact. I don't have to
go to them. As soon as they find out who I am and what
I'm doing they're going to follow me around like a
pack of lost dogs. I'll be able to say anything I want to
them anytime that I want. I will be able to pick up the
phone and speak to the entire world in about half an
hour anytime I want. So can you. But what I have to
say, at least in the United States, will become a rallying
cry. And that's what they're going to do. I'll give them
your address and they'll stand in front of your house all
day and all night. They'll rally to me, and they'll be all
over you like stink on dog shit. Pardon my French."

He was suddenly humorless. "I don't believe that is a
French expression. What is it you want to do if you see
these American servicemen?"

"I want to have a privileged conversation with them.
Unless you don't recognize the attorney-client privilege, and eavesdrop or record what attorneys and their
clients say to each other."

"Of course not. We give them complete freedom
once they are admitted before this court."

"Monsieur Magnette, I think you should give me a

provisional admittance before this court, subject of course to your later disapproval, so that I can see my clients and began advising them on these very serious matters."

He measured the box he was in. He thought in silence for perhaps a minute. "I accept your recommendation. They are being held at a prison outside town. I will have a car pick you up out front. Please wait in the lobby."

I stood, expecting to shake hands, but he turned and walked out through a side door to his office and left me standing there. I picked up my briefcase, walked back down the hall and back out by the security officers, and waited in the lobby.

# FOUR

The car that picked me up was a black Peugeot with tinted windows. It looked like a government vehicle of some kind, but was probably one of the fleet of cars of the International Criminal Court itself. What an enormous budget this court had. It was like its own small country.

After a twenty-minute drive we pulled up in front of a prison straight out of the dark ages. I was shocked a building like it was still being used anywhere in Europe for anything, let alone the place where prisoners were kept by the International Criminal Court, the worldwide focus of international human rights. From the outside it looked like a torture chamber. It was old, and made from large stones or bricks. It looked to be in good shape, but clearly was originally built hundreds of years ago. It had high turrets like the Tower of London, with barbed wire. It looked like a maximum security prison fast-forwarded from the 1500s. The driver dropped me off in the parking lot near a door that was the likely entrance. I got out, closed the door, and looked around uncertainly. I wanted to appear unsure about how to enter the prison, which wasn't far off, but I really wanted to examine the security, to see how I might get into the prison without invitation if I were so inclined. I wouldn't admit that such thoughts occurred to me often. The kinds of things I did in my former, active days.

I walked to the massive wooden door and stepped through the smaller door that had been cut into the medieval structure. As I got inside the receiving area, I noted there were guards all around inside, but none outside. The room was small with a hard floor, the kind you might see in a hospital, probably vinyl on concrete. There were a few paintings, but no chairs. There was a high desk behind which sat an official in some kind of uniform. I didn't recognize it. I approached. "Good morning. My name is Jack Caskey. I'm here to see the two Americans."

"Yes. We know. Please wait."

I looked around the room. There were no chairs, no benches, and nowhere to wait for any length of time. The implication was that if you had to wait very long, you were in the wrong place. I went to the small window overlooking the courtyard of the prison and stood there in amazement. There was what passes for a typical prison courtyard, with fairly nice grass, but it was surrounded by a steel fence with barbed wire on top. Outside that fence was another fence that was equally intimidating. Inside that was a covered passageway entirely encased by steel bars. The bars rose from the concrete up overhead and arched into the stone wall close to the door where I was standing. You could fit a tennis ball through the bars perhaps, but not much else. I looked back at the desk where the guard was sitting there doing nothing. I crossed back over to them. "Is there some problem? Some delay?"

"No sir."

"So then may I see the Americans?"

"Yes. The guard is coming."

I nodded, and continued to walk around the room, waiting. Finally I heard a loud bang as the massive lock on the large steel door behind me was thrown open electronically. The door swung open toward me and two men entered. One was a large prison guard, the other a dark-suited man who had to be a warden or supervisor. They approached me. "Mr. Caskey?" the warden type said.

"Yes."

"Please come with us."

I followed him down the hallway past several dark rooms and doors, around the corner, through two other hallways, then into a room that was cavernous and dank. The warden said to me, "We will bring the two Americans here."

I looked around. "We'll be alone?"

"Of course. But their guards must have them in sight at all times. They will be outside, at that window."

I saw the window he was indicating. It was thick with steel wire running inside it like a chain link fence within bulletproof glass.

The warden turned and headed toward the door. "I will bring the two Americans."

The two men left and were gone for about five minutes. I could hear chains dragging on the stone outside the door before they got close to the room. Finally the door swung open, and the two Americans were brought in, still in their flight suits, with leg chains around their boots and their hands cuffed behind them. They looked frightened. They looked at me expecting an inquisitor, I thought. I said to the warden, "Take off their handcuffs. Give them some time to talk to me and the dignity of having their hands."

The warden nodded at the guard, who released their handcuffs. They rubbed their wrists. I waited, and the warden and the guard stepped out and closed the door behind them. They threw a large bolt closed and stood watching us through the window.

I looked at the two officers, who examined me. Even though they were both in their flight suits, they were as different as they could be. The one I came to learn was Rawlings was tall with dark eyes and hair as long as you could wear it in the navy. His face had a brooding, angry look. The other officer was shorter, about my height, had blond hair cut closely. He had an open, bright "seen-it-all" ironic look on his face. He actually looked kind. I said, "Good morning. My name is Jack Caskey."

The taller one interrupted me. "You American? What in the hell is going on?"

I motioned to the table in the middle of the room. "Let's sit down."

They went around to the other side of the table and

sat. I held my hand up to forestall their flood of questions. "I've been hired by your wives to represent you." I took out the two letters of engagement, and handed them to them.

They looked at them, then at me. The tall one said, "My wife doesn't know any lawyers. How did she hire you?"

"Well, actually it wasn't initially your wives. They were referred to me by someone else. First, tell me your names."

"I'm Doug Rawlings," he answered.

The shorter one said, "My name is Bill Duncan. They call me Dunk. They call him Raw, and not without reason. But who referred you?"

"Chris Marshall. He's on the staff of the national security advisor at the White House."

"JAG officer?" Dunk asked.

"No, actually he is the officer in charge of special operations and counterterrorism operations."

Dunk frowned and looked at Raw. "I still don't get the connection."

"I used to be a SEAL. Like he still is." I went on. "But now I'm a criminal defense attorney in D.C. I worked for the Justice Department for a while. While I was there I did some research on the International Criminal Court. I guess he heard about it. I've tried a lot of big felony cases in federal courts around the country and know my way around a courtroom. I guess he thought I had the right combination of skills."

Raw jumped in. "So what the hell are we doing here?"

"Your last mission in Pakistan."

"Well we were flying in Afghanistan initially. We got a late vector."

"Right. But the ultimate target was in Pakistan."

"And?"

"Well apparently it was a refugee medical facility. The bomb killed a bunch of Afghans, and aid workers. Most of the people killed were women and children."

"No way," Dunk said, sitting up. "That was a legitimate al Qaeda target. We had good intel."

Raw looked concerned. "You had a good target, right? Good image? Match the lat/long?"

"Perfect. Good cross-hairs, right in the middle. No issues. This isn't collateral damage, unless someone happened to be standing right next to the building. No doubt we hit what we were aiming at."

I nodded. "Well then, you had bad targeting information, if what they're saying is true. They're saying sixty women and children were killed, and something like six or eight medical workers from a European medical group. The tribal chiefs from the area—and some others, obviously—are saying it was intentional. A statement of some kind by the United States to the Taliban and al Qaeda operating in Pakistan; and to the country of Pakistan that we were coming in, and it didn't matter what they thought or said."

"That's just complete bullshit. Who's making the shit up?" Raw asked, getting red.

"I don't know who's making this up. But this whole thing feels rigged to me. So I think your instincts are correct—somebody is making this up, and doing a good enough job that the whole world is buying it. At least for now. Including the ICC. That's why you're here. But let's go through all this methodically. Let's start from the beginning. I want to get all the facts while they're fresh in your mind. What was your mission?"

They told me everything, from the brief, to the flight, to the drop. All routine from their perspective. Then the Stingers. No idea how that happened, but one or more got into their engine and down they went. The capture and humiliation was just how it looked, except there were some arguing for the carpet knife, but others with more authority prevailed. After a ride, they suddenly found themselves sitting in the plush leather seats of a brand-new Falcon 7X.

"What did you think then?"

"We thought finally sanity has prevailed and we're going to get flown to Qatar and sent back to the carrier," Dunk said.

Raw added, "Except they kept us handcuffed. That was not a good sign."

"And no one would talk to us."

"And they were talking in a foreign language."

I started wondering. "What language?"

Dunk said, "Not sure, but sounded French."

"Not Dutch?"

"I don't think so. I've only been to Holland once. It sounds more like German, if I recall right. French is pretty distinctive."

"What else did you notice?"

"Nothing really."

"Who else was on the plane?"

"Security guys. Tough guys."

"The whole plane? Just pilots and security?"

Raw nodded.

Dunk frowned. "No. There was one other guy."

"Were you blindfolded at all?"

"No. Not for the whole flight."

"So who was this other guy?"

Dunk shook his head. "Don't know. Old guy. Sitting in the back all by himself. The security guys didn't talk to him at all. But he seemed to be in charge. Sitting there in his suit. I only got to see him once, when we got on. He was sitting there. After that we were facing forward and couldn't really look around."

"An old guy?"

"Yeah. Maybe seventy. White hair. Suit and tie."

"Who was he?"

"No idea. Never got up that I saw."

"He wasn't worried about you seeing him."

"No. Not at all. In fact he had sort of a look on his face. Like 'Now you will get yours, Americans.'"

"Like he wanted you to see him. His look."

"Exactly. Like he'd finally done it. And he wanted us to know."


As I walked out of the prison I walked into an army of reporters, television cameras, and microphones. I knew they'd catch up with me at some point, but I didn't expect it yet. I glanced at them, and they rushed me. I was surrounded by journalists yelling at me. Several of them were yelling my name. I stopped. I heard the question of one of them. "What did the American pilots say? Why did they drop bombs on the refugee building? How are you going to defend them from these charges? Are you qualified to represent someone before the International Criminal Court?"

The cameras were already rolling. If I walked away without saying anything they'd accuse me of avoiding them. I'd had enough encounters with the press in some of my cases in the States to know that there was no good solution. The last thing I wanted to show my clients was their attorney responding to journalists saying "No comment." I put down my briefcase, and turned toward the journalists. They grouped around me and jammed microphones toward my face. It was one of those scenes that you see on the news all the time of somebody surrounded by journalists with arms being used as booms to extend microphones toward your face. "I'll answer a few questions, but then I have to go."

The man closest to me yelled, "Did your clients bomb the refugee camp?"

"Let me say something preliminarily. I do not plan on giving you a recitation of whatever it is that they are ultimately going to be charged with. I have not had the benefit of seeing any charge or indictment. I don't know what the allegations will be. Based on the information of the press it sounds like a building that was being used for refugees, and in particular for medical attention, was struck by a bomb. I don't know that, but that's what I have heard. Obviously the question is how did that happen and why. Anyone who asserts that that was done intentionally is wrong. I am confident that the two American aviators will be exonerated. But first we will have to challenge the jurisdiction of this court to try individuals from a country which not only has never signed the treaty, but has protested its existence and refused to be bound by it because they predicted that something just like this would happen. And here we are. Some prosecutor's idea of what constitutes a war crime may not coincide with the general understanding of war crimes, and such a prosecution could in fact simply be a political act. I don't know if that's what we're dealing with here, but I intend to find out."

"Did your clients bomb that building on purpose?" one man yelled with a German accent. "Whether they knew it was a refugee camp or not, did they hit the building they were trying to hit?"

"As I said, I am not going to get into the details of what they were or were not trying to do, or how this could have happened. There is much that I need to learn about the facts. I need to examine the entire series of events. I for one would like to know how it is they ended up on a private jet in Peshawar, Pakistan, and that night were flown to The Hague. How did that happen? And without even a conversation with the United States government or any indication of intent to hold American aviators. Do you know? Find out how there was a private jet waiting for them in Pakistan before the bomb was even released. Don't you find that puzzling? I intend to find the answers to all those questions."

A journalist toward the back of the mob yelled, "Why you? Are you qualified to defend these Americans?"

"I have been retained by their wives. I have tried numerous criminal cases in the United States, but certainly nothing before the International Criminal Court. Whether or not any individual believes me to be qualified, I am the one who's going to do it, and I will do my best to get them off these charges."

"Did you see what the American president said this morning?"

I looked at him and realized that I had not seen any news this morning. Noting the time, the president might have only recently said something that made the morning news shows. "No, I haven't seen his comments. What did he say?"

The man with the German accent continued. "Your president has said that this is an outrage, that the Americans have done nothing wrong, and that the court has no jurisdiction over American servicemen. He said he would try and get this resolved without charges being pursued."

I nodded my agreement. "That makes the most sense to me. We should get this resolved before it gets any further down a road from which we cannot return easily. Now if you'll excuse me . . ."

The car that had brought me to the prison was still there. I crossed the parking lot to it, climbed in, and closed the door hard.

"Where to?" the driver asked.

"Can you take me to my hotel and then the airport?"

"Yes, of course."

When I landed in Dulles I knew it was time to meet the two wives who had "retained" me. When the bus pulled up to the main terminal I headed straight to the Delta counter. As I walked through the terminal I got a sense of the infinite focus of the American press on the bombing incident. It had everything they could want. The military, politics, injustice, war crimes, hazy and questionable accusations, humiliated Americans, an international incident, outrage everywhere, and possibly a trial—confrontation. They were already pushing at every door they could find to learn more about what happened, and who was to be involved. Although my face had been on televisions all over the world, no one in Dulles recognized me. I bought a ticket to Norfolk, Virginia, sat in the gate area for two hours, and finally boarded. Two hours later I was at the Hertz counter heading to the two addresses on the engagement letters. I called Marshall.

"Chris Marshall," he answered

"I hope it's okay if I call you."

"You can call me anytime."

"You may regret saying that someday. But I'm on my way to meet the two wives. What do they know?"

"They know you're representing their husbands, and that the government is paying for it. That's it. They also know what you look like because I'm sure they saw you on television."

"Okay. You should know that I called Kristen at Covington and Burling in New York. Classmate of mine. I told her I needed their firm to go to bat for our boys just as hard as they did for the terrorists at Guantánamo who they were so keen on representing for free. I wanted to get some of that righteous indignation working for a couple of American servicemen. You okay with that?"

He paused. "Why do you need them? I told you half the Justice Department is already working for you. You have whatever you need."

"Look, I have a lot of respect for Justice. Lot of good people there. But Covington is one of the best firms in the country. Probably have some of the smartest lawyers the country has ever produced. I need that extra creativity, that cleverness. I need people outside the government who aren't thinking of their next promotion or moving to a private firm to finally cash in on all the years they've been underpaid at Justice."

"Fine with me. Whatever you think you need."

"So what's the thinking in Washington on all this?"

"Everything is on the table, Jack. We haven't taken anything off our decision tree. We might just go get them."

"Meaning?"

"You know exactly what I mean."

"Chris, I've been in that prison. It can't happen. At least not without a lot of casualties."

"We'll talk about it later. You'd better call those two wives before you get over there. I'll text you their phone numbers." Marshall hung up.

I continued down the toll road toward Virginia Beach. As soon as I saw Chris's text, I opened it, highlighted the first phone number, and dialed.

I asked them to be at the same house so we could meet once. The house was in the Kings Grant section of Virginia Beach, a pretty, peaceful neighborhood of brick houses and mature trees. I knocked on the door and it opened immediately. I was met by a beautiful woman who clearly had been crying. I could see another woman standing behind her. She was slightly taller but equally attractive. I introduced myself, and they invited me into the dining room, where we sat down around the table. I heard a noise in the back of the house and the first woman, who introduced herself as Sarah, Dunk's wife, said, "That's Parker. I just put him down for a nap."

"You have children?"

"Just one. He's nine months old. Would you like some coffee?"

I looked at my watch. It felt like the middle of the afternoon, but was only 10:00 A.M.

"Yes. Absolutely. Black. Thank you."

The other woman, Carolyn, Raw's wife, watched me take a sip, waiting. She finally said, "We saw you on television. You saw our husbands."

"Hope I didn't make a fool of myself."

"Not at all. But who are you? How did you come to represent our husbands? There's so much we need to know."

I nodded. "I got a call from a gentleman at the White House. He asked me to represent them. It's obviously ultimately up to you, but he offered to pay for it."

"How much do you charge?"

"You don't really need to worry about it because it's all taken care of."

Sarah asked, "Why would they do that? Why would somebody else pay for our husbands' defense?"

"Because in case you haven't figured it out yet, it's very likely they're just pawns in an attempt to manipulate the United States. Someone has planned this out. The United States therefore takes an interest, and they want to make sure this comes out right."

"How can they do that?"

"By doing whatever it takes to get your husbands off, including paying me to defend them."

Sarah had already moved on to what she really wanted to know. "How are they? How do they look? Are they being tortured? What is the prison like?"

"They're uninjured and fine. They told me they even have computers with Internet access. They aren't allowed to do e-mail, but I can get word to them for you. If you want to write letters the postal service will deliver them, or I can take them, but they'll get them."

"Can we go see them?"

"You know, I'm really not sure. I didn't ask that question. It seems reasonable, so I'll ask. Can you get over there?"

They both nodded. "We'll find a way," Carolyn said.

"I need you to understand a little who I am, and what I'm doing." They nodded. "I am a criminal defense lawyer from D.C. Before I went to law school though, I was in the navy."

"Did you fly?"

"No. I was in special operations."

"A SEAL?" Sarah asked.

I hesitated. I didn't want to get into too much detail. But I had gone out of my way to gain their confidence by mentioning my navy experience. One of those trade-offs you make that on reflection might have been better left unsaid. I answered, "I did a lot of work in the

Middle East with the SEALs. Different assignments, different places. Can't really go into most of it, but I understand the military. And I also understand how people don't always look out for you when they say they're going to. So I want you to know that I will not abandon your husbands, no matter what. If you want me to represent them, I will do so to the best of my ability. I'll take every position that I can that is to their benefit, even if it goes against what I'm being told to do by those in Washington who are paying me. I want you to understand that." I looked directly into their eyes as I stopped to make sure they were listening. "My loyalty is to your husbands, and indirectly to you. I will do every single thing I can to get them off. I will embarrass whoever needs to be embarrassed. I will chase whatever needs to be chased.

"I expect to get some resistance from the military, because I will ask for operational orders, targeting information, intelligence available, anything I can to show that they were operating within their orders and did exactly what they were told to do based on intelligence that was given to them. So if the government starts to pull away, I'll press them. That doesn't mean they'll do what I want, but I am not here to make the government happy. In fact, that's one of my flaws. I wasn't a SEAL to make the government happy. I'm a little too much of an idealist and sometimes I made my superiors unhappy. I'm a little too independent. That's one of the reasons I got out. But I am loyal to my clients, and I will fight for them."

They were weighing my words carefully, not sure

what to make of me. "I do have to tell you though, I don't have any experience before the International Criminal Court. I'm not sure any American attorney does. There may be one. But we don't usually show up there and don't represent clients there. It's a European thing, a continental thing. Their rules are a little different than ours, and I'm sure I will make some missteps. But we will do all we can to prevail, and I will get your husbands off. Or at least I'll try."

They looked at each other with concern. Carolyn said, "You don't sound very confident."

"I'm not very confident. This whole thing feels rigged. How did they even get shot down? How does an F/A-18F, the most advanced fighter in the navy's inventory, get shot down? I think we've only lost a couple of F-18s in the early 90s in Iraq. So do I really think that a bunch of al Qaeda jerks sitting in caves in western Pakistan have the ability to shoot down an F-18? I don't think so. That means either they got unbelievably lucky, or they had some help. And I don't believe all that much in unbelievable luck. If they had help, where did it come from? Who in the world would provide al Qaeda with the ability to shoot down an F-18? Money can certainly purchase a lot of things, and Pakistan is a notorious market for American uniforms, computers, weapons, and equipment. You literally can buy an American M-16 rifle in a sidewalk bazaar. But antiaircraft equipment—particularly Stinger missiles, which I have heard were used—would be *really* difficult, even in a market like that. So I kind of doubt that. But it's something I'm going to be tracking.

"And I've got to tell you, your husbands told me that

they hit the exact target they were told to. That means our intelligence was terrible—and believe me, we have had bad intelligence in the past—but this is horrific. How did we get a specific building as a target for an al Qaeda meeting that was to take place, hit that building on the button, and it turns out to be full of refugees, medical personnel, and women and children? How does that happen? Was it just a mistake? I don't think so. That's why it feels like a setup. But the thing that really convinces me someone is behind all this is how your husbands got to Holland. There just *happened* to be a Falcon 7X jet waiting for them at the Peshawar airport to whisk them off to the ICC. That's one of the newest, fastest, longest-range business jets in the world. And one of the very few that could fly from Pakistan to Holland nonstop. Coincidence? The very night they are shot down they get in a jet and fly to Europe? I don't think there are Falcon jets just sitting around in Pakistan waiting to be hired to fly to Europe. Maybe it's just me, but that feels like something that was planned. This whole thing stinks to me."

I sat back and drank from my cooling coffee. They said nothing, and tried to absorb what they had heard so far. I went on. "So how do I prove these things? How do I get the evidence to show this was a setup? Especially, if the International Criminal Court was part of the setup?

"It feels like some cases I've had in D.C. where the federal prosecutors and the Washington police are a little too cozy. It's like entrapment, only worse. And I don't know what the United States is going to do about it. I don't really know whether they will be as behind me as they say they're going to be. At the end of the day we have to assume that they will let your husbands rot. Rather than embarrass the International Criminal Court, as they ought to do, instead of confronting Europe head-on, they'll let this go, let it go to trial, let your husbands get convicted, and argue for a reduced sentence. And I've got to tell you, if I sniff that coming I'll run up the bullshit flag and go right to the press. I'll scream bloody murder and accuse everybody of acting in bad faith. But I will be there beside your husbands until the end, whatever that turns out to be.

"You just need to understand there's a lot in play here other than the trial. I'm going to find out what really happened here and who is pulling the strings."

# FIVE

As I drove back to the Norfolk airport I called Marshall on my cell phone. He answered on the second ring. "Chris, Caskey."

"How'd your meeting go?"

"Fine. What's going on in Washington?"

"You been watching the news?"

"No. What's up?"

"The press finally got ahold of this, and they're shaking it like a rag doll. They can't believe what a sexy story this is, and all the different ways this might play out. They're in full alert."

"What about the government? What's the official reaction?"

"The president was supposed to have another press conference this morning but it got moved to this afternoon at three. It's all about the ICC."

"What's he going to say?"

"Quite a bit. I can't go into the details. It will be worth your while to watch."

"I'll try. I've got to run up to New York. I'm going to lean on Covington and Burling to help me."

"Right. Your classmate. Why are they so special again?"

"Because one of their partners when they were representing seventeen Yemenis being held at Gitmo for free is none other than our current attorney general, Eric Holder. So not only are they bright, but I'm thinking they may let him in on what we're doing. And I need the DOJ behind us, not conspiring against us—"

"Why would they conspire against you? Come on."

"Why? Because the president is on record of being in favor of the ICC. I don't want this to take a bad turn. So maybe Holder will hesitate to go against his old firm, if they're on board and visibly for our guys. It's sort of a trump card."

"You're overthinking."

"Maybe. But it won't hurt us."

"I guess. Look, we should talk as soon as you get back. There are a couple of other things we need to discuss, but not on the phone."

"What about tonight?"

"Maybe. You going to your office?"

"Probably later. I'll give you a call. You keep your cell on?"

"Always. I might bring somebody with me this time. Not sure he can make it, but I'll try."

"From DOJ?"

"Not even close."

"Sure. Whatever. I'll catch up with you tonight."

I tapped my Bluetooth to disconnect Marshall, and dialed Kristen. Her cell phone rang and she answered. "This is Kristen."

"Caskey. What did the committee say?"

"You are just unrelenting aren't you? The committee doesn't do something just because I say so."

"Did you submit the request?"

"Yes. And they'll deal with it as they see fit. It's a bunch of partners with a few associates, Jack. And I'm not one of the associates."

"So when are they going to decide?"

"I don't know. I don't even know how often they meet."

"So all you did, really, is fill out a piece of paper and slip it under the door to the mysterious pro bono committee. That's dedication."

"Well I'm not dedicated, Jack. I am reluctant and unenthusiastic. I am not on board. I'm doing this for you as a favor. Maybe you can get someone else from this firm to work on this with you, but frankly I'm not interested."

"You going to be there for a while?"

"I suppose. Why?"

"I'm coming to New York. Call the chairman of your pro bono committee. Tell him I want to meet with him."

"No."

"In fact why don't you tell him to put a committee meeting together on an emergency basis. Tell him this is an opportunity for the firm to gain some much needed patriotic publicity, and if they don't jump on it, I'm going to walk right down the street to Skadden Arps, or MoFo, or Weil Gotshal and they'll jump on it."

"It doesn't work like that. I can't call the committee together."

"Have you seen this partner? Is he there today?"

"I saw him this morning. I don't know if he'll be here all day."

"What about the chairman of your firm? Is he going to be there all day?"

"It's a woman."

"Fine. *She* going to be there all day?"

"I believe she's here. But I don't know. She doesn't run her calendar by me every morning, which she certainly should."

"I'm on the next flight to New York. I'll see you there in a few hours."

"You don't need to come here, Jack. It's not going to make any difference."

"We'll see. I want to talk to these people and look them in the eye. I still think your firm is going to do the right thing here. And we need to get working."

The cab ride from JFK was uneventful, but it was later in the day than I had hoped. It was almost four by the time I arrived on Eighth Avenue where the New York office of Covington and Burling was located. I got out of the cab, paid the driver, and looked up at the building. It never ceased to amaze me how much bigger New York felt than Washington just because of the size of the buildings. There was no height limit in New York, no maximum height, like in D.C., measured by the top of the Capitol. That made for the unmistakable New York skyline known around the world as the center of commerce. And this law firm was right in the middle of it. Eighth Avenue and West 40th. In the beautiful new New York Times Building. In the highest floors of one of the tallest buildings in New York. The rent was probably twenty times what my office cost per square foot. But they made ten—or twenty—times what I made. I went into the lobby, checked in with security, and they called Kristen.

I wondered if she would claim to have never heard of me. I waited for a few minutes, and finally she came out to the reception area. She smiled, crossed over to me, and extended her hand. She was exactly as I had remembered her: five feet eight, thin, with casual yet classy clothes. I didn't know if they were expensive, but they looked very good on her. She had the thin figure of a model, so everything looked good on her. I was still in the suit I had worn on the airplane all the way back from Holland, to Virginia Beach, and now to New York. It was starting to look like I had decided never to take it off and was going to wear it until it fell apart. My beard was stubbly and I was sure my hair was starting to look oily. Kristen's presence made me very self-aware, something I hadn't anticipated.

I shook her hand and looked at her eyes. She was prettier close up than I had remembered. Her blond hair hung down to her shoulders. She probably colored it, but it was truly beautiful. Her pretty blue eyes were full of curiosity. "Thanks for taking the time to see me. I know I've been pushy, but I'm here to take my pushiness to a whole new level." I smiled.

She smiled and rolled her eyes.

We had been close friends since we were members of the same study group at law school. She had done better than I had, but we both had done well enough to say that we had succeeded. She was in the middle of the class politically, which meant she was liberal. I would say probably 80 percent of my law school class would self-identify as liberal. I was one of the few that didn't. It made me something of an odd man out, and most people assumed therefore that I wasn't very smart, and would join the JAG Corps after I left law school. When a few of them learned that I had been a Navy SEAL, they thought I was some kind of freak or crazy person. That was okay. I'm used to people not knowing what I am about. I use it to my advantage. Kristen knew everything about me though, as we had spent hours studying together. We had grown extremely comfortable with each other in spite of our political differences. We spoke directly, so we thought, and thought about dating. But we were both ultimately sure it would never last long term, so we never started. I said, "Take me to your leader."

"Not that easy. I told him that you were coming, that you are the one they had seen on television, and that you wanted to meet with the pro bono committee immediately. I got the response that I expected. We don't just have committee meetings because someone demands it. We submit the information, and it goes to the committee in due course. They think that decisions that are rushed are often not good decisions."

I laughed out loud. "Damn, Kristen. That's just so impressive. They should run a school for bureaucrats."

"Can I get you a cup of coffee or something? I really do need to get back to work, but I have a few minutes for a cup of coffee if you'd like."

I stared at her without answering. We stood there in the reception area, with me staring at her, and her trying to avert her eyes, but not really able to. I waited a little longer. "Is that what this is? You think you can pacify me and I'll go away? And you're a little bit afraid that I'm going to make a scene. Something really noteworthy and regrettable. And that it will fall on you because you know me, and you greeted me here. You'll be made to look like a fool." I waited; she said nothing. "That's fair. I have seriously considered making a scene. So what I would suggest we do right now, instead of talking about coffee and other equally important things, is for you to walk down the hall to the office of the chairman of your pro bono committee. Your only other choice is to have that person come here now."

She shook her head. "There's no way I'm going to walk you into the office of the partner who's the chairman of the pro bono committee unannounced. That would be rude and improper."

I shrugged. "I'm okay with rude and improper." I looked out their large picture windows over the skyline of New York City and noticed how bright and clear the day was. It was just getting to the point where the sun was descending toward New Jersey. "I am *totally* okay with inappropriate and rude right now. Let's go," I said, waiting.

She turned and walked over to the receptionist. "Would you call Thomas McInnes for me please?"

The receptionist dialed while she looked at Kristen's face. She was seeing something in Kristen's face which I couldn't see but she didn't like. McInnes answered the phone and the receptionist handed it to Kristen. She spoke softly where I couldn't hear her, with her back to me facing the receptionist and the large picture windows behind her. The conversation lasted no more than a few seconds. She handed the phone back to the receptionist and turned to me. She walked across the tile floor and said, "He's coming. *Now* would you like some coffee?"

We sat in a cavernous conference room on the fiftieth floor overlooking central Manhattan. The conference room probably had more square footage than my entire office including my secretary and paralegal. Thomas McInnes turned out to be a nice fellow. He was younger than I had expected, in his early forties, had straight brown hair, and wore round wire rim glasses. A very intelligent, if dated, look. He seemed far more forgiving than I would expect a litigator in a big New York law office to be.

I started telling myself to behave, not to be a jerk or too demanding. Thomas—not Tom—had what I needed. The manpower and depth that came from a big firm, and the prestige to be respected before you said or did anything. I needed their help. I couldn't do this case by myself.

Kristen sat quietly at the end of the table, and Thomas and I sat across from each other, next to her. He spoke. "So, Mr. Caskey, you were just in Holland. I saw you on television. You looked quite annoyed."

I smiled. "Probably was. Not as annoyed as I would have been if they had done what they were inclined to do. They weren't going to let me see my clients—I wasn't admitted before the ICC yet. I told them I was going to throw a tantrum on television, and accuse them of injustice and obstruction. Much to my surprise they relented and I got to see them."

He nodded. "I'm impressed. Most prosecutors are unmoved by threats of going to the press. They know you're going to do it anyway."

"Better than that. I told him the press would stand in front of his personal house until he relented. And he knew that I'd give them the address."

He raised his eyebrows. "You know where the prosecutor lives?"

"Actually it was the court administrator. And no, I didn't know. But I sure would have found out and stood in front of it myself if he hadn't let me see my clients."

"Well I'm glad you got in to see them. So what can we do for you?"

"First, thank you for taking the time to see me. I know I didn't go about this in the normal way. I didn't send letters and requests and official correspondence, and I probably took a little advantage of Kristen's friendship. I hope I didn't get her in trouble."

He shook his head vigorously. "Not at all. What do you have in mind?"

"I assume Kristen told you the basics. I need help. This is going to be a major international trial. I have been retained by the families to represent them. I know a little bit about the International Criminal Court, and there aren't *any* American lawyers who have ever tried a case in front of the International Criminal Court. So I'm not outside of some elite group—there is no elite group. At least not in the U.S. All the attorneys who have tried and defended those accused in front of the court have been European. In fact the whole event is pretty much a European thing. So I'm going to do the best I can, but I need help. I have to file motions, argue jurisdiction, find witnesses, prepare for trial—everything you can imagine. So I wanted to see if your firm would be willing to work on a pro bono basis to help these two men."

He played with a paperclip in his hands, and stared down at the table. He said nothing. I looked at Kristen, who looked back at me, unclear what was happening. After an extended pause he looked up at me. "This is not the usual kind of pro bono case that we take on. We don't usually defend the military from charges of war crimes."

I waited to see if he was going to say anything else. Apparently not. "Yes, I know. In fact it is somewhat un-common for American service members to be charged with war crimes. I did not come to your pro bono com-mittee in the hope that we could find someone who had experience defending at a war crimes trial. The point really was to have smart people from a very capable law firm help in the defense. Perhaps what inspired me was the article that I read on Law.com which outlined your firm's vigorous defense of terrorists, mostly Yemenis as I understand it, at Guantánamo. I guess I was hoping that you would be willing to extend the same courtesy to American servicemen that you extended to terrorists."

He looked across the table at me intensely, with a look that showed a transformation from the nice guy he had been five minutes before. I was shocked. He said, "In fact that's your whole point, isn't it? You hope to leverage our representation of those who were without representation at Guantánamo Bay into helping you assist those who do have representation, and, as I understand it, are entitled to representation from the Department of Justice. You essentially are trying to shame us into helping you. You think that by bringing up Guantánamo Bay, we will feel bad and chip in to help in a case that we normally would not be involved in. Isn't that really what we're dealing with here, Mr. Caskey?"

I could transform a little myself. "I don't think I would call it shaming you into it. I guess I would call it giving you an opportunity to show that you truly care about justice and fairness. And that you don't operate based on an agenda. Firms like yours, in fact yours specifically, stand up tall in full righteous fury, patting yourselves on the back for representing terrorists. You published a pro bono report about last year where that was one of the first cases cited by your firm in tooting its horn about what great pro bono work it had done. Spent over three thousand attorney hours on Gitmo cases in one year. I'm not condemning that work, I don't really know much about it, just that it happened and your firm has now worked maybe ten thousand hours for free on behalf of the Guantánamo detainees. And in fact one of your partners, former partners, dropped his pants and held a chubby press conference in his underwear to emphasize how horribly your Yemeni clients had been treated. But sometimes the people who most need representation are those who are not the darlings of the New York bar who make you feel righteous and indignant. Sometimes it's those who've been wrongly accused or, in this case, set up. So yes, I'd like to give you that opportunity to show that you truly care about justice and fairness and American serviceman."

"Well sir, we are definitely interested in justice and fairness, but we don't usually look to sole practitioner criminal defense lawyers in Washington to tell us what that means."

"I'm not telling you anything. I'm giving you an opportunity, and asking for your help. You can say yes, or you can say no. If you say no, I will go elsewhere. And the *American Lawyer* article that will ultimately be written on these cases, and on this trial, will certainly feature your firm prominently as being unwilling to help."

He sat back and smiled wryly. "Ah, I see. Your threat of journalists again. It must be your favorite gambit."

"No, actually it's not. I generally hate the press. They don't get very much right, but they can be helpful in accomplishing an objective. So, the question is, are you willing to help or not?"

He changed the subject. "Kristen tells me you used to be a Navy SEAL."

That little piece of information usually went one of two ways. Either people had an overinflated opinion of SEALs and thought they were supermen, or they thought they were evil and part of some special operations criminal conspiracy to subjugate the world. Here he may have just been making conversation, but I didn't think so. "True enough."

"How long were you in the navy?"

"About eight years."

"Why'd you get out?"

"It was time."

"Meaning?" He stared at me.

"Meaning that it was time."

He smiled. "You probably saw a lot. Did you ever go to Iraq or Afghanistan?"

"Yes."

"So you've probably seen and done some things that you aren't proud of."

So. One of those. "Like what?"

"I don't know. Killing civilians, torturing people, you know, the stuff that seems to happen in war that we later regret."

"We? Did you serve in the military?"

"No."

"That's too bad. You might have a little more respect for those who have."

"I didn't say I didn't respect people who serve in the military. So did you see anybody commit any war crimes?"

"What the hell is this all about? You have something against the American military?"

"No. Absolutely not. They are important. I just don't like it when they get carried away. So I guess I would have to say that I think that the International Criminal Court is a good thing. They ought to be there to take care of the times when the military, ours or anybody else's, or governments, or even civilians, get carried away and commit war crimes. Someone ought to hold them accountable."

"Well, I didn't really come here for this discussion, but I guess I'd have to say that if some American did something wrong, committed an atrocity, intentionally killed a civilian, they *are* accountable and they are prosecuted. There are many cases of Americans being put on trial for that very thing, and going to prison. We don't need somebody else telling us how to do it. It's a violation of the UCMJ, the Uniform Code of Military Justice. I don't care what Holland says about it."

"Maybe I do. Or at least that we should hear what they have to say."

"Look, I'm not here to tell you how to think, I'm here to ask for help. Are you going to help these two Americans or not? It's a pretty simple question. Just let me know your answer."

Kristen spoke, probably trying to keep him from rejecting my proposal with his next sentence. "Thomas, perhaps we should submit the request to the full committee. They can consider it, take a look at my memo, and vote on it. Perhaps we could have a special meeting today, so we could get back to Jack."

Since he had just been ready to tell me no, I was willing to wait for a committee vote. He said, "Good idea. Mr. Caskey, I will call a meeting of the committee today, get some of the people from D.C. on the phone, and we'll get you an answer by tonight. Is that satisfactory?"

"Completely."

By the time I got to my apartment it was close to midnight. I was completely exhausted. I sent Marshall a text, knowing he was not at his office, and asked for the meeting first thing in the morning. I had to find out what the hell had gone wrong in Pakistan.

When I woke up after what felt like thirty minutes of sleep, I checked my phone and found a text from Marshall. He asked to meet at a restaurant that I knew near the federal courthouse for breakfast. I glanced at my watch, jumped in the shower, threw on a suit, and headed to the restaurant. He was there waiting for me when I arrived, sitting in the back reading the *Washington Post*. He looked like a typical Washington bureaucrat. We shook hands and I sat down.

I gestured to the waiter, who came to the table and poured me some black coffee. I drank it quickly.

Marshall said, "You didn't waste any time in stirring up a hornet's nest did you?"

"They didn't want me to see our two guys. They thought real hard about shutting me out. I told him that that would be unwise, that they were already suffering in the eyes of the American public, and if they refused to allow their prisoners to see their attorney, they would look even worse. Surprisingly, they relented and I got to see them."

"How are they doing?"

"They're doing fine, I guess. It's a bit disconcerting to launch from your carrier on a semi-routine mission, complete your mission with one diversion that was not only authorized but directed, get shot down, and end up in a prison in Holland. That was probably not on their list of things to do that day. They're being fairly well treated, the prison is sort of old and smelly but it's not inhumane. I guess I would describe their state of mind as general bafflement."

"No doubt. You going to be able to defend them?"

"That's what I need to talk to you about. I will certainly be able to *defend* them, but the real question is can I get them off. I will put on whatever evidence I can, but you've got to help me."

"Absolutely. What do you need?"

I lowered my voice slightly. "You have to help me figure out what in the hell happened here. This is just bizarre. How did they get targeting information on something that probably, based on the video that we're now seeing on television, was a refugee facility? How did we not know that? And why the diversion? Why did *they* have to go hit that target? Why not a Predator? We don't have fighters drop on targets in Pakistan, at least we didn't used to. This is not just some average case of bad intel. Something malicious happened here. And I need to find out what happened and who was behind it."

"And how do you propose to do that?"

"You tell me. Who ordered this strike? Who got the intel? Where did it come from? Who approved of a JDAM strike based on that intel? What other assets did we have in the area that either confirmed or didn't? And then probably most importantly, how do I get this evidence in the trial? I mean if in fact they did exactly what they were supposed to do, and they hit the target they were supposed to hit, and it turned out to be full of civilians, how is that their problem? Seems to me they got the wrong guy."

Our food arrived and I put my napkin in my lap. "So tell me what you've got. I have to know *everything* you know."

"Sure. Best I can tell so far, routine operation. We have outfits chasing the Taliban and parts of al Qaeda through the mountains of eastern Afghanistan and of course western Pakistan where they go to hide. They have tribes that are ruling part of the western area, the Taliban took over the Swat Valley for a while, then got pushed out. The Pakistani government goes from pretending like the Taliban isn't there to sending the army after them. And one of the things we've always been afraid of is a joint effort between al Qaeda and the Taliban. Well occasionally we get a very good piece of intelligence from Pakistan and we act on it. So here, as I said, routine operations, the *Reagan*'s air wing was operating from the Gulf over Afghanistan, along the border with Pakistan, and one of their F-18s was about to head home. Then somebody, not sure who, got a flash message that Pakistan had identified a high-value target, a leader of al Qaeda, someone from the inner circle, who had called a meeting with the Taliban in a hut in western Pakistan. We were told the reliability of the intelligence was ninety percent. We were given the latitude and longitude, and we pulled up a photograph immediately. It was a large hut with no windows, and a large flat roof. It looked like it could hold forty or fifty people. We thought this was it. They vector in the F-18, which had a JDAM, and transferred the latitude and longitude to them by data link. They confirmed the target, confirmed the latitude and longitude, and as a double check, we had a predator in the area that flew over and laser-illuminated the target."

"I thought a JDAM was GPS-guided."

"Generally. But the new model has GPS guidance and laser terminal guidance. It takes the best of whatever guidance it has to hit the target."

That puzzled me. "What if there's a conflict?"

"It has a very large brain for conflict resolution. It does it just as you would if you were doing it."

"Okay. So what happened?"

He looked over my shoulder at someone who was approaching the table and remained quiet. The person passed and he spoke again, quietly. "They vectored the F-18. They got the target, accepted it, the GPS checked out, so they flew in at normal altitude and dropped on the target. Hit it right on the bull's-eye. It was obliterated. Then after the fact, we see the videotapes of the arms and legs of the European doctors and the women and children who are being cared for there."

"So the intelligence was wrong."

"To say the least."

I pondered that for a second, then asked, "How in the hell did they shoot down an F-18?"

"Apparently somebody got ahold of Stinger missiles. This target was in a valley. No problem, they drop from 25,000 feet. Way out of the range of any shoulder-fired missile. But they were flying right down the middle of the valley. And of course they're 25,000 feet above sea level, not above ground level. They turned away from the target and headed south for the carrier, then out of nowhere five or six missiles were fired at them simultaneously. Apparently from a high peak on the side of the valley, the side they turned toward and were belly-up to as they were about to roll out to a southern heading. We have no idea how they got six Stinger missiles; we watch every one of those like a hawk. Stingers were what ended the Russian war in Afghanistan. We weren't going to have the same thing happen to us. Anyway, the pilot dumped a bunch of flares, and a couple of the stingers hit the F-18. They went down like a ton of bricks. They ejected and were captured. You've seen the rest."

"Pakistan has Stingers."

"Yes. But how would these shooters have gotten them from Pakistan?"

"A lot easier than they could have gotten them from us."

"True enough."

"And if I recall correctly, Pakistan makes their own version of the Stinger. Could have been those."

"Possible, but they'd have to have awfully good connections to get those out of the Pakistani army."

I had to agree with that. It gave me something to

think about. "Didn't you have any satellite photos on target?"

"Not really. It'd never been listed as a target before. We hadn't ever concentrated on it. We had some old satellite photos we were able to dig up, but none of them are significant. We were told the hut had been selected the night before for the meeting. That's pretty much how you'd expect them to do it. So we got the intel, acted on it, and here we are."

A lot of it didn't make sense. "And them getting shot down just *happened* to coincide with a Falcon 7X being in Peshawar and its owner being willing to let it be used to fly two U.S. naval officers to Holland to put them in prison." I paused. "Have we crawled back up the chain of intelligence to see who gave us this information?"

"We're trying. The key is Pakistan. They're not exactly falling all over themselves to cooperate. But we're leaning on them. We'll get through."

"Shit, Chris. Too many coincidences. Somebody was driving this whole thing."

"I think so too."

"So is the president going to say that?"

"He's going to say that we had intelligence of an important meeting and that we acted on that intelligence."

"Is he going to put the damned Pakistanis on report?"

"Probably not. We still have to work with them. And we need information from them on this."

"That's not the way to do it." I sat back for a minute and thought. I asked, "Is it possible the intelligence was right? The Taliban and al Qaeda *were* meeting at the refugee camp? It'd be good cover. Maybe they figured we'd find out about it, and knew we'd never drop on a refugee facility."

He nodded and drank from his water glass. He put it down. "Yes. In fact," he looked around, "we had a team on the ground near there. We knew there was going to be a meeting. A high-level meeting. And we knew it was to be in western Pakistan."

"The same source that told you about the building?"

"No. HUMINT."

"You must've had pretty hard intel to put a team on the ground. We never inserted unless we were sure."

"We were sure. We are sure. We think the meeting happened. We just think we got called off to a different location at the last minute. So rather than being near where the team was, the location we got was too far away and they had to take it out with the JDAM."

"You have to put me in touch with whoever was in charge of the team on the ground."

He frowned. "I'm not sure he'd know anything that would help you, but I'll find out who it was."

# SIX

When I got back to my office, much to my surprise Kristen was waiting for me. She was sitting in my small, dingy reception area. She stood up and crossed over to me right away, with a smile, but it was a semi-ironic smile. She extended her hand.

"What are you doing?" I asked.

"I'm ready to go to work."

"So . . . I take it the committee decided to let you lower yourself to do work with me."

She picked up her briefcase. "You should be grateful, not cynical."

"So you're serious? The mighty Covington and Burling voted to let you do this?"

She nodded. "Not only me, but anybody else you need. If you need a whole army of associates, we can get them. If you need another partner, a former U.S. attorney, or an appellate partner, just say the word. We're ready."

I looked over at my receptionist, who was hanging on every word. I turned back to Kristen. "I'm not sure where to put you. My paralegal is in the only other office. There's an office behind you. Technically it's not actually in the space I rent. The landlord owns it, but since you can only access it through my reception area, he can't rent it out without my permission. And I never seem to quite return those phone calls when he has someone who is willing to rent it. Let me talk to the landlord and we'll get you set up in there." I put my briefcase on the chair, took off my jacket, folded and laid it on the briefcase. "I've got to tell you, Kristen, I'm surprised. I thought the chairman of your committee hated me. I didn't make it easy for him, I'm sure. I thought he was one of those left-wing 'America is always wrong' kind of guys."

"Actually no. He's one of those left-wing 'do what's *right*' kind of guys."

"And he thinks this is right?"

"Actually, he is one of the most well read people you'll ever encounter. He has difficulty with trying to enforce a treaty against the citizen of a country where that country never signed the treaty and protested its language."

"Good enough for me. I take back half of what I said about him."

"That's real big of you."

"You have a travel budget?"

She nodded. "Just like representing a real client. The money though comes out of the firm's pro bono account. Whenever we win a pro bono case that results in attorney's fees we put it into our pro bono account to fund other cases just like this one. So my expenses will be paid by the firm."

"Excellent. Tell you what, you go get yourself organized wherever you're planning on staying. I'll get the landlord to spring for this office, I'll meet you back here at five. We'll eat some Chinese food on your new desk. Then tonight we're heading to Holland. I've got more questions for the clients, and I want you to meet them."

There wasn't anything electronic in her office yet. No phone, no computer, not even a standing light. Just the annoying buzzing overhead fluorescents. I had had the landlord move his boxes out of the room, and set up her office before she came back. Once he heard what I was doing, he agreed to give me the office for no charge. I placed the Chinese food containers on her desk and spread out the two thick paper plates. We sat around her wood veneer desk on the two government surplus chairs I had borrowed from the landlord. She sat in the desk chair, and I looked around the room as I handed her one of the food containers. I said, "I'm not a big fan of fluorescent lighting. I'll get you a lamp." I went to my office and unplugged my Georgetown University lamp. I put it on her credenza, plugged it into the wall, turned it on, and turned off the overhead lights. Although it wasn't very bright, it made a much more pleasant environment for dinner, and felt less stressful.

Kristen handled the chopsticks with great dexterity. She pushed her hair back, which hung on her black turtleneck sweater as she ate. I had to admit she looked beautiful. I started thinking about our never quite started relationship in law school. It made me question my own motives in contacting her, of all people. Sure, she worked at Covington and Burling, but I could have picked from hundreds of people who were better qualified. I probably wanted another chance to be with her. Not the right reason to pick someone to help you in what was likely to be one of the most important trials in your lifetime. We ate hungrily, and said nothing for a few minutes.

Finally she said, "So tell me what your plan is on defending this case. First, how did this all happen?"

"There's a lot I don't understand yet. I am very confused on how these two naval officers ended up in The Hague. Who did this? Who chartered the airplane? How did it happen to be in Peshawar? This whole thing feels like a very large and very well executed plan. You can certainly encounter things like that here and there, but I don't know that I've seen the Taliban or al Qaeda have a Falcon jet waiting to fly somebody to Europe. Somebody is behind it. And I don't mean somebody who is accusing them of war crimes from Pakistan. I mean somebody big. Perhaps even a government. I've got a feeling when we run this snake all the way back down to its hole, it's going to lead us somewhere completely unexpected. But for now, we have to treat it for what it is. An accusation—soon to be a released indictment—by the International Criminal Court under the Treaty of Rome."

She nodded, took a drink of her Diet Coke, and put down her chopsticks. "And what will the charges be?"

"They haven't released the indictment yet. But the charge is almost surely to be killing civilians. It's a defined war crime under the treaty."

"So theoretically if you kill a civilian intentionally, it's a war crime and you can be dragged to Holland to defend yourself?"

"Not only theoretically, but exactly. And that's exactly what has happened here. This was an accident. They got bad intelligence. Plain and simple. In fact, I am beginning to think that the bad intelligence was intentional. But I cannot imagine who could have done it. I'm sure as hell going to find out. One way or another."

"You think you have to prove who set this up in order to get them off?"

"Well, the evidence is going to show pretty clearly that they hit the target they were aiming for, and that target contained refugees and aid workers. All civilians. So they intentionally hit a target that included civilians. The only question is whether they *knew* the civilians were there. Or maybe—I'm not sure of the standard yet—should have known there were civilians there. A lower standard than actual knowledge. Our clients say no, and if I get the Americans involved in the targeting, *they'll* say no, but the prosecutor will call everyone from the mountains of western Pakistan to say *everybody* in the region knew that that building was a refugee camp and medical facility for weeks before the bombing. It's not possible the U.S. didn't know, and anybody who says anything to the contrary is a liar, and the United States always lies, and they were trying to send a message to Pakistan and to Europe that al

Qaeda and the Taliban were infiltrating western Pakistan, and if they didn't get their act together, it was going to get worse. That will be the story."

"This will be tougher than I thought."

"A complication for us is that President Obama is a fan of the International Criminal Court. But the *real* kicker, for us, is a law that is on the books in the U.S. It could make this thing blow up completely."

She picked up her chopsticks again and scraped the bottom of the container, piling the rice on her plate. "What law?"

I had to smile ironically because of the name it had been given by the press. "Passed by Congress and signed by President Bush right after the International Criminal Court treaty was ratified by enough countries to make it effective. It was called 'The Hague Invasion Act' by European press at the time."

"The Hague being the city where the International Criminal Court is."

"Exactly."

"I don't get it."

"Congress was so pissed that the International Criminal Court claimed jurisdiction over people who didn't sign the treaty—the United States, for example—that they wanted to make their rejection clear. They passed a bill saying that if Americans were ever captured and taken to the International Criminal Court, the president of the United States was authorized to use whatever means were necessary to get the American service members out, including force."

"Well, but that bill never passed, right?"

"Wrong. Passed both houses of Congress, and President Bush signed it."

"Truly? I mean this isn't really the law. Not currently."

"Absolutely is. Still on the books. The president has the power to do whatever it takes to get our clients out of the clutches of the International Criminal Court, including using force."

She wasn't buying it.

"You don't believe me."

"Not a chance. I would have heard of it."

I stood. "You still remember how to use Lexis?"

"Very funny."

"Log on." I pointed to her laptop.

She opened it, accessed my wireless network, and logged on to Lexis using her Covington and Burling ID and password. "Okay."

"Go find 22 U.S.C. Section 7401."

She accessed the U.S. Code, where all the federal statutes are found. "Okay. Let's see . . . The International Criminal Court . . . Subchapter II, the American Servicemembers' Protection Act."

"There you are. Now go to Section 7427."

She scrolled down and read. "Okay . . . holy shit. You weren't kidding. This is still the law? How can that be?"

"Because it has never been rescinded. Obama doesn't want to touch it. Too much animosity about the ICC, and he'll look weak."

"That's literally unbelievable. That came down when we were in law school."

"Yep."

"I don't remember anybody talking about it."

"I remember a few newspaper articles, but mostly in Europe. They went nuts about it. It was mostly ignored here."

"So what will Obama do? That's why he's in such a pickle. He has American servicemen in the custody of the ICC who are going to be put on trial and face imprisonment for the rest of their lives for doing exactly what they were told to do. And he will have the specifically authorized power to get them out, but won't use it."

She nodded as if she now understood something. "That's what that journalist was asking him about in his press conference today."

"He waved the question off like it wasn't relevant. Well believe me, it is relevant, and you and I are already working with somebody inside the National Security Council who would be very happy to use that law. This thing could go sideways in a bunch of directions, and I have no idea where this is going to end up. But I hope you're ready for the ride."

"Absolutely." She glanced at her watch. "Should we head to the airport?"

"Let's go see our clients."

Kristen and I sat in the Admirals Club at Dulles Airport and I checked the latest Internet reports on the president's press conference, any news about our case, and the building public hostility against the International Criminal Court. Numerous law professors had been requested on the usual news shows to give their opinions on the enforceability of the ICC treaty. One of them noted that he was surprised that the ICC had chosen these events to make their big move and try to subject U.S. citizens to their jurisdiction. When pressed on what was so surprising about it, he commented that Pakistan hadn't signed the Treaty of Rome either forming the International Criminal Court. And the court didn't have jurisdiction over actions in the territories of countries that hadn't signed the treaty. So the Americans would have a good argument that there was no jurisdiction over them.

I was impressed. So at least there were two of us who knew that. I also agreed with him that it was a real reach to assert jurisdiction over an American, but an American in Pakistan? That was a two-armed reach. I hoped I'd be able to make them look silly for having done it.

Of course nothing precluded the prosecutor—self-appointed determiner of all war crimes—from charging someone and issuing an indictment. That prosecutor would then try that person. And the International Criminal Court would then hear it, and there was no appeal, well at least not outside the ICC system itself. What a great system. I took another sip from my preflight scotch and turned to Kristen. "Come on. They're calling our flight." As we headed for the gate I said, "And while we're over there, we can see how hard it will be to break them out, just in case President Obama decides to do it. "

She stopped. "You're not going to tell me that you're still some secret Navy SEAL, and this trial thing is all a ruse for you to go over there and play superhero and get them out, is it? Because if that's what we're doing, I don't want any part of it."

I smiled. "Nope. My superhero days are over. But if I see something interesting, maybe I'll pass it on." I shrugged. "Who knows."

Kristen sat next to me in the cab from the airport at The Hague to the prison where our two clients were being held. It was a crystal-clear morning with beautiful blue skies. I could tell we were close to the sea by the salt in the air. She asked, "Who are you texting?"

I looked at the taxi driver and looked at her. "The guy I told you about on the airplane."

"What about?"

"Tracing the ownership." I opened my pad and drew a rough sketch of an airplane while pointing at the driver so she knew why I wasn't telling her everything.

She nodded in understanding. "It's a little early."

"He doesn't sleep."

"Oh. Is he a former SEAL like you?"

"Current."

"Made out of titanium like you were."

"Actually he's a newer model, mostly made of composites. Us older titanium models are considered too heavy and inflexible." I looked at her and saw her pretty smile. "So you have a boyfriend?"

She looked at me strangely, wearily. "Men are all the same."

"Meaning?"

"Meaning you just want to get into my pants. You wanted to in law school, and you still do."

"You women are all the same—you think all men are the same."

"They are."

"I didn't want to get into your pants in law school, and I don't want to get into your pants now. I just want to know whether you're going to be able to devote twenty-four hours a day to this work, or whether you're going to be worried about whether somebody's calling you back soon enough."

"No. No boyfriend, not married, no prospects, I'm married to the law."

"Right. I remember you used to say that in law school. You were married then to the *Law Review*."

"Of course I was. That's what allowed me to get the job that I now hold in New York."

"Where they work you like a gerbil, tease you for ten, or twelve, or thirteen years, and then say they're *shocked*, but you are not going to make partner and they hope that you have a really great legal career."

"Very funny."

"Well I'm a partner in my firm. How about you?"

"There's only one attorney in your firm. We have eight hundred."

"Yes, but I am an owner. And you're an employee."

"Very funny."

"So I guess your prospects at partnership are dimming."

"Actually my prospects are bright."

I chuckled. "That's what they tell all of them."

She said, "So tell me about this prison."

I looked at the driver again. I never trusted anyone

to not be listening. I didn't like discussing client matters in front of anybody, I didn't care who they were. They may know somebody who knew somebody that might benefit from their information. It's far better to be careful. "You'll see." I looked ahead and saw the prison coming into view. I pointed. She looked.

The prison looked different in the bright daylight. The red was more intense, the years less flattering. As the cab approached, I began filming with my miniature palm-size digital recorder.

Kristen hit me in the leg and looked at me intently, clearly telling me to put down the recorder. I ignored her and continued filming. We stopped in front of the gate, I stepped out and continued to film, sweeping up and down in front of the prison, and then put the recorder into my briefcase. I paid the driver, and we walked to the front door. We went to the same window where I had been before to announce ourselves. The guard nodded, and picked up the telephone. An older man appeared behind him, and came out into the reception area. He was wearing a black suit, and was well groomed. He said, "Good morning, Mr. Caskey. May I ask who it is you have here with you?"

"Yes, this is Kristen Chambers. My co-counsel."

He turned to her. "Good morning, Ms. Chambers. I am Jan Stam. I am the director of the prison. May I see your credentials please."

She opened her purse, took out her wallet, extracted her driver's license, her New York bar card, her passport, and her business card and handed them to him. He examined them and handed them back. "So I take it like Mr. Caskey, you are not admitted before the International Criminal Court."

"Not yet. I was hoping for the same preliminary acceptance that he received so that we can meet with our clients."

His gaze was fixed. "Which of the two defendants will you be representing?"

"We will both be representing both defendants."

He turned to me. "Mr. Caskey, I need you to give me the memory card or tape that is in your video recorder. It is illegal to videotape the prison. I am informed by our guards that you videotaped the entrance and this entire side of the prison. That is not approved."

I had expected something like this. "Are you serious?"

He nodded. "Of course. It is not negotiable."

I reached for the recorder inside my briefcase, took it out and held it in my hand. I extended the recorder to him briefly, then drew it back. I said, "Tell you what. I'll give you this memory card, if you can show me the discs or tape that you retrieved from all the journalists who were here the other day when I held a press conference in front of the prison. I personally saw, as I'm sure you did, the journalists repeatedly filming the prison, all the walls, the entrance, the guardhouses, and everything that I just filmed. So if your rule is so inflexible, so 'nonnegotiable,' then please show me those tapes, and I will gladly give you mine."

He stared at me coldly. "If you promise not to film anymore, I will see what the status is of that effort. If I have those, you will turn yours over. Yes?"

"Yes."

"The two Americans are eating. We will let you in when they are done."

He turned, went back into the guarded enclosure, and disappeared. After fifteen minutes we were finally escorted into the same room where I had met with them before. We sat at the table waiting, and finally the door opened and the two Americans were escorted in. The guards released their bindings and left the room. We all stood somewhat awkwardly. I finally introduced them. Raw said to Kristen, "How did you get roped into this?"

"John asked us to help. My firm has agreed to help you on a pro bono basis."

He frowned. "What does that mean?"

"Well, literally, for the benefit of the public. But it means for free. We won't charge you anything. We will even advance the costs necessary for us to complete our job."

Rawlings was surprised. He glanced at me, and then back at Kristen, not sure what to make of her. He looked her up and down, which was awkward, but then said, "How much would it cost us if we were paying you?"

"A lot."

"What's your billing rate?"

"For most of the cases I'm working on, it's 575 per hour."

"You a partner at your firm?"

"No."

Raw asked, "Why is your firm really helping us for free?"

Kristen glanced at me. I said nothing. She said, "We have a little bit of experience in controversial cases."

Duncan chimed in, "What does that mean?"

Kristen was trying not to say it, but knew she had to. "I went to law school with John. He knows that my firm represented some of the Gitmo detainees pro bono. We tried to get them into federal court to make sure that they were being held properly. And that they should get a trial. So when this came up, he thought we should help you just like we had them."

Rawlings's face got red and he put his hands on his hips. "You think we're just like Gitmo detainees? Are you shitting me?"

Kristen shook her head. "No. Can we sit down?"

He shook his head. "I don't want to even be in the same room with somebody who chose to represent Gitmo detainees for free. What in the hell were you thinking?" He glared at Kristen.

"We were trying to get them protection under the law. So they couldn't be held without any charges indefinitely. The same rights anybody else would have."

"The same rights?" Raw yelled. "These are the guys who are blowing people up, and cutting off their *heads*. You have any idea who those guys are, or were?"

"Yes. We learned a lot about them. More than probably anyone else knew. We wanted them to be charged properly, and make sure that the people being held are the ones who should be held. You can't just hold people without charges."

Dunk was amazed. "Of course you can! Where are

you getting this crap? We held thousands of German POWs in the U.S. in World War II. In prison camps. Can you imagine dragging all of them in front of some judge to make sure that we were *holding* them properly and give them a trial? What's the charge? Being a German? Being a soldier? That's not how you do it. You capture somebody, you put them away until it's over. End of story. What kind of law firm do you belong to?"

"I think our reputation is that we are one of the best law firms in the country. We have over eight hundred lawyers."

"And how many of those eight hundred are assholes that think like that?"

Kristen gave it right back to them. "Probably most of them do think people should be given the protection of the law. Probably most think that you should be sure you have who you think you have. Probably most think that you shouldn't engage in torture." She was getting hot.

Raw looked at me. "This is who you brought to help us? Somebody who's sympathetic to al freaking Qaeda? How do you know she won't sabotage us because she thinks *that's* the right result? She probably thinks we're guilty. Have you asked her that?"

I couldn't stand by idly anymore. "Let's sit down. I'll tell you all about her, and her firm, and how important it is that we have their help. Raw, you need to relax a little bit. She's on our side. She has chosen to do this personally. I asked her, yeah, but she didn't have to. And she has set aside all the other work she was doing to devote her time to this. She's even moving down to

Washington, to work out of a broom closet in my office so she can help you. So you can back off a little bit, give her some credit, and give her firm a little bit of room to believe something different than you do about where the rule of law applies in this weird place we find ourselves, which is not exactly a standard war with armies and uniforms. Let's leave ourselves some space for differences, okay? Our job is to get you out of here."

Rawlings stared at me. He was still angry, and obviously still had little regard for Kristen. He sat. "So what's the plan?"

"Have you been around the prison quite a bit? Do they let you walk around?"

Raw's eyes narrowed. He knew where I was going. "Little bit. It's quite a fortress." He glanced at the door. "Thick stone walls, high barbed wire and electric fence, minimal courtyard, and lots of cells that are almost completely empty. They move us every night to a different cell. We haven't slept in the same place two nights in a row." Rawlings leaned across the table and lowered his voice. "You're a former SEAL. Right?"

"Yeah."

"Can't some of your pals come get us out of here?"

"No, we're going to do this right," I said. "The reason I'm here today is to introduce you to Kristen, and to tell you what our plan is. We're going to challenge this court at every turn. We are going to challenge their jurisdiction, their indictment, their definition of war crimes, and if it goes to trial, we will challenge everyone who testifies against you. But first," I said, opening my notebook, "I need to know the names of everybody who could testify on your behalf. Who gave you your orders? Who issued the operational order? Who gave you clearance to drop? Who gave you the coordinates you had? Who confirmed those coordinates? Who was operating the Predator that was nearby?"

Duncan smiled. "We've got a lot of work to do."

# SEVEN

Kristen slumped in the cab next to me as we headed away from the prison.

"You tired?" I asked.

"I don't think I've slept a minute since you just dropped by in New York. You've sort of turned everything I was doing upside down."

"It's good for you. You're getting too set in your ways."

"As if you know anything about what I'm doing. We heading to the airport?" she asked without opening her eyes.

"Nope. Now that they've released the indictment, read it to the whole world, printed it in every newspaper known to man, it's time to have a chat with the prosecutor."

"Who is the prosecutor? I didn't even look."

"An Irishman. Liam Brady."

"Know anything about him?"

"A little. He actually is from Northern Ireland. U.K.

He became famous for prosecuting IRA terrorists in Belfast. He claims to be very antiwar and a big believer in nonviolence."

"And now he's prosecutor for the International Criminal Court?"

"Yes. He's the one who prosecuted Maluta from Nigeria."

"Let's go see him." She sat up, and reached down to her briefcase to review the indictment.

The release of the indictment acted like bellows on the firestorm already blazing in the United States. The more people realized what was happening and that the United States had never approved of the International Criminal Court, the more confused, perplexed, and angry everyone got. Now that they had read the entire indictment, those opposed to the ICC were in full roar. These two American F-18 aircrew had simply been doing their jobs, as the American press generally thought. They had accidentally dropped a bomb on a refugee facility, but it wasn't a war crime. It was terrible accident. One of the many that occur in wartime.

We entered the lobby at the International Criminal Court building where I initially stopped on my first trip to The Hague. We went up to the reception desk. "Hello. I'm John Caskey. This is Kristen Chambers. We'd like to see Liam Brady."

"Do you have an appointment?"

"No. We are the attorneys for the Americans in the indictment he just released yesterday. We would like to meet with him about that indictment."

"So he is not expecting you?"

"No."

"One moment please." We walked away from the reception desk as she called his line. She was speaking with someone, at some length. I had the feeling we were in for the usual run-around. Brady was going to have to deal with me at some point though; he may as well start now. The receptionist gestured for me. I crossed over to her on the hard, beautifully polished tile floor. "Yes?"

"Mr. Brady is in a meeting. He will not be available for an hour. He suggests that you get something to eat, and come back at 1430."

"That'll be fine."

Kristen and I found a small sidewalk café nearby and had ham sandwiches and coffee. We tore through the lengthy indictment again, made notes, reviewed the procedural rules for the International Criminal Court, and prepared for our meeting. We were doing a lot of it on the fly, but we had to do things quickly whether we fully understood the implications or not. There was some risk of a misstep, but there was much more of a risk that this court would settle into its comfortable, tedious, paper-driven process and not have to deal with the case in the public eye. We wanted to keep everything front and center in the newspapers—and on the backs of the politicians.

We returned to the court building and were told that Mr. Brady was available. We were escorted to a conference room on the second floor near the prosecutors' offices. Like the rest of the building, it was ultramodern, with minimal furniture or decoration. There was a piece of modern art on the wall in the hallway outside the conference room, but nothing else for the entire length of the hallway. It was hospital clean, and quiet. The conference room itself was medium-sized with a significant glass table in the middle and stainless steel framed leather chairs on either side. It looked expensive. The receptionist closed the door behind us and we waited for Brady. I looked at Kristen. "This ought to be interesting."

"Do you know anything about him other than what you said?"

"No." Before I could say anything else, the door opened and a man walked in. He was about my size, with brown hair over his ears. He had quite an intensity about him, nothing feminine or soft. He appeared tough and could probably be mean. He looked at me and walked directly toward me. It was as if Kristen didn't even exist. He put out his hand. "Liam Brady."

"John Caskey. And this is Kristen Chambers."

Brady looked at her momentarily and then back at me. "Caskey." He thought for a moment. "Is that Irish?"

I shrugged. "Don't know. We've never been able to figure it out."

He obviously wasn't listening. "I understand you would like to talk about the two American navy pilots. Please have a seat." He walked to one side of the table and we sat on the other. He carried no papers, no briefcase, no phone, nothing. Just him and his dark suit.

I spoke, "Thanks for taking the time to meet with us. Yes I would very much like to talk about the two navy fliers. Only one is actually a pilot, not that it matters. The other is called a WSO, a weapon systems officer. But my question to you is why are they here? What has happened that has resulted in them being in the custody of the International Criminal Court? I want to talk to you about the charges, but I would first like to understand the details of how they came to be here."

Brady smiled. "We became aware of the horrible events in Afghanistan and Pakistan and filed charges. Simple as that. We evaluated those charges and agreed that there were war crimes at issue and we needed to issue an indictment."

"When did you evaluate the charges?"

"The night of the events."

"How? Who was it that gave you the information?"

"That will all be made known in more detail, but it was tribal leaders from Pakistan who referred the case to us, who told us about it."

"Well you said referred. You didn't mean referred as in requested that you prosecute under the ICC treaty, right? Because nonstate parties can't refer, and states who haven't signed it can't refer—and Pakistan hasn't signed it. So I'm not following you."

"Correct. I meant referred in that they gave us the critical information on what happened."

"Who did? Who claimed to have all this information?"

"As I said, tribal leaders."

"What are their names? And how did they claim to

know the intentions of the Americans immediately after it happened?"

Brady took a paperclip out of his pocket and began playing with it. "I don't recall their names as I sit here."

"Well I want to know who they are."

"It doesn't really matter. It's not a formal referral and the charges will stand or fall based on the evidence, not—"

"How do you even know who they were? How do you know it wasn't al Qaeda or the Taliban on the phone claiming to be some tribal leader? And how do you file a case in the middle of the night and happen to capture these men and fly them here in a few hours? How in the hell does all that happen in one night here in Holland?"

"All your questions will be answered in due—"

"Well then the best thing then would be to answer them now. While the information is still warm in your brain. Who did you talk to?"

"I did not come here to be cross-examined by you."

"Mr. Brady," I said, leaning forward and looking directly into his eyes. "You have taken a very risky gamble in this case. You have taken on the United States and charged two naval officers with war crimes because a bomb apparently went into a refugee facility. You've stabbed a very angry dog in the eye with a stick when that dog is already involved in a couple of fights. But worse, you don't have any business messing with that dog. You don't have any jurisdiction. There's no referral from Pakistan or the U.N. Security Council, and the events didn't occur in a country that signed the treaty. So you need to dismiss this case right now."

"We do have jurisdiction, and you will learn why."

"Then tell me now, or are you afraid I'll have too much time to respond to what obviously must be a doubtful theory?"

"Not at all. We have jurisdiction because the crime occurred not just in Pakistan, but also in Afghanistan. When your clients made the decision to bomb the target, they were in Afghanistan airspace. So the crime occurred in two places, Afghanistan and Pakistan."

I was stunned. "Seriously? That's your theory? That's unbelievable. What's the authority for that?"

"Do you think that if the Taliban, the ones based in Afghanistan, went over the border and murdered everyone in a village in Pakistan to teach the country of Pakistan a lesson, do you think that we would not have jurisdiction over that war crime?"

"No, you wouldn't."

"I disagree. In that case important elements of the crime occurred in Afghanistan, just like here. *Where* the crime occurs is not defined in the treaty, and is subject to interpretation and good judgment. The judges obviously agreed with me, as they approved the charges and the indictment."

"That's just unbelievable," I said. I looked at Kristen, who was equally surprised.

"Yes, you already said that. But it has been approved. So you may make your argument before the same judges who approved it when we have our pretrial hearing."

"I intend to."

"And you expect a different result?"

"I always expect judges to do the correct thing. So yes, I will expect a different result."

He chuckled and broke the paperclip in half.

I asked, "And the fact that the United States hasn't adopted this treaty is of no concern to you."

"Correct. It is clear that we have jurisdiction over those who commit war crimes regardless of whether their state has signed the treaty or not."

I sat back and thought. "So if Kristen and I formed a treaty between ourselves, and agreed that we had jurisdiction over ICC prosecutors, we could arrest you and charge you with prosecutorial misconduct."

Brady smiled. "Very clever. Of course incorrect under any international law standard."

"So how do I challenge the jurisdiction of this court? How do I get this before whatever judges will be appointed to this court a motion to dismiss this case for lack of jurisdiction and lack of a proper referral?"

"Have you not read the procedural rules of the court, Mr. Caskey?"

"Yes."

"And you could not find the answer to that question in there? Did you want to meet with me to give you more clarity on how the rules work?" His Irish accent became more pronounced the more aggravated he got.

"I'd just like to hear your answer."

"Well then as I said, unlike many European courts, we do allow for pretrial motions both for evidence and jurisdiction. So you may bring such a motion anytime you like. But I would recommend that you bring it so the motion can be heard at the pretrial hearing, where most of these kinds of things are discussed, and where the court determines whether there is enough evidence to proceed with the trial. Like what you Americans call a preliminary hearing."

"Will do. Until then I'd like to have the two naval officers released on bail until such time as the trial occurs."

Brady shook his head. "Bail is theoretically possible in our system, but I can tell you that it would not be approved in this case."

"Really. Have you already spoken to the judges about it?"

"No. I have not."

"Well you could. I mean this is a cozy setup you have here. The judges are right down the hall. Right?"

"Some of them. Others are appointed specially."

I took out my notebook and pen. "Who are the judges that have been assigned to this case.?"

"They have not yet been assigned."

"Do you have e-mail?"

"Yes of course."

"Will you let me know as soon as they are?"

"Yes."

I handed him my business card. "Sorry, I should have given this to you earlier. You can just send the information to that e-mail address." I acted as if I was about to stand up. Then I paused. "Can you help me understand something?"

"Maybe. What is it?"

"I don't understand how these two men have been charged."

"We just went through that."

"Yes, but the *timing*. How did you get these charges issued and approved by judges—since there was no referral—in *hours*?"

"No great mystery. It was widely known that I was investigating many allegations of war crimes—by all the parties—in Afghanistan. I already knew much of what has gone on there. So when this happened, I was called immediately. The criminals—your navy officers—were in custody in Pakistan, and it was known that our time frame to act, to decide, was short indeed. We didn't want to act rashly, but we didn't want the opportunity to pass either when those who might be accused were already being detained. So we examined the information, and made our decision."

I felt the heat rising that I had to control. "That's remarkable. And where did you get all this critical information that allowed you to make a decision so quickly?"

"I told you. From tribal leaders. The sovereign leaders where this happened. Where Pakistan has ceded control, and allowed the imposition of Sharia law. They must be protected too. So they gave me the information, and we learned of the track of the American jet involved from Pakistan, which gave us jurisdiction."

"And you had evidence. How did you get all this evidence?"

"Electronically. They gave us witness statements,

and photographs. All transmitted over the Internet. Just minutes after the event. Then we learned the Americans had been captured."

Kristen asked, "I'm new to all this, so forgive my ignorance—"

"No, I expect your ignorance. It's exactly how I expected the Americans to be defended, with attorneys who didn't know the court, who aren't admitted here, and who are ignorant of its procedures. Go on."

Kristen was shocked. "I appreciate that. But my question is how do we challenge all this? How do we ask the court to dismiss these charges for, oh, ten or twenty different reasons?"

"I just answered that too. Were you not listening?"

"Yes, I was. I guess I was indirectly asking whether *you* would rather deal with these issues earlier, or separately from the preliminary hearing."

"No, no need. The preliminary hearing as we'll call it is set for Monday at ten A.M."

"That's six days."

"Correct."

"When were you planning on telling us this?" I asked.

"As soon as you have submitted all your paperwork and the chief administrator has *admitted* you to *practice* before the ICC."

"Our clients are entitled to be there and hear the evidence, I assume."

"Of course."

"Where will that hearing be?"

"In the trial courtroom, third floor."

We stood. "See you then." I stopped and turned back as I shifted my briefcase to my other hand. "By the way, I assume you have all the evidence for me to take with me—the file that has your proof."

Liam stood as well. He stretched, then put his hands in his pockets. "Of course."

We flew home on the latest flight we could get and went straight to my office. When we got there, Marshall was waiting for us. "What are you doing here? How did you know we'd be here?"

"I checked your flight."

"How?"

"Your secretary."

"Oh. Good idea. She must trust you. I'll have to talk to her."

I introduced him to Kristen, but could tell from Marshall's face that it wasn't the time for a full introduction. I told Kristen he was with the government and was involved in helping with the defense. I invited him into my office and Kristen was right behind us. He told her he needed to talk to me alone, which left her surprised and frustrated. He closed my door and walked around the office, looking at the walls and windows. "How's your security?"

"I've never needed any. But I know where you're going."

"Get some. Right away. And at your apartment."

"You think the Dutch are going to come here to find out what really happened?"

"No. But lots of people suspect we're not just going

to sit by and let them string up two officers who did nothing wrong. They know we're likely to act. And they'll want to know how and when, and they'll suspect that you will know about it, and may be complicit in it, particularly once they discover your background."

"Good point. Can you help me out? A real security system would cost a lot of money. You could get some fed guys to do that in half a day."

"I'll take care of it."

"I'm going to start some coffee. Want some?"

"Sure. Black."

I came back from my closet-sized kitchen and gave him his coffee. I put mine down on the desk and sat in my chair. I could suddenly feel the heaviness my body was carrying. I breathed deeply and rubbed my eyes. "I haven't had much sleep lately. Lots of flying to Holland."

Marshall said nothing.

"I'm going to hold a press conference. I told Kristen to get her firm's PR machine warmed up. We are going on the offensive. Against the ICC, and against the U.S. government."

"Careful."

"The president hasn't done shit, Chris. He's had what, two press conferences? He keeps talking about the *deep* respect he has for the ICC, and how he continues to consider whether to submit the treaty to the Senate when all this is cleared up, this misunderstanding, obviously pandering to the very court that has kidnapped two naval officers. Well that's double bullshit, Chris. This isn't a misunderstanding, and we can't possibly ratify it, and this case is a perfect example of why. But what I'm going to take him to task on is the Ser-vicemembers' Protection Act. It's time to send a battle group to Europe and get my clients out of that medieval prison. I'm going to call on the president to exercise it."

"First, you will *not* call on the president to do any-thing. You can rag on the ICC all you want, but you will not challenge the president. We will go public with any military action when it's time, and not before. Right now he's asked me for an evaluation of the likelihood of success of a covert operation. That's why I'm here."

I looked at him with surprise. "Shit, Chris. I thought you were worried about security. You're talking some big stuff here."

"I asked you about *your* security. I'm not worried about mine. I had this place swept after everyone left. It's clean, and I've been here ever since. I won't be con-fident about your security here after I leave though.

"I've asked a 'friend' of mine to join us. He should be here any minute."

I nodded. "You serious about trying to break them out?"

"Of course."

"I—" My phone buzzed. It was Kristen using my secretary's phone. "Who is it? Sure. Show him in."

The door opened. The man came in. I stood and greeted him, as did Marshall. I gave him a cup of cof-fee, and pulled a chair away from the corner so he could sit. He was casual, wearing jeans and a sweatshirt with longer hair than was common among Navy SEALs, although sometimes some would have longer hair to blend in with the community, particularly those with DEVGRU, the primary counterterrorism unit of the navy. He was larger than me by a good bit. Perhaps six feet three and 220 pounds. He was humorless and cold. I said to him, "Sorry, I didn't get your name."

"Richard."

"Richard what?"

"Just Richard."

Marshall said to him, "He," indicating me, "used to be on the teams too. We can speak freely with him."

Richard looked at him. "I don't speak freely with anybody."

I said, "It doesn't matter. We're here to try and get these officers out of this bind. I'm going to try legally, but I can already feel that that task is an uphill one. Not only uphill, but basically straight up. I don't know how this happened, and I don't know who's really behind it, but I intend to find out. But I think what Marshall would like to know, and why you're here, Richard, is to see if we can grab these guys before this ever gets to trial."

Richard looked at Marshall. "Do we have authorization?"

Marshall shook his head slightly. "Not yet. But we expect to get it."

Richard looked at me and then around the office, then back at me. "We won't do anything without written authorization. But assuming that's coming, tell me about the layout."

"Well I'm not sure how or when you do it, I'll leave that up to you. I'll tell you whatever you'd like to know. Here's one thing you should have." I opened the drawer of my desk, and pulled out the video camera and attached it to my laptop. I turned the screen around so they could see it and came around to their side of the desk. I used the small remote from the camera to run the videotape. I narrated as we watched. "Here is the entrance to the prison, there you can see the walls going down the left—that's the wing where the conference room is where we see them when we go, the central area is walled off and is separated even from the prison itself by two fences with electrical wiring along the top. Each section is divided by steel walls with solenoid-controlled locks. There are video cameras in three positions in every room, one on the floor and two in upper corners. The guards are generally inattentive, but not stupid. They clearly have never contemplated that anybody would actually try to break into this prison. It is at least two or three hundred years old, but has been upgraded for security, electronics, barbed wire, video surveillance, and motion detectors."

Richard and Marshall watched carefully, sitting forward in their chairs. Richard said, "Hold it right there. Go back a little bit." I rewound and he said, "Stop." He looked closely at the image. "Can you zoom in on that?"

"I think so. I think if I freeze it . . ." I zoomed in on the front door where we had entered.

He commented, "The door looks weak. External hinges. We can blow that off easily. If we went in that way where would we be in relation to our guys?"

"That's the thing. They're never in the same place. They are moved to a different cell every night. No pattern. There are hundreds of cells, the vast majority of which are empty. This is a huge prison run to hold a handful of prisoners. Because they're the worst prisoners in the world. The war criminals, the genocidal maniacs."

Richard said, "We could clean out the entire prison. Open every cell door, but that would take a long time. Whatever security this prison has, I'm sure it will be backed up by the Dutch police, and probably the Dutch military. I don't think we would have time. We need to have a fixed location, and go from there. I don't see that."

"What about on the way?"

Richard considered. "How are they transported?"

"Don't know. They've never been transported except from the airport to the prison. The first time will be when they go to the preliminary hearing."

"When is that?"

"Next Monday."

Richard said, mostly to himself, "Wow. What are our rules of engagement?" He looked at Marshall.

Marshall said, "Don't know. The president hasn't authorized it. He wants to hear the mission, and then he'll determine whether it's a go. But I think he's going to restrict us. I don't think we're going to be able to just go in there and start killing Dutch prison guards, or Dutch police. You think we have an uproar on our hands now, can you imagine what would happen if we do that?"

Richard almost smiled. "So we go into a major European city, break people out of a prison fortress, and make sure no one gets hurt. That about it?"

Marshall knew the reaction his information would

get. "I'm just the messenger. You guys know I've been there. In fact I'm sort of still there. But that's what I think is coming."

Richard sat back. "You can tell the president based on current information we're not going. I'm not going to put my men in a position of violating an order of the president and getting thrown in our own prison in Leavenworth. Unless we have freedom to do the mission, we're not going."

Marshall said, "Then he might force me to send Delta."

Richard shook his head. "You know better than that. They'll tell you the same thing. Unless we have clear rules of engagement, and freedom to accomplish the mission, we're not going on a pretend mission or a mission that's from some children's video game where nobody gets hurt. They want a guarantee? Tell him to call somebody else."

Marshall said, "We're working on the ROE. I'll let you know when we have what the actual requirements are."

I said, "Look, let me say what I want to say. Let me go public and challenge the president to invoke the Servicemembers' Protection Act. It says he can use *whatever means are necessary* to get American servicemembers away from the ICC. Let's *use* it. We can use force if we need to. If people get killed that's just too bad."

Marshall smiled. "You're so unpolitical, Jack. You don't get how this stuff works. It's not about what you can do, or what laws have been passed, it's about looking good, and satisfying an international image. This president has to be seen to be in favor of the International Criminal Court. To attack it with the military, overtly, will never work."

I was puzzled. "But sending a group in there to grab them is okay? That's even worse. It looks sneaky."

"I think he is planning on a private negotiation for their release before this happens."

I was surprised by this, say the least. "What? What kind of private negotiation? With who?"

"The prosecutor. He's going to call him."

I shook my head. "That's a really bad idea. I've met him. He's not giving up for anything. This is his big deal, his chance to be famous. If the president calls and begs him he'll say no, and then tell everyone how he resisted the undue, improper pressure of the president of the United States. It'll make his day. He'll probably record the conversation and post it on the Internet to show what an idiot the president is. To show how when Americans get in trouble, their president will grovel before some self-appointed prosecutor who's out to rip them a new asshole. It will be seen for what it is, pathetic. It's shameful. Our president shouldn't be calling anybody."

"I'm just telling you what is likely. Maybe he won't do it. I don't know."

Richard stood. "May I have that video from your camera?"

I gave it to him. He slipped it in his pocket and said to Chris, "Call me," and left the office.

I said to Chris, "Who's he with?"

"It's best you not know. You're just a civilian lawyer."

"Right. That's why you picked me."

"I'll be in touch once we have something in mind. But I think we better start looking toward grabbing those guys on their way to the preliminary hearing. Next week. Stay loose."

# EIGHT

The idea of grabbing the two pilots on the way to the hearing was both a good idea and a bad idea. I had no idea how they would do it; maybe they'd be able to gain enough information between now and then to actually pull it off. I'd probably just learn about it in the newspaper. But I had a suspicion that I was going to be involved. I wasn't naive. Marshall had probably picked me for this job because of my SEAL experience. And at just the right moment, when I least expected it and they most expected, they were going to call on me to do something well outside my lawyerly duties. Or at the very least see some pretty risky plans as well within the bounds of what might be considered. That gave me a lot of pause. But for now, I knew what I had to do. In spite of what Marshall had said, my duty was to my clients. And I had to put President Obama on the hot seat. I needed to stir up whatever I could, to make as much heat and steam as I could, and bring as much difficulty to bear on the International Criminal Court that I could.

The next morning, after I finally had a night's sleep, right on time the head of Covington and Burling's outside PR firm arrived. A tall thin woman with very short hair died bright orange and large red glasses swept into my office. She took in my entire office in a second. I knew her thoughts without her saying a word. What in the world kind of law firm has Covington gotten itself tied up with? And how could an attorney operating from such a slipshod shop be in a place to defend two Americans in what was likely to be the show trial of the decade in Europe?

She finally turned her attention directly on me. She was bizarre-looking, but professionally comforting. She knew exactly what she was doing. She sat down in my office next to Kristen with her assistant on the other side of her. She introduced herself. Her name was Patty Robbins and her assistant was Jonathan Hill. She was probably fifty-five years old, and was in very good shape, with the energy of three people. She talked incessantly and had an infinite amount of advice that she was ready to give at any moment.

I told her the whole story, from start to finish, telling her everything I thought was relevant. She was fascinated, and acutely aware not only of the public relations implications, but also the American and international political implications. What she didn't really understand was the role I had in mind for the press; to use them to achieve my objectives. I saw the press as a tool, she saw the press as an echo chamber to make us look larger than life and terribly important.

After considerable discussion, I said, "I want to call a press conference in two hours. At four o'clock. Just in time for the local stations—and the national news—to put it on the evening shows. It'll be hard-hitting. I'm going to let people know about the International Criminal Court, and how they're railroading our navy fliers, but I'm also going to challenge the president. I've been cautioned against that, but I'm going to ignore that caution. I have to put him on the spot. I have to get the American people to rally around us, around me, and force Congress and the cabinet and the president to invoke an act that was passed during the Bush administration. President Obama will grind his teeth privately, and if he has a way to squeeze me, will do it. But I'm going to squeeze him first."

Patty adjusted her red horn-rimmed glasses and looked at me disapprovingly. "Jack. Is it okay if I call you that?" I nodded. "Jack, that's not the way we operate. We don't use our public relations skills to insult the president or, as you put it, put him on the spot. We use our skills, our tools, and our context to make our law firms and our clients look better, to control the media frenzy that is building around this case, and to use it to our advantage. Confronting the president at your first U.S. press conference is not how that is done."

I looked at Kristen, who I could tell was in agreement with Patty. She even may have had a discussion with Patty on this very subject before Patty arrived. I nodded as I turned my pen in my hand and my attention back to Patty. "I understand that. But *you* have to understand that I'm not normal. I don't operate like a big firm would operate. I do whatever I think is right, and trust my instincts. I know that's not how PR folks do it, everything is calculated with an agenda, with an objective, with a prepared statement or press release, and with controls so that nothing can come back to bite us. Well, this certainly could come back to bite us. Believe me, I get that. But I'm willing to take that chance. Because I think the upside, of getting the president to act, even in a preliminary way, far outweighs whatever risk I'm going to take. Plus, people expect attorneys in high-profile cases to be vague and self-serving, and not to say what they're really thinking. Well in my experience, the American people love it when you speak the truth directly to them. Even if you're wrong, they appreciate the attempt.

"So the asshole Irish prosecutor is going to hear from me today, and every day that I can make his life more difficult. And the president? He's got to stand up to the International Criminal Court. He can't start by pandering to them, as he apparently is currently planning on doing. I frankly am hoping to torpedo that idea right now. So, Patty, if this means you've got to leave me here dangling and swinging from my own rope, if your true allegiance is to Covington and Burling and not our two naval officers, that's fine—but you've got to let me do this. Call your contacts in the media, get them to set up in front of the Justice Department, on the steps right there by the entrance, and I'm going to hold a press conference at four o'clock this afternoon. Tell everybody that you know."

She didn't know what to do with me. She stared, angry, frustrated at being unable to control my clearly misguided intentions. But she was there to help us, so help us she would. Whether she would ever help me again remained to be seen. Jonathan, her assistant, had remained silent through the meeting. He looked at her with obvious fear. Apparently people didn't usually talk to her that way. When it came to determining how to deal with the press, most people hung on every word she uttered and he wasn't accustomed to seeing anybody tell her what to do.

She stared hard at me, undoubtedly going over various options in her mind. Finally she said, "I'll see you there."

As four o'clock approached, I learned from Chris Marshall that the president intended to go forward with his call to the prosecutor. He thought he'd be able to talk him out of pursuing the charges, or if not, that he might be able to talk to the head prosecutor who might release them on bail. I told Marshall it would do more harm than good. He understood my position but stood behind the president. I understood that; his job was at the White House. But it was my time to start shooting.

When I arrived at the Justice Department there were at least a hundred journalists waiting. Patty had set up a lectern in spite of the Justice Department marshals asking her not to. She shooed them away and told them to call her friend in the Justice Department who would certainly authorize it if asked. They were puzzled, but went off to make the call.

There were probably twenty microphones strapped to each other so that I could be heard directly into the feed of each organization. At exactly four o'clock I walked up to them. Kristen stood right next to me. I waited until there was some semblance of silence, and began.

"I am going to make a brief statement, and then would be happy to take questions. As you know, I am a criminal defense lawyer in Washington, D.C., and have been asked to defend the two navy officers being held by the International Criminal Court by their families. I have visited them twice now, and am happy to report on their condition, and their location. They are being held in an old prison on the outskirts of The Hague. The prison is run by the International Criminal Court where they hold those being charged with war crimes. It is the same prison where Thomas Lubango Dyilo, Jean-Pierre Bemba Gonbo, and Ahmad Muhammad Harun were held during their war crimes trials regarding the Congo, the Central African Republic, and Darfur respectively in 2009 and 2010. Those are the kind of people that such a court is intended to prosecute. And to put your minds at rest, I have no problem with the International Criminal Court charging war criminals who have committed genocide or ethnic cleansing or who have devastated an entire region through their evil acts. Particularly when the countries where they lived were signatories to the convention or there was a referral from the U.N. Security Council. That is all ordinary, and a correct application of international law.

"But to hold two American officers in the same prison as genocidal maniacs, and charge them under the same law as those who have murdered hundreds of thousands of people, and to hold those who are from a country—the United States—that not only never approved the International Criminal Court treaty but objected to it during its founding, is obscene.

"They have been charged with several violations of the Treaty of Rome. Let me review the charges for you. The definitions of these charges are found in the ICC's Elements of Crimes. The first charge is the war crime of attacking civilians, Article 8(2)(b)(i). The second is Article 8(2)(b)(iii), the war crime of attacking personnel or objects involved in a humanitarian assistance or peacekeeping mission. The third is Article 8(2)(b)(iv), the war crime of excessive incidental death, injury, or damage. The fourth is Article 8(2)(b)(ix), the war crime of attacking protected objects, one of which in this case, allegedly, was a 'hospital.' The fifth is Article 8(2)(c)(i)-1, the war crime of murder, which includes killing medical personnel or those who are hors de combat." I put down the paper I was holding where I had summarized the charges for reference. "I could go on. Notably, each charge requires actual knowledge of the target's condition—that it is a medical facility, for example—or actual intent. The ICC is saying that these officers intentionally killed civilians and medical personnel.

"How did this happen? These two aviators were flying off the USS *Ronald Reagan*, conducting normal operations inside the country of Afghanistan. Late in their flight they were vectored to a new target given to them by the control aircraft flying in the airspace of Afghanistan. They asked for and received verification of the target. They asked for the latitude and longitude of the target, which was not only told to them over the encrypted radio, but sent to them by encrypted data link. They were the same coordinates, which were then entered into their targeting and weapon, a JDAM. They had additional confirmation from laser target designation from a Predator which was being operated by the United States Air Force. They dropped their bomb on the target they had been given. They hit the target directly, and were in the process of returning to base when they were shot down. We don't know the details of the shoot-down, but we will find out. It makes one wonder how that happened.

"After being shot down, they were immediately captured, and were driven in a truck to Peshawar, Pakistan. You have all seen what happened there. They were paraded through the streets and humiliated with dog collars around their necks. Yet curiously they were not kept in Pakistan. They were whisked to the Peshawar airport where they were loaded aboard a Falcon jet that happened to be waiting for them, and flown nonstop to Den Haag—The Hague—in Holland.

"How is it that a Falcon jet, a very expensive top-of-the-line business jet, just happened to be waiting in Peshawar to rush them to The Hague? How is it that the target that was so well confirmed turned out to be something completely different? How is it that an F-18 is shot down and the two Americans are rushed to Holland? How does that happen?

"And perhaps even more curious, while the Americans are being shot down, evidence is being faxed and PDF'd to the International Criminal Court in The Hague so they could make a determination of whether war crimes charges were going to be brought. In the middle of the night. Photographs, documentary evidence, testimonials, all sent to The Hague, just in time for the prosecutor to meet with the court and issue a sealed indictment. All in less than twelve hours. This from a court that takes months to do anything. This from a court that has taken two and three years in the past to respond to demands to indict war criminals from Africa. Twelve hours?

"So the indictment is issued, the Americans are arrested, transported to The Hague, and thrown into a medieval jail. This is a dark day for international justice. War crimes are being made a mockery. Now people who have disagreed with the American participation in the ongoing wars in the Middle East have their prisoners.

"I have visited them. They're in good physical condition and in good spirits. They are completely baffled by these charges. All they did was complete their mission. They feel, as do I, that they have been set up. That this was all arranged somehow and somebody is behind it. We don't know who, but I promise you I'm going to find out.

"The next thing that happens in this case is that my two clients will be brought to the courtroom to hear the charges in what in America would be called a preliminary hearing. We welcome this airing of the charges, both so that the world can see how ridiculous they are, but also so we can challenge the court's jurisdiction and right to bring these charges at all. It will be our first opportunity to be heard, and we ask the world to follow this case closely, to hear the evidence and reasoning for these charges.

"But because I have also met with the prosecutor, and seen the zealousness with which he intends to pursue these claims, and realize that the deck is stacked against my clients, I don't believe they will get a fair trial, and I do not believe they would get a fair appeal—which is heard by the appellate division of the ICC itself. Same building. So I hereby call on President Obama to put an end to this. The United States anticipated this very event. We saw it coming. We knew that someday some American would be indicted with phony charges, which the court would use as a political tool to chastise the Americans for their so-called rogue behavior in the world. That time has now come. That's the reason for this case.

"During the preceding administration, Congress was so infuriated by the International Criminal Court treaty's refusal to respond to our concerns about the formation of this court, and would not fix the problems with the court—like no jury trial, like no acknowledgment of American sovereignty, like no appeal to a court outside its own building—that the United States withdrew its support. We knew that Americans would one day be charged, even though that violated every tenet of international law that has ever existed. So Congress passed the Servicemembers' Protection Act. Not only did the act pass, but President Bush signed it into law in 2002.

It is the law of the United States right now, as I stand here. It gives the president the tools that he needs to challenge the International Criminal Court directly. If Americans are taken captive by the court, the president has the power to take *whatever means are necessary* to extract those Americans from the clutches of the International Criminal Court, including *force*.

"I call on the president right now, before the whole world, to tell the American people what steps he is going to take to free these two Americans from their prison in Holland. I call on him to send a battle group to the North Atlantic to be off the coast of the maritime country of Holland, and the seaport of The Hague, to be prepared to go ashore to take control of these two Americans and bring them home.

"President Obama, send the Marines. Do it. Let's watch the prison guards try and stop the Marines when they come to bring their comrades home. I call on the president to stand tall in this hour of need for justice, to not allow Americans to be dragged through months of procedural nonsense only to be put on trial on trumped-up charges that have been created by some European and Middle Eastern conspiracy. We need to free the Americans, and we need to free them now. We need to send the battle group and the Marines and get the job done."

I looked at the faces of the journalists. They were stunned. I could tell that most of them had never heard of the Servicemembers' Protection Act. That didn't really surprise me. It was not well known. Even though it was actually passed, and the president had in fact signed it as I had said, *no one* had ever expected it to be used.

Except perhaps in Holland, and other places in Europe, where they monitored its passage and signature with horror. But it was the law, and the president had the affirmative power to do whatever he needed to get them out of that prison. We could go in there with guns blazing, and nobody could say we didn't have the right to do it.

"I am happy to take a few questions at this time."

Reporters around me tried to edge closer so they could ask the first question. Hands shot up, and reporters yelled my name and other things to try to get my attention. Some tried the age-old trick of simply asking a question loudly and not stopping regardless of whether they were going to be the ones to ask the question. I pointed to a female reporter directly in front of me. "Yes."

"Do you really think the president will send American troops to Europe?"

"I've heard his statements. I've not heard him say anything that indicates that he would. That is why I felt compelled to mention the act, which he has not mentioned, and indicate to the American people that it is my belief that he should employ it immediately to stop this charade. But do I think he will? I don't know."

I selected a man in the back who was tall and able to project over the entire group. "Why do you think you are in a position to tell the president how to handle this crisis? Maybe he is planning things that you don't know about."

"I suppose that's possible. If he is, then we'll learn about it, but right now, I'm not aware of any such effort."

A man in the front yelled out, "Who is behind all this? Who flew the Americans to Holland?"

I nodded my head. "That's a question I'd like to know the answer to. And I intend to find out. This is not some random event. This was a carefully planned series of events that occurred quickly. Things were in place. So that's a great question. I will find out the answer before this is over."

Another asked, "Pakistan seems to be losing control of the mountainous areas. Is it now what Afghanistan was when President Bush first invaded there?"

"That's a great question too. I'm not really sure. I think that Pakistan is on the verge of becoming a failed state that just might take the place of what Afghanistan was in 2001, a haven for the Taliban and al Qaeda. But with nuclear weapons and 170 million people. It could be a catastrophe."

"Are you going to be able to get these two navy fliers off if the president doesn't go in as you are asking?"

"I'm going to do everything I can to defend them. I will do the best job that I can within the bounds created by the International Criminal Court. I don't see how they can ever prove intent, or knowledge against my clients. But right now I feel like they are on a rail and I'm not sure I'm going to be able to stop it. I would call on the International Criminal Court to transfer these men to the United States. They certainly know that if our people have committed crimes, war crimes, that would be a violation of the Uniform Code of Military Justice and they can be prosecuted in the United States. I'm sure a full and complete investigation would be done, and if they deserve to be charged, they would be. But one way or another, we're going to bring them home."

I went straight back to my office hoping that the other attorneys from Kristen's law firm would already be there. Much to my surprise, rather than coming to the press conference, some journalists camped out in front of my office, hoping to get a private press conference or statement of some kind. I was already thinking about our next move. I didn't have any more time to talk about it.

I walked past the journalists without comment, and closed the door behind me. Kristen was waiting for me, and next to her were several other people. I said, "Who do we have here?"

"Two from our D.C. office, and four from New York. These are the ones that have the time and the willingness to help out. I hope they're okay."

"Come on in to my office, everyone." They followed me into my larger office. They stood around aimlessly while I took off my coat. I looked at them quickly. "Did any of you see the press conference?"

One raised her hand. "I did. I think we all did actually. Tristan had the television on in her office, and we all stood in there watching."

"Then why are you the only one who raised her hand?"

She smiled with some embarrassment. "I don't really know."

I took some papers out of my briefcase. I spoke quickly. "Do you all understand the difficulties that lie in front of us? We are going to have a lot of people against us."

One of the men, with his hands in his pocket and floppy hair hanging down to his eyes, said, "Probably including the chief legal officer for the State Department. I think his title is actually legal advisor to the State Department."

I looked at all of them. "Why don't you all grab chairs, and bring them in here. We have a few things to go over." When they had all taken their seats in a rough semicircle around my desk, I said to the one who'd spoken, "What do you know about the legal advisor to the State Department? What's your name by the way?"

"Todd. Todd McCarthy."

"So what are you talking about?"

"You don't know about him?"

"I don't have any idea what you're talking about. Get to the point."

"Yeah. Well, if you follow international law stuff at all, he's kind of famous. He was at Harvard Law School, and basically takes the position that international law should trump the Constitution, and that by ignoring the International Criminal Court and the International Court of Justice, and by making treaties subject to the Constitution, that we are sort of a stand-alone country. We're not really good international law partners. He has always said he wants us to come around to international law norms."

"How do you know that?"

"That's what I do. International law. It's mostly commercial, but once in a while I get involved in treaty stuff. I was the editor of the international law journal at Harvard. He was one of our heroes."

"So this guy is your hero?"

"Well, he was in law school. Sort of. He had really big ideas that we all thought were pretty good. I haven't thought about that much since."

"How many years have you been practicing?"

"Five years. But just so you know, in the interest of full disclosure, I do transactional work. I mostly work on international mergers and acquisitions."

"What the hell are you doing here? You don't do litigation? You don't do criminal work?"

"No. I don't. But I know how to do research, and I had some time. I just got off a deal that closed last week, and I was going to take a three-week vacation to Australia. But I decided to do this instead."

"That's mighty nice of you. You sure you want to do this? Are you sure you're going to be on the right side of this?"

"I'm here to help. Whatever I can do. I'm not here with some preconceived idea of how all this is to go. Just tell me what you want me to do."

"What about the rest of you? Tell me what kind of work you do, and why you're interested in helping out."

They all told me their levels of experience, all of which were less than seven years, and none of them had ever tried a case of any kind anywhere under any circumstances. That was okay, I didn't really expect them to be part of the trial. I just needed some sharp minds helping to draft some of the motions and papers that I expected to file. It was good to have some help.

"Kristen is my number two. All of my assignments to you will go through her. She knows you a lot better than I do, probably knows who is best placed to do each thing we need to do. Todd, you ought to start working on the jurisdictional motion. You may already be familiar with the vocabulary, and the hearing is in just a few days. It's going to be right on top of us before we even know it. You had all better start planning on working eighteen-hour days. We've got a lot of work to do. Kristen, you and I need to put together a document pretty quickly. All the rest of you, let's get to work."

After the others had filed out, Kristen said, "What do you have in mind?"

"We need to do the best we can to draw a diagram of the prison, the entrance, and the International Criminal Court building."

"That's not legal work. Why do we have to do that?"

"Because some of our friends may need to take advantage of any weaknesses we can find. Let's go upstairs."

I led Kristen to a conference room I rented six floors up. It wasn't very nice, sort of nondescript and not decorated. But it had a wooden table and six chairs, and electric power. That was all I needed. A man was waiting for us. It was Richard. Kristen was surprised to see him. I said to him, "This is Kristen, the other attorney I told you about."

He didn't move; he just stared at her, assessing her. He had an intense look. He said nothing.

Kristen looked at him, then back at me. She said, "Can I speak?"

"He's on our side. Let's get to work."

"Who is he? And doing what?"

"Like I said earlier. Drawing the prison."

She looked at him. "Why do you need to know what the prison looks like?"

He spoke softly. "In case I ever find myself arrested for a war crime."

She wasn't amused. "Seriously. Why do you need to know?"

"To keep our options open."

"Who are you?"

He looked at me. "A friend of John's. We play water polo together."

She looked at me skeptically. "You play water polo?"

I went to the table and opened a map of The Hague. It was large, three feet by four feet. I walked around to the other side of the table, the same side that Richard was on. We examined the map carefully. I had marked the prison and the possible routes from the prison to the court. He opened a backpack and pulled out a packet of eight-and-a-half-by-eleven photographs in full color. They were from the high-def video I had taken. He spread them out. Kristen walked around to our side and looked on noncommittally. The photos showed the prison from every important perspective, from the approaches that one might take to break in and two possible routes of escape. There were additional photos that I couldn't account for, photos of streets, buildings, exterior shots of the court, and vehicles. As I examined them I asked, "Where'd you get the rest of these?"

"Quick overnight flight. My camera."

I picked up one photo of what looked like a SWAT van. "This their van?"

He nodded. "One of 'em."

Kristen asked, "What van? For what?"

I replied, "For transporting prisoners."

Something clicked and she was horrified. "Are you going to try and stop the van and take our clients?"

He was stoic. He looked at me. "What is she doing here? Send her out to get some food or something."

Her face flushed. "Get food? Get *food*? Who do you think I am, your mother? I am here to *represent* these men. Not be part of some illegal operation."

He ignored her and pulled a small laptop from his backpack. He powered it up. He spoke to her while watching his screen. "If this makes you uncomfortable, whatever it is you think we're doing, maybe you should go do something else."

She turned to me. She looked as if I'd betrayed her. "Are you part of this? Is this what you want to do?"

I said, "Why don't you go downstairs and start working on those motions with the others. I thought you might be helpful in giving him some of your observations from the times we were there, but don't worry about it. I'll take care of this."

She put her hands on her hips, clearly deciding whether to do what she was contemplating. "Maybe my firm's attorneys should just go back to what they were doing before. We're not going to be part of some violent event."

She had a very tight sense of right and wrong, on which she stood with great confidence.

"We'll talk about it later. Just go join the others."

She walked out and closed the door behind her harder than she needed to.

He said, "What's her problem?"

"She's always right."

He nodded. "Think we can get them in the prison, or are we going to have to do this on the street?"

I imagined the scene of an American special operations team breaking into the prison. "It can be done, but it's not some lightweight county jail. It'll take a lot of force. Probably have to kill several guards. If you go after the van, you should be able to pull it off. I don't know if they travel with guards inside the vans, but I assume so. They've got a huge budget, and realize there may be people out there who want to free the war criminals they're holding. Not our guys so much, but the usual African tyrants. They have lots of guys who might try something, so they're prepared. It won't be a soft target. And I would assume they'll be expecting you. That means they may have extra guards, and decoy vans. All kinds of things. But I also expect the last thing they want to face is an op by DEVGRU."

He glanced up from his screen. "Who said I was with DEVGRU?"

"Nobody."

"You used to be with them."

"Yeah. Two years."

"You've got a rep. A lot of people still talk about you. Best planner anyone could remember. Always had some clever, unexpected angle. You did some live ops too."

He was testing me. But I had assumed Marshall would have filled him in on everything. "Sure."

"Where?"

"Iraq and Afghanistan, mostly. We went in to Afghanistan before the invasion. Same for Iraq, and stayed for a while. Did one op in Pakistan too."

He looked up. "In 2001?"

"Yep."

"I'd love to hear about that someday."

I smiled. "You're not cleared."

He chuckled. "So why'd you get out?"

"Long story."

"Let's hear it."

"Nah."

"Why not?"

"I don't like talking about it."

"Do something stupid?"

I hadn't talked about it since I'd left the navy. Not even to my parents. Most guys who got out had a simple story. They needed more money, wanted to get on with an education, wanted to save their marriage, the usual reasons. I could have said I wanted to go to law school, but it wasn't really true, at least not at the time. I could have just said I didn't want to go to sea anymore, but I didn't go to sea that much, and actually I loved going to sea. I could have said it was killing my relationship with my family, but I didn't have a family. I wasn't married, had no prospects, and still didn't. So I didn't have a crisp little story. And every time somebody asked why I had gotten out, the events that made me get out came flooding back.

During the invasion of Iraq, after the Iraqi army collapsed, dropped their rifles, and jettisoned their uniforms, my SEAL team was tasked with looking for the HVTs, the high-value targets, or units. The biggies in the Iraqi government or military. The famous Deck of Cards, where the more important targets were the face cards, and Saddam Hussein was the ace of spades. We were very good at finding them and went through the deck like card sharks.

We had a line on the jack of spades, one of the most important figures in Iraq. We were on the outskirts of Baghdad, by ourselves, in the middle of the night. We could call in an attack helicopter if necessary, but we were basically on our own.

We approached the house where he had been sighted. Our intel was very good. We'd gone into several houses before that one, on other nights. We were good at it. But each house was different. Any one of them could be full of armed men waiting for us or booby-trapped. We were on the house within minutes of the target arriving. It was nearly 1:00 A.M. and the neighborhood was still. We split the block, surrounded the house, and covered all entrances and exits. Six of us approached the front door along the wall. We checked the door. It was made of thick wood and bolted. We examined the hinges, looked to where the bolt was and smashed it with a sledgehammer on a full swing. The door broke open and we rushed in. We knew each other's movements and assignments.

No muzzle flashes, no explosions. They thought they were safe and hidden but they weren't. We were all over them before they even knew what was happening.

We grabbed the jack of spades and jerked him up off the floor. We illuminated his face while we videotaped and photographed him and zip-tied his hands behind him. The other men sat or stood silently, hoping we weren't going to drag them out of the house too. We didn't want them, we wanted him. They knew if they interfered it would be their last act.

I put my 9mm back in its holster and put a hood over the jack of spade's head. No doubt on the ID. I started pulling him out while the others covered our exit, when our radios came alive. Our comm specialist had gotten a call from a Marine squad that had been patrolling nearby. They had been walking down a street when they were ambushed from houses on both sides. They were crying for help, lying in the street fighting for their lives.

The bad guys had gone into occupied houses and when the Marines approached, fired their AK-47s out the windows in a deadly crossfire while holding unarmed civilians in the windows so the Marines wouldn't shoot back; women and children were visible and more were inside the houses making the use of grenades impossible.

I handed our prisoner to one of my men. I indicated to the others with me to follow, and with half our team ran the mile to the Marines. We could hear the automatic rifles from half a mile a way. The deeper, distinctive sound of the AKs, and the powerful but higher-pitched reports of the Marines' M-16s. Hundreds of rounds were flying back and forth.

We stopped at the corner and I flipped down my night vision goggles. I squatted and looked down the street where the firefight raged. Half the Marines were already dead, their weapons lying next to them. The other half were in a desperate fight. We had to get them out. The only way to beat an ambush is to go right at it, but the shooters were hiding behind civilians.

I motioned for my men to take both sides of the street and go in after the shooters. Avoid the civilians and stop this ambush. We took off down the street. I was on the right, and our man with the sledge and another man with him went right for the first door on the other side of the street. They smashed in the door and took out the first two shooters. Three civilians lay dead on the floor, either killed by the shooters or the Marines trying to stay alive.

We went to each house, staying by the walls and returning fire as we could. Inch by inch we cleared the houses, and took out all the attackers. I secured the last house with two of my men, and waited until a shooter got greedy. He was out of targets, and leaned from the window to aim his AK down the street. I grabbed the barrel of his AK and pulled him out of the window. I shot him and kicked in the door. As I went in we realized there were three more shooters inside. They fired wildly, unable to see us in the dark. We were on the floor shooting back. We took out all three of them, and then noticed several civilians huddled in the corner. Two others were dead next to them. They were crying and holding each other. I went outside and looked across the street where three of my men came out. There had been five shooters in the house they entered and they had ended up in a point-blank firefight. Two of them had taken rounds in their bulletproof vests, but were okay.

At the end of it there were two dead children in their house.

We had saved the Marines, had risked our lives in a mission that we hadn't planned or had time to talk through, but we had done the right thing. But sometimes that isn't good enough.

Word got out about the dead civilians. I say that as if it was coincidental. It wasn't. Somebody took pictures and circulated them all over Baghdad, saying the Americans had broken in and murdered the civilians. The American command sent a forensic team to investigate. They recovered the civilian bodies and did autopsies. They found that the two children in the house across the street had been killed by the much smaller M-16 bullets. American bullets. The bullets were too mangled to match them to a specific weapon, but because of the wound paths in the children, the investigators concluded they had been killed by my team members when they entered the house.

Sometimes civilian deaths are unavoidable. That was one of those times. Anyone who thinks they shot children on purpose doesn't know my men. Never. But that knowledge wasn't good enough. The navy put them on trial.

And that's what set me off. I didn't want any part of a navy that would put brave men like that on trial for incidental deaths from a deadly firefight in an ambush. Most SEALs on active duty when I got out knew the story. They knew why. Richard didn't. But I didn't feel like telling him.

I walked over to stand behind him to see his screen. "You know their van routes?"

He looked at the map. "I've got every one they've ever used. So we might have the one they'll use this time, unless they really think I'm coming, in which case they'd be stupid to use one of these."

"You talk to Marshall?"

"Sure."

"The president going to authorize this?"

He closed his laptop and put it in his backpack as it powered down. He stood and zipped up his North Face fleece. "You tell me."

"Don't know. I put him on the spot, publicly. That could cut either way."

"Yeah. I saw it. That wasn't well received. You knew Marshall had some things in the works. He asked you not to go public. You did anyway. Called attention to the idea that we might take this into our own hands. That made it harder, Jack. Marshall's pissed."

"Not the first time I pissed someone off."

"Well, you made it harder on me. And I don't appreciate it. So no, I don't know if we're going to get authorization. What's your cell?"

I gave it to him.

"Does it work in Holland?"

"Yeah."

"Keep it on. I may be in touch. Or someone may."

# NINE

Kristen was waiting for me in my reception area. Her face was full of indignation. "Are they seriously going to try to grab our clients? I absolutely will *not* be part of anything illegal."

I didn't answer. I walked toward my office.

"So what, are you just a setup? A front?"

I stopped. "What is your problem?"

"What's my problem? Are you kidding? You bring some man in here to pick our brains on the best way to blow up a prison and get people out and you wonder what I'm worked up about? We're trained to *uphold* the law, John. Not violate it. We're lawyers in case you've forgotten."

I raised my voice. "And which law is it that you want us to uphold, Kristen?"

She squinted through eyes full of disbelief. "I can't believe we're having this conversation. How about the law of not breaking into *prisons*."

"You need a little orientation. We are Americans, not Dutch. We are not Europeans. We are not bound by the self-appointed courts of the Europeans. We are not bound by the International Criminal Court, a point we are about to make in a motion that is being written by your colleagues right now."

"I need an answer."

"To what?"

"Is he, that man who wouldn't introduce himself to me, is he the reason that you were chosen to be the attorney for these two navy pilots? So you could help him? Who exactly is it that selected you? Did the wives call you? Answer me that?"

"What difference does it make?"

"Answer me!"

"Chris Marshall called me. He's the Deputy Director of the National Security Council for counterterrorism operations. A former Navy SEAL."

"So *that's* what we're doing? A counterterrorism operation? Are the Dutch now *terrorists*? Is the International Criminal Court now a terrorist organization?"

"No. But they're working directly with terrorists, or the Taliban, if it's what I think happened here."

"So a counterterrorism director selects you as the attorney for these pilots, and then what, promises to pay you from the government coffers?"

"Something like that."

She laughed as we got to my office. We walked in and I closed the door behind her. I sat in my chair and took a deep breath. She said, "So *we* work for free, and you get paid by the United States government to run

cover. We make up this operation that looks just like
attorneys representing clients, but is in reality a front
for a special operations mission to rescue these men from
the International Criminal Court. That about it?"

"No. You're way off. I'm not involved in any operation. I am not—"

"Do you think there's any doubt that they chose you
because you were a former Navy SEAL? You think
that was irrelevant?"

"I don't think it was irrelevant, but I don't think that
was the reason. I have a good reputation—"

"John, you've been practicing law for seven years.
There are criminal defense attorneys in Washington
who have been doing this for thirty years with reputa-
tions fifty times bigger than yours."

"Sure. But I can't name one who has any military
experience, let alone someone who understands the International Criminal Court, or who has worked at the
DOJ and written about it. I may not be the best criminal defense lawyer in Washington, but I may be one of
the few people who can do what we're doing."

She rubbed her eyes and checked her watch. Her fatigue was starting to show. "Are you involved in this
operation? Are you just some undercover Navy SEAL
or CIA special operations person pretending to be a
lawyer?"

"No. I am not just pretending. And I'm not some
undercover Navy SEAL. I left that behind a long time
ago. I haven't had anything to do with them since. I
stay in touch with some people, I pay attention to what
they're doing, I go to the bars that we go to when one of

us is killed, but I'm not still involved in anything. You have to trust me, Kristen. I have been completely straight with you, and I always will be. There may be a time when I can't answer a question that you want me to answer, although I doubt it. I don't have anything to hide. But to get to your real question, yes. I *absolutely* will help them try to break these guys out. I hope they do it on Wednesday when they're being taken to the initial or preliminary hearing. I really hope they do. But I don't know if they'll get authorization. It's going to be ugly. I don't see how they can do it without killing a few guards, and that will be an international disaster. But you've got to remember, Kristen, Congress has authorized the use of force. So if President Obama wants to rescue these men by the use of force, he is authorized to do so. So when you start screaming about doing something illegal, you're off base."

"Well it sure as hell would be illegal in Holland."

"No doubt. So which law is it that you plan to follow?"

"I plan on following all the laws. I don't violate laws."

"Then you'd better stay out of the way while some other people do. Because they are going to get our clients out of Holland."

Kristen's questions had forced me to consider what I was actually trying to accomplish, and whether I even knew what I was doing. Was I being used? I knew that "The Government," that mixture of truth, justice, the American way, reckless self-promotion, and random haphazard destructive will, could use and consume me or anyone else for its purposes. But what was I, personally, doing? Was I a stooge? If they tried to free the navy fliers, what about me? They'd be whisked away by helicopter, or boat, and I'd be standing there in my briefs. I'd be arrested by the outraged Dutch and charged with obstruction of justice, or murder. I'd be the one in a Dutch prison forever. And there was no American law authorizing the use of force to free a stupid American lawyer caught in an attempt to free "war criminals." Did I trust The Government to even pull it off? Going into Egypt or Thailand was one thing. But Holland? Europe? They had all the sophisticated equipment we had. They had a small but well-trained military. They wouldn't be caught napping. People would get killed, and the outrage the Europeans already had right now would explode.

I had gotten out of the navy for a lot of reasons. But one element was a desire to do justice through the system, not to resort to violence, or killing people. I hadn't become a pacifist. Hardly. Sometimes there wasn't any alternative to war. But I had seen law school as a chance for me to use my mind to find ways make things better, to achieve justice. I had studied international law, written papers on how to make all the international institutions better, how to fix the U.N., how to achieve international justice against war criminals. How to make the ICC treaty better so the U.S. could sign it. But after years of study, after working at the DOJ to try to actually accomplish something, I'd become a cynic. I had hardened. International institutions were all corrupt and full of people who hated America for completely irrational reasons. Everything was our fault, and every international institution was to be used as a string to tie the giant to the ground.

I walked away, wishing a pox on the whole endeavor. So I quit reading foreign policy quarterlies and started defending criminals. One case after the other, one day after the other, fifty cases at a time, paying the bills. And now where was I? Nowhere. I wasn't a highly trained tough guy pushing back the dark evil of those who wanted to reduce our country to rubble, and I wasn't trying to fix the institutions that might have made it better. I guess I had quit caring. Instead of trying to change the world I had decided to build my own instead. But I hadn't done much of that either. No wife, no children, a few friends, and no real *mission*, except to get the latest gang-banger back on the street because the U.S. attorney had failed to gather the evidence properly, or was too young and incompetent to get the evidence admitted at the trial.

So that, all of it, is why I had jumped at the chance Marshall offered me. It wrapped it all up in one neat package. The chance to do justice, the chance to challenge another self-righteous corrupt international institution, and the chance, maybe, to set the whole damned thing on fire. And I wanted to be right in the middle of it, from all directions. And maybe, if I was smart enough, I'd figure out how all this happened. How these two naval officers ended up on the ground in Pakistan and in prison in Holland with a midnight indictment. Somebody set this up, and I was going to find him.

\* \* \*

Monday dawned cloudy and cool. The Hague was buzzing. Everyone in the city knew what was going to happen that morning, or at least thought they did. I hadn't heard from Marshall or anyone else. I went for a walk around the city center, stopping at a couple of cafés for coffee. I didn't speak Dutch, but knew what everyone was talking about. The Hague was the center of the world today, and would be at the trial. The city was thrilled with the attention, the press, and the innumerable people who had flocked to the city to support and to criticize the court and the charges against the Americans.

A café I stopped at had several empty tables on the sidewalk. I ordered another double espresso. A bad habit of mine, drinking too much coffee. But I hadn't picked that street, or that café, at random. I had made an educated guess on what time they would transport the two Americans to the ICC. And then I'd studied the map of The Hague and figured out about five probable routes from the prison to the ICC that any caravan carrying them would take. I'd been part of dozens of PSDs as a SEAL. Personal security details. We'd transported and provided security for numerous people, from heads of state to the chief of the CIA. I knew what they'd be thinking about, how they would try to make the transport of my clients as safe and invulnerable as possible.

But I also knew nothing was invulnerable. The job was to reduce the exposure, reduce the opportunities, reduce the likelihood of an attack or a kidnapping. Lower the odds of success so they wouldn't even try. But no matter what route they took, I knew their destination.

A huge advantage. At some point, their caravan had to come to the ICC. They might use dummy caravans, several identical vehicles, only one of which was the true caravan. I didn't know if they'd go to such lengths, but I was intent on finding out.

The street I had picked for my morning stroll was the one they'd use to approach the ICC in three of the five routes I had considered.

So there I sat, wondering whether I'd guessed right.

The waiter placed the coffee on my small table with its smooth white top. I checked my watch. It was two and a half hours before the hearing, and about the time I would expect them to be on their way. Most people would expect them to arrive perhaps thirty minutes before the hearing. Not me. I sipped from my espresso and heard several engines roaring in the otherwise quiet morning. Knowing I guessed right, I looked up and saw two vans tearing down the street followed by two armored cars, which were being followed by two more vans. They were moving fast and close together. Well executed so far, I thought. My eyes looked at a man I saw emerge from a café a block down, closer to the ICC. He was talking on a cell phone and gesticulating wildly. He glanced toward his left, where the vans were racing toward him from a quarter mile away, and didn't see them at all. He stepped right off the curb, engrossed in his conversation, and started across the street. The van saw him and blasted an ear-splitting horn for him to move. He froze, looked up standing in the middle of the street, and pulled the phone slowly away from his ear.

The lead van screeched to a stop and five men armed with submachine guns jumped out and pointed them at him. He put up his hands as they yelled at him to get the hell out of the street. He nodded and quickly moved to the far side of the street.

The other vans and armored cars stood restlessly behind the first van. Perfect I thought. I looked around and saw another man walking on the other side of the street toward me. He was in a business suit, carrying a soft briefcase with a long strap over his shoulder. He coughed as he continued to walk but I noticed that he kept his hand near his mouth a little longer than necessary. He was talking into a microphone in his sleeve. An American. No doubt. He was relaying information to the rest of the team, who were probably elsewhere, giving them the makeup of the caravan. We were about a half mile from the ICC building. He was probably telling them what I could see.

It was a very heavily armed caravan, with a separate armored car for each prisoner and probably twenty security guards, not to mention whoever was in the armored cars with the American. It could be taken, but it would be a bloodbath. They might have something in place a couple of blocks away.

I stood, put some euros under my cup, grabbed my briefcase, and started walking in the direction the caravan was moving. The likelihood of an attack was higher than I had thought. I knew they were there, the question was whether they would execute. I walked as quickly as I could without appearing to be in too much of a hurry. I didn't want to get too close if firing started. That would be the ultimate irony.

The caravan turned left, still driving very quickly. It took me ten to fifteen minutes to get to the ICC building, where the press had set up a perimeter of satellite vans, cameramen, and reporters from all over the world. Kristen was to meet me there at eight, a full two hours before our scheduled hearing. We wanted to get into the courtroom, get a feel for it, see how the setup would play for our examination of witnesses, and get comfortable.

I came up behind the CNN setup and to a reporter I recognized from television. "Did the prisoners arrive okay?"

He was looking at his script and holding his microphone and paid very little attention to me. He clearly didn't recognize me. "Yeah. They pulled in about five minutes ago."

I nodded, and kept walking without him ever knowing who I was. I crossed through the crowd. They were too busy getting prepared for my expected arrival an hour from then. I went to the receptionist, showed her my credentials that had been issued, and she nodded without smiling. "You may proceed to the courtroom on the third floor."

"Thanks. Has Ms. Chambers arrived yet?"

"No sir. You're the first."

I passed through security and crossed to the elevator in the stark hallway and rode to the third floor. I studied every part of the approach, from the type of the elevator to the ceilings. I now thought of the ICC building as an extension of the prison in which my clients were held. It might have to be right in the courtroom where some unexpected people came to get them and take them home.

I pushed open the heavy doors to the ultramodern room that was the courtroom. Anyone on first seeing it would assume it was some kind of scientific lecture room, or corporate meeting room. It had a European sterility to it. It was a carefully crafted architectural eunuch. It was full of blond wood. It had a very high ceiling yet felt confined. There were desks everywhere with multiple computer screens at each. The bench, or what we would call the bench, which looked to me like a heightened computer screen viewing station, had three seats for the three judges. Permanent tables were placed for attorneys on each side of the bench, facing each other and not the judges. The judges faced the witness bench, behind which were a two-story wall of glass and several rows of audience seats. There was room for perhaps one hundred audience members. It was medium-sized in the world of courtrooms, windowless, with a lot of glass and a feeling of hardness. It reminded me vaguely of a wood-paneled surgical center, except for the modern, striped—but in a modern artistic way—green carpet.

There were technicians all around checking the lights, the computer screens, the microphones, and the flooring to make sure that there were no wires or protrusions over which someone might trip. It was clearly designed for people to remain stationary and talk to each other across the computer screens with headphones so each person from a different part of Babel could understand the others with the help of translators. Thankfully the trial and all proceedings were to be in English. All trials at the ICC were either in English or French.

It was a very strange setup, and not something you would ever see in an American courtroom. But we weren't in America. That was becoming ever more clear. I wasn't sure which table was mine. I asked one of the technicians in English, "Do you know which table is for counsel for the defendants?"

He was wearing dark blue overalls. He looked up at me surprised. Either he didn't know I was there, or he didn't expect me to speak English. But in any case, he said in a heavy accent, "Yes. That one." He pointed to a bench that was to the left of someone who was facing the judges' bench, and close to the glass.

I put down my briefcase, took out my copies of motions that we had filed before the hearing, and prepared my checklist for the points to be argued.

This first hearing was to "confirm the charges," as they put it. I thought the likelihood of them not "confirming" them was about the same as at a preliminary hearing in the U.S. They'd be confirmed. My job here was to learn as much as I could, make a little noise, and see if I could find a weakness I could capitalize on. The prosecutor wouldn't show his whole hand. I didn't know what we would hear, but had some sense based on what Liam had already disclosed to me. I didn't know whether Liam would bring live witnesses. European continental courts—to be distinguished from English common law courts—mostly dealt in affidavits. They used sworn written evidence as opposed to live witnesses. That of course is a problem. In the United States, affidavits are generally not admissible in trial. The common law tradition, started in England, and perhaps kept even more alive in America, believed that a witness's demeanor, tone, and ability to withstand a live cross-examination was a far better determiner of the truth than someone who signs an affidavit in a room far away observed by no one other than those presenting his evidence. It's easy for an advocate to write an affidavit for a witness so that the nuances of the testimony all fall his way. But that was what we were likely to face, unless Liam decided to start trying to win over the international press, including the American press. He knew it wouldn't be that hard. If he showed what many thought was a war crime, the press wouldn't worry too much about arguments over jurisdiction.

As I removed my notebooks from my briefcase I was trying to figure out why my friends from DEVGRU had decided not to grab the two pilots. No explosions, no gunfire, no screaming, nothing to indicate an attempt had even been made. Maybe they were just checking the formation and the security, and planned to hit them on the way out. I doubted it, but it was possible. My guess was Obama asked whether it could be done without killing anybody, and they wouldn't guarantee it.

I heard the door open behind me and turned. Kristen walked in wearing her gray suit and white blouse. She had her hair up and looked very official. She also looked both excited and concerned. She walked over to me and put her briefcase on the table and began unpacking her notebooks. She looked around the room, saw that it was full of only technicians, and said, "You ready?"

"I think so. I'm actually kind of surprised that we're still here."

She frowned. "Meaning?"

"I thought our president might act boldly this morning."

"Maybe he has more respect for Dutch law than you thought."

"Maybe."

The door opened again and Liam walked in. Just the sight of him annoyed me. He struck me as superficial; someone who thought he knew a lot more about the world and the operation of power, particularly American military power, than he actually did. He walked around with a suitcase full of prejudices and stereotypes about the way the United States operated. Sometimes it was even informed by a few facts. But it was my sense he had a deep-seated hatred of what we stood for. Maybe it was premature, and maybe my bias against him was just as unfair as the prejudice that he had against the United States. But that's what I felt.

I sat down with Kristen at my side and placed my notebooks in front of me. It was a strange feeling. It was a very un-American courtroom. There was no jury. There would be no argument to ordinary people. The people who were my audience, or who would be once this hearing began, were trained professional jurists who almost certainly were somewhat cynical, and had preconceived notions not only on how the hearing should go, but what would come out at the other end. There had never been a pretrial hearing at the ICC on whether to confirm the charges in which the charges weren't confirmed. And every single case had ended in conviction.

Finally Liam crossed over the room to me. He put his hands on my desk and leaned in. "This won't be like your American courts. You leave everything in the hands of uneducated people. Like O.J. and Michael Jackson." He snickered. "No persuading people who don't know any better, and let the defendants go because they like their music or the way they run on a football field."

I stood up and extended my hand. "Morning, Liam. Nice to see you again. And thank you for your comments on our justice system. I'm sure you're right. This system is far better, and I am here to learn, so thank you for reminding me of our primitive system, which of course is based on the British system, where you were trained."

He seemed put out, like I'd interrupted his speech. He abandoned whatever else he was going to say and walked to his side of the courtroom. I wondered why he had gone to the trouble. Most experienced prosecutors didn't waste time trying to intimidate defense counsel. He wasn't impressing anyone.

I studied my notes and outlines while the courtroom filled. A door opened to the side of the judge's bench and our two clients walked in. They were dressed in ill-fitting suits but notably were not restrained. The guards escorted them to their seats and one stood to the side and behind each of them. The few remaining seats behind the glass were now filled. Everyone was in place and there was an audible buzz of people getting ready for the big hearing, which was to be carried live throughout the world. Finally the three judges entered the courtroom. Everyone stood. Kristen stood next to me. The judges stood behind their seats until the one in the middle told everyone to take their seats. We sat after they did.

The lead judge was a German by the name of Dietrich Hauptmann. He had spent his entire legal career as a judge under the German system, and had been selected through a comprehensive selection system to be a judge of the International Criminal Court. According to the sources that I had found, he was highly respected, but considered very much a "European," as opposed to a German. The second judge, who was sitting to his right and my left as I looked at them, was from Brazil, and the third judge was from Egypt. They looked distinguished. They wore black robes, and had long blue collars, almost scarves, that draped around their necks and halfway down their chests. The royal blue was accentuated by a decorative full white collar underneath the blue collars. It was a sophisticated look and unlike any other judge's robes I had ever seen.

After the preliminaries and introductions, the reading of the charges and the judicial statements, the hearing began in earnest. Judge Hauptmann looked at me and asked, "Mr. Caskey, as lead counsel for the two defendants, do you have any preliminary issues or motions that we need to deal with before we hear the prosecutor's evidence to determine whether there is sufficient evidence to conduct a trial?"

"Yes sir. I believe you have our motions before you."

The clerk in front of him gave him a subtle nod. He looked at his computer screen, scrolled down, and clicked on something. "Yes. We have them. The first is a motion to dismiss the charges based on lack of jurisdiction of this court. I take it you want to argue these motions?"

"Yes sir."

"We understand your arguments, as we have read your papers. Do you have anything that you wish to add?"

I looked around the courtroom, trying to decide how to proceed. I felt unsteady. I hesitated. The judge seemed to sense my quandary.

He said, "You may argue your motion, sir, if you choose."

I had to argue our position, particularly with members of the press sitting in the audience. Part of my strategy had to be to stimulate outrage, at least in the United States, if nowhere else. I stood. "Thank you, Your Honor. Our first motion, and the one that you have already referred to, is the most important of the three. In fact I will submit the other two on the papers and not argue them. But fundamentally, this court does not and cannot have jurisdiction over citizens of a country that did not sign the treaty. It is a fundamental tenet of international law. Treaties only bind countries that sign them. The United States has never signed the Treaty of Rome that formed the International Criminal Court. The United States recognized at the time the treaty was being considered that this very possibility existed—that this court could take jurisdiction over a military operation that it didn't like, or the outcome of which it didn't like, and charge Americans with a war crime. It is true that President Clinton initially signed it, but he told the Senate not to ratify it. And the United States subsequently decided to 'un-sign' it. The concerns the United States had were never addressed, and still haven't been. And now this court has done the very thing the United States feared. It has asserted jurisdiction where there is none, and over Americans.

"In addition to a jurisdiction concern, the crimes listed in the treaty are broad enough to cover just about anything, which when combined with this court's lack of jurisdiction requires that these charges be dismissed. The jurisdiction of the court is inconsistent with international law, and the fundamental concepts of fairness, and, equally important for American citizens, contrary to the United States constitutional guarantees of due process. Frankly, Your Honor, this entire event is an outrage to international law and to the American people, and most particularly to the American military, which finds itself sometimes fighting the wars of others, including NATO, one member of which is Holland, where this court sits."

The judge nodded, not in agreement but rather out of recognition of the argument that he expected, and looked at the prosecutor. "Mr. Brady?"

Brady stood, looked at Lieutenants Duncan and Rawlings, glanced at Kristen and me, and then addressed the court. "Thank you, Your Honor. We have heard this argument before. It is the most common argument of those accused of war crimes—no one outside their own country can tell them what to do or stand in judgment of any conduct, no matter how egregious or outrageous. Of course that would be the argument, because they, or the ones ordering them to commit war crimes, would never hold them accountable for war crimes. It was for that very reason this international tribunal was established. Not only have 110 countries agreed to be bound by this treaty, but they all agreed at the same time that international law called for jurisdiction over all countries because otherwise war criminals in nonsignatory countries would simply not sign and continue inflicting mass crimes around the globe with impunity. It is that impunity, that attitude, which must be subject to international understanding of human rights and war crimes. We cannot tolerate hubris in the enforcement of war crimes.

"The United States, for example, if I might remind the court, was one of the founders of the entire concept of enforcing war crimes as exemplified by the Nuremberg trials in Germany after World War II. By what jurisdiction did the United States impose its morality of war crimes on Germany? Sure, Germany was defeated, but many of the highest leaders of the country were put on trial for war crimes. Numerous people were dragged before an international tribunal at Nuremberg, and held to a standard that was said to be universal. There was no treaty. There was no prior agreement by Germany to submit to such trials. They were just imposed on a defeated country. How is it then that the United States now comes here, through its criminal lawyer from Washington, D.C., who is well steeped in the constitutional protections available in the United States, and argues that this court has no jurisdiction over crimes committed in a clear act of war in the mountains of Afghanistan and Pakistan? A country with which the United States is not at war? The argument is specious and the international community has long recognized that it is without merit. This court has heard this tired argument repeatedly by each war criminal brought before it, and this motion has been denied each time. It should be denied again." Brady sat.

The judge looked at me. "Mr. Caskey? Anything else?"

I considered my options and decided to charge ahead. "Your Honors, this court is in something of a dilemma. Mr. Brady argues that my assertion of lack of jurisdiction is specious because others have made it before me. The fact that the argument was made poorly in the past—and I have read the arguments in the previous trials—does not mean that the argument is invalid. And the fact that the court has found a jurisdiction in the past, again, does not mean it has proper jurisdiction in every case. Jurisdiction is based on the facts of a given case. I think the court needs to seriously consider whether it truly intends to assert jurisdiction over members of the armed forces of the other country, which has not only not ratified the treaty, but was party to the drafting of the treaty and affirmatively chose not to. In fact, the United States has objected to this treaty at every turn. Saying the very things I am now saying, that this court cannot assert jurisdiction over it, that it violates the United States Constitution. And in fact the United States Congress was so incensed by these assertions that it passed a law authorizing the president of the United States to use force to extract prisoners—like my clients—who are captives of this court."

The judge held up his hand, "Your threats are not appreciated, and not relevant to our inquiry."

"It was not my intention to threaten this court with anything, Your Honor. To completely ignore the will of the United States, whose citizens are now in the dock in this court, is to risk reducing the legitimate jurisdiction of this court—to the states which have signed it—to an irrelevance. I request my clients be released immediately because this court has no jurisdiction."

The judge nodded. "Your motion for dismissal is under consideration. Anything else?"

"Your Honor, one other thing. I move to dismiss these cases based on the fact that the prosecutor does not have a case referred from a sovereign state that was a signatory to the convention in Rome or from the U.N. Security Council. There is no evidence of any other referral to this court, and therefore the case is not proper and must be dismissed."

"Mr. Brady?"

Brady nodded. "As Mr. Caskey knows, there is a third way of obtaining an indictment. A prosecutor may refer charges to the judicial committee if the prosecutor believes there is sufficient evidence to bring charges. If the committee confirms the charges, the indictment may

issue. That, as is known, is what happened here. As this
court knows, I had been conducting a long-standing investigation into the war crimes, or potential war crimes,
of the United States, and others, in the conduct of the
wars in Afghanistan, Iraq, and Pakistan. There were innumerable situations where civilian casualties occurred
from aerial bombings in particular, and about which the
United States said only that it was 'collateral damage'
and not 'intended.' After our systematic review of these
incidents, we concluded that they were not 'simply coincidental,' but in fact part of the war plan of the United
States. We detected a pattern of bombing civilian out-
posts, and in each case it was believed by those on the
ground that there was a direct reason for the attack. Just
like the United States bombing of the Chinese embassy
in Kosovo during President Clinton's administration, it
was immediately perceived, rightly, as a statement to
the Chinese. Likewise these attacks in Afghanistan and
Pakistan have been interpreted by the people who have
been attacked as statements to them. In this case, statements to aid workers to stop helping those who are participating in the war against the United States. Simply
put, they want the medical aid to stop. They want the
people they are fighting to suffer, and not have help from
Europeans. However the European relief organizations
do not choose sides, they help those who need help. Because of the timing of the shoot-down of the Americans, charges were referred to this court immediately,
and were issued. The charges are legal and proper, and
Mr. Caskey knows that."

I knew they thought so. A single prosecutor may refer charges, and if they're confirmed, off we go. Just like that. No involvement with any country at all. If the prosecutors and the judges of the ICC don't have enough to do, they can read the papers, start an investigation, and send themselves some business. Bad setup as I saw it. I was at Justice long enough and fought with enough prosecutors to know that prosecutors are not more sure than the rest of us. I said, "Your Honor, a midnight rush to issue charges about two men who had *just* been shot down smacks of a system with a judgment in search of a trial. It's outrageous. It's a sham. One of the principles of this court is that it is the court of last resort. It only prosecutes if the country that would otherwise have jurisdiction refuses to. Here, if in fact the pilots committed war crimes, they would be tried in military courts in the United States. But the United States wasn't even given time to find out what had happened, let alone determine whether some 'war crime' had been committed."

"Thank you, Mr. Caskey. We will consider your briefs and issue a written ruling. For now, the charges are proper, and we will now determine whether there is evidence to hold the defendants over for trial." He turned to Brady, "The prosecutor may begin his evidence."

I sat down, adjusted my papers in front of the screen and took out my pad to take notes.

Brady rose slowly, finally in his moment. He looked around the room, and nodded to a man sitting to his left. He then addressed the court, "I would like to begin by showing a videotape of the event in question. Please begin the tape."

The overhead lights dimmed, and the screens came alive. It was a grainy but clear image of a large flat building on a hillside. There were cars around it, and it seemed perched in the outskirts of a village in a valley, surrounded by distant mountains. I assumed this was the target. The image continued, people came and went from the building, and darkness came. The tape advanced, but the image stayed fairly clear. I could tell the video was shot through a low light lens, which takes the minimal light and amplifies it. Even a sliver of a moon was enough to light up the countryside through the lens. Pretty sophisticated equipment for a Pakistani village.

The camera stayed focused on the building. Nothing much happened; occasionally you could see someone walking into or out of the building. Suddenly there was a slashing blur at the top of the screen and the building exploded into dust and mayhem. In complete silence. There was no audio. We watched the dust cloud settle. After some time the camera operator carried the camera to the building and continued filming with his night vision lens, but at close range, now illuminated by small flames and smoldering embers. Arms, legs, body parts, bodies, and medical equipment were strewn everywhere. It was a grisly sight and was somehow more horrifying in the green and white of the low light lens.

The next scene came quickly. It was a first-aid station set up near the building caring for the wounded, which included a number of children and people who appeared to be European. Two of the patients being worked on were Caucasian women, clearly not Pakistani or Afghan. It was a horrible scene. Whoever was operating the camera left the sound off, or at least we weren't able to hear it. No interviews, no identification of the people involved, just pictures of devastated lives. After the twenty-minute video, the lights came back up and the room was quiet. Brady let the images linger while he prepared his next evidentiary presentation. The chief judge looked at me, "Any objection, Mr. Caskey?"

"Yes, Your Honor. Several. First, there's no indication who took this videotape, or where, or how. It has not been authenticated. I might note that it is taken with a very sophisticated night vision lens. I would like to know how it is that the person taking the video happened to be there with the night vision lens attached to a video camera. That is an uncommon arrangement. It makes me think that the person knew to be there, that the person was aware that the event was about to occur. How is that possible? If this is a war crime by American forces, how did someone on the ground in Pakistan know it was about to occur? And if he knew, how could he stand there filming, instead of warning the people in the building of what was about to happen?"

The judge nodded. "You may ask those questions during the trial." He turned to Brady. "Mr. Brady, the next evidence?"

Brady stood and said, "The next two pieces of evidence will also be videotape, and supported by affidavit." He walked across the courtroom and handed the two affidavits to the clerk, then crossed over and handed them to us both in the original language and in authenticated translation. "The first is Mohamed Moardi. He is a villager who lives in the house directly next to the building that was struck. His house was destroyed. Thankfully he was not in his house. He was visiting his brother perhaps a quarter mile away; but he had a clear view of the entire event. He saw the bomb hit, and saw the building implode. He saw the damage done to his house next door at the same time. He is outraged and furious that the United States is not willing to compensate him for his lost house, and has come here by videotape to testify at my request. As I said, the same essential content is in the affidavit which is before you."

He nodded to the technician and the videotape started. The lights came down slightly, and the image of a Pakistani or Afghan man in his fifties came on the screen. He looked like someone out of a *National Geographic* photo. He was rugged and had bad teeth, but overall seemed to be saying what he thought. Brady had put the translation of the interview at the bottom of the screen so that you could hear the audio but read in English what was being said. He recounted he was sitting on the porch with his brother talking about their families when they heard a whistling sound. They didn't hear it for very long, only for a couple of seconds before the bomb hit the building. The concussion shook his chair on the ground where he sat. He thought he was going to be knocked off his seat. It felt like an earthquake but one started by a massive sledgehammer. He and his brother both shouted and jumped up, and immediately ran to the site of the bombing. They found themselves looking up into the sky for airplanes or any other bombs that might fall, and as they made their way to the destroyed building, saw what they thought were rockets streaked up from a mountain into the dark sky. They seemed to explode, and then he saw the silhouette of an airplane as it tumbled to the ground. He did not see any parachutes but has talked to people who did and who ran to the location where the parachutes touched the ground. He spoke of the carnage, the death and destruction all around him. He said that this was a refugee facility, where people who had fled from the fighting in Afghanistan came for medical treatment. The building had been set up a few weeks before the attack; everyone in the region knew its location and its purpose. He said there was no chance that anyone could possibly believe that it was an al Qaeda headquarters, or that there was some secret meeting going on that night between al Qaeda and the Taliban. He said it is a small village, and there could be no such meeting without him and everyone else knowing about it. Strangers are noticed immediately, and people find out who they are.

The man began to sob as he described the devastation. His house had been ruined, and his life changed forever. He was a sympathetic figure. The video ended with a lingering shot of him weeping.

The second witness was essentially the same. Another man from the village who had actually been nearer the explosion and had some damage from debris or shrapnel on his face to prove it. There was a large cut on his forehead, as well as burn marks across his left cheek. He said they were received the night of the explosion as he was sitting in his living room across the street from the building that was hit. Debris had come flying through the window both in large and small pieces, some of which struck him in the face as he sat at his table reviewing his weekly sales at his shop.

Brady then submitted five additional affidavits including some from those who had captured the Americans. They were labeled anonymous, as they did not want any retaliation from the United States military. They describe how they had taken the two aviators into custody, and had delivered them to men who they didn't know but believed to be with the Taliban and who had then thrown them into the back of a pickup truck and driven them away. They were very proud of their role in capturing the Americans. They showed the photos of themselves with their faces covered holding AK-47s on the Americans.

I objected to the admission of anonymous affidavits, but the judge said it was common at this stage of the proceedings. The court accepted the assurances of the prosecutor that these were real people who would testify at trial if called.

Brady then stood up, again nodded to the technician, and displayed a PowerPoint chart on the screens. It showed the number of "collateral deaths" from American military action—from airplanes, drones, even artillery—during the conduct of the Iraq and Afghanistan wars. It showed the number of stray bombings, and the number of civilian deaths associated with each such bombing. He went through pages of charts broken down by distance from an actual target (as far as he was able to identify one), the number of women and children, the number of bombs, broken down by Pakistan, Afghanistan, Iraq, Kuwait, all the way back to 2002. Although I was impressed by his thoroughness, this had no part in a trial over a specific incident. I stood and immediately objected to all the so-called data.

Brady was waiting for it. "I expected Mr. Caskey to object to this, Your Honor, but frankly as was revealed earlier, the charges against these two individuals are simply the end of a very long and painstaking process to identify the systematic way in which Americans 'accidentally' drop bombs on civilian populations, and how curiously those accidents correlate to general population intimidation and war objectives. Is it is very clear that these two aviators are participants in a long-standing scheme to intimidate Middle Eastern populations, particularly of Afghanistan and Pakistan, into doing America's bidding in its war with the Taliban."

I jumped to my feet. "This is outrageous, Your Honors. Instead of proof of a supposed war crime of which they have no evidence, they have phonied up a bunch of supposed data of errant bombs and claim a plan to intimidate civilian populations. It is ridiculous on its face. And if that is in fact their theory, then it would seem that the ones charged should be the ones who concocted this complex scheme, not two naval aviators who simply did what they were told."

Brady looked at me and smiled. "Those indictments are being considered as we speak, Mr. Caskey."

The rest of the evidence was more of the same. More videotaped witnesses supported by affidavits. More photographs of dead bodies and body parts strewn around the village, even some grizzly pictures taken of a head found a quarter mile away from where the bomb hit. I particularly remembered a hand lying in a bucket on the stoop of a hut five hundred yards away. There was a great deal of graphic evidence intended to inflame whoever saw it. Copies of the photographs were immediately released to the press.

Then came more videotaped interviews, again accompanied by affidavits, of people from the European aid organization who explained how they came to be in the village of Pakistan, how long they had been there, and how they were there simply to care for the refugees both from Afghanistan and from the Taliban's war against the Pakistani army.

According to them, it was widely known that they were there, they had been there for two weeks, and nothing had happened there that even remotely could have indicated that it was a hideout for al Qaeda or the Taliban, or the location of an important meeting between them. One woman testified that she had been there since the facility opened, that she had never seen anyone from the Taliban or al Qaeda that she knew of, that most of the people who passed through as refugees were women and children, that many of the aid workers were women, and that the only way that she had escaped death was that she had chosen to grab some sleep nearby outside the building, as she had worked herself to exhaustion.

The entire event, all of the evidence, felt canned or like it had been prepared, or could have been, weeks before the event. The outrage, the photographs, the conveniently located night-vision-equipped video camera, the whole thing smelled. Of course none of the witnesses was in the courtroom to be subjected to cross-examination, nor was there any evidence that there had been any *intent* to attack a refugee medical facility. The only thing that they had proved even indirectly was that a bomb had been dropped on a building and that innocent people had been killed. I probably would have stipulated to that. But accidentally killing innocent people is not a war crime. What seemed to me to be absent from all of their evidence was any indication of any intent or gross recklessness that might be subject to war crimes charges, let alone a scheme or plan or system of attacking innocent people.

And of course the people who would interpret the ICC treaty were the same ones who were sitting in front of me, the judges. They would decide what constituted a war crime under what circumstances, and then apply their standard of the facts before them. Almost certainly, if they were outraged enough, my clients were going to prison.

# TEN

At the conclusion of the hearing, I asked to speak to my clients in private. The court told the guards to put them in the secure room behind the courtroom. Kristen and I went into the small room where our agitated clients were waiting. They were pacing back and forth. Rawlings asked, "What the hell is this about? I thought you were going to get us out of here."

I looked around and up at the ceiling for recording devices or cameras. I saw nothing, but moved cautiously. "I think we'll beat these charges."

They got it; they knew I was speaking cautiously, concerned about recording devices. Duncan said, "These charges are complete bullshit. You know that."

"Of course I know it. Everybody knows it. But here we are. And they're going to continue forward, and the court is going to find that there is enough evidence to have an actual trial. So this is only a step. The trial is probably a few months off, and I'm going to do what I can to find more evidence, to find what the heck has happened to set this up."

Kristen said, "Believe me, we'll do whatever we can to get you off."

Rawlings roared, "Off? We want out!"

I nodded, picked up my briefcase, and asked, "Did anything happen on the way here? Anything unusual, unexpected?"

They both shook their heads, then Duncan said, "We did have to stop suddenly once. That was a bit odd. Kind of slammed us into the front of the truck, but no harm. I'm not sure what that was about. We can't see out of the truck."

I nodded again. "They'll take you back to the prison. I'll come out there later, or maybe tomorrow, and we'll go through everything we know so far. I also want to get any thoughts from you on what other evidence I need to get." I looked to Kristen and then at them. "But one thing I know already. I have to go to Pakistan."

The rest of the hearing went as predicted. Indirect testimony, much of it sympathy-generating, and a decision that there was enough evidence to hold the two Americans over for trial.

I was exhausted on the flight back to the United States. We got in to Dulles at 10:00 P.M. I rubbed my eyes as we landed and felt my phone buzzing. I opened up the text dialogue box and looked at it. It was from Kevin Crane. It said, "Nice work. You're doing us proud."

I texted back. "Bunch of rubbish. What the hell have you been up to?" Crane was a fellow former SEAL.

We'd served on the teams together. He had always been one of the sharpest operators, so no one was surprised when he got out to start his own company. At least that's what we thought he was doing. No one really knew what he did, other than running a company, jetting around the globe, and texting or calling many of the rest of us to ridicule us or remind us of the good old times. He was funny, full of energy, and extremely dangerous if you were on his wrong side. My phone rang. It was Crane.

"Crane! How the hell are you doing, man?"

"I saw you on the news! 'Course I've seen you on the news a hundred times, but this time I decided I couldn't resist anymore. I had to call and make fun of your haircut."

"What's wrong with my haircut? Just because you're losing your hair doesn't mean you have to make fun of me."

"You look gay. I was just making sure you're okay. This is a pretty damned high-profile thing. You all right?"

"Sure. How's it coming across in the news? You following what's going on?"

"Definitely. The Europeans are up in arms and all offended that you challenged their ability to put Americans on trial. They should just go piss themselves."

"Yeah. It's a load of shit, but they aren't showing any intent of stopping."

"No doubt. You need anything from me? Anything I can do for you?"

I thought for a moment. "You been to Pakistan since the last time you and I were there?"

"Maybe."

"You familiar with things over there enough that you could go with me to talk to some witnesses, examine the scene of the supposed crime?"

"Wow. You really are gonna throw yourself into the furnace, aren't you?"

"You got any time?" I stood up and got my bag out of the overhead. I turned my Bluetooth on and put my iPhone in my pocket. "You want to go on one more adventure with me? I may need somebody like you."

"Like me meaning what?"

"You're still sort of in the active security business. Right?"

"Yeah, sort of. What do you have in mind?"

"I need to go find the people who are swearing out these affidavits against my clients. I need to find the guy with the video camera that just happens to have a night vision lens. I need to prove that these charges are totally false. But you know what that place is like. If I turn the wrong way for a second, I'll get a knife in the back, or a bullet in the head. Do you have a few guys that you could bring, and come with me?"

"Whoa. You're serious. That's a big deal, Jack. That's the kind of thing where people get hurt, or don't come back."

"I've got to do it. I sure could use your help. How's your Urdu?"

"Good as ever. Nonexistent. You know I don't speak Urdu. Just some Pashto."

"Yeah, but you can get by. And you speak Waziri."

"That's just a Pashto dialect."

"So what do you say?" I was hurrying down a tiled hallway at Dulles nearing the main terminal.

"Sounds like a government-supported gig. Where are you?"

"Just getting out of the airport."

"Where you heading?"

I looked at my watch. It was 10:30 already. "My office. I've got some stuff I need to figure out."

"I'm in my office downtown too. I'll meet you there in an hour."

"Thanks. This thing is a real goat rope."

"Kind of fun to watch. I want to hear all about it."

"See you there."


Kevin was one of my best friends when we were in the teams together. He was one of those unusual guys who were gregarious, funny with a big smile, but were completely lethal. Women were always hanging all over him because he had this big toothy grin and reassured everybody just by his presence. He wasn't particularly imposing physically, he wasn't small, but he wasn't the kind of guy that made people sort of check to see if he was angry at them. He just had a presence. He was maybe six feet two and 210 pounds. Extremely athletic, and always the one that we would choose to do a particularly tough thing in a mission. He was a physical artist, and yet again, more than happy to pull the literal trigger. He wasn't afraid of anything. He saw any new mission as another challenge, an opportunity to excel as he called it. I had a similar mind-set, but less skill. I could've continued on, as could he have, but we'd both decided to get out after a couple of tours. I changed direction and went to law school, but he wanted more adventure. More adventure with more freedom and less accountability. He started his own security company, one that allowed him to go pretty much anywhere and do pretty much anything. I really had no idea who he worked for. I only believed about half of what he told me about his customers and clients. There are always various shades gray between the government and private companies in the world of international security.

He was waiting for me at my office when I arrived. I wouldn't have recognized him if I hadn't been expecting him. He looked like a salesman at REI in jeans with running shoes, a zip up fleece, and a baseball cap on backward. He was wearing black horn-rimmed glasses, and leaning against the door.

"Come on in," I said.

He said nothing and followed me into my office. He asked, "Anyone watching your office?"

"Why would they be? Who would bother?"

"Never know," he said, glancing out my office window. "You've said some things to anger the European press. They may be watching."

"I really doubt it. Plus the feds are watching out for me." I put my briefcase down heavily, took a deep breath, and removed my tie. I sat down in my office chair and closed my eyes. "Damn, I'm tired."

He sat across the desk from me. "Can't imagine why. You haven't been doing anything, no travel, no pressure, no publicity, no stress—you're just losing your grip. You're getting old and fat."

"You're as old as I am."

"Not true. You've forgotten my first tour was your second. I was the noob. You were the old veteran. You're probably four years older than me. Plus, I've stayed active. I didn't dedicate the rest of my life to getting rapists off."

"Save it." I was too tired. "So can you help?"

He studied my face. "What do you have in mind, exactly?"

I leaned toward him. "The evidence they're bringing to the ICC is just a little too convenient. I'm going to find their witnesses, and find the guy with the magic video camera. I want to know who told him to be there. Why was he filming that night with a night vision lens? Just happened to? Makes no sense."

"And?"

"I need somebody to go with me. I need a few guys, actually—probably no more than four—who you can count on if things get ugly."

"How ugly?"

"You know how it goes. Word will get out that we're there and either they'll come to get us or they won't. If they do, they'll come in force. So we have to be ready to respond and get the hell out of there."

Kevin put his hands behind his head and looked at the ceiling. "You got funding for this?"

"I doubt it. I can ask Marshall."

"Who's he?"

"Works for the national security advisor. Counterterrorism. He's actually the one who retained me and is making sure I get paid."

"He may have some money for this, but I doubt it. So it would probably be me going with you, and some of my men, right into the lion's den, for free."

I considered whether there were any other options. I could call Marshall at the White House, but I knew he would not only not fund it, he'd tell us not to go. Too dangerous. If it truly needed to be done, he'd want to send active duty military or CIA; but he wouldn't take the chance of sending them now, because of the risk of capture. "Yeah, probably."

Kevin put his hands down and nodded. "Well my timing is just impeccable. What if I hadn't called? What was your plan?"

"Don't know. Hadn't formed one yet."

He finally nodded vigorously. "Why the hell not. Business has been good. I've got some extra dough. And what better cause than to help get a couple of Americans out of the International Criminal Court?"

I loaded clips of Brady's videos from the night vision camera onto my iPhone, as well as the affidavits, and the videos of the witnesses. I knew it was the right thing to go to Pakistan. Right for the case. But it might be stupid otherwise. I might find the witnesses, but they were unlikely to talk to me. And what more would they say? I might find whoever took the videotape of the bombing. But I wouldn't get the true story. But I also hoped that I might find out from somebody, just one person who would tell me the truth, what really happened. I had to find out who was behind all this, who had a Falcon jet at Peshawar just so they could fly these two navy officers to Holland. Who funded it? Who gave the Americans the intelligence on which the strike was based? Who told them that al Qaeda was meeting with the Taliban in that hut at that time? It was someone with such credibility that their word was accepted and the strike was launched without even checking. Somebody burned a very big card when they played that hand. I needed to push back through the United States intelligence, but I thought there was a chance that we'd find something else while we were there. I knew I had to go even though I had doubts.

We flew together, the five of us, myself, Kevin, and three of his men, who were dispersed throughout the airplane in nondescript clothing looking like graduate students or businessmen. There was no conversation, no contact between us on the airplane. We flew through London, and then a nonstop flight to Peshawar on British Air. We had agreed that we would rent two cars. We rented a couple of Fords. They were about the size of the Fusion, only less roomy. After we got our cars we drove right back to the terminal. It was hot and dusty, with people everywhere. Pandemonium is too strong a word, but disarray isn't. The airport was full of people going and coming on smaller planes, airlines I've never heard of, airplanes that looked older than me, and a few First World airlines. Kevin and I thought we should start where we might find something about the Falcon jet. It was the thing that yelled at me the most.

We pulled up to the decrepit charter terminal where business jets would refuel. It was separate from the main terminal, and had a couple of King Airs parked on the tarmac. Kevin and I went inside. As we walked through the glass door I saw the three men who had come with us leaving in one of the rental cars. I asked Kevin, "Where are they going?"

"Shopping."

"For what?"

He adjusted his baseball cap and took off his sunglasses. "It's been too long since you've been here. You can't bring in the stuff that you need, so you have to buy it. They know where to do that. They know the city like the back of their hand."

"All right. Let's find out what we can about the Falcon jet."

We went to the counter. The man behind the counter stared at us. I glanced around the terminal. There were maybe twenty people there, all watching us. Kevin spoke to the man behind the counter. "Do you speak English?"

The man nodded slowly. "A little." He had a slight British accent as was common with those in Pakistan who spoke English, since it was part of British India when it was a colony.

Kevin said, "I need your help. A few weeks ago, there were two Americans who were shot down. They were friends of ours, and we're trying to find out what happened to them."

The man's eyes got big. "I don't know anything."

Kevin nodded understandingly. "We're not here to ask about the shoot-down. We just have an airplane question. That night, right here at this terminal," Kevin said guessing, "there was a Falcon jet. A three-engine

Falcon jet—a 7X—that flew from this airport to Holland nonstop. Do you know anything about that jet?"

The man shook his head before Kevin had even finished his question. "I don't know anything. You need to leave." He turned to another man, who was standing at the end of the counter looking out the window toward the tarmac. They were speaking quickly in Pashto.

Kevin understood him, but gave no indication.

He said to the man behind the counter, "You must have books, records of the aircraft you refuel. I'm sure you weren't here that night when that airplane was here, so I'm sure you don't know anything about it personally, but maybe there's some record of it. All I'm really looking for is the side number of the Falcon. That's it. Do you remember the side number, or can you look it up?"

"I was not here. I don't know anything."

Kevin grew less patient. "You keep records don't you?"

"I don't keep any records. I am just at the counter."

Kevin understood. "I understand completely. Who would know about the records?"

"I don't know. I only just started working here."

Kevin glanced to his right and saw the other man on a cell phone. He assumed what I did. Others were coming to chat with us. Kevin was unconcerned.

Kevin glanced to his left, behind me. He said to the man across the counter, "Never mind. I'm sorry we bothered you." Kevin turned to his left barely winking at me as he did and we headed outside. The man behind the counter glanced at the other man in satisfaction.

Kevin was up to something, but it had been too long

since I had been in the field. I wasn't picking up on all the signals, but he told me everything that was being said. As Kevin stepped through the door a Land Rover pulled up. A distinguished-looking man got out of the right side of the car and walked directly at Kevin. Three other men climbed out of the back seat armed to the teeth. The driver also got out and cleared his handgun for easy access. Kevin walked directly at the man with a smile and extended his hand. Before the man could say anything, Kevin spoke to him in Pashto, and told him he was glad he was here, as the man inside had said we needed to talk to him.

The man was taken aback, and replied harshly in English, "Who are you and what do you want?"

"My name is Jonathan Livingston. Is there somewhere we can talk?"

The man was suspicious, but thrown off by Kevin's smile and calm demeanor. "What is it you want?"

"The answer to one simple question. That's it. I'm unarmed, I will not harm you, I have no bad intentions. I have one question. And I think you're the one who can answer it." He added quietly, "And I can make it definitely worth your while to answer this simple question."

The man turned to his guards and yelled at them to search Kevin and me. They ran forward and began patting down Kevin. Another one took me and checked for weapons. They seemed surprised not to have found any. I'm sure they assumed we were with the CIA.

The man nodded at Kevin and said, "Come with me."

I began to follow, but they stopped. The man put up

his hand and said to me in English, "You stay here. Do not move."

I stood there on the stoop of the building looking at the men, who were studying me carefully. They clearly wanted nothing to do with me. If I was with the CIA, nothing good could come from it. Two pickup trucks pulled into the parking lot a good distance away. The windows were tinted, which struck me as odd. I hadn't seen any tinted windows since we arrived.

In what seemed to be less than two minutes Kevin and the man came back out to the front of the small terminal. Kevin thanked him. The man got back into his Land Rover. The others joined him, and they drove away.

Kevin said, "Come on." We headed for our rental car, and the other rental pulled up next to us. Kevin reached into the back seat, pulled out his backpack, and retrieved a GPS. I'd never seen one like it. It looked far more sophisticated than any other I'd seen. He turned it on, and said, "You drive."

I got into the driver seat, and started the car. We headed out of the airport and I asked him, "What the hell happened back there?"

"Oldest trick in the book. Find that guy in charge, tell him what a hero he is and how important he is, then pay him a whole bunch of money and he'll tell you whatever you want to know."

"You just bribe them?"

"Bigger than hell."

"How much did you pay him?"

"Five grand."

"You paid him five thousand dollars?"

"Of course." After staring at the GPS while we made our way down the road, he reached into his pocket and handed me a slip of paper. "And here's your side number for the Falcon jet."

I took it in my hand and looked at it. "So it was here at this terminal."

"Yep."

I looked at the number. "I don't recognize this kind of number. Must be European."

"He said he didn't know where it was from. The side number on the fuel log is bogus. This is the real one. They didn't talk to the pilots, just gave them fuel. He didn't know who they were, or where they were from, just that he guessed they were probably Europeans. He didn't think they were Russians or Slavic. Probably Western European."

"You do know that if you bribe somebody overseas it's a violation of the Foreign Corrupt Practices Act."

Kevin smiled and shook his head. "Whatever. I didn't know going to law school could make you such a weak dick."

"I just wanted to make sure you knew."

"You're looking out for me? Now you're *my* lawyer, trying to keep me out of trouble? If I were you I'd be worried about the ICC, which is going to put your clients away for life. You should charge *them* with foreign corrupt practices. I didn't figure you'd drink the legal Kool-Aid, Jack."

"Spare me." I dodged a broken-down car that was sticking out into the traffic lane.

Kevin said, "If you're going to be so touchy about a little bribe, how exactly were you planning on getting this information when you were coming here by yourself? You think you'd walk in to some Third World airport and ask some poor guy for a side number and he'd just look it up and give it to you? When you're obviously an American, and probably there to make trouble? You think that's gonna work? Jeez, Jack, how long has it been?"

"Where am I going? And where'd your men go?"

"We're going to the village where all this happened, and the guys are right behind us. I told you, they went shopping. They got a couple of trucks, a lot of weapons, and a lot of ammo. And as soon as we get to the place where I'm planning on stopping, we're gonna shift and get everybody armed up and ready to go."

"You think somebody's gonna come after us?"

"Are you serious? Have you regressed? Of course they're going to come after us. You think somebody sets up something this big, puts out this much bullshit, and we're just gonna come down here and expose them? Is that how you saw this happening? Shit, Jack. That's not the real world, man." He looked closely at his GPS, then at the road. "Okay, see that intersection up there?"

"Yeah."

"Turn right, and whatever you do don't stop."

"Why not?"

"Just do what I say. I know this area."

I turned right quickly at the intersection, running a stop sign amidst the confused traffic, and headed quickly down the poorly paved two-lane road. There were houses on either side as we reached the outskirts of Peshawar.

"Slow down."

I slowed and he said, "Turn left here into that dirt strip."

I turned hard onto the dirt and the other rental car followed. The two trucks were right behind.

"Go to the end. There is a big warehouse on the left, with the door open. Turn into it. See it?"

"Yes." I turned into the deep warehouse and into the darkness. I turned the headlights on and saw a huge empty room with a dirt floor. The last truck came in behind us in a cloud of dirt; a man jumped out and closed the warehouse door behind us.

I got out of our rental car and surveyed the building. Completely empty, not a cobweb or rusty piece of machinery anywhere. There were older Toyota pickups already in the warehouse. The men got out of their vehicles, all eight of them, and came to where we were standing. They were heavily armed with AK-47s and handguns, bulletproof vests and black steel-toed boots. They wore local shirts and scarves. Some even wore the colorful caps of Waziristan. They were all very comfortable in western Pakistan, but they were all Westerners. Probably Americans. On their boots the leather had been cut back to reveal the steel in the toes. Kevin saw me looking at them. "It's our thing. For some reason it intimidates people. I guess they think we're going to kick them in the balls. People notice it, and remember us. People talk about it. And when they're asked to describe us, it's all they remember."

I thought for a minute. I considered everything that had transpired since I first talked to Kevin. As two of his men spread a large chart on a table, I said, "Who are these other guys? We came here with you, and me, and three others. Now there are five more."

"Friends."

"They work for you."

"Yeah.'

I looked at them, then at Kevin. "You guys are awfully comfortable around here. You didn't pay that guy anything, did you?"

Kevin looked up at me. "What guy?"

"The guy at the airport. You didn't pay him anything."

He stood straight up. "What makes you say that?"

"He didn't come at us like I would have expected. He wasn't upset. He knew you, didn't he? And your men didn't go shopping for all these weapons and trucks. They were already stashed somewhere."

Kevin came over to where I was and looked me in the eyes from a foot away. "We were here, Jack."

"Where?"

"In the hills. The mountains. We'd been operating in very eastern Afghanistan. Near Camp Salerno. At another camp run by the Agency. Remember when that son of a bitch Jordanian double agent walked in and blew up a bunch of Americans? Killed my buddy, former team member, father of three. Well we came to help make that right. And we were here."

"When were you here?'

"When your boys dropped their bomb. We were sitting ten miles away in a wash. We had the same intelligence they had. Big meeting. Al Qaeda and the Taliban. It came late, but we were in position. If the bomb didn't get them, we—and some others—were to take them on their way out of the hut. It would have been ugly, but we'd have gotten it done. So we have a little bit of a personal agenda here too. I guess I should have let you know that. We got had just like your boys did. And we don't like getting had."

I started thinking back. "So you called me hoping I was going to Pakistan."

"Either that or I was going to persuade you to go. I was coming back regardless. Unfinished business."

"Who were you here for? Who were you working with?"

"Well now that's a very personal question, asking me about my company's clients," he said smiling. "It doesn't matter. We were just here doing a job. Now it looks like the whole thing was a setup, so I'm pissed. I want to know who had the credibility to turn the head of our entire intelligence community to do that strike. Who makes that call and has us all buy it? Only a few people. I'm kind of surprised they didn't find a way to send in the American special ops teams first, then get *us* blown up too.

"I've started pushing back to find out. So far I'm not getting anything. But coming back here and starting at the ground level will be a good start to chasing that rabbit from a different spot."

I was surprised, but I guess I shouldn't have been. It was the very kind of thing I used to do, but never as a civilian. I was just not used to looking for those kinds of angles anymore.

Kevin said, "I think we try to find the cameraman first. The one with the night vision lens."

I nodded. "I agree. But if we start asking around, you think someone will come looking for us?"

"Sure."

"So what do we do about that?"

"Well what would you do about it?" Kevin asked, smiling again.

"I'd ask quickly and keep moving, and be ready if someone decided to take us on."

"*Exactly.*" Kevin yelled at the others, "Let's go!"

# ELEVEN

Our caravan of now four Toyota pickup trucks with low-profile camper shells on the backs and tinted windows approached the village of Danday Saidji where the fateful bombing had occurred. Kevin noticed what I did. "Lot of new vehicles around here," I said.

"Probably still part of the cleanup. Or the pretend investigation."

"Probably makes it more likely the bad guys won't come get us." I studied the village as we approached. It was very poor with dirt streets. The low buildings were arranged haphazardly with rutted streets between them. I said, "Let's try to find where the camera was stationed first. That perspective had to be on a straight line from the image. Let's start maybe three hundred yards away."

"Why so far?" Kevin asked as he slowed and stopped outside the village.

"He had to know what was coming. That's why he was filming. If he knew it was going to be a bomb, no way he'd be inside a couple of hundred yards. Depends on his gear too. Couldn't have had more than about a 200mm lens. A 1000mm would be very odd attached to a video camera. So an image of the size we saw with a maximum zoom of a 200mm lens would probably be back about three to five hundred yards. So let's look for signs of a tripod."

"You've been thinking about this."

"Ever since I saw those images in court."

Kevin pulled over and stopped. The others stopped behind us, but no one got out. They sat in their trucks with tinted windows. He got out and started climbing up a hill toward the village. "Up here," he said. I followed him. He looked back at me as I crested the hill. "You're not in too bad a shape."

"I try."

"Think you can still shoot an AK?"

"Sure. Why?"

"Just in case we need you. If too many bad guys come after us, we'll need all the firepower we can get."

"I forgot to check my AK in my luggage."

He smiled as he looked down toward the village. "No worries. We've got you covered." He pointed. "This it?"

I ran the video from the hearing on my iPhone. I watched it carefully to match the line of sight. "Yes, this is the line the camera sat on."

He looked around, then up at the high hills. "This really is at the end of a long valley. The mountaintops are high."

I looked at the hills and then down at the village. It was dusty with low buildings made of dirt-colored brick with roofs of bundled sticks or slats. Not much color, some reddish brown, but mostly dirt color, the same as the narrow streets. The village had probably two thousand residents, with no obvious city center. Just streets, buildings, and houses. People were walking in the streets, with a few men on carts pulled by oxen. There were some cars and trucks, but few were moving. I saw a man on a motor scooter swerve to avoid a woman walking with two children. I turned away from the village and evaluated the valley in which the village sat. I had to say it was beautiful. There were snow-capped mountains in the distance and more green than brown as the valley curved up onto the rocky mountains. They were much higher than I expected. "Damn," I said.

"What?"

"Normally a shoulder-fired missile would never hit an F-18 at altitude. But even if he was at 25,000 feet, men standing up there," I said pointing to the highest mountain peak, "could reach it. And if you had several of them, like they've told me there were, they'd be in trouble." I looked back to the village and the black hole where the refugee building once was. "This was elaborate. They had to have a lot of pieces in place. And it wouldn't have worked if the Predator wasn't out of missiles. No one to shoot down or arrest. It *all* had to come together. They had to lure an airplane here they could shoot down. Who could do this? Who could pull this off?"

Kevin considered. "Somebody inside Pakistani intelligence. Had to be where they got their info." He looked back at the hole. "See those people down there going through the wreckage?"

"Yeah."

"How far? Sniper range?"

"Sure. Less than a thousand yards."

"That's how I see it. That camera was between us and the building. There's only one hut between us and the village. Let's walk." He looked down at the trucks first, then all around. No one was approaching. He set off.

We walked directly to the lone hut. Kevin looked over his shoulder and saw that one of his men was on his belly in the hill behind us with a high-powered rifle. Kevin was making a lot of noise, talking, laughing, kicking rocks, approaching the house with obviously empty hands. He stopped short of the entrance to the house and looked around for signs of a tripod. He stooped down and moved some dirt around. A large man came out of the hut behind him and started yelling at him. He was wearing the traditional Waziri garb of loose-fitting trousers and a long tunic of the same color. Both were worn but clean. He had on a colorful cap, distinctive to the mountain region. Kevin stood up slowly and turned to greet him. He spoke to him softly in Waziri. The man quieted. Kevin pointed to the place where the bomb had hit. He then asked the man something. The man nodded. His name was Mahmoud. Kevin asked for my phone, which I gave him. He showed him the clip of the hut in the daylight, before the bomb hit. He held it up so the man could see that they were standing in what could have been the camera position. He put the iPhone in his pocket and pretended to be filming.

Mahmoud got it and started nodding vigorously. He

pointed toward the village from his hut. He started walking. Kevin followed with me right behind. He stopped fifty yards from his house and began pointing at the ground. Kevin looked around and saw evidence of many footprints and activity. This was the place.

He asked Mahmoud how many people had been there. Three. How long? All day. Setting up, measuring the distance to the hut, filming, waiting.

He told Kevin he had tried to approach them to ask who they were and what they were doing. But he was not allowed to come anywhere near them. They had come over the hill just as we had, from the same place. Kevin asked if he had seen how they had gotten to that spot, and the man said yes. They had come in two trucks. And who were they?

The man claimed not to know. He was animated; he waved his arms, raised his voice. They wouldn't talk to him, but he had heard them. They were speaking Urdu and were not from his village or anywhere nearby. They spoke like they were from Islamabad. They were very serious, and left as soon as the bomb hit. They knew something was going to happen. They had never been there before, and never since. They had a camera on a stand. They waited, it got dark, and he quit watching them. They got bored. As darkness settled in he forgot about them and went to bed. Then the bomb hit. He had never been so scared in his life. It was so loud he thought it had gone off right in the front of his house. He was terrified for his children. He got up and ran to the front of his home, and confirmed everything was intact. He ran outside and saw the fire and the glow from the hole where the bomb had hit in the village. Just as he was trying to understand what had happened, the three men with the camera had run by him back over the hill. But there was so much confusion and screaming no one was paying attention to them. Since then some from the village had wondered if they had been responsible. They wondered if what had looked like a camera had been some kind of guidance device for the bomb.

Kevin asked him again. Who were they? He didn't know. But he didn't like them. They brought trouble to the village. He didn't know how, but he knew they were somehow responsible for the trouble. How could they not be? They had known what was going to happen before it happened. He didn't know how the camera men knew the building would blow up if they hadn't been part of it. The whole village was angry. They had welcomed the refugee medical facility. It meant jobs for some of them, carrying water, helping inside the building. But now, many people from the village had been killed. The people were very angry.

Kevin told me everything Mahmoud had said. He asked him if he had been down to where the bomb had hit since it happened. He nodded vigorously. Kevin asked him if he would go down to the site with us. He immediately agreed and pointed to the path.

Kevin told him to wait for a minute. He walked back up to the top of the hill and looked down at the approaching road. No cars, no activity. He looked at the two trucks. The driver from each was leaning against the hood. Each nodded. It was still safe.

Kevin, Mahmoud, and I walked down the dirt path

to the main part of the town. He walked ahead of us with authority and determination. As we came into the town people who might otherwise have stopped us or asked us questions said nothing; they stared at Mahmoud and the strange Westerners who were with him. They had seen plenty of Westerners lately, and these were simply two more they wished would leave.

We arrived at the crater of what was once a good-sized hut. Based on the debris it looked to have had cinder block walls and a weak roof that collapsed quickly under the incredible force of a JDAM.

I'd seen JDAMs used before, even close up. I'd felt the concussion from a half mile away. I knew well the destructive power of a highly accurate big bomb. I knew people usually died when they were dropped. But I was usually happy about it; the ones who died deserved to die. But I hadn't seen anything like this. I looked back toward the mountaintops, toward where my clients' F-18 had flown and had dropped the bomb that had created the scene in front of me. The destruction was complete. Whoever was in that building was dead. No doubt about it. And many who weren't in the building. The crater was roped off and people were sifting through the debris, still looking for body parts, documents, anything of note. It was a sobering picture. Many of the workers were European and wore shirts and hats that identified them as being with the AMI, the Aide Médicale Internationale, a medical relief organization based in Geneva. The organization whose workers had been providing medical attention to the refugees at this facility.

I looked over the site as Kevin asked Mahmoud how many villagers had been killed.

He didn't know, but thought about thirty. Plus all the people who were inside as refugees, he didn't know that number, plus the Westerners.

Kevin told me to show him the first witness. I pulled out my phone and pulled up the first video. He asked Mahmoud if he recognized him. Sure. Of course. He confirmed his name. He is from the village. And where is he now? No one knew. He had left the town with some other men a couple of days after the bombing. They had said they needed to talk to him, and a couple of others. They said the government needed to talk to them.

Government? Who from the government? You didn't ask that question to those kind of men. You just hoped they would go away. The village had heard that they were needed as important witnesses in the investigation of what had happened. So the men went willingly. But they had not been heard from since. Their families saw their videotapes on the television from the trial. They were relieved. It was them. They looked fine, and everything they said was accurate. But still no one had seen them. They were very concerned. Kevin asked if he could take us to their families. He said of course he would.

As we turned to walk, a woman approached us. We continued, but she called out to us in English. "Excuse me!" she yelled, clearly at us.

We turned. I replied, "Yes?"

"Who are you?" she asked in accented English. Probably Dutch, or German. She was about my size, had short blond hair and an AMI baseball cap. She looked angry.

"Who are you?"

"I am Elizabeth Vos. I am with AMI. Now who are you?"

"My name is Jack Caskey."

"What are you doing here?"

"What does it matter to you?"

"Because I am trying to find out what happened. And if a Westerner comes here, they may know something I don't know. You with the military, CIA, what?"

"No, none of those."

She looked at Kevin. "You military? You with the Pentagon?"

He looked at her and said nothing.

"You don't even reply?"

"Why should I? Who appointed you the grand inquisitor?"

I said, "We're here to find out what happened, maybe you can tell us. Because if I'm reading all this right, your people have been sacrificed to the greater good of intimidating the United States."

She was furious. "We were sacrificed? How can you say that? You Americans dropped a bomb on my colleagues. You killed them."

I nodded. "That's true."

She waited.

I took off my sunglasses and looked her in the eyes. "You think some American somewhere, the pilots or someone else, knew that this building was full of AMI

people, medical workers, refugees, local village workers, and dropped that bomb on them intentionally. That's
what you think? Some evil American conspiracy to kill
Europeans? To teach them a lesson?"

She nearly snarled. "Yes, that is exactly what I think.
You Americans step on people all over the world to extend your empire, you don't care who gets killed in the
process, and if a few Europeans and refugees have to be
sacrificed to teach everyone a lesson, so be it!"

She had moved up the slight hill overlooking the crater to make sure her eyes were at the same level as mine.

I said, "What if you're wrong? What if the Americans
got very reliable—or so they thought—intelligence from
someone who guaranteed this hut was the place where
top-level al Qaeda people were meeting with the Taliban? One of the very rare times we could confirm an actual meeting, and that it would only be for an hour. If a
strike was to happen it had to be immediately. What
then?"

"That's just what you want to believe. Nobody
from the American government has said anything
like that."

"Yes they did. That's exactly what they said."

"But gave no proof. No names. Nobody who told them
this. It's just talk. Always an excuse. They haven't even
said they were sorry."

"Yes, they did. President Obama apologized the next
day. You just didn't want to hear it."

"My friends were killed here, Mr. Caskey. An apology will not fix them. It will not reimburse their families! In fact the families have asked me to file a claim

against the United States for their loss. Maybe then I will find out what really happened here. But it is clear, and I am sure, that two of your navy fliers dropped a very powerful bomb on my colleagues and they are dead." She stopped, took off her hat, put it back on, thinking no doubt of some other way to express her indignation. "And who are you, anyway? I've told you who I am, I've told you everything. You've not said why you're here if you're not with the U.S. government."

Kevin spoke first. "I'm just a private citizen. A concerned citizen." He looked away from her, checking the surroundings, looking for any unusual movement.

Before she could say what she thought about Kevin's comment, I said, "I'm an attorney. I'm defending the two navy fliers in the trial in Holland."

"You are him? The one who was on television?"

"Yes."

"How can you defend them? Why don't they admit it? The facts are before us," she said, waving her arm across the entire disastrous scene.

"No they're not. And maybe you saw the witnesses who testified by videotape. They're from here. And maybe you know that the government, someone from the government, took them away. And now they're nowhere to be found. Their families don't know where they are. Doesn't that strike you as odd?"

"I don't know. But probably so your American agents don't track them down. That's why."

Kevin pulled on my sleeve. He whispered to me, "You're wasting your time."

I continued, "And how did there just *happen* to be a

photo team on that hill up there to film the bomb when it hit? And how did there happen to be a long-range business jet in Peshawar to take the two Americans to Holland? Your name is Dutch. Are you from Holland? Maybe you know."

"No, I'm not from Holland. I'm from Belgium. I'm Flemish."

I shook my head. "Look, I'm sorry about your colleagues. I really am. And when this is all over, I think you'll find that the U.S. was set up, and your people were sacrificed. And as far as Belgium goes, I like Belgium. I really do. But you guys have indicted about every swinging American dick who had anything to do with Iraq, from Donald Rumsfeld to George Bush— before the International Criminal Court was even *set up*—in Belgian courts. The U.S. had to persuade you to get rid of your laws of universal jurisdiction. So it's particularly ironic that you are the ones who got *used*. But the only 'bad' guys in the world you seem to worry about are the Americans. Funny you never indicted Osama bin Laden. Why not?"

"I have nothing to do with any of that. I am dealing with body parts of my friends. So I hope your clients are convicted and you Americans finally learn your lesson. And leave this area! You think the people of Pakistan or Afghanistan want you here?"

Mahmoud had remained expressionless throughout the English conversation. He hadn't understood a single word. He shrugged as Kevin told him to lead us to the first house of the families of the missing witnesses.

\* \* \*

The family could only be described as skittish. They were very happy to see Mahmoud, but not us. Mahmoud spoke quickly to calm them. He assured them we meant them no harm. Their panicked eyes ran all over us, looking for weapons, threats, any indication of what we were about.

After Mahmoud told them who we were they were even less interested in us being there. Kevin began talking to them. They were shocked at his ability to speak their language, and well. Before he went on they wanted to know how he could speak their language. Did he have family from there? Did he study in Pakistan? He told them he used to be an employee of the U.S. government, as a "translator." They accepted that. He showed them a short clip of the video. Yes, they said, that was the father of this family. He had been outside that evening and had seen the bomb drop. He had tried to go help, but there was too much destruction.

After that, some men had come to find them, and taken them to they didn't know where. Maybe Peshawar, maybe Islamabad. They didn't know. But the big question Kevin pressed them about, was who were the men they had gone with? Who had come looking for them?

They didn't know.

Who did they suspect? Who did the village think they were?

From the Pakistani government. They said they needed all the information on the bombing, and needed to do an investigation on what had happened.

Who in the Pakistani government?

The woman I assumed was his wife and the young

woman who was probably the oldest child, maybe eighteen, looked at each other. They were afraid to say. Kevin encouraged them, as did Mahmoud. They weren't sure. But they believe it was Pakistani intelligence. The ISI, they had heard, but they didn't really know what the ISI was.

I did. They were like a mix of the FBI and CIA, and a tricky enigmatic organization. They had helped the U.S. in the war on terror, but they had also set up the Taliban, and, some say, continued to secretly support them and slipped them critical intelligence. They were a very deep and difficult mixed bag from our perspective.

We asked why the man of the house hadn't returned. They didn't know. They were afraid. Ever since his face had been on international television they were very concerned for his safety. They believed that the Pakistani government was keeping him away from the media, away from anyone else who might hurt him until after the trial was over.

"Who would hurt him?"

"The Americans."

The story of the second witness was about the same as the first. He happened to see the bombing, ran to the scene, confirmed that it wasn't a car bomb or any other terrorist activity, that it in fact did fall from the sky—how he would know that I have no idea—and like the first had been taken away by Pakistani government officials immediately after the event. He hadn't been seen by his family since either. And they understood he was being safeguarded by that same government.

We walked back up the hill, dropped off Mahmoud, and headed back down toward the trucks. The small radio in Kevin's pocket crackled. He pulled it out and held it up to his ear. It was about the size of a pack of cigarettes and had a transmit button on it. He listened carefully, and then said, "We'll be right there. Get ready to roll." Kevin looked at me. "Three vehicles are headed toward the village at high speed. They're coming after us."

We picked up our pace and hurried down the hill to the road. We looked past the Toyota trucks and saw the vehicles racing toward the village. One was a full-size white American Chevy pickup, the only one I'd seen since we'd been in Pakistan, and the other two were Land Rovers. All of them were full of men. We ran to the first Toyota and the rear door was thrown open. We jumped in and the door slammed behind us. The driver accelerated quickly, spinning the wheels on the dirt road. The other three Toyotas fell in behind us. We raced out of the village toward the other side, toward the mountains. I thought we'd head back toward a city, but realized that was where they were coming from. It was the only road to the village. We had to go the other way. I looked at the two men sitting in the front seat. One I recognized; he'd been with us in the warehouse. I hadn't seen the other one before. I had no idea where he'd come from. The third man crammed into the back seat with us was also one that I had seen at the warehouse. He had an SR-25 Mk 11 sniper rifle. It was a serious weapon that could also serve as a carbine in close quarters. He asked to switch places.

I was sitting in the middle but was happy to do whatever he wanted. He climbed over me and I slid underneath. He turned around, got up on his knees, and opened the small window. He leaned back until the barrel of his rifle extended through the window. I could see that the man in the middle seat in the back of the other pickup was doing the same. With three carloads of men determined to do us harm, a couple of guys with rifles were unlikely to make the difference. All the men around me appeared calm. It reminded me of my days with the teams when we would go ice cold in the middle of an operation.

The three vehicles behind us were two hundred yards away and bounced along the dirt road with abandon. They were very determined. The Chevy was four-wheel-drive and had a big V8 engine. It was closing on us quickly. We quickly rounded a bend and were into the hills outside the village. The road narrowed and became more rutted. I bounced off the seat with my head occasionally hitting the roof. The driver drove expertly, but was on the edge of us rolling over and down the hill, leaving us exposed like a fish on a pier. I gripped the handle of the door and held on. I strained to see what was going on behind us as we went around one hill, then another, and climbed up steeply. There was nowhere else to go. There were no other turns, no intersections, and no options. We could perhaps turn off the road and careen down the small mountain, but that would certainly end in disaster. We took the next corner even quicker than we had taken the last. We were on the ragged edge of control. The men inside the truck were arming their weapons, pulling the slides back on their handguns to chamber rounds, and making sure their rifles were ready. I had no weapon, and no one offered me one.

I yelled at Kevin, "You know where we're going? There a plan here?"

He nodded and yelled, "We'll confront them uphill a little way."

"They've got to outnumber us two to one."

He shrugged and nodded. He wasn't worried.

The road now had only ruts, no tracks. It headed almost directly uphill. The driver downshifted noisily and floored it. The Toyota lurched but accelerated. We came to a sharp right turn and took it quickly around a large hill to our right that rose two or three hundred feet above the road. The white Chevy and the two Land Rovers were closing on us. They were within seventy-five yards. For the first time I could hear supersonic rifle bullets cracking past our truck. The man sitting next to me with his sniper rifle was calm and took careful aim but fired not a single round.

We jerked around another curve and the road disappeared. There were no tracks, nowhere to go. Our driver kept going and the other Toyotas followed, fanning out at the end of the road. They all slammed on their brakes. Dirt from the ground under the locked wheels clouded the air around us. Kevin yelled, "Everybody out!"

I threw the door open and jumped out.

Kevin moved to let our sniper out, then yelled, "Jack!" He threw the back of the seat down, revealing several weapons. He grabbed an AK-47 and two clips and handed them to me, then grabbed one for himself and took two more clips.

The Chevy came around the curve first and saw us stopped. We had fifteen men heavily armed pointing our weapons at him. He slammed on his brakes and skidded to a sideways stop seventy-five yards away. The two Land Rovers almost ran into him as they came around the bend, but were able to steer around him. They skidded to a stop, and just as they did my heart almost stopped as I saw out of the corner of my eye the smoky trails of several RPG rounds fired simultaneously from the top of the hill we had driven around. Shit! I stumbled as I tried to back away from the Toyota pickup that had to be the target. I didn't want to be anywhere near it when it blew up. I ran sideways and threw myself on the ground, trying to keep my AK pointed at the men below us. As I waited for the impact, I realized that the rocket-propelled grenades were heading for them. All three of the vehicles chasing us were hit. One of the Land Rovers rolled down the hill in black oily smoke. The other sat on melting tires in white-hot flame as two men trapped inside tried to get out. The white Chevy had only been hit in the bed and tried to back up. Our man with the sniper rifle, who was ten yards closer to them than me and lay quietly, waiting, fired once and the driver slumped over the wheel just as another RPG round screamed down directly into the cab killing the other two still in the truck.

Several of them though had seen the RPG coming at their vehicles and had jumped out. They were looking for cover and shooting at us. What they had thought would be an ambush had been turned on them.

Kevin's men coolly picked them off as soon as they showed themselves. I got on all-fours and hurried closer, next to Kevin. "What the hell is going on?"

"Get whoever you can! We have to get past them and get out of here before any more come."

I took a prone position with my AK and started shooting. The AKs I had shot in the past weren't that accurate, maybe a five-inch grouping at a hundred yards. But this one was perfect. It was zeroed in to the sight and could hit a teacup at a hundred yards. I saw two men firing at us from behind a rock formation on the left and fired in between the rocks, hoping the 7.62mm bullet would splinter rock and ricochet around inside their hole. One stopped firing and the other tried to move to his left. I picked him off with a head shot and he dropped like he'd been poleaxed.

The firing slowed and Kevin held up his had to stop shooting and evaluate. We waited. No one moved. Suddenly four men with helmets and body armor came down from the top of the hill with M4 rifles at the ready. They approached from the back of the burning Land Rover and checked each body. They were all dead. They gave Kevin a sign and disappeared

Kevin stood up and said, "Let's move. We've got to get out of here."

I stood with the others. I surveyed the carnage. This was a very well planned op. He had lured the bad guys into a box canyon with his grenade shooters prepositioned. If they made it out of their trucks they had to come uphill to get us, and he had four snipers ready, which meant none of them had a prayer.

We got back to our truck and I was about to climb in to the middle seat as our sniper waited for me.

Kevin said to me, "Nice shooting."

I stopped with one hand on the roof of the pickup as I faced him. "You didn't need me. I could have stayed in the truck and read a book. Those shitheads didn't have a chance."

"Yeah, but you got him."

"Why me? All these shooters? Seems strange. You wanted me to get one of 'em. Get me back into it. Get my hunting tag going. What's the annual limit for shit-heads?"

He smiled. "No limit out here. Look, you got him. It's just that simple. Somebody had to. Let's go."

I slid into the back seat. "Where we going?"

"Wherever you want. You're the boss."

I took a deep breath. "If we're gonna get to the bottom of this, we need to go right to the source. We need to go talk to the ISI. To Islamabad."

Kevin nodded and jumped in next to me.

# TWELVE

We returned to the warehouse, got our rental cars, and made our way to Islamabad. The men I was never introduced to disappeared.

We drove to the capital of Pakistan on highways, trying to look inconspicuous. It wasn't very hard to blend in. Vehicles of all sizes and descriptions, new, old, Mercedes as well as manufacturers that I didn't even recognize—probably Russian or even Chinese. There were buses with people hanging out the windows, and little respect for lanes or traffic signals. The closer we got to Islamabad, the crazier things became. While on the way, I sat in the left front seat with Kevin driving from the right seat—Pakistan followed the English driving pattern of driving on the left side of the road. After I had settled down and thought about the day so far, I decided to call Marshall, even though it was the middle of the night his time. I dialed, and much to my surprise he answered. He sounded tired. "Yeah," he said immediately.

"You know who this is?"

"Yeah."

"I need you to make a call. We're going to talk to the folks at intel. You know where I am?"

"Yeah."

"Then you know who to call. We're going to go stay in a hotel tonight, and I'm going to walk into their headquarters tomorrow morning. Make it so that I can talk to whoever the hell knows what happened over here. Whoever gave us the intel we relied on. As we like to say in the legal world, I want the person most knowledgeable. Can you do that?"

He sounded curious, but pessimistic. "I'll make the call. I can't guarantee you'll get anywhere; we sure haven't."

"Tell them to humor me, or I'll hold another one of my press conferences and have a tantrum."

He breathed in deeply through his nose, which was audible over the international cell line. "I think you flatter yourself. They'll probably be about as afraid of that as we were."

"Maybe. But maybe they'll think I'm crazy and will do something unexpected that they don't want."

"You alone?"

"No. I'm with someone."

"You might want to leave them behind."

"Not a chance."

"Your choice. I'll make the call."

I turned to Kevin. "Where are we going to stay?"

Kevin nodded as he looked in his mirrors. "I know a place."

"I figured you did. And if you know a place, do you know anybody at the building where we're going? Anybody with Pakistani intelligence who could tell us what the hell happened?"

Kevin thought for a moment, then shook his head. "Yeah. I know people. I can ask around, but we can't meet with them. I'll see if they know what happened, but it'll have to be on the QT."

"Whatever you have to do. I think they slipped us some bad intelligence, and I think they did it on purpose."

"That would be malicious."

"Oh, it's way worse than malicious. They basically signed the death warrants for a bunch of people just to give us a black eye."

Kevin nodded. "There's more at work here than just Pakistani intelligence. We've got to figure out who took them to Europe and propped up the court so they were ready to launch on this charge as soon as the bomb hit. This is way bigger than just Pakistan."

The hotel that Kevin knew about wasn't a hotel at all. It was an apartment building with hundreds of units in a high-rise. It wasn't high-class but it wasn't low-class either. Something of a quiet family building, for postal clerks and bus drivers. Kevin led the way, and opened the door with keys that were handed to him by one of his men. He stepped into the apartment, and stood still, looking around for any signs of tampering. He crossed over to the hall closet, opened the door, and touched a panel on the wall. The panel opened and he removed a recording device. He pulled out the digital tape and looked at it. He showed it to me. "None of the tape was used."

"Motion-detector-triggered camera?" I asked.

He nodded and replaced the tape. I saw no camera or lens anywhere. It was very well disguised. The other men were waiting in the hall and came in. The apartment was a three-bedroom, with three twin beds in each room. The furniture was of poor quality but clean. "How do you happen to know about this place?"

Kevin smiled. "I use it in my business."

"You come here a lot I take it?"

"Often enough. You ever been to Islamabad?"

I shook my head. "No, just the mountains, Peshawar, a few other places. I went to Karachi once; sort of a combination of Norfolk and Mexico City."

Kevin chuckled. "More Mexico City and full of bandits."

I sat down on the couch and put my feet on the cheap coffee table. "So you want to tell me what happened in the mountains today?"

"That worked out okay."

"You lured those guys right into that ambush."

Kevin went to a cabinet, opened it, and pulled out a bottle of twelve-year-old Macallan scotch. Probably illegal in Islamabad, but what the hell. Compared to what else had happened that day, a bottle of scotch wasn't going to make any difference. He offered me a glass but I declined. He poured himself a couple fingers in a small glass and sipped it slowly. He finally said, "You know the routine. You know about missions like this. You may have seen this as a mission to go ask a couple of witnesses some questions, but you don't go into Indian Country without a lot of contingencies. Like I said, I operate here a lot. I don't take a lot of chances on getting on the wrong side of men who are coming in numbers to get me. I *always* assume they're coming to get me. I'm usually wrong. But when I'm not, it doesn't go well for them. And that's not because of luck, it's because of planning." He sat down and drank the rest of his scotch. "So let's talk about tomorrow."

I got up early, or what I thought was early, to find Kevin and the others already standing fully dressed, drinking espressos. My head was still a little foggy. I said, "What's up? Why is everybody up?"

Kevin shook his head and smiled a little bit. "Good morning, sunshine. You really have lost your touch, haven't you? We're always up. Or somebody is. How many people slept here last night, Jack?"

I shrugged. "I don't know. Four?"

"No. Seven. And we had two of them up in shifts all night. And they were armed and alert, and watching your pretty ass to make sure nobody snuck in here to do us harm. And we had people at the perimeter of the building. And we had people in other buildings. Have you forgotten how this is done?"

I looked at my watch. "So we have about an hour before we need to leave?"

"That's right. It's currently seven. We're going to

leave at eight, and we'll be knocking on their door at nine."

I checked my iPhone for texts but saw nothing from Chris. This could be a very short meeting if he didn't get somebody to make that call for us. But we had to give it a try.

At eight o'clock sharp, Kevin and I went down the stairs of the apartment building. We walked out and stepped directly into a waiting car. But it wasn't one of the rentals from the day before. It was a beater Camaro, probably 1985, that looked like crap. But I could tell by the sound of the engine that it was highly tuned. Behind the Camaro was a Renault station wagon. It had tinted windows—the Camaro did not. As I tumbled into the back seat I asked Kevin, who was sitting in the front, "Where the cars come from?"

"Friends loaned them to us."

"Friends?"

"Yeah. Don't worry about it. We know where we're going. Just sit back and relax." The door slammed and the Camaro took off and worked into the stream of traffic at the main intersection one block from our apartment, which I now realized was on a fairly quiet street. The traffic was insane. Even if I had been able to drive there, I don't think I would have. I would have had a wreck and spent the next month trying to explain myself. We drove through miles of Islamabad trying not to distinguish ourselves and making sure we weren't being followed. Finally we headed for a building that Kevin seemed to know about. The Camaro made a hard left turn, stopped in front of the entrance, and the doors flew open. The driver got out on his side; Kevin got out on his and threw the seat down so I could climb out. He grabbed my arm and pulled me. The driver jumped back in and floored it, pulling away from the building with the Renault right behind him. Kevin went over and opened the lobby door of the unmarked building and we walked in. It felt like we were working hard to make sure nobody saw our faces. The door closed behind us and I could see now that no one could see inside the building. It wasn't exactly shaded as much as mirrored—that cheap glass covering from the inside that appears to be for reflecting the heat but acts equally well reflecting unwanted eyes. I checked my iPhone but still nothing from Chris. I crossed over to a man sitting behind a desk in the room which passed for the lobby. It was not a normal lobby. There were no seats, and the large room was stark. The walls looked normal but I could tell by the corners that they probably had metal interior sections. There were cameras in both corners behind the clerk, and the glass behind us looked bulletproof. Also notably there was no name or indication of what organization was inside the building. This may not have been the actual ISI headquarters but it was clearly something closely related. It might have been their equivalent to our Directorate of Operations at the CIA.

Kevin leaned close to me as we walked in and said, "This is your deal. I'm going to go quiet."

I said to the man seated behind the counter, "Do you speak English?"

He looked at me with some contempt, "Of course."

I said, "I am here to see someone, but I am embarrassed to say I don't know his name. He should be expecting me."

The man looked at me perplexed. "What is your name? Do you have a passport?"

I removed my passport from my jacket pocket and handed it to him. "Jack Caskey. John Caskey, actually."

He looked at my passport and looked at me. "An American?"

"Yes."

He looked at Kevin, who was standing with his back to him looking out the glass doors to the street. "And him?"

"What about him?"

"Is he with you?"

"Yes."

"I need his passport too."

Kevin heard him, turned around, and handed him his passport. I saw that it had the name of Kevin Johnson.

The man looked at him, took both our passports, and disappeared through the door behind him.

He came back after a few moments and said, "Someone will be with you. I'm not sure when. You may wait."

And wait we did. For two hours. We stood in the lobby, with the corner cameras trained on us, with nowhere to sit, no water, no coffee, and no one to talk to. But we knew the game. They were checking our backgrounds, checking with American intelligence, checking our passports and passport numbers, and seeing if we were a threat to anyone. Finally, after what seemed like an interminable time the door opened from the side. I was surprised that I hadn't even seen the seam for that door before it opened. A man walked out. A small Pakistani man with an intense look and a small wispy mustache. He crossed over directly to me. "Mr. Caskey."

I extended my hand and shook his. "Yes. I'm Jack Caskey."

He handed me my passport and held Kevin's out to him. "And Mr. Johnson."

Kevin took his passport, put it in his pocket, and said nothing.

The man looked at me. "Why don't you both come with me." We followed him through the door and down a dimly lit hallway. He turned and went up a stairway and we followed him to the second floor. It was much better lit and had substantially more activity. Several men were furiously working on something and noted us with some concern. They looked at the man leading us, as if to ask whether he knew what he was doing. There were no labels, no nameplates, and no indication of what was going on there, only that it was intense. He turned down two more hallways and opened a door. We walked into a conference room that was completely bare except for a metal table and six chairs. He indicated two chairs for us to sit in, and sat on the opposite side of the table himself. Shortly after we sat, a young Pakistani woman arrived with a tray of coffee and biscuits. She looked at us. "Do either of you prefer tea?"

We both shook our heads. The door opened again and another man came in. This man was younger than the first, but equally intense. His hair was combed back and oiled. He wore glasses that were new and fashionable. He was wearing a Rolex, although it was fake; the second hand ticked between the seconds, like a quartz watch, instead of the smooth works of a Rolex. He sat next to the first man.

The Rolex man leaned on the table and looked at me. "What is it that you want?"

I said, "What did you say your name was?"

He smiled. "I didn't. Tariq Qazi. Pleased to meet you."

"My pleasure. I'm Jack Caskey, and this is Kevin Johnson. I hope that you knew that we were coming, at least a few hours before we arrived."

"Yes. We received a message of high importance from Washington asking that we meet with you. So here I am. What can I do for you?"

He was not very happy that we were there, and was even less happy that he had been compelled to talk to us. As I began to speak, he turned to Kevin and said, "I know who this man is. He is the attorney for the two pilots that have been arrested. But who are you?"

"Just a friend. I am a businessman. I sell electronics internationally, mostly radios. I have a contract with the Pakistani army for high-tech radios for special operations teams, for example."

The man almost sneered. "You are actually a CIA operative."

Kevin laughed out loud. "No, not even close. I am a private U.S. citizen. I have nothing to do with the CIA."

"And your name is not Johnson."

"That's true, you got me. My real name is Kevin Crane, but that's the passport I've been traveling on for years so I just stick with it."

The man looked at us both. "You are both formerly with the Navy SEALs."

I looked at him, unsure of where this was going. "True."

Kevin nodded. "Yes. Used to be."

Qazi looked very unhappy as he said, "And yesterday you were in the village of Danday Saidji. You were asking questions of many people, examining the place of the bombing. And then you killed many Pakistanis in an ambush."

Kevin shook his head vigorously. "No sir. Yes, we were at the village, because Jack here wanted to ask some questions of the witnesses who have already testified in the trial in which he's involved. And I speak the language, so I was helping him. But then a bunch of men came for us in jeeps and a truck. We ran for our lives. We were in the hills, and frankly it was getting sketchy. Dangerous. But somebody took them out."

He didn't believe a word of it. "A remarkable coincidence."

Kevin nodded as if he were accepting the sarcastic assessment as true. "Unbelievably lucky. I don't frankly think we'd be here if it weren't for whoever that was. My guess is they thought we were in the back three cars and were trying to take *us* out. Their lead pickup truck was American-made, which is probably why they got hit. But who knows. I wasn't going to stand around and ask them."

He turned his attention again to me, showing the contempt he felt. "So what do you want?"

I took a deep breath. "Well, first, where are the

witnesses? The ones who testified by videotape at the hearing last week?"

Qazi smiled almost imperceptibly. He played with his watch and said, "I do not know. I do know that they are being guarded, as there are many people who do not want their testimony to come out."

That made no sense to me. "Their testimony is already out. I just wanted to ask them how they came to be witnesses, and who it is that asked them to testify. I'm just doing my background checks. Just like I do on any witness at any trial."

He said, "This isn't any trial."

"Well, I can't argue with that. And I thought that would probably be your answer. Can you put me in touch with whoever it is that's guarding them? I want to ask them a few questions."

He nodded, but I could tell he didn't mean it. "Yes, let me make a note of that and I will get back to you."

Right. "And I'd also like to talk to whoever it was that was filming that night. Somebody had a camera with a very sophisticated lens on it and just *happened* to catch the bomb smashing into that building. A really remarkable coincidence. Who was doing the filming?"

"I do not know."

"Well maybe you know this. Why was he there? Was he one of your guys?"

He looked at the other man, then back at me. "We had information that al Qaeda was meeting with the Taliban there. We wanted to track anyone who came in and came out who was connected with either of them, and when we saw the men we wanted, we were going to arrest them, or track them. It depended on how they presented themselves. We did not know the bomb was going to be dropped. He just happened to be there when that happened."

I sat back and studied his face. I glanced quickly at the other man, who was not looking at anyone. They knew more than they were saying, and were good at not saying it. "It's curious that you put your man a few hundred yards away, so that he was out of any blast pattern. There were many houses much closer to that building from which he could have filmed much better. Why didn't you put him there?"

"If he was closer it would have been much easier for him to be discovered. We wanted to see anyone approaching, not just a close-up of the door."

"You say that you had information that al Qaeda and the Taliban were meeting there, but you knew it was a refugee facility. You knew there were European medical people there."

He leaned forward and nodded. "Of course we knew that. That's why they were choosing to meet there. No one would attack a refugee medical facility. The Europeans would have no idea who they were. They intended to go in and pretend to be Afghans looking for injured and wounded people from their village. Then they would meet together in the corner as they supposedly discussed patients' conditions and identities. The Europeans would know not to approach these men in such deep discussions. And they knew no one within that building would turn them in."

"You told the Americans about the meeting. You

gave them the latitude and longitude of the building and told them the Taliban would be meeting al Qaeda there."

"Of course. We wanted them to know. It was our understanding that they had special operations teams on the ground ready to act. Instead, they chose to drop a bomb on the building. We had no knowledge of this, and did not expect that. If they had asked us the wisdom of this, we would have told them not to do it."

I replied, "You knew they had airplanes and Predators in the air, armed and ready to go."

He leaned forward. "They *always* have airplanes and Predators in the air, ready to go. And they usually drop on targets without consulting us. Often, it results in civilian casualties. It is a big problem for us, because they don't trust us. They challenge our intelligence, and challenge our loyalty. So they make decisions without our input, which then result in the deaths of people of our country. It is a terrible thing. I'm not sure we can cooperate much anymore. You Americans don't understand how difficult this is for us."

"Do you have the tape of the man on the radio giving the Americans the coordinates?"

"No. We only keep tapes for twenty-four hours."

"Do you know his name?"

He looked up at me. "Yes, but I am not at liberty to tell you. His position is very sensitive."

"Well, is he going to testify at the trial?"

"That is being discussed. If he decides to testify, I will tell you and perhaps we will allow you to speak with him then. You must inform your American intel-

ligence people that we have cooperated, and that this
was not of our doing."

I paused, trying not to show my frustration. "Tell me
about the Falcon jet that was parked at Peshawar waiting for the Americans to be captured. Tell me about the
men in the mountains who happened to have Stinger
missiles. Tell me how the Falcon got them out of the
country without you knowing about that, and without
you right now being able to tell me who owns that
aircraft—who registered it."

He responded, "It was a false registry. Or, rather, the
number we were given was taken from the records at
the airport. It is a false number. The number we have is
not a real aircraft. We are trying to find out about the
airplane, but don't know."

I sat back feigning surprise. "So you allowed a Falcon 7X to land at Peshawar, take two Americans to the
International Criminal Court—to which Pakistan had
not referred them—and then disappear? You don't know
who that was?"

He glared at me. "I just said we didn't. The number
we have is not a correct number."

Kevin jumped in. "So isn't it maybe a little possible
that somebody inside your organization who had the
same coordinates for this meeting you did, gave you
those coordinates knowing exactly what was going to
happen? And then told whoever it was that was going
to bring that Falcon jet in that this was going to happen? Isn't it possible that somebody inside ISI set this
all up and you got duped just like we did?"

I thought Kevin was actually being generous. He had assumed that ISI was the grand conspirator in this whole thing from the minute it happened. He was now at least allowing them an out by thinking about the possibility that somebody else inside their organization had used the intelligence in a very different way than they had— and in fact maybe created the very intelligence they passed to the United States.

"No," Qazi said, "that is not possible."

"Let me ask you something," I said. "If your camera guy was there because you wanted to see who was going into and out of a meeting, then you must have had special operations guys nearby to grab whoever you filmed, right?"

"We don't discuss our operations."

Kevin made a fist. "Bullshit. You didn't have anybody anywhere near there."

The man with the wispy mustache stared Kevin down. "You don't know that."

Kevin stared back at him. "Yes I do. *I* was there, and as you know we don't do anything inside Pakistan without your approval and participation. We whipsaw the press, so you can pretend to the crazy extremists that you're not helping us, and we tell everybody that you are so we can continue to give you too much money. So don't play bullshit games with me. You didn't have any teams anywhere nearby."

The man smiled. "I did not know that you were there. I thought you were an importer of radios."

Kevin smiled slightly, but not in a humorous way. "I have many jobs. Have to support the family."

"You don't have a family."

"True."

Qazi asked, "So perhaps you should ask the people *you* work with whether they know this airplane that came to pick up the two Americans. Where it came from. Maybe they already know."

I said, "If they knew, I would know, and I wouldn't be asking you. But I sure do want to know whether somebody in this building had something to do with them getting here and getting out with a phony tail number. It doesn't even make sense. The tail number is painted on the side of the airplane in huge block letters. Are you telling me nobody wrote it down?"

"They did write it down. And it is wrong. The tail had been repainted."

I knew it was time. "I need the name of your cameraman—the one who took the video of the bombing."

"For what?" Qazi frowned.

"Because I want to talk to him. I want to see if there is any other footage around, and I would like to discuss with him what his job was and what he saw."

"That is not possible."

I pressed. "So as I understand it, you have the two eyewitnesses that will be used at the International Criminal Court, and you have the camera operator, and you're not going to let us speak to any of them, right?"

"Correct. You can examine them when they testify at the International Criminal Court."

"So you're cooperating with them fully? You're

providing them with whatever information they need. Is that right?"

I felt Kevin move as if he felt threatened.

"What I'm saying is, we are not giving any witnesses to anybody. If they have already been videotaped, you have seen what they have said, and they will testify at trial. That is all. Very simple. No one will have access to them before the trial to try and manipulate or change their testimony."

I stood up and Kevin followed me. I turned and looked at Qazi. "If what you've said is true, somebody inside the ISI gave those coordinates to the United States. And the information was completely bogus. There was no meeting. There's never been any evidence of a meeting and nobody showed up on your videotape. Right? And whoever passed those coordinates just happened not to mention that it was a refugee facility. Something you well knew. So somebody inside your country, inside your organization, is working for the other side. You better find out who that is, and when you do, I want you to tell us so we can have a chat with him."

Both the Pakistanis stood up. The one with the mustache said emphatically, "Mr. Caskey, you are completely wrong. We gave the coordinates to the United States with the full understanding that there *was* to be a meeting. But we never expected the United States to bomb the facility. We even told them it was a refugee facility. They acted without telling us about it, and the blood is on your country's hands. Not ours."

I was about to fire back when I felt my phone buzzing in my pocket. I pulled it out and looked at the text message. It was from Chris. It said, "Big developments. Call me."

We said our goodbyes and headed out. The Camaro was waiting for us.

As I climbed into the back of the car, I dialed Marshall's number. He answered it immediately and said, "Yes?"

Our driver pulled away from the curb and merged into the heavy city traffic. The other car was right behind us. "What's up?"

"Where are you?"

"Islamabad."

"This isn't a secure line. Come see me when you get back." He hung up.

# THIRTEEN

After we touched down at Dulles Airport in northern Virginia, I turned on my phone and it immediately buzzed with a text message from Kristen. I read: "When are you back? All motions denied. Trial in three months."

"Shit." I hadn't expected anything else. I knew all of our motions would be for naught. We had to try though. Now we were going to have to put on a case. That would be tough since I had no witnesses and my basic theory was that the prosecutor was insane and the entire case was a setup. I had to get Chris to find the people on the inside who *got* the intelligence from Pakistan that was passed to my clients. The problem was they would claim state secrets privilege and limit what they could say by claiming that anything more detailed was classified.

I grabbed my bags off the carousel and texted Chris to meet me at my office in an hour. It was just after noon and it was a spectacularly beautiful day. The drive into Washington from Dulles was the kind of drive that makes you proud to live in the United States. Such a beautiful country and so inspiring—to see the Washington Monument, the Jefferson Memorial, the Lincoln Memorial, the Capitol, all reminders of what I have always thought to be the greatest country in the history of the world. We had our issues, we had our quirks, we had our darkness and sin, but no other country had ever come close to creating what we had created. Even though half the country at any given moment, depending on which half you were talking about, seemed to be trying to tear everything down, I was glad to be home. I was thankful I didn't live in Peshawar, or Islamabad, or Danday Saidji.

When I arrived at my office, Kristen and several of her associates were there. Chris came several minutes later. I looked at the stack of phone messages, and invited Chris into my office with Kristen. We sat down. Kristen said, "So how was Pakistan?"

"Crazy. Chris, how are you doing?"

"Good. Lots to discuss. How was it?"

"Colorful. We got the side number of the Falcon that picked our guys up. The real side number. The one on the records there was fake." I wrote the number down on a piece of paper and handed it to Chris. "Can you find out who owns this airplane?"

He barely glanced at it before putting it in his pocket. He seemed uninterested. "Tell me about your conversation with the ISI."

I sighed. "Is that why you came over here?"

He shook his head. "No, I came over here to tell

you about something. But not with her here," he said, glancing at Kristen.

"What does she have to do with it? She's part of the team."

Kristen looked wounded. "What have I done? Seriously?"

He stood up, and walked toward the door, as if he were going to open it for her. He said, "It has nothing to do with you as an individual, it has to do with limiting the number of people who know a given piece of information. The fewer people who know the information, the less likely it is to appear in the press before it's time. And I'm not ready for this to be in the press."

Kristen stood up and walked toward the door, clearly furious. "Oh, and I'm the one who would tell the press. Is that what you're saying?"

He shook his head, bored with her attitude. "I never said anything like that. It's a matter of statistics. I don't really care whether you understand this concept. I'm not going to tell him what I have to tell him unless you're out of the room. And if you're not going to leave, if you're going to have a little mini–attorney tantrum, then fine. I'll just leave and catch him another time."

Kristen looked at me to rescue her but I couldn't. "Give us a second, Kristen."

She walked toward the door and Chris opened it and closed it behind her. He crossed back over to my desk, sat down, and leaned forward with his elbows on my desk.

I asked, "What's up?"

He glanced around the room, looked at the ceiling,

thought about something, and then said, "Let's go for a walk."

I looked out the window and saw that it was growing cloudy and ominous. A storm was probably on the way, and the sunlight that had been illuminating the room was obscured. I said, "Sure."

We walked out of my office. I glanced into the room that I called the annex, where there were three associates, including Kristen, who saw us and looked away as soon as she did, and went directly outside to the sidewalk. We turned right and headed toward the Capitol and then turned right at the corner. Chris waited until we were well away from the office and said, "Thanks for stepping outside. Tell me what happened in Pakistan."

I gave him a complete rundown from the minute we landed, to the conversation with the ISI.

He asked, "Did you know Kevin was working for somebody over there when the bomb hit?"

I stepped around a man carrying a backpack in his arms and said, "No, how would I know that? Did you know that?"

Chris shook his head. "News to me. 'Course I'm not exactly in the middle of some things outside of my area."

I frowned at him. "What do you mean outside of your area? You're supposed to be the guy who knows everything about special operations."

"Yeah, that's the idea. But sometimes I don't get clued in."

"You mean that Kevin's working for the Agency?"

"I mean that the mission he was on when the bomb dropped was not anything I was aware of. Could have been the Agency, could have been anybody. He could have been working for a private contractor that I don't know anything about. One of those off-the-books kind of missions. I have no idea."

He slowed as we approached the intersection. The weather continued to worsen. I looked around to see if there was anybody that looked suspiciously interested in us. I didn't see anybody. "He's not still on active duty, with DEVGRU or something is he?"

Chris shook his head. "No." Chris thought for a minute. "How did Kevin manage to have those men prepositioned there? That's impressive."

I nodded. "Yeah, a lot of strange things. He seemed to know a lot of people. He's the one that got the right side number in Peshawar. They were going to give me the complete stiff-arm. For him? They rolled over. He said he bribed the guy. I don't think so. I think the guy knew him, and owed him one."

Chris asked, "Do you trust him?"

I glanced at him quickly. "What's that supposed to mean?"

"If we don't know who he's working for, then we don't know why he's doing what he's doing. How do you know the side number he gave you from that guy at Peshawar is legit?"

"I've known Kevin for years. There isn't a straighter guy out there."

Chris shrugged. "Money talks. Some of these independent types get lured by big piles of cash. It sounds like he's got many piles of them, with the trucks and weapons and men and connections he has over there.

Where else does he have people prepositioned? What other countries does he operate in where he lays big piles of cash around for other people?"

"Beats the hell out of me. But I tell you what, I worry about a lot of people, but not him."

"Because a Navy SEAL would never do anything wrong after he gets out. Right? They are *immune* from temptation."

"Not saying that. Just that he's not taking anybody else's money. But enough about that. Why did you text me in Islamabad?"

"That ambush has been in all the intelligence briefings at the White House. People are a little bit confused as to who was involved but your name came up. That left a lot of people puzzled. Some think you're the one who had people prepositioned."

"Yeah, that's pretty funny. Mr. Lone Wolf Criminal Defense Lawyer has a secret special operations team operating in the mountains of Pakistan. Actually it was my paralegal and three secretaries that I put over there before I got there."

"Don't be a smartass. They asked me your rep when you were a SEAL. I told them you were average."

"Thanks."

"Average with weapons, but the best planner they'd ever seen. Came up with clever stuff nobody else ever thought of. So they thought it sounded like you."

"Whatever. I'm out of the planning business, except for planning for trial. But your text said big developments. What's up?"

Chris looked around but said nothing. We walked

across the street and stepped onto the path that led down the Mall from the Capitol to the Washington Monument. "The president doesn't like how the hearing went in Holland. He knows your motions have all been denied. That means that they're gonna be put on trial."

"He didn't actually think the ICC would *start* this process without being able to finish it, did he?"

"No." Marshall lowered his voice to where I could barely hear him. "We were almost able to snatch them on the way to the court."

"I know. I was there. They had them. What happened?"

"Pretty well organized motorcade. Would have taken a lot to get them."

"Could have been done. Why wasn't it?"

"Too much bloodshed."

"You expected it to be bloodless?"

"I didn't. But that was the requirement."

"Whose?"

"President's."

"That's impossible. But that's what the whole Servicemember's Protection Act is all about. It would give him cover."

"Maybe so. But there is the *ability* to use force, and the . . . *willingness* to use it. No doubt it's authorized. No doubt it's U.S. law. But that sure doesn't make it acceptable."

I stopped and turned to him. "Are you saying international law trumps U.S. law? I can't believe you're saying that."

"I wasn't saying anything trumped anything. I'm just saying what may be legal in the United States, or may be legal for Americans to do—even overseas—doesn't make it legal in the country where it's going to happen. Nor does it make it acceptable . . . based on political concerns."

I started walking again. "So what are you saying?"

"I'm saying the president knew that we had them in our sights. He knew our team was in place, and he knew we could get them. I was *with* him. He said he wouldn't authorize the use of force unless they could *guarantee* him no one would be killed. Killed *or* seriously injured. But with that he gave them authorization to hit the motorcade. Our man on the scene said it was a hard target, but they were in place and could take it. But it would require a lot of force, much of it deadly force. So the president nixed it at the last moment."

"Unbelievable." We were approaching the end toward the Washington Monument. I glanced around and looked at the sky. "You want to keep going down to the Jefferson Memorial?"

Marshall also looked around, glanced at his watch, and put his hands in his pockets. "I've gotta get back. But I still haven't told you what I need to tell you. And what you can't tell anybody else. Even Kristen. Even your clients. Nobody. Agreed?"

"Yes."

"The president didn't like the fact that he couldn't get our two navy men out of their possession. He also didn't like that at the hearing they mentioned the possibility of indicting other Americans, even for other things. He wants to make a statement."

"How?"

"He wants them to see that if they're going to play this game of political football with American prisoners, that we have a playbook ourselves. He's going to send the *George Washington* battle group to the North Atlantic for 'exercises.' Currently unscheduled exercises. And notably, going with the battle group will be an entire Marine Expeditionary Unit, and an entire SEAL team. We will have all our options, to go in with force, to go in with special operations, or to do whatever else we might do. Even blockade Holland."

I chuckled. "The Europeans will go apeshit." I thought about the battle group steaming up to the North Atlantic and waiting off the coast of Holland and going through some phony exercises when everyone in the world would know why they were there. "You really think the president will use force with the Marines when he wasn't going to with special ops a week ago?"

"He told me he was dead serious. I guess we don't know for sure, but he's sure going to stir it up. I think he believes the ICC will want to talk when they see this move."

"I doubt it, but I like the move. But one other thing. I still don't know the name of the person who initially authorized this target. Who gave the go-ahead. Why is this so hard? He's the key to the whole thing."

"I've been on it since before I first called you. I've heard two different names, but I think I've got him tracked down. I'll get it to you as soon as it's confirmed.

# FOURTEEN

Two days later, after asking Chris and everybody else I could think of, I'd made no progress finding this now elusive air force officer involved in the targeting.

While I was standing in the annex talking to Kristen and reviewing the first of about twenty briefs the DOJ had sent over, my cell rang. It was Chris. I answered. "Chris. You find him?"

"I'm calling about something else. You got a second?"

"Sure." I stepped out of the annex into my reception area. "What you got?"

Chris lowered his voice a little. "The president sent the *Washington* battle group to the North Atlantic two days ago."

"Sure. Just like you said he would."

"Right, well he hasn't announced it to the public. He was going to wait until they were halfway."

"And?"

"And he called all the European leaders to privately announce that these previously unscheduled exercises will be ongoing and have nothing to do with the International Criminal Court."

I laughed out loud. "He actually said that? That it has nothing to do with the International Criminal Court?"

"Yes, he did. I drafted it—with the national security advisor—we knew that piece would be particularly pointed."

"So of course they then know that's exactly the reason for the exercise. It gives him a military option to exercise against the International Criminal Court itself."

"Exactly."

"Except, he won't use it. He had a military option ten days ago when Raw and Dunk were en route. They had picked out the right spot, they were about to execute, and the president called them off. You told me so yourself."

"Who knows. But the point is that your prosecutor is going to hold his own press conference in about five minutes. We think he may announce they're going to release your clients on bail. And of course they'd never go back. We think he heard about the battle group, and the ICC blinked."

"Five minutes? Are the networks carrying it?"

"Of course. I just wanted to let you know your job may about be over."

"Fine with me. Let me go watch it and I'll get back to you. Well done, Chris."

"Don't thank me. It was really the president's idea."

"I'll call you." I hung up and hurried back into the annex. I said to Kristen, "Go to CNN online. Brady's holding a press conference. Marshall thinks they're going to grant bail. Sort of a halfway measure. They'll never go back, and the ICC—wait, there it is. Turn it up."

Kristen turned her screen so all four of us could see it. Wolf Blitzer was staring back at us from the television with a "special news bulletin" graphic superimposed in the upper-right-hand corner. Blitzer was already talking. He said, "The prosecutor has called a press conference which is about to begin. Let's go to The Hague."

Brady stepped up to a lectern where numerous journalists had gathered. Just seeing his face made me angry. Brady looked tired, but delighted. He looked around the room until it was mostly quiet and said, "As was disclosed and discussed during the preliminary hearing of the two naval officers that will soon be tried by the International Criminal Court, we have long been contemplating additional indictments. That process has been ongoing, and a large folio has been prepared of the various war crimes that will relate to the charges I am about to describe. Let me first say, that as everyone who has studied the International Criminal Court knows, we only act when it is clear that the country responsible has no intention of acting. We are a court of last resort. Most countries claim to oppose war crimes, and promise to take care of their own who have committed such crimes. Occasionally that occurs, but too often it does not.

"In this case, the United States has been accused of ongoing activities that are clearly violative of the

International Criminal Court definition of war crimes. As everyone knows, Article 8 of the treaty defines what constitute war crimes. In this new indictment, the charges include charges under Article 8(2)(a)(ii)-1, the war crime of torture. It also includes, in Section 2 of that subsection, the war crime of inhumane treatment, primarily related to those who were captured in various locations in the Middle East, transported to Guantánamo, and treated inhumanely. The indictment also includes the war crime of denying a fair trial, Article 8(2)(a)(vi). These charges additionally include the charge of unlawful confinement, again, mostly related to Guantánamo Bay and the prison established there by the United States. Such a prison in the estimation of the International Criminal Court violates Article 8(2)(a)(vii)-2. There are numerous other articles involved in the indictment and a full copy will be made available to the press as soon as this conference is over. But it includes attacking civilians, attacking civilian objects, and excessive incidental death.

"The court understands that these are serious charges. This indictment is not being brought lightly. With the election of the new president of the United States in 2008, who was sworn in in January 2009, it was hoped that there would be changes, that the truth commissions or investigations promised by numerous senators and human rights groups would actually occur. That there would be investigations and congressional hearings on what had transpired in the previous administration that allowed for and even endorsed torture, forced rendition of individuals overseas to be tortured by other countries with the full knowledge of the United States, and violations of international law, all premised on various opinions of attorneys within the previous Department of Justice.

"But the United States has done nothing to bring to justice those who planned, executed, and hid these acts from the public eye. Not even an inquiry to see if additional steps were called for.

"In light of that vacuum of justice, that vacuum of truth, the International Criminal Court has issued its indictment. The individuals will come to The Hague voluntarily, or if they are found in a treaty-signing country, will be arrested and brought to The Hague. Now I would like to present to you the names of those indicted.

"Number 1. Former President George W. Bush. Number 2. Former Vice President Richard B. Cheney. Number 3. Former Secretary of Defense Donald H. Rumsfeld. Number 4. Former Chairman of the Joint Chiefs of Staff General Richard B. Myers. Number 5. Former Attorney General Alberto Gonzales. And Number 6. Former Director of the Central Intelligence Agency George Tenet. We expect the United States to voluntarily surrender these individuals and have them sent to the International Criminal Court. We expect to have some negotiations on the requirement of their presence prior to trial which can be discussed. But I want to make one thing perfectly clear. There will be a trial, and these men will have a judgment. One way or another, whether they are here or not."

Kristen was stunned. "They indicted Bush? A lot of people think he ought to be indicted, but seriously?"

I replied without even looking at her. "This is the ICC's response to Obama telling them he was sending a battle group. He wanted to give them a chance to respond before he publicly announced it. They responded all right."

I thought about the implications of indicting a former president of the United States. "Unbelievable." I stepped out and called Chris. "Well. That's a real nice up-yours."

"Didn't see that coming. Well, I guess you're still employed."

"I guess so. What's the president going to do now? Recall the *Washington* battle group?"

"No. At least not right away. He's evaluating his options. Oh, we got the Falcon owner."

"Who is it?"

"European Executive Charter. It was leased. Somebody leased it from them for three weeks."

"Who?"

"They're not talking."

"Where are they based?"

"Brussels."

"Belgium?"

"Yeah. We've made informal contact, but they're not saying a word. They apparently anticipated this. We may never get to find out who leased it from them. They acknowledge owning the aircraft, acknowledge it was gone for three days, acknowledge that it's back, and won't tell anybody anything about the in-between."

"I'll find out." I hung up.

Personally I was pleased the ICC had hit back at

Obama instantly. It showed how uneasy they were about the law passed under Bush. They knew it was a tool, and that Obama could use it if he chose to. These indictments were an attempt to keep the United States military at home. It might have been a mistake for President Obama to call them ahead of time to tell them what he was going to do. That let the ICC take the first public step.

It made me wonder if Dutch intelligence had noticed the same things I had, the Americans in place to snatch the prisoners from the ICC's guards on the way to court. Maybe that's why Brady had fired a warning shot by mentioning other possible indictments during the preliminary hearing. But the president hadn't been intimidated. Instead he had decided to send an entire battle group with all the capability necessary to the North Atlantic to be ready to do the very thing the ICC most feared. And if he sent the Marines, it wouldn't be with the assurance of no casualties. If the Marines stormed the fort, all bets would be off. People would die. And American relations with Europe would be broken for a very long time.

So the ICC had to play the biggest card it had. Indicting a former president and secretary of defense and others; a slap in the face to the United States and to the Bush administration in particular. But since they had done it, they had to mean it. The indictment had been issued and arrest warrants were prepared. If they were found anywhere other than U.S. soil they could theoretically be arrested and sent to the very same prison where Raw and Dunk now sat.

* * *

The new indictments seemed to get Chris even more activated. He called me with the name of the air force officer who was the go-between with Pakistani intelligence. He didn't know where he was at that moment, but was trying to find out. I decided to make a couple of phone calls of my own. My connections within the navy were pretty stale, and few people that I knew closely were still on active duty. But I did know one guy I had met early in my career. I had met him in BUD/S training, the basic SEAL training, but he hadn't made it. He had gone into navy intelligence after that and was now a commander stationed at the Pentagon doing detailing. The detailer is the person who assigns you your next job. He can be a friend or an enemy depending on how well you are regarded within the navy. I had stayed in touch with him, and we even got together now and then for drinks. I called him. He answered on the third ring with his name, Jacob Denton.

"Jacob, it's Caskey."

"Well, Mr. Television Star! Aren't you the big international lawyer now? I've seen your face all over the place."

"Yeah, I haven't actually done much, but when you show up in a trial like this, you're immediately notorious. Loved by some, hated by many."

"That's the big leagues."

"No doubt. Look, I'm trying to defend these two navy guys."

"More power to you. I assume you have the full support of the entire federal government behind you. But why are you calling me?"

"Actually I have the full support of a very small part of the federal government, and I can't really tell if it's attached to the rest. I need some information. This is all about hitting that target in Pakistan."

"Yeah. No doubt. Bad deal to hit a refugee medical building."

"Yeah, but how did they do that? Why would they hit a refugee facility if they knew what it was?"

"They wouldn't."

"Exactly. Yet I just spoke with the Pakistani intelligence officer who said they told them it was a refugee facility. So I need to talk to the American who got that information and passed it to my clients. The guy I'm working with at the White House claims to not be able to find him right away. He's still checking. I need somebody to get on the big mammoth I-know-everybody federal computer and find this son of a bitch. And since you are in the detailing shop, I figured you had access to the worldwide where-is-everybody network."

"I do. Is he a navy guy?"

"No. Air force."

"Shit. I don't have access to the air force guys. But I know the air force detailers. Give me the name and I'll see if I can track this guy down for you."

I looked at the piece of paper Chris had given me. "All right, his name is Major Russell Curley."

"Curley? Figures. Good air force name. Probably a targeting geek."

"He's supposed to be an intel officer. He relayed the information up the chain and got the target approved for the F-18."

"I'll see what I can find out and get back to you."

I hung up. While he was looking for Curley, I had to find other witnesses. I wanted the commanding officer of the F-18 squadron, I wanted the commanding officer of the carrier, I wanted the admiral in charge of the Middle East, and I wanted an expert witness on operating in a war zone and taking orders from the targeting center. Now I had to go find them.

When I got back to the office, the television was on and all the associates from Covington and Burling were glued to it. It was a press conference by Jerzy Buzek, the president of the European Parliament. He was talking about the decision by President Obama to conduct "naval exercises" in the North Atlantic. I sat in the conference room with the other attorneys and listened carefully.

Buzek stood in the press room for the European Union in Brussels. It looked like a standard setup, with a lectern and a large European Union flag behind him. He had silver hair and a stern look. He was a former engineer from Poland. He said, "It is understood by all of Europe, and by the European Parliament, that the recent activities by the United States Navy and the declaration by the Obama administration that they are going to conduct previously unscheduled naval exercises in the North Atlantic is simply a threat to the International Criminal Court. It is an attempt to impose the will of the United States on the rest of the world. It is

an attempt to avoid a fair trial under the Treaty of
Rome of which 110 states are members, and another
thirty-eight have signed and are awaiting confirmation.
This is not some unknown organization; it is recognized
throughout the world as a legitimate court with exten-
sive jurisdiction.

"The threats of the United States have not gone un-
noticed. It is fully believed that the United States is
simply preparing to exercise what it has authorized itself to do under the so-called Servicemembers' Protection Act. It is nothing of the sort, it is simply a preemptive
declaration of hostilities by the United States against
the International Criminal Court. The court has done
nothing to antagonize the United States, it has simply
executed an indictment that was issued by the court. If
there has been no wrongdoing, if there has been no
crime, then there will be no conviction and no harm has
been done. On the other hand, if the United States takes
matters into its own hands, and attempts to forcibly release the Americans from the prison in which they are
currently being held pending trial, then Europe will not
stand idly by. To attack Holland, as the president is apparently contemplating, would be a violation of international law, and the Treaty of Rome, whether or not the
United States has signed it.

"Second, the United States itself has acknowledged
jurisdiction for war crimes whether there is a treaty
signed or not. I would refer them to their imposition of
a war crimes trial on Europe. Particularly Germany,
after the cessation of hostilities in World War II. The
United States, with other Allies—established the highly

esteemed court of justice in Nuremberg, Germany, to try German war criminals at the conclusion of that war. There was no treaty, there was no signature of Germany on a treaty prior to that war that it would subject itself to the jurisdiction of an American war crimes trial. Yet the trial went forward, people were convicted, and executed. I would like President Obama to explain to me the difference between Nuremberg and the Treaty of Rome, which not only had years of discussion and debate but was carefully drafted in Rome with numerous countries present—including the United States—and then signed by 148 countries. This is not an ad hoc war crimes tribunal as Nuremberg was.

"But when the Americans are accused of a war crime, they react with threats and saber rattling. They send their military to intimidate the other signatories to the Treaty of Rome, the prosecutor, and the judges and the court itself.

"Because of the provocative military measures undertaken by the United States, I have asked the European Union members to take a heightened level of military readiness in case of attack by the United States.

"Lastly, I would remind the United States that it is a member of NATO, the North Atlantic Treaty Organization. The NATO treaty binds us together. It expresses that we have similar interests in Europe and the United States. That while we have our differences, our goals are the same. The United States is opposed to war crimes but differs with some elements of the International Criminal Court. That is understood, but to threaten the legitimacy of the court with military action is intolerable. Moreover, if the United States were in fact to carry out any military operation into Europe in any way related to the International Criminal Court, that would be a violation of the NATO agreement, and would force the other NATO members to come together to defend themselves, from another member of NATO. The NATO agreement of course requires that an attack on any member of a NATO country is an attack on all of them. So the United States, ironically, would not only be violating the NATO treaty, it would be in essence attacking itself and would be required to defend itself from its own attack pursuant to the NATO treaty.

"So, President Obama, I call on you to stop this provocation. Withdraw your military forces from the North Atlantic, and give us your assurance that there will be no attempt to release the American prisoners by force."

I looked around at the others. "Did I miss much?"

"No. You pretty much got the whole thing. Everything Obama is doing is a bad idea and is simply going to make things worse," Kristen said.

"Anybody else see the irony in all this?"

Nobody said anything. I said, "President Obama ran on a campaign that indicated—although admittedly not in the clearest terms—his support for the International Criminal Court. And now he is threatening to blow them up.

"This is what you would call an international crisis, and it is *exactly* what the ICC wanted to create. And it's been engineered by somebody else, somebody who is pushing this who is not a member of the ICC directly, some outsider."

Kristen asked, "Who, who could be behind this but the court itself?"

"Whoever sent that airplane to pick our fliers up, that's who."

"And who is that?"

"I don't know, but my guess is whoever that person is has been working closely with Brady, trying to set this up. And I think he's probably been working with contacts inside Pakistan. They had to get us bad intel for us to act on it."

Kristen didn't like the way I was talking. "Jack, we are trying to prepare for our defense. We're not supposed to be dreaming up schemes to or expose somebody. This is crazy."

"Really? Do you not really get that this is all a big plan?"

"You mean a conspiracy?"

"Do you really believe this just *happened*? Some prosecutor woke up in the middle of the night, drafted an indictment, got the court to issue it, and arranged for a flight all in about three or four hours? Is that what you think happened?"

"No. Of course not."

"Well then, who do you think did this? Who do you think pushed this?"

"I don't know. For all I know, it could be some Americans."

That thought had never occurred to me. It hit me like a thunderbolt. The fact that some wealthy American might throw a few million dollars at the problem left me literally speechless. It was beautiful, at least from their perspective. Could they do that though? "What made you say that?"

She sat back defensively. "I don't know. You're talking like there's some grand scheme. I just don't see the Europeans doing that. But maybe they would. I don't know. With this kind of money—"

"There are a lot of Europeans with this kind of money."

"Maybe, but the way this is turning out? With Bush and Cheney getting indicted? There are a lot of Americans who would have paid a lot of money to see that happen. They put a lot of money into campaigns of people who promised to have hearings."

I nodded my head. "And maybe have a truth commission. Where there wouldn't necessarily be criminal charges, but the 'truth' would come out about what happened during the war in Iraq, and prisoner treatment, and secret rendition missions. Shit, Kristen, that's brilliant. You may have really hit on something there. You guys hang out with a lot of smart people in New York. You ever hear anybody say anything like this before now?"

She shook her head. "No."

I nodded. "Well start asking around, see if you can hear anything, in any blog, anywhere, anything." I looked around the room. "We have to think outside the usual case preparation. We have to think much bigger. If we can show everybody what really happened, and our clients had nothing to do with it, they're going to get off. No matter what the evidence is that the prosecutor puts on." I looked at my watch. "I've got to go make a call. I'll see if I can line up more witnesses. We need to go into full trial preparation mode. I need everybody here at seven in the morning and you should expect to work until nine at night. We'll provide meals and whatever else you need, but we need everything you've got for the next ninety days. Is everybody up for that?"

They seemed to have been energized. Except for Terry, one of the quietest associates from Covington. He was turning a pencil in his hands. I said to him, "What's with you?"

He smiled sarcastically. "What if you'd rather be part of the conspiracy than the solution?"

I looked at him coldly. He was pissing me off. "Meaning what exactly?"

He looked at me equally coldly. "I think Bush and Cheney and the others *should* have been indicted. I think they're a bunch of lying assholes. I think they took this country down a road it never should have gone. We never should have gone into Iraq, we never should have opened Guantánamo, we never should have sent prisoners to countries where they would be tortured, and we never should have tortured people ourselves. We completely lost respect in the world, and it only came back when Obama became president. I think that is absolutely undeniable. And if two guys have to be put on trial to get the United States to join the International Criminal Court and agree with the entire international community that war crimes should be punished, and indict Bush and Cheney, then I'm all for it. And if some clever American has figured out how to make that happen, then I'm all for him."

I looked at him for a minute trying to decide between three or four different fates, one of which included violence. I controlled myself. "And what if it wasn't an American? What if it was a Pakistani or a German?"

He shrugged. "I'd still say more power to them. Seems like the right thing to do."

"To set up two Americans and send them to prison for life? To kill sixty-five innocent people? That's the right thing to do?"

"No. It's never right to kill innocent people. But sometimes there's, as Rumsfeld used to say, collateral damage."

I put my hands on my hips and fired. "Go back to New York. We don't need you here."

He stood up chuckling. "You only work with people who agree with you? Maybe I missed the indoctrination."

"Don't give me any of your bullshit. Just go home." I looked around the room and not many were looking at me.

Terry packed up his computer, shoved it into his soft-sided leather briefcase, and began walking out of the room. As he got to the door, he stopped and looked at the others. He said, "Anybody else? You all going to stay and work for this losing cause?"

Two others at the end of the table nodded their heads, packed their computers, and followed him. I stared at them in disbelief. I didn't say anything. They worked their way out of the room and closed the door behind them. I glanced at the faces now all looking at me. "Anybody else have anything they want to say? Anybody think we're on the wrong side of this? I'm not going to give you the usual lecture about criminal defense and that you defend your client no matter what. I want people who are with me." I saw subtle nods. "All right, let's get back to work."

# FIFTEEN

After a couple of hours, I went down to my office and called Marshall on his cell phone. He answered right away. "I need witnesses, Chris. I need the guy's CO, the admiral, the location of that air force intel officer, and I need somebody else from the squadron to testify as an expert on targeting. When you accept a target and when you don't. You've got to help me out."

"Of course. I've been working on it. All the people you need are still at sea."

"Will they be back in time for the trial?"

"No. The trial is scheduled to begin toward the end of their cruise, but before they come back. They should still be deployed during the entire trial."

"What the hell am I supposed to do?"

"We'll get whoever you need off the ship to go to trial. That's what we have to do. But talk to them first. See if they have anything to say. Right now all we were saying is that we got bad information from the Pakistanis but we don't have anybody to say it."

"Great. Put me in touch with them. Set up a video conference. I'll go to the Pentagon."

"No. I think you need to go out there and see them."

"To the Persian Gulf?"

"Exactly. In fact, I was just in a meeting with a certain chief of staff. People in the White House are seriously lit up about this. The speech by the president of the European Parliament has gotten people activated. We've got you on a flight tomorrow morning to Dubai, then you'll get on a COD out to the carrier."

"Seriously?"

"Yup. The entire ship has instructions to cooperate fully."

"I need Kristen to come with me."

"I thought you might say that. I have a ticket for her too."

Kristen coming with me was key. First, when Terry was having his political tantrum, Kristen didn't abandon me. More importantly, I'd been on enough ships. I'd seen enough naval officers in enough meetings. When there is a beautiful woman present, they behave differently. I don't mean beautiful women who are in the navy. That didn't count. I mean someone outside their normal sphere. Someone they couldn't order around or intimidate. Most of them, perhaps without even knowing it, wanted to please the woman. And Kristen was nothing if not beautiful. Frankly, I thought she was growing up a little bit in this case. She started off with an attitude that wasn't very conducive to our working together, but as time had gone on, she seemed to have bought into what it was we were trying to do. She seemed enthusiastic about attempting to get our clients off. I even thought she believed that getting them off was the right thing. That it would mean justice had prevailed. I was even starting to get over the attitude I had toward her. I was starting to like her again. And the fact that I had never been married, never close, was starting to haunt me. I guess if I was completely honest, I looked forward to spending a little more time with her.

I'd had girlfriends in the past, both in the navy and after. But none very serious. I never let anyone get that close to me. It was my own fault, and I knew it. And my lack of serious relationships caused me to withdraw inside myself more the older I got. I assumed everyone would find fault with me, so I never really gave them a chance to find it. Kristen was intriguing though.

She met me at Dulles and we sat next to each other on the American Airlines flight to Dubai. It was a hell of a long flight. On the way, after the passage of the short darkness that passed for night when flying east, we went over the entire case and the evidence that we had so far. We were both acutely aware of the holes in our case and the need for witnesses and documents. We had also hoped for a longer time between the preliminary hearing and our time to prepare a defense. Unfortunately our time was as short as the International Criminal Court could make it, which pushed our preparation time up dramatically. The court clearly wanted to push this case. It caused me to have a touch of anxiety, like battery acid in my stomach, as I thought about the implications of leaving two Americans stranded in a foreign prison for life because we hadn't found the right evidence to get them off. It was completely up to us. The good news was the United States government was now fully behind us.

As we descended into Dubai I could see the Burj Tower from a long way off. Not only the tallest building in the world, but the tallest man-made structure ever built at 2,700 feet. It was enormous. It was also beautiful. It set Dubai apart from the rest of the Arab world. Dubai was attempting to be to the Middle East what Hong Kong was to Asia.

We landed and I turned on my phone. I got an immediate text from a Lieutenant Dan Cruz, my point of contact to get aboard the *Ronald Reagan*. It said to call him on his cell phone when I landed. We finally emerged from customs, and I dialed. He answered right away, and said he'd pick us up at baggage claim.

When we walked out from baggage claim to the sidewalk and the desert heat hit us, a white sedan pulled up. A man jumped out of the passenger seat and walked toward us. He was clean-cut and wearing casual clothes. He extended his hand, which I shook, and he turned to Kristen to introduce himself. "Let's put your gear in the trunk and get over to the COD."

We did and went to a smaller terminal on the international airport property. It was unmarked and unremarkable, but clearly was an outpost for military flights to and from the carrier. There were a couple of navy helicopters parked there as well as the navy COD, an

ugly two-engine propeller plane that looked like a boxy
little brother of a C-130 Hercules. Cruz directed us toward the COD, where we were briefed and given seats
along with fifteen or so other people, mostly military.
There were a couple of other people in civilian clothes
but it was essentially a military flight. We sat in our seats
facing backward, and immediately taxied to the runway
and took off. Cruz had told us the flight was less than a
hundred miles so it wouldn't take very long. It didn't.
Before we knew it we were flying through the milky sky
over the Persian Gulf and descending on our approach to
the *Reagan* floating somewhere off the coast of Kuwait.
The COD's landing on the carrier was exactly as I had
remembered from before. It slammed into the deck. The
two engines roared as the pilot went to full throttle and
the airplane strained against the steel cable of the ar-
resting gear. Our heads and shoulders were thrown
back. It was an unsettling feeling even though I'd experienced it before. The COD folded its wings as it taxied
off the landing area of the flight deck and over toward
the island where the rear ramp was lowered. We were
escorted off the COD and directly into the island.

As the others were being led away by various escorts,
Cruz turned to Kristen and me and said loudly, "I know
that you were in the navy, Mr. Caskey, so welcome back.
I'll be your escort during your time aboard *Reagan*. If
you need anything at all, you can call me. I'll be with
you throughout your entire time here, if you have to interview anyone, I'll be there. Not to oversee it, but to
help you; I'll also guide you to meals and wherever else
you need to go. I will be accessible twenty-four hours a

day and you can feel free to call me for anything. Since it is only 1430, I've lined up the first interview as the one you wanted the most, Mr. Caskey. We're going to go see the admiral. We have an appointment at 1530 in the admiral's mess. They'll have coffee and snacks available and you are free to ask the admiral anything you'd like." He gestured toward the passageway. "Let me take you to your staterooms. They're right next to each other on the 03 level."

Kristen said, "Thanks very much. May I take a shower?"

He nodded. "No problem. I hope you brought a robe. The women's head is about a hundred yards down the passageway."

At 1525, Cruz was standing outside our staterooms, in his khaki uniform. I noticed the wings on his uniform. "What do you fly?"

"F-18s."

"What's your job now?"

"Hard to describe. I'm kind of like an aide, but I'm an extra. I don't wear the gold braid of an aide, but I'm assigned to the admiral. He calls me his special projects officer. I don't know what that means, but I do what I'm told."

"Sounds better than some jobs."

"It is. Some of the special projects are quite special. It varies all the way from intelligence to making coffee."

Kristen came out of her stateroom wearing slacks and a blouse that complemented her figure. As soon as Cruz saw her, he involuntarily looked at her clothes and figure and then caught himself and turned down the passageway. "Follow me." He began walking. He said over his shoulder to Kristen, "Watch out for the knee-knockers as we step through these hatchways, you can really rack your shin if you're not careful."

After a couple hundred steps we started walking on blue tile. Everything in the area was noticeably different. All the railings were wrapped with stiff, immaculate white rope. There wasn't a speck of dust anywhere. Cruz went to a door and knocked sharply twice and stepped through it. We followed him. We were in a part of the admiral's area that looked like a living room. There were couches and chairs. The admiral, with two stars on his collar, sat on one of the couches with his legs crossed talking on the telephone. When he saw us, he ended the conversation, hung up, and stood to greet us.

Cruz said, "Admiral, may I introduce to you Mr. John Caskey and Ms. Kristen Chambers." Cruz turned to us. "Mr. Caskey and Ms. Chambers, Admiral Michael Lewis."

He was average size with short-cropped gray hair and dark brown eyes. They were the darkest brown I'd ever seen. He was extremely tan and fit. He barely glanced at Kristen and walked to me. "Mr. Caskey, welcome back to the navy."

I smiled, took his hand, and said, "Thank you very much. I have to tell you I never expected to be in admiral's country again, sir."

"Well, we're glad you are. I can't think of a person better situated to defend our two men in Holland."

"Thank you, sir. May I introduce Kristen Chambers.

She's another attorney, from a big firm in New York and D.C., who is helping me."

He turned and looked at her and she extended her hand. He took it and said, "Nice to meet you, Ms. Chambers. Welcome aboard. Thank you for helping out in this case. I understand your firm has agreed to do this for free."

"Yes sir, we're honored to do it."

He smiled and his demeanor softened. "Well, I have to say that I'm surprised by that, but I appreciate it." He looked at me. "Please sit down. We've been instructed from the highest levels to cooperate with you in any way we can. So I take that to heart. I've asked a few other people to sit in with us. They'll be here shortly. I've asked Captain Cassidy, my intelligence officer, as well as Commander Bishop, the air wing intelligence officer, to join us. I've also asked Commander White, the ship's intelligence officer, to come, because frankly this is mostly about intelligence, isn't it? But I've also asked Captain McDonald, my air wing commander, to be here. I wanted to have you get here first so I could tell you who they were going to be and you could start writing down the names and the like." He looked at Kristen. "I see you are already doing that."

He looked at Cruz. "Lieutenant Cruz, why don't you go see if you can round them up. They should be in the admiral's mess."

Cruz nodded, disappeared, and reentered less than a minute later with all the men just mentioned. The admiral stood. "Gentlemen, please come in and have a seat."

We found ourselves surrounded by the collective brains of the battle group that had been in place the night the attack occurred as they took seats at various chairs and couches. The admiral directed his attention to me. "So, Mr. Caskey, fire away."

"Well, Admiral, let's begin with you. You were the commanding officer of the battle group when this all occurred?"

"Yes."

"What was the mission?"

He spoke softly but very clearly. Very precisely, as if he were considering each word just before he said it. "It was a night of multiple missions. As I'm sure you know, we have a rolling target list depending on where we're operating and what we're trying to accomplish. When there is an assault ongoing, there are targets of response within many kill boxes, such as troop movements and mortar positions and the like, which are determined by people on the ground and radioed to the CAOC, the combined air operations center. We also have close air support for active engagements. But then of course there are the targets off the target list. That list is compiled over a lengthy period of time and refreshed every day. It is based on intelligence, knowledge, anything else we can bring to bear to give us the right targets. We're always looking for high-value targets from al Qaeda and the like. If there is good information developed it makes it onto the list. But we have to have confirmation that the target is a good one, and preferably active photograph intelligence confirming the target location. We can then correlate all that targeting information. Then we prepare the air tasking order and execute our attack plan."

"I think I got most of that."

The admiral continued. "But let's get to what you're interested in. How did we have the target that turned out to be the refugee facility. I'm going to ask Captain Cassidy to explain that to you."

He turned toward his intelligence officer. Cassidy nodded, his face contorted. He was very unhappy. "In short, Mr. Caskey, we got had. But the exact specifics of how that all happened required that several things come into play at once. We had multiple platforms airborne that night in, as the admiral said, multiple kill boxes—restricted attack locations designated for each platform. There was a lot of Taliban and al Qaeda activity in the mountains of Pakistan and the eastern mountains of Afghanistan. As you know, we're right back into the Vietnam and Cambodia situation. The Taliban retreats into the mountains of Pakistan where they are usually left alone—unless they do something stupid like try and take over the Swat Valley as they did in 2009. Then they forced Pakistan's hand and they had to get them out. But if they stay in the tribal areas, the essentially ungovernable mountains, they're left alone. Well we don't leave them alone as long as we can get away with it. Pakistan tries to tell us what we can and can't do, which we try to listen to, but we go after them where we can find them. We've had some bad luck with some of our UAVs"—he looked at Kristen—"those are unmanned aerial vehicles, or drones. Many of them are armed and do some of the dirty work in areas that are more dangerous." Kristen nodded and he continued.

"So we had some navy and air force assets airborne in Afghanistan, and the Pakistani missions were being flown by the UAVs we had airborne—Predators. We had been aware of a potential meeting between al Qaeda and the Taliban. They have not worked well together in the past and there were indications that they were going to start working together. Obviously, if they're going to start working together, they pretty much have to be together physically, since they know we monitor any radio or telephone traffic. So they have to send messengers and arrange meetings. Sometimes we hear about those meetings in advance, but they don't happen very often, and never at the highest level. Well, this was supposed to be the big meeting. The chief of the Taliban from the mountain region of Afghanistan and Pakistan was going to meet with somebody from al Qaeda. We weren't sure who, but it was somebody within the top circle of the organization. If they were going to meet, we had to be there. In fact, we had several special ops units in the area from all the services. We didn't know where this meeting was going to occur, but we had fairly good intelligence—"

I interrupted. "From whom? Who was this great intelligence from?"

"Several sources. We had HUMINT from Afghanistan, as well as some confirmation from Pakistan. We were confident that this was real. We were ready depending on when this meeting was going to happen, but we didn't know." He looked around at the others, who knew what was coming next.

"We got a flash message just before the meeting was supposed to take place. Timing was critical. All our Predators were winchester—out of weapons—and when we got the coordinates from the ISI—Pakistani intelligence—with a satellite photo of the building, we knew we had to go for it. None of our ops teams were close enough. So we had an expected meeting, confirmation of the meeting, a latitude/longitude that was correct and correlated to an area that we expected them to meet in, and a satellite photo of the building in which the meeting was to occur. All we had to do was forward the latitude and longitude to the target aircraft, and they were given the order to drop. We sent it, and they dropped a JDAM and hit the target exactly like they should have done. They did absolutely nothing wrong. They hit the intended target—"

Commander McDonald, the commander of the air wing, interrupted. "And only then did we find out that it was a refugee medical facility." He looked at the three intelligence officers. "Why did we not know that was a refugee medical facility? That's the question I have."

I looked at all the others. "Why did we not know?"

The intelligence officers looked at each other. Finally Bishop, the air wing intelligence officer, spoke. "Basically because we didn't have time. We had to drop on the meeting or we were going to miss it. The decision was made to execute."

I looked at the group. I could feel the tension between them, because obviously things had not gone as they expected. Everyone thought they had one of the leaders of al Qaeda trapped in a meeting with the Taliban, and hadn't done their homework. They had skipped a step, and it had come back to bite them. And I was about to find out who was going to get bit. "Who gave the go-ahead?"

The admiral spoke immediately. "I did."

I asked, "Why didn't you get confirmation from our own targeting database? Or check more photos of the building, to see if we had any?"

There was no immediate answer.

I asked, "Has anyone checked since then?"

The admiral answered, "We've now looked at everything. We had one photo, but we didn't check our other image files as that building had been listed as a target several times. Each time it was listed, the target was ultimately pulled because nothing had happened there. It was, apparently, a well-known building. One of the larger buildings in the area, sort of a multipurpose place. Sometimes inhabited, sometimes used for tribal council meetings, that sort of thing. But it was not always a target. Only when there was going to be a meeting, and those meetings were very fleeting."

I was puzzled. "How do you know any of those meetings were legitimate? How do you know you hadn't been told about all of these supposed meetings by the ISI just so you could get this image in your database? Just so this could be listed as a target, which was all part of this long-term plan to get you to drop on it at exactly the wrong moment?"

The admiral shook his head. "It was based on our own intelligence, as well as the Pakistanis'. What I want to know is who gave the European refugee association the building for their medical facility. How did that happen? We have no idea. It may be that they moved in there on their own."

I shook my head. "No, I was just there. They were set to go in there for a couple of months."

Bishop, the air wing intelligence officer, said, "Well . . . we don't know that for sure. It's possible. Our one photo was at least six months old. But we thought we had good intel on the place, and even retrospectively our intelligence looks good. Although in retrospect it appears a little less perfect than we thought at the time. The flash message only gave us the latitude and longitude. But as you said, we had the latitude and longitude of that building for a long time. The confirmation that it was a meeting, and that we only had thirty or forty minutes—whatever the time was—came by verbal radio message from Pakistan."

"It was from a gentleman within Pakistani intelligence with whom we had dealt many times. We had no doubt."

"Do you remember his name?"

"Yes. He was identified as," he looked at the others, "I don't remember his name. He used sort of a nickname."

"I just met with Pakistani intelligence in Islamabad. They say they told you that there was a refugee facility at that location, and that the meeting was going to go on with the refugees present."

Commander White, the *Reagan*'s intelligence officer, spoke up. "I don't think that happened. I wasn't on the radio call, but that's not the information that we were working with."

Kristen looked shocked. "Surely, you guys record these conversations?"

They all shook their heads. "No. Radio communications are not recorded."

"You've got to be . . . are you sure?"

"Yes. But you must understand. When we say 'we' had a conversation with him, it wasn't anyone on this ship. The conversation was between him and the air force intelligence officer at the center in Qatar."

Kristen asked, "Why there?"

The air wing commander said, "That's where the air tasking order is published every night for the next twenty-four hours. All the information goes to them and they issue targeting instructions to all of the available platforms, including navy. So the actual conversation was between an air force officer and the Pakistani."

I sat back on the couch and took a deep breath. I thought about how this all would play into the trial, and what if any of it was going to be admissible as evidence. I turned to Admiral Lewis. "Sounds to me like the only thing that went wrong was that the target was not understood to be a refugee center and that we weren't given time to sort it out. Both of those things feel intentional to me."

He agreed. "No doubt about it. We were set up. And it's not just about this attack. And it's not just about these two naval aviators." The admiral sat forward. "This is about trying to humiliate the United States. This is about indicting President Bush and the others, and now trying to intimidate President Obama into backing off from freeing our men. They have us right where they want us."

I said, "I have a line on the air force officer, I think he's on his way back to the United States. He's been rotated out. My contact in the White House is helping me track him down. But what do we do now, Admiral? How do we prove any of this? Will you testify?"

The admiral said nothing. He sat back, looking at the others around the table, probably wondering whether he should have had his JAG officer present, and finally said, "I'd do anything to get them out of there. If you need me to come to Holland to testify, I'll be happy to do it. I'll tell them exactly what I told you."

I nodded. "I may take you up on that, Admiral. But before I go and find that air force officer, I want to do two things. First, I want to see all the message traffic that you can let me see; if it's top secret, please line out the stuff I can't see, but I've got to see the traffic. Then we have to go to Qatar to see if they record these conversations." I turned to Lieutenant Cruz. "Can you send them a message and let them know we're coming and have somebody there to meet us just like you did here for us?"

"Better than that. I'll go with you. I'll get the message traffic together and we can look at it tonight in the admiral's wardroom. We'll make copies of whatever you need, and either the admiral or somebody else can authenticate it for your trial."

# SIXTEEN

Kristen and I stayed up late that night reading piles of messages. They gave us everything, even messages that were labeled top secret and had not been redacted. It was amazing information. Most of it had to do with the entire targeting plan, and they had also shown us the air tasking order, the ATO as it was affectionately known. A lot of people thought the ATO didn't give them enough flexibility in responding to a crisis or a target that revealed itself late in the day. But it seemed that this very event showed that the tasking order was flexible enough to respond to whatever arose. And that had been the Achilles' heel of the entire operation. They had accepted the intelligence from a Pakistani they thought they could trust and had executed on that intelligence immediately.

The message traffic was exactly as they had said it would be. Everything was exactly in order, and everything lined up perfectly. The one missing piece was what the Pakistani had said to the air force officer. None of the men we had spoken with was on the radio. They had all heard it relayed, but none had heard the communication itself. I had been assuming that what they had said was accurate, that the Pakistani intelligence officer had told them it was a clear target and that they could hit it. But I had to at least consider the possibility that he had told them exactly what Qazi had told me had been said. I thought that possibility was so remote as to be nonexistent, but I had to consider it. It was hard for me to imagine that they had heard that it was a refugee medical facility, that al Qaeda and the Taliban were going to meet there while it was manned by Europeans, and that we would attack it anyway. That was not possible. If that were the case, we would have sent in special operations teams and surrounded it, and taken anybody who exited the building. And fundamentally, how did anybody know that the meeting was going to take place? It had to come from human intelligence inside either al Qaeda or the Taliban. And who was to say *that* was reliable? I'd seen enough issues with intel in my days, particularly HUMINT, to know it was tricky in the extreme to know what was true. Usually you looked for confirmation.

Equally important though, how was the prosecutor going to prove what the knowledge, then intent, was of the Americans when the bombing occurred? Without the Pakistani intelligence officer testifying for him, he wouldn't be able to show any particular state of knowledge.

I continued reading the messages and thinking

about the implications. I marked thirty of them for copying, and Lieutenant Cruz had them duplicated for me. A couple of them had redacted sections because of their classification, but the rest were fairly clean. They would definitely show that the targeting coordinates were identified only thirty minutes before the attack occurred. It then took those thirty minutes to run it through the targeting group at the CAOC, as well as assign the target to the only available platform, Raw and Dunk. It was a pretty clear story. But I needed to follow up in Qatar.

Kristen and Cruz and I got up early the next morning and had breakfast in the aviator's wardroom. I had eaten on carriers but had forgotten how good the food was. They had fresh eggs and bacon, orange juice, and coffee in large urns. Many of the pilots were there with us long before the usual duty day as they were on the first launch of the day, set to go at 0715, so at 0500 the wardroom was much fuller than I had expected. We were scheduled out on the COD on the first launch and Cruz wanted to make sure we didn't miss it. He had made arrangements to have sailors carry our gear up to the island so we could be ready to go out to the COD first thing. We would be the first airplane off the deck. Other strikes were heading out to Afghanistan and some flying over northern Iraq.

As we went up to the island after breakfast, Cruz reiterated to us the admiral was willing to testify, more than willing. I told Cruz that I planned on calling the admiral to testify. I also told him that based on the

ICC's indictment of Bush and the others, they might indict the admiral as the one truly responsible. And put him in the hoosegow. Cruz said the admiral had already considered that and would take the risk.

I was surprised. I didn't expect him to step up to that extent. Too often admirals went political at the worst possible moment. Not this one.

We boarded the COD on the silent but windy flight deck as the aircrews manned their aircraft for the first launch. Our COD was positioned on catapult three, pointed down the angled deck into the darkness, where the sea and sky were indistinguishable. We put on our helmets with ear protection and our flotation vests— which should be called burial vests on a COD, because that's the only function they would have if this airplane didn't get airborne off the catapult—and the pilots started the engines. We took our aft-facing seats and strapped in. After taxiing forward slightly, the engines went to full power. The catapult fired, the hold-back released, and the COD rattled down the catapult as our feet flew up off the deck of the aircraft involuntarily in response to the rapid acceleration forward. Noise lessened and the acceleration stopped as we reached flying speed and pulled away from the ocean.

I was sitting next to one of the few portholelike windows on the airplane and could now see the deep blue water next to us, maybe sixty feet away. We had settled slightly off the angled deck, but I could feel us climbing away from the ocean. The COD rattled again as the pilot raised the gear and flaps and we turned toward Qatar.

\* \* \*

We flew directly to Al Udeid Air Base, the massive air force base in Qatar where the CAOC was located, the Combined Air Operations Center. It was where the air force intelligence and targeting officer had been stationed, and where all the intelligence was gathered for preparation of the nightly air tasking order. The COD's air-conditioning was poor but was still better than the furnace that existed outside the aircraft. After a two-hour flight we landed without incident. When we came to a stop and the engines were silent, we stepped onto the blistering tarmac. It wasn't even 7:30 and it was already over a hundred degrees.

Cruz had arranged for a car to pick us up. Kristen and I jumped in the back and Cruz got in the front with the navy petty officer driver. He took us to a large building in the center of the base. As we came to a stop he said, "They're expecting us."

We followed Cruz out of the car and into the wonderfully air-conditioned building. Cruz pointed to a hallway to the left of the lobby, and opened the door for us as we passed through it. After a long walk, we entered a conference room. There were two men and one woman waiting for us. They were all senior officers, a navy captain, an air force colonel, and an army lieutenant colonel. They stood as we entered, offered us seats. An air force sergeant in the corner was preparing a tray of coffee cups and muffins.

Cruz said, "Colonel Wright," indicating the female air force colonel who must be senior to the navy captain, "Captain Surrey, and Lieutenant Colonel Black." He then pointed to us. "This is Jack Caskey, John actually, and his associate, Kristen Chambers."

Colonel Wright was staring at me, and not in a friendly way. The kind of look when someone has to deal with you but wishes you weren't there. We exchanged greetings and small talk, as the coffee was placed around the table. Lieutenant Cruz, who was adept at controlling meetings, said to Colonel Wright, "I'm sure you've seen the message traffic about Mr. Caskey and how we are all to cooperate with him to our fullest capability."

Wright nodded but said nothing. Cruz continued. "He's already met with the battle group commander, and the air wing commander, and the heads of intelligence of the admiral's staff and the air wing, as well as the *Reagan*'s, but the air tasking order—and the specific target assignment—came from here, and the conversation with the Pakistani intelligence officer was also from here. Now it's my—"

Colonel Wright interrupted him. "We know all that."

Cruz was surprised. Cruz had mentioned her specifically when we were eating breakfast. He had tried not to say too much, probably in the hope she'd behave herself. She had graduated first in her class from the Air Force Academy, had wanted to be a pilot but was physically disqualified. She went into intelligence and had a chip on her shoulder. She was incredibly bright, but mean.

Cruz waited to see if she was going to say anything else, and seeing that she was not, continued. "Rather than me restating everything then, why don't I just let Jack here ask whatever questions he has."

Colonel Wright sipped from her coffee and said nothing. She continued to stare at me. Never being one to dodge an issue, I asked her, "Is there some problem here, Colonel Wright? You seem annoyed."

She paused, then said softly, "That's your first question? We took a break in the prosecution of the war to meet with you to answer your questions—which I don't really have an interest in doing—and you want to know whether I'm *annoyed*?"

I nodded slowly. "Yes. Because it seems you have something against me, or against what I'm doing. And if you do, I want to address that first and get it out of the way."

She breathed in audibly through her nose and then exhaled. "I didn't know that I was exhibiting hostility. If I had to trace it back, it is probably my antipathy toward attorneys."

I was surprised. "You hate attorneys?"

"Yes. I think they are a scourge. I think they are parasites. I think they take a lot of what's good about our country and make it bad. I think they are liars, and evil."

I stared into her eyes. I thought for a moment and then said, "So you're divorced."

She looked as if she'd just been Tasered. "My personal life has nothing to do with this."

"Maybe. But I'm thinking your personal life may account for this opinion about attorneys. I don't really care. People can hold irrational opinions all they want. I just don't want you holding it against me right now. Can we get into the issues here?"

"Yes," she said icily.

I glanced at Cruz, who looked like he was going to throw up. I looked at the other three and said, "Let me cut to the chase. What can you give to me that shows how the decision was made to attack this target?"

Kristen added, "Documents and message traffic would be most helpful. We have to prove this, not just assert it."

Lieutenant Colonel Black said, "Thought you already had the message traffic."

Kristen responded. "We do. We have the traffic that was available on the *Reagan*. But you may have traffic we haven't seen. We'd like to look at whatever message traffic you have before and after this event to see if there's anything in there we could use."

Wright said sarcastically, "A fishing expedition I take it?"

I looked at her with renewed intensity. "Fishing is one way to put it, I guess, but I would put it that we are looking for evidence that will help us. Do you have some problem with that concept?"

She leaned forward on her elbows. "We're fighting a war here. We don't have time for this."

I said, "Well do you have time to get the two Americans out of prison in Holland without looking for evidence? Can you think of how we're going to do that? Can *you* do that?"

"Does this surprise you when we keep killing civilians accidentally that at some point someone has to be held accountable?"

I glanced at Kristen and then the two intelligence officers, who were surprised by the colonel's response.

I replied, "Are you implying that we've been reckless? That we don't care about civilian casualties? Because that's the opposite of my experience. So if we've been out there throwing bombs around and not caring whether we kill a bunch of innocent civilians, I guess I should know that right now."

"Of course not. That's not what I'm saying at all. It's just the way the world works, when bad things happen, somebody has to be 'accountable,' whether they're responsible or not. There always has to be a sacrificial lamb."

I frowned. "It sounds like you're okay with that. That it doesn't matter who's accountable, or whether there's any evidence to support it."

She looked at Cruz, then at her watch. "I have to get back to work. What else can I tell you?"

I said quickly, "Let's start with what you know about the night this attack occurred. Was the attack on the target that ended up being a European medical facility authorized?"

"Yes," she said.

"Was it based on intelligence that was authenticated by you? The people sitting in this room?"

I saw them squirm ever so slightly. No one wanted to answer the question. Finally, Colonel Wright said, "We accepted the intelligence from Pakistan, and acted on it. There was no way to verify it. The verification comes from spending years relying on information from given sources. You begin to trust the source. That can lead you down what you think is a rosy path that turns out to be full of thorns."

I said, "My understanding is that Major Curley is the one who actually spoke with the Pakistani intelligence officer. Do I have his name right?"

They nodded.

"And where is he now?"

"He's been reassigned to Washington, working at the Pentagon for the Air Force ISR Agency. Intelligence, Surveillance and Reconnaissance."

"When is he due to report there?"

"He's taking thirty day's leave."

I looked up at them. "Who knows where to find him?"

Black said, "He's getting married. He's from Wyoming and his wife is from Nevada. I think they were going to Vegas on their honeymoon."

I was writing. "Anyone have his cell?"

"I do," Black answered.

"All right. Was anyone else on the line when he spoke with that Pakistani intelligence officer?"

Black said, "May have been somebody from the *Reagan*. We thought it would be their tasking as it was late in the day."

I looked at Colonel Wright. "Why aren't these conversations recorded?"

"Because you're creating a top secret recording with a foreign intelligence officer's identifiable voice. They requested that we not record them. They don't believe the United States can keep anything classified, let alone their identities, if recorded. So it's better to never create the recording in the first place."

Black had a thin file in front of him. He opened it

slowly and took out a single piece of paper. "Since I thought we'd be talking about this, I wanted to bring you the notes Major Curley took from that conversation." He handed me the piece of paper.

I looked at it, looked up at him, looked back at the notes. "He took notes?"

"They're really just notations. I don't think they reflect the entire conversation."

It was a single piece of paper, unlined, like printing paper, on which he had made numerous notations. There were some doodles, but most of the notes were abbreviations and made no sense. There were two lines across the page and in the middle of those two lines was the information about the critical conversation, or so I thought. "This stuff here in the middle between these lines . . . is that where he made notes during the conversation with the Pakistani intelligence officer?"

"Yes."

I stared at them and thought I understood them completely, but asked, "What do you think they mean?"

"Well, if you look right there, he's got the time, which is 1816 Zulu, which local time, since we're east, is 2216. Then in the middle after that he says, 'new target—AQ/T.' I think by that he means, in fact I'm pretty sure, al Qaeda/Taliban. This is the meeting we had been waiting for for a long time. There is a little bit of a power struggle between al Qaeda and the Taliban particularly in the mountains of western Pakistan. We'd been expecting this meeting, and it had been confirmed by several separate and independent intelligence sources. When we got this call that this meeting was going to happen, we weren't surprised at all. Nor were we surprised by the location, at least in general. So I think that's what that means." He looked up at me and made sure I was looking at the right section of the paper. "You can see the latitude and longitude. He has it down to the second."

"Did you check those coordinates on a chart?"

"He did. We wanted to confirm it was an actual target."

"What did he find?"

Colonel Wright interjected, "It wasn't a previously identified target, although it had been mentioned before as a potential target. It wasn't on our target list that day at all. So we didn't really have time to check it out."

"Was there a targeting folder for that building?"

"No. No targeting folder. Just a few old photos."

Kristen asked, "Have you looked at pictures and intelligence on that location that we had at the time?"

"Yes."

"Can we see them?" Kristen asked, looking around innocently. "Can we also see the satellite and photography of the building after the bombing?"

The three intelligence officers looked at each other reluctantly. No one spoke. I didn't intervene. I didn't give them an out. I said nothing. Finally, they had to say something. Wright said, "Those are classified."

I nodded understandingly. "Yes, but you received the message that you are to help us in any way you can. So we'd like to see them. Could make a big difference."

Lieutenant Cruz interjected. "Why don't you let me

take a look at them and see if they're so classified that they can't be released."

Wright looked at him with contempt. "Do you think that we don't have a better feel for that than you might, Lieutenant?"

Cruz shrugged. "I was just trying to help. I think you ought to bring these photos into this room and a navigational chart so we can get what we can out of this."

Colonel Wright said, "Let's bring them in. Get the folder."

My ears perked up. A folder, something which was currently not in the room. The only thing we had in front of us was a single piece of paper that Lieutenant Colonel Black had decided to let me look at. He knew Wright was talking to him, so he got up, left the room, and returned in two minutes. He had a file, possibly an inch thick, and sat down where he had been. He opened the file, and slid it across the table to Kristen and me. It had pre-bombing photos, post-bombing photos, the aeronautical chart that would confirm that location, and other message traffic that would correlate to the night of the attack. I leafed through it and looked up. "Can we have this?"

"We made that copy for you, but weren't sure whether we were going to give it to you," Wright said reluctantly. "I'm still not sure we're going to give it to you. There is classified information on there."

"I don't really see any. There are satellite photos which I suppose could help someone determine what the quality of our satellite photography is, but these are not particularly high-resolution photographs. They are certainly not maximum-resolution, which I could tell you as a matter of fact. They look like generic satellite photos that you might get off Google Earth. So I don't think we would raise any eyebrows if we produced these. But I like that they show what the building looked like before and after, and that the bomb hit is dead center in the roof of the target. No one can argue this is reckless. We hit the target we were aiming for. The message traffic seems to be the same as what we saw aboard the *Reagan*, but I'd like to be able to study it. And I don't need to be here wasting your time doing that."

They looked at each other and finally Wright nodded. "Yes. But you need to get clearance before you put those into the public as exhibits in the trial."

I nodded. "I will."

As I closed the file and prepared to put it in the briefcase and looked at the single sheet of paper with Curley's notes on it again. I looked at Lieutenant Colonel Black. "I have one more question about these notes."

"Sure."

"Look at the bottom of the center section. Where the line is. Do you see in the bottom-right-hand corner it has two initials. RG. What is that?"

He frowned. "I hadn't really thought about it, but I assumed those were his initials."

"He initialed the middle of the page?"

"I assumed so. His first name is Russell."

"What's his middle name?"

"I don't know." The other intelligence officer, not

Colonel Wright, said, "It was McNamara. Everybody used to ask him if he was related to Robert McNamara, which he wasn't. So his first two initials would be RM, and his last name was Curley. So that would be RC."

I looked down more carefully at the writing. It was clearly "RG." I looked at everyone in the room one at a time. I said quietly, "Is it possible it's his abbreviation for 'refugee'?"

As we rode in the white navy car back to the airport terminal everyone was silent. Cruz, Kristen, and I all thought about what the meeting we had just completed meant. Cruz finally spoke first as the air-conditioning in the car finally began to take effect and push back the Arabian heat. Cruz couldn't take it anymore. "So did that meeting help us or hurt us?"

I glanced at him. "Who's us?"

"The prisoners. The defendants."

"Well, it helps us unless RG means refugees, in which case it kills us."

Kristen said, "Unless he said there are *occasionally* refugees there, or there *used* to be refugees. Depends on what it means."

"There's no 'used to,' or 'formerly,' or 'sometimes' near those initials."

"Nobody needs to see them at all," Kristen said, thinking about whether to even offer them this document into evidence.

I looked at her. "We've got to talk to Curley."

"Now?"

"Yes. Right now. We're going to go find him."

"In Vegas? I don't have any more clothes."

"I'll buy you some." I said to Cruz, "Have the driver take us to the terminal. We've got to book tickets to Vegas."

# SEVENTEEN

By the time we got to the airline counter I was asleep on my feet. The entire case hung on what was said to Curley. My clients' lives were at stake, and to have any chance of exoneration, I had to get *irrefutable* evidence. Russell McNamara Curley was the key. I bought tickets in business class. I needed to be able to talk to Kristen without anyone overhearing.

We boarded in order and were assigned our seats, although seats don't quite capture the idea. More like pods. They had little curved walls behind and to the sides of each seat with a foot rest in front and a leather seating area that had a thousand different adjustments and buttons. It was amazing. I had never flown business class in my life. The cost was ridiculous, but I was starting to think maybe after this I could write a book or give a speech somewhere. Maybe I could get paid to discuss what had happened at the International Criminal Court, and maybe I'd be able to pay for these seats. Certainly my clients couldn't, and I didn't really have authorization from the United States government to fly business class, and knowing the government, they would far rather have me suffer than pay me to fly business class, even if it was a two-hundred-hour flight. Of course my speaker's fee would probably be less if I showed up to tell everyone how I got my clients convicted of war crimes and incarcerated for life.

We got airborne as the sun was setting. After we leveled out, the beautiful flight attendant offered us drinks. I ordered a Stella for myself and a Chardonnay for Kristen. I got up from my pod and went around the wall to hers. I sat on her immovable footstool and handed her the wine. She smiled and put her head back. She took a sip of the Chardonnay and a deep breath. She had her shoes off and her feet were crossed on the side of the stool to my back. She was wearing a very lightweight black blouse with fitted gray slacks. Her hair was a little bit straighter than usual, probably due to the dry heat. She wore no makeup, but didn't need any. The faint freckles on her cheeks showed pleasantly. Her usually bright blue eyes looked subdued. I said, "You tired?"

"Exhausted. I don't think I've put my feet up, let alone had a glass of wine, since we started this whirlwind."

"Neither have I. I feel sort of guilty right now for not poring through documents or researching international law."

She nodded and took another sip. "How do you think we're doing on our case preparation?"

I studied her face and decided to go in a different direction. "I'd rather talk about you."

She looked surprised. "What about me?"

I looked around as I saw the flight attendant dim all the cabin lights. It left us in near darkness, with only the reading lamps illuminating the pods in the nearly full business class section. "Why didn't you walk out when Terry stormed out in his fit of righteous indignation?"

She shook her head. "He was being an ass."

I pressed her. "You didn't agree with him?"

"I've met these two guys. They deserve a lot better than this. Who could possibly say that they deserve to go to prison for life? Even if you disagree with the war in Iraq, or Afghanistan, or even going into Pakistan. They were just doing what they were told."

I held out my beer for her to touch with her wineglass. She did. I said, "Thanks for sticking with me. If you had left, the whole room would have come unraveled, and I wouldn't have had any help. I can't do this by myself."

She smiled. "We do have a whole army of DOJ lawyers helping us, and my firm has a lot of people on it. So you're not exactly alone."

"True. And frankly I don't want to play second fiddle to someone else. I keep expecting to be replaced by some super big shot because I've said something they don't like."

"You *are* the super big shot. You are the hero of the D.C. criminal bar and you got those Marines off last year. You are the guy. You have recent game experience and you're former military. Who else would they go to? Some government lawyer who has never defended anybody? Just prosecuted? I don't think so." She took a sip. "Think we'll find Curley?"

"I texted Chris from the airport. I told him to do whatever it took to find him. Even if we had to interrupt his freaking honeymoon." I leaned forward a little bit and hesitated. "But what about you and me?"

"What about us?"

"Do you still think I'm a right-wing lunatic crazy person like you did in law school?"

She looked at my face, evaluating it carefully. The hundreds of tiny little watchmaker gears inside her head were spinning almost inaudibly. "Probably."

I laughed out loud. "Yet somehow I'm more tolerable now?"

"I never thought you were evil. In law school I thought you were hot. You were older than the rest of us. And you were—and still are I might add—in phenomenal shape, and have seen things and done things the rest of us don't understand at all. But we probably, myself included, thought it was morally questionable. 'Course we don't know that. I just like to assign myself to the side of moral superiority, it makes me feel better about myself."

"You're still single though, right?"

"None of your business."

"I'm making it my business. Are you dating anybody?"

She leaned her head back momentarily, then closed her eyes. She took another sip of Chardonnay. "I already told you I wasn't. I'm a little surprised it took you this long to get around to asking. I figured I'd be fighting you off with a stick on day two. You thought about asking me out in law school."

"I did think about it. But thought you'd say no because we disagreed about everything politically, so it was pointless. Probably a bad idea then. May still be."

"I don't think you have to be completely compatible. If you were, it might be a little weird. "

I studied her pretty face and her soft features. "Maybe. So what do you think? Think we might get together?"

"You're pressing a little, Jack."

She was right. I said, "I can see forty from here. If I'm ever going to get married . . ."

"Oh, so I might be the solution to your aging problem."

"Just need one available female. You were the closest one in business class likely to speak English when this thought first hit me."

"You really want to go out with me? Seriously?"

"Maybe."

She exhaled slowly for a long time. "It would complicate things. I don't think we have time for the emotional complications. Plus, I'm not living in Washington."

"Well that's getting ahead of ourselves a little bit. I just said go out, not get married. And if somebody had to move, if it ever got to that point, I'd probably be happy to move to New York. I don't make any money, so it wouldn't be like I'd be giving up a huge thriving practice. I get by, but I'm not really getting ahead. I need a change. I really need a change. I'm starting to vanish into my own unremarkable life."

"Representing these two navy men in front of the

whole world ought to change your profile quite a bit."
She changed the subject deftly. "Would you send the
military in if you were the president?"

"Yes. Well, probably. I might wait till after the trial.
If they were actually convicted, then I might break them
out. If they're exonerated, everyone can claim victory.
But I sure wouldn't let them go to prison for life. I can
tell you that. And we can't do any kind of an exchange.
You can't exchange one spy for another or one prisoner
for another. I mean frankly, they are political prisoners.
Nobody can really dispute that. And the Europeans are
going to make whatever they can out of it. The problem
is if you wait until they're convicted, you'll have to
break into the prison to get them. And if the president
does that, a lot of people are going to get killed."

"You think we can get them off?"

"I don't think it matters what we do."

"Then why go to all this effort?"

"Because we have to. We have to show the world that
they're innocent. I don't want them to just take our word
for it, because they wouldn't. We, America, never get
the benefit of the doubt. And since this will be broadcast live around the entire universe, if we show they did
nothing wrong, and they're convicted, it will do what it
should, undermine the legitimacy of the International
Criminal Court."

"I think it is legitimate. I just don't think they should
be able to try somebody from a country that didn't sign
the treaty."

"I've got no problem either if they charge someone
from a country that signed the treaty." I looked around

for the flight attendant, and saw her in the galley. I lifted my Stella and pointed to it. She nodded. "So, are we going to get together or not?"

"I don't know." She paused. "If I'm honest, I kinda doubt it. We seem to be on different paths. But who knows."

# EIGHTEEN

I'm not a fan of Las Vegas and don't like going there.
I'd passed through a couple times in my military days,
but not since. As we landed I could see it had changed
a lot. I turned on my phone and checked for texts. I had
one from Chris that said, "Found him. He's ready to
talk. Call him."

I turned to Kristen. "Chris found him. I'll call him
as soon as we get out of the airport."

"You promised I could go shopping before we meet
him. I'm starting to smell."

"I promise."

"And you're buying."

The concierge at the Mandalay Bay said if we couldn't
find what we were looking for at the shops within the
hotel property that we should go to the Forum Shops at
Caesars Palace. I'd been to those shops once before. It
was an indoor mall with no windows, air-conditioning
everywhere, and a ceiling painted like the sky. Many

of the shops were designer shops and ridiculously expensive. Nothing a normal person would ever buy in a normal setting. Only in Vegas where money didn't seem real because you lose so much of it so quickly. Five hundred dollars didn't seem like that much money. You could lose that in five minutes at the craps table. Actually, you could lose it much faster than that if you were determined.

Kristen was determined to lose my money on some of the designer clothing that she now lusted for. I didn't really have much patience for clothes shopping. My head was spinning with all the information that we had received in our stops in the Persian Gulf. As she tried on yet another blouse I said, "I can't do this anymore. I feel like I've been drugged. Can't we just go to bed?"

She looked at her watch. "It's only seven-thirty. We haven't even eaten."

"What is it you want exactly?"

"I want an outfit that looks nice but casual. I want to impress him. He's an important witness."

"He's a major in the air force. He wouldn't know designer clothing from Target."

"I'll bet his wife would."

"Okay, I'll bet you. Let's go to Target."

"Very funny. I'm going over to Michael Kors."

I looked at my phone for any new e-mails or texts, and checked the time. I slid it back into my pocket and followed her into the shop. I stood there looking bored while she tried on several outfits. I did have to admit that she looked good, but the outfit she ultimately picked about broke me. It was a pair of jeans that looked like a thousand other pairs of jeans I'd seen on women, although tighter, and a sort of fluffy blouse with a neckline that I can't describe. It was layered and low-cut at the same time, and then a short jacket that, as she put it, "completed the outfit." All I know is that it cost me $843. I pretended like it was pretend money, and smiled as I handed the clerk my credit card. I was probably going to get a call from American Express pretty shortly due to my business class tickets all over the world and now women's designer clothes in Vegas. Not my usual spending patterns of automatically renewing *Outside* magazine, my annual national park pass, and Netflix.

Kristen looked pleased, although her fatigue was starting to show. She said, "Buy me dinner. I think that restaurant right over there would be fine." It was an "outdoor" sidewalk café kind of restaurant under the painted ceiling of the Forum Shops called Trevi, and, of course, had an elaborate fountain that was incredible. We sat on the patio, next to the "Fountain of the Gods." It was cool, quiet, and gorgeous.

We ate in near silence. We were both starving, and tried not to show it as we forced ourselves to eat slowly rather than shoveling the delicious food into our mouths. I had ordered a nice Chianti as well, which may not have been too smart. It was acting like a sedative on my already exhausted body.

As we finished our dinner my phone rang. I looked at the number and glanced up at Kristen. "It's him."

I answered it. "Jack Caskey."

"Hi, this is Russell Curley. I understand you're here

and want to meet with me." His voice sounded confident and annoyed.

"Hi, yes. Thanks for calling. I'm here with my associate, Kristen Chambers."

"I'm on my honeymoon."

"Yes. I know. I'm really sorry to intrude. But as I'm sure you know, there are two Americans about to go on trial for war crimes in The Hague."

"I saw that."

"Listen, we don't want to interrupt. All we need is thirty minutes of your time. Do you think you could meet with us to see if you could help these guys get off?"

"Would that mean I'd have to testify in Holland?"

"I don't know. It depends on what you say."

"And then I would just be the next guy indicted, right? Right behind President Bush and Donald Rumsfeld."

I closed my eyes and tried to avoid telling him what I had to tell him. I looked at Kristen, who looked at me wondering what I was doing. I finally said, "I'm not going to lie to you. The prosecutor is . . . difficult. He may very well indict you. I don't think they would arrest you on the spot though. I don't think they want to escalate this thing with the U.S."

"Really? That's why they indicted our former president?"

"I hear you. But they're not trying to arrest him exactly."

Curley paused. "I'd love to help you, but like I said, I'm on my honeymoon. You have my cell number, just text me in a couple of weeks and I'll think about it." He hung up.

I looked at my phone and then at Kristen. I said, "The son of a bitch hung up on me! He doesn't want to meet with us." I dialed his number and it went straight to voicemail. "That *ass*hole. He's turned his phone off. Dammit!" I stared at my phone for a minute, then dialed Chris's number. He picked it up after the first ring.

"Yes?"

"Curley says he doesn't want to meet with us. He said I should text him in a couple of weeks after they're off their honeymoon and he'll think about it."

"Well, I guess you could wait until—"

"No. I'm not waiting for shit. Find out where the hell he's staying. You've got your ways. Have the freaking FBI look for him. Look under his wife's maiden name. And then send me his photo."

"I'll see what I can do."

"You have any contacts in the Las Vegas police?"

"I said I'll see what I can do." Chris hung up.

I put my phone back in my pocket as I stood up and picked up the bill. "Let's pay for this on the way out. We've got to go find him." I paid in cash and started walking quickly, heading back toward the main door where we could grab a taxi back to the Mandalay Bay. As we walked Kristen grabbed my arm and walked quickly with me, but restraining me slightly.

"You know why he doesn't want to meet with us, don't you?"

"No. Tell me."

"Because if what that Pakistani intelligence officer

said is true, then *he's* the one who screwed up. This whole thing would be his fault."

I looked at her. "It's not his fault. This is a setup." I pushed us on.

Kristen said, "Unless RG means . . ."

I was up all night drinking coffee and evaluating the implications if Curley disappeared. Disappeared as in became "unavailable." The air force wouldn't let him just go away, and I knew I could get him through the Pentagon eventually. But the question was before trial. I sent a new text to Chris that asked him not only for Curley's picture but also for his wife's. He told me he didn't have one, and I told him to go find one. Find the best man. If he's on his honeymoon there are about ten thousand pictures of both of them that are about a week old. Use every asset within the United States government to help me find these people.

Finally, I sat down in the leather chair in front of the television and put my head back, intending only to rest and went into a deep sleep. I was awakened by the tone on my phone that meant I had a text. I shook my head, and grabbed the phone and looked at the text. It was from Marshall. Curley and his wife were staying at the Paris Las Vegas hotel and pictures were attached. I clicked on the picture of Major Russell McNamara Curley, then on that of his wife. She was very attractive and should be easy to spot. She had very long blond hair.

I called Kristen. She was clearly asleep. I said, "I heard from Chris."

"What did he say?"

"They're staying at the Paris hotel. I've got photos of both of them."

She paused. "So what do you want to do?"

"We're going to go over there tonight. Why don't you get some sleep."

"That's what I was doing."

"Let's have breakfast around ten-thirty, then I'll go over to the Paris and scout it. Then tomorrow night, I will wager that they go out to dinner. When they do, we'll be there."

When we got to the Paris the next evening at 5:30 Kristen was wearing her new outfit and looking beautiful. She looked rested and eager for what was about to happen, although she had a lot of reservations. From my perspective by that time it was much less about hoping things would turn than forcing them to.

I was wearing an open-collared shirt and my suit coat as a poor man's sport coat. The casino section of the Paris was, like most casinos, in the front so that you had to walk through or by the casino to get anywhere, including the elevators.

Kristen stood next to me as I played craps on the table closest to the door. I made sure that from where I stood I faced the elevators and that to my left was the area that led to the restaurants in the hotel's self-contained sky-painted shopping area. It was actually quaint in a phony sort of way; it was made to resemble a French village with brick walkways and iron lampposts.

Kristen asked, "How am I going to recognize these

people? I've never seen them in real life. I don't think the pictures will do it."

"You'll recognize them. Look for a woman with long blond hair and a clean-cut guy who looks like he's in the military. If you see a couple like that at all, we'll check them out."

Kristen said, "She'll probably have her hair up."

"True. But if she does, there should be a good bit of it. She had a lot of hair."

"You don't know when that picture was taken and whether she's cut it. Or worse, dyed it."

"It was a wedding picture."

"Why is he being so elusive? Why so—"

I interrupted. "I think that's them. Come on." I picked up my few chips and put them in my pocket and indicated to the croupier that he could keep the bet that I had on the table.

Kristen began walking right at the couple. I pulled her back, and turned left toward the bakery. I grabbed her right hand and held it like we were a couple. She looked at me with some concern but also amusement.

Curley was in an ill-fitting Hawaiian shirt, black slacks, and sandals. It was a bad look. His wife was in a very small, tight black dress that fit her perfectly. As Kristen had predicted, her hair was up. She had a fabulous figure and was much more beautiful than I had expected. It was one of those couples where you wondered what she saw in him.

We walked behind them toward the exit about three yards back looking just like another couple heading toward the taxi stand. They didn't look around and didn't see us behind them. They walked out the two sets of automatic glass doors and stood behind several others waiting for cabs. The doorman came up to them and asked if they were waiting for a taxi; I heard him say yes. The doorman saw his wife, looked back at his face, then glanced over his shoulder. He caught my eye. I nodded to him. I walked to the side of the taxi line with Kristen away from the others standing in line. Kristen asked, "What are we doing? How are we going to stay with them if we don't get our own taxi?"

"You'll see."

As Curley and his wife approached the end of the group of people waiting for cabs, the doorman approached him. We could barely hear him as we were about ten feet away, but he said, "Sir because you are on your honeymoon, we have arranged a special limousine."

They both smiled as the large stretch limo came around the circle. As the doorman held the door for the limousine, I grabbed Kristen's hand, started walking, and said, "Come on."

Curley and his wife stepped into the limo and sat facing forward. Just before they closed the door I grabbed it, stepped into the limo and pulled Kristen in behind me. I sat by the door and closed it behind me.

They looked confused as the driver pulled away. Finally Curley said, "Excuse me, but I think this was our limo, it was arranged for us by the hotel. We're on our way to dinner."

I looked at him and smiled. "So are we! We're not

on our honeymoon, but we are going to dinner. In fact, we're going to dinner with you."

"To the same restaurant?" his wife asked.

"No, we're going to have dinner together, the four of us."

Curley suddenly got it. "You're him. The attorney representing those navy pilots."

"I hate to crash your party, but I really need to talk to you. And I don't have a few weeks to wait until you get back to Washington."

He looked at Kristen. "And who is she?"

"She's another attorney working with me. Her name is Kristen Chambers. She's actually with a large Washington firm called Covington and Burling. She's in the New York office. She's working for our clients for free."

Now he was angry. "I can't believe that you interrupted my honeymoon." He looked around at the car. "And I suppose this limousine was actually your doing, not the hotel's?"

"I hope you don't mind. And the restaurant was more than happy to make a reservation for four instead of two."

"You even know where we're going to eat?"

"The concierge was nice enough to allow your good friend to surprise you. She was very helpful. She even made the call for me."

He shook his head. "I don't appreciate you stalking us, and we're not gonna have dinner with you."

I looked at Kristen and nodded. "I understand that completely. That's fine, we'll just ride around in the limo then, because this driver isn't going to stop until I tell him to."

"Oh, I get it, so now we're your prisoners?"

I looked offended. "How could you even think that? I just knew that you wanted to see the sights and I was happy to accommodate you."

He turned to his wife reluctantly. "What do you think?"

She smiled slightly. "Make him pay for dinner. Plus, I've seen him on television. I'd kind of like to hear what's going on."

Curley frowned. Not the response he wanted. He said to me, "You're buying, big time, whatever we want. And if I say we're done talking, then we've got to stop."

I looked at him in the darkened limo and said, "Happy to buy."

We drove until we reached the base of the Stratosphere and got into the elevator to take us to the top.

The maître d' at the Top of the World Restaurant seated us at a table right at the window. He placed us where I had asked him to, which had cost me a lot of money. As we took our seats and looked out over the strip, even I had to admit it was incredible. There is something beautiful about the lights of a city at night, even if that city is Vegas. It made the newlyweds pleased despite the fact that they had been shanghaied. We ordered drinks and appetizers.

I said mostly to his wife, "Thanks for letting us join you at dinner. I know it was ridiculous of me to do it that way, but I can be persistent. I really needed to talk to you."

The major said to me, "I didn't really have a choice. If what they've said about you on television is true, you're a former Navy SEAL."

"People make too much of that. It was a long time ago."

"Yeah, but you would have thrown me out of the limo onto the pavement. I'd have bounced around on the street while you took my wife to dinner."

I laughed. It was the first time I'd seen him exhibit anything close to humor or normal human behavior. "Nah, I would have picked you up after you bounced around a little bit. No problem."

Curley's wife said to Kristen, "How did you get involved in all of this?"

Kristen introduced herself first. "I'm sorry. We never really introduced ourselves. I'm Kristen Chambers. What's your name?"

"Melanie, well now Curley. Melanie Curley."

They smiled and shook hands. "I went to school with Jack. I've known him for ten years. Three years in law school and seven years of law practice."

She asked Kristen, "Are you married?"

"No."

"Dating someone?"

Kristen shook her head.

Melanie looked at me. "You?"

"Married?"

"Yes."

"No. Never have been."

Melanie sat back with a smile on her face. "I get it.

You guys are fooling around, and someone else is picking up the tab."

I shook my head and smiled. "I have proposed fooling around, but she hasn't been interested yet. I'm continuing to work on her."

Melanie laughed. "Well keep at it. She might be the right one for you."

"Why would you say that?"

"I don't know. I think you're looking for something."

"You mean something other than a wife?"

"Yes."

"What are you, a psychologist?"

"Yes. Actually I am. I do marriage and family counseling."

I smiled ironically. "Figures. But enough about me. I'm really here to talk about you. Actually, him," I said, turning my attention to her husband. The main courses arrived and were placed quickly on the table by the waiter. When he left I said, "Now can we talk about what happened in Pakistan?"

He put his knife down, rubbed his forehead, looked up at me reluctantly and said, "What would you like to know?"

I looked out over the Strip and thought about my two clients still sitting in the medieval prison in Holland. I said, "Our clients are charged with war crimes because they dropped a bomb on what turned out to be a European medical refugee facility in the mountains of Pakistan. The tribal area."

I paused. I watched as he nodded. "You and everyone else in the world know that. But we've just come from the *Reagan*. We met with your colleagues. What you particularly know is that we received intelligence from Pakistan that this meeting was going to occur. We had some background intelligence that a meeting was likely, but we didn't have a location. We had special operations teams in place all over the area, including the tribal areas of Pakistan. All they needed was the word and they would have been on that meeting like stink on shit." I looked at the psychologist. She shook her head.

I continued. "So as you know, they were captured and sent to Holland for war crimes trials. I won't bore you with the legal part. Just know that in a few weeks we're going to trial, and I've got to defend them. And right now the amount of stuff I have to defend them with is not good enough. I need a witness who was involved in the intelligence, who knows what was received and what was said, to testify about the targeting. Everybody I've talked to from Pakistan to the *Reagan* to the intelligence center at Qatar all say that you're the man. You're the one who spoke to the Pakistanis. You're the one who passed on the latitude and longitude and approved the target. Obviously, you didn't give the final approval, but you gave the initial intelligence and targeting endorsement and the immediate need for a strike and passed it up the chain. Those above you approved it, but they didn't have anything other than what you told them. Frankly, it's all on you. So what happened?"

Since I was paying he had purchased the lobster and

steak plate. He had attacked the lobster first and clearly wanted to go for the steak. He was debating with himself whether to answer my questions or try and defer until he was done eating. He cut a bite off his steak and placed it in his mouth. He chewed it slowly and swallowed, and put his knife and fork down. "I think you're pretty much right. I was the one who talked to Pakistan. I was the one who did the emergency targeting package, set the latitude and longitude, did a quick check for images in our targeting database, and passed it up the chain of command. All true."

"And the way you heard about it was by encrypted radio communication from Pakistani intelligence, the ISI, right?"

He looked around to make sure no one was listening and said, "Initially yes. But then we had a radio conference. Sort of a telephone."

"Did you take notes during this conversation? Well let me back up, who was on the radio?"

"Just me and the gentleman from ISI."

"They said on the *Reagan* someone there may have been on the phone too."

"No."

"Do you remember his name?"

"We don't use names. But I recognized his voice. I've spoken with him before. He had sort of a call sign that we used."

"What was it?"

"Wazi."

"As in Waziristan?"

"Exactly. He was an expert on what was going on in the hills."

"So did you take notes?"

"Yes. I always do."

"Where are those notes?"

"They should be in the file."

"Okay, I may have some of those, but what did he say?"

"That this was the meeting that we had expected between al Qaeda and the Taliban. They've had a long series of issues of controlling the Waziristan area, as well as incursions into Afghanistan, general strategies, all that stuff. There have been a lot of disagreements between the Taliban and al Qaeda. This was supposed to be a high-level meeting between some of their top people. As I said, we all expected it to happen, we didn't know when. All of a sudden everyone gets all activated. The ISI sends us a flash message telling us to get on the radio with them, that they have emergency targeting information."

I interrupted, "Why wouldn't they just tell you in the message? Why wouldn't they tell you the latitude and longitude and the nature of the meeting in the message itself?"

Curley took another bite of steak and with half of it still in his mouth said, "There had been an issue with leaks inside the ISI. Targeting information was getting to the bad guys. Places that were targeted based on their information seemed to be empty by the time we got there. We thought it might be someone in their comm center who was passing on what he typed in as a message. So we went with the radio. It was at our request. Typically it was a twenty-four-hour turnaround from targeting to making it part of the air tasking order, but still, we thought there was a leak. So rather than pass it to one of their comm techs, who could have been passing it on to somebody else, they just picked up the radio and told us directly. There's nothing like recognizing somebody's voice to know what you're dealing with."

"Okay, so you got on the radio with this guy. What did he say?"

"That the meeting was on. That we needed to get there within a half hour and the latitude and longitude. They also gave me a description of the building, and said they did not have an image of it. It turned out we only had an old stock image. Nothing too exciting. We had that latitude and longitude image from a high altitude, so we had the whole village, but we didn't have a high-resolution photo of that building."

I thought about everything he had said. It all made sense, it all fit together, and it all should have worked. But something had gone wrong. "So how in the hell did we hit a refugee facility full of refugees and Europeans?"

He shook his head. "You tell me. We hit where he told us to hit."

I reached into my suit coat and extracted the folded piece of paper and handed it to him. He opened it and pressed it flat on the table next to his plate. He nodded as he looked at it. I asked him, "Are those your notes?"

"Some of them."

"Is that your handwriting?"

"Yes."

"That has the latitude and longitude on it, and some other comments. Look on the bottom right. It says, 'RG.' See that?"

"Yes. Sure."

"What does that mean?"

"It means refugees. That's my abbreviation for refugees."

I looked at him, looked at his wife, looked at Kristen, looked at the notes and back at him. "So the ISI guy told you there were refugees there?"

"Yes. He said there were."

"Were, as in when the place was going to be bombed?" I couldn't believe my ears.

"No, were, as in past tense. Had been. When we were talking on the radio he said there were refugees there. The clear implication was that they used to be there."

"Look, Russell, if I can call you that, you were talking to a Pakistani with quite an accent, on an encrypted radio channel in a big hurry, is it possible he said there *are* refugees there?"

He shook his head. "No, he said *were*."

I said in a heavy Pakistani accent, " 'There are refugees there.' So which did I just say?"

"You said 'are.' "

"Can you see how you might have misheard him?"

He shook his head. "No, I didn't mishear anything. He said were."

I looked at the notes and thought for a minute. "You said there were other notes. I didn't see any other notes in the file. These were the only handwritten portions of the entire file."

"I had another page, another partial page of notes."

"What happened to them?"

"I don't know. They didn't give them to you?"

"No. Any ideas?"

"Well we shred a lot of stuff at the end of the day; it's possible that it got placed into the shredding pile."

"Perfect. Just what we needed. So as far as you know, this is it. Your notes indicate that he discussed refugees with you and that you then cleared the target to be bombed by our navy F-18. Is that about it?"

"Afraid so."

# NINETEEN

It was another nearly sleepless night as I contemplated whether my clients were going to go to prison for life because a targeteer had misheard "are" as "were." The implications were chilling. But I refused to surrender. I had started to fall into the evidentiary trap of thinking that everything was about the trial. But this was much bigger than the trial. This was about giving the United States a bloody nose. This was about somebody in Europe. Someone trying to pull a lot of strings to make this happen. And they had succeeded. I needed to redouble my efforts to figure out who that was. I had to keep pressing the other side of this equation. The real moving force behind this play.

We flew back to Washington the next morning and I was back at my apartment by four. I called Kevin. He answered his cell phone. I said, "Where are you?"

"I'm in D.C. Nice of you to call. Long time no see."

"I've been thinking."

"Always a good idea."

"Would you be willing to help me find out something in Europe?"

"I love Europe. Don't speak the languages. But love how green it is. Kind of crowded."

"It may not be legal."

"What do you have in mind?"

"That chartered jet. I need to find out who *really* owned the Falcon. I need to find out who the hell is behind all this. You got the real side number, now we need to find out who really owned it, and who was using it when it flew from Pakistan to Holland."

"I thought you knew who owned it. That charter company."

"They had the registry apparently, but may not have been the actual owner. And they're not talking to the U.S. about who chartered it, or why, or who owns the aircraft and I don't even know it's a real charter company. Could be a front for the freaking Belgium CIA—if they still have one."

"They do, it's called the Belgian State Security, the Sûreté de l'Etat specifically. But they're not a big player."

"I need somebody to get in there and find out the real story behind that Falcon 7X."

"Sounds like something where somebody could end up in jail."

"Not you though, you're a genius."

"Let's talk."

The closer we approached the trial with no political resolution, no shaking of hands and good friends all the way around as some had expected, the more attention the public paid to every turn of events. The press covered the story at every news cycle, and some were spending two or more hours a day on it. And now it was coming to a head. The question that most people wanted answered was what President Obama planned to do with a battle group still steaming off the coast of Holland. They were supposedly running military exercises, which is what battle groups always do, particularly when they want to have an answer as to why they're in a given location, but everyone knew they were there in case President Obama decided to use force to get the Americans out.

The president was still implying that he was willing to use force if the ICC didn't back off, but he was clearly reluctant to pick a fight with the ICC, let alone greenlight an operation which would result in the deaths of Europeans.

As Kristen walked into my office with both of us looking bleary-eyed and overwhelmed, my desk phone rang. I picked it up. It was Kevin.

"You there?" he asked.

"Obviously."

"Lunchtime. J.B.'s, fifteen minutes."

"It's only eleven o'clock."

"Fifteen minutes."

I rolled my eyes as I hung up. Kristen asked, "Who was that?"

"Kevin. I'm to meet him for lunch in fifteen minutes."

She looked at the clock on the wall a little surprised. "I'm coming with you."

"Fine. We've got to go now though; it's a fifteen-minute walk."

"Where we going?"

"J.B.'s."

"Never been there."

"It's a loud sports bar that's always crowded."

"Why there?"

"Because we will not stand out, and there's not a chance anybody can overhear what we're saying. The place is deafening with ESPN and rock music all the time."

We left the other attorneys working in the conference room upstairs and the small annex where Kristen had her office. Although it was early, J.B.'s was already half full of people there to watch some English soccer match. I looked around for Kevin, and saw someone sitting in front of one of the large screens watching the game with a baseball cap on backward. That had to be Kevin. He was always wearing his baseball caps backward. I approached him from behind and I could tell he knew I was there five feet before I got near him. He was good. He turned around. Moved his hat so it faced forward, and I barely recognized him. He was wearing his thick black-rimmed glasses like Elvis Costello and an Arsenal hat. I said, "Oh, so you're a soccer fan now?"

"Go Gunners!" he said. "Have a seat."

"What's going on? Why the clandestine meeting?"

He looked at Kristen and at me. "Who invited her?"

"I did," I said, getting a little irritated. "She's working with me every step of the way."

"That doesn't mean she gets to know everything. You know that, Jack."

"I know that. But she needs to know about this."

He looked at me. "I talked to a friend. I need to tell you what he said. But I don't trust her. She's probably taking notes, and she's going to write a book when this is all done and rat us all out. I don't want any part of her."

Kristen said, "What is your problem? What have I ever done to you?"

"Simple. You and our now attorney general who used to be with your firm, what's his name, Holder? You defended the people who are trying to murder me and my friends. People like you and people like your firm just want to hurt America. Whatever is good for America, you're against it."

Kristen was getting visibly angry. "That is ridiculous. Defending somebody's right to be sure that they're being properly held is not anti-American, it's pro-American. It's pro-Constitution."

"Yeah, whatever. You just keep on believing that. I don't really expect to persuade you and I'm not here to debate you. I was here to talk to Jack about some important things, and you're not welcome to hear them."

He got up, turned from the game and walked out.

I stood up and looked at Kristen. "I'm going to catch up with him. I'll see you back at the office."

I caught up with Kevin as he stepped onto the sidewalk and switched out his horn-rimmed glasses for his Oakley sunglasses. He walked quickly down the sidewalk.

"What you got?"

He turned and looked behind us. He saw that Kristen wasn't there. "How do you know she's not undermining you? How do you know she's not secretly hoping that Raw and Dunk get convicted? That'd probably make her firm happy. That would make all of New York happy."

"Oh get off your horse. Save that for some officer's club bar. What do you have?"

People passed us on both sides as we hurried down the sidewalk. There was not a chance anyone was recording what we were saying. No one knew we would be there and we weren't stationary. No vehicle could get near enough.

Kevin said, "This thing about the charter company. I called a friend. He works with the French counterterrorism people. Or he used to. Now he's sort of a loosely associated person with some of the things I do. I can't really go into it."

"And?"

"He checked out the company. He said they're legit. A legitimate charter organization that has access to dozens of aircraft. Some of them are based at their headquarters at the Brussels airport. He had a friend of his in Brussels take a look at the building supposedly because he was interested in a charter. They showed him all around, showed him the hangar, showed him some of the aircraft. They've got a lot of security. He can get inside, probably find their records, but it is not risk-free."

"Is he willing?"

"He wants money."

"I suppose you do too."

"Nah, I'm in this for the good of the cause. I'm so pissed that I didn't get those boys that were supposedly at that meeting. But it sounds like the meeting was bogus anyway."

I stopped on the sidewalk. He stopped with me. I said, "I've got to tell you that there's a scenario here that makes it all fit, even if the Pakistanis are telling the truth and the Americans are telling the truth. This whole thing may come down to a Pakistani intelligence officer saying 'are' and the American targeteer, a major in the air force, hearing 'were.' If you think for a second," I paused as a taxi honked at a homeless man staggering across the road and stopping traffic. I studied the homeless man to see if he was who he appeared to be.

I continued. "That the Pakistani was telling the truth and gave a legitimate target to the air force, and the air force legitimately passed it on, but misunderstood the implications, then there really *was* a meeting between al Qaeda and the Taliban at that village or in that building. The JDAM blew everybody to hell, so finding who was there and who wasn't is nearly impossible. The refugee building was cover for them. They knew nobody would attack it. They were in there. And they were killed. Nobody has even thought about that. We've all assumed from the beginning that this was a misguided attack from the outset. That it was bad information, a bad understanding, or the meeting never occurred. But if everybody I've talked to is telling the truth—and again, I don't know if they are—we may have gotten one of the top al Qaeda operatives and one of the top Taliban operatives. I don't think we'd ever be able to sort it out because they're blown to complete dust. Do you know what the concussion of one of those JDAMs is?"

"Yes. I do."

"Anyway, sorry I was digressing and thinking out loud, but I'm telling you that those guys may have been there. So you didn't blow a chance to get them, they may have been gotten."

He nodded with his hands in his pockets. "Except your new scenario isn't what happened."

"How do you know?"

"Because if it was all legit, if the intel was right, they wouldn't have been there waiting for your clients with shoulder-fired missiles and a Falcon jet."

"Maybe, but what better way to trap someone than with a legitimate target?"

"So what do you want to do? Want me to talk to this guy to get into that company? It's going to be illegal as hell, and we're starting to stick our necks out here by going over the line of European law."

"Yeah, I know. I've got to get the information though. How much does the guy want?"

"Ten thousand euros."

"Shit. I don't have that kind of money."

"I do, but I'm not gonna front it. I think I've done enough for the cause. You gotta come up with it, if you want this stuff."

"Are you going to go with him?"

"Not a chance. It's a pissant little mission, that could end you in jail for a couple of years for something that's not worth it. Get the Europeans to do it. He's a pro. But it will look like petty theft to anybody that catches him. Not that they will."

"Tell him I'll get him the money. I'm going to give it to him through you though."

"Where you gonna get it?"

"I don't know. If I have to take a cash advance on my credit card, I'll do that. Whatever it takes. I'm going to find the son of a bitch that set this up."

Kevin looked around on the street for anything unusual, then stopped. "Are you going to Holland soon to prepare for the trial?"

"I don't know, probably in a month or two. Why?"

"Just wondered. This friend of mine seems to be on our side. He thinks the Dutch and the ICC are full of shit. He said he knew of a good office complex right across the street from the ICC. I'll get you the address."

"Thanks."


When I got back to the office Kristen was, of course, already there. She was in the conference room with the others, all working madly on their laptops drafting briefs, witness outlines, research, putting together factual information from available Internet sources on the bombing, helping me prepare. When I walked into the conference room, I closed the door behind me. "How's everybody doing?"

Most uttered "fine." I noticed that Kristen not only didn't say "fine," she wouldn't look up at me. I wasn't in

the mood for drama. I turned around, left the conference room, and went down to my office. I grabbed the
phone messages, went into my office, and closed the
door. As I was leafing through them, noticing that most
of them were from the press, someone knocked on my
door loudly and opened it before I said anything. It was
one of the younger associates. She said to me, "Jack, I
think you should see this. There is a news bulletin on
CBS about the battle group up near Holland."

I dropped the messages and followed her to the annex. The television sat on a table in the corner and was
loud enough for everyone in the small room to hear.
The reporter on the screen was Mara Meyer, the chief
White House correspondent for CBS. I had found her
reporting so far in this whole thing to be pretty fair
and straight. She stood with the White House over her
shoulder and spoke into the microphone she held in her
hand. I listened. ". . . somewhat surprising development in that the two American fliers are still in prison
in The Hague. There has been no indication that they
are to be released, or that their charges will be dropped.
But in spite of that, President Obama has agreed to
withdraw the battle group, and not only withdraw them
into the Atlantic, but has agreed to return them to the
United States. The White House issued a statement
that the battle group's training exercises were complete
and they were returning to port for routine mainte-
nance. Several people inside the administration who
asked not to be identified have said that the president is
simply making a gesture of reconciliation to the International Criminal Court. Others outside the adminis-

tration have said that he blinked. He didn't achieve any of his objectives by sending the battle group; the Americans are still in prison. And, a former president of the United States has been indicted along with several members of his cabinet and military staff.

"The trial for the two Americans is set. President Obama has said that he will make a statement later in the week, but has confirmed the return of the battle group to the United States. John Caskey, the attorney for the two Americans charged, was unavailable for comment."

I recalled that one of the messages I had just read was from her. Unavailable for comment. Unavailable in the ten minutes they had given me to get back to them. I couldn't believe that President Obama had just withdrawn the battle group. I took my phone out of my pocket and dialed Chris. There was no answer. I was fairly certain he saw it was me and refused to answer. I left him a voicemail message: "I sure hope we got something in exchange for this withdrawal. Call me and let me know what it was."

I didn't hear back from Chris. That was ominous. If he now went cold on me I had no other real contact within the government. He was the one who set up the representation, he was the one who made sure I got paid, he was the one who gave me access to witnesses, he's the one who gave me insight into the White House strategies. My mind ran away with me. What if the administration was using this crisis to achieve a political objective? What if they allowed this entire thing to escalate? What if they had just gone through the appearance of being tough? Sending a battle group up there to make noise, and stimulating the very thing they knew might come next, an indictment of a former American president and members of his administration. To what end?

To the end that I could feel coming. To reach an accommodation with the International Criminal Court. To make the United States a signing party and to submit to its jurisdiction. The very thing that the self-appointed human rights advocates had been screaming for since the ICC was founded. And in exchange the ICC would dismiss the indictments of Bush and the others.

But that would be so damned sinister. My mind raced. I reviewed everything I knew, every fact I'd encountered. Every conversation I'd had. I was not a believer in government conspiracies. Inside every supposed government conspiracy was someone who thought they could become the next Deep Throat and tell the *Washington Post* everything they knew. So calling it a conspiracy was too much. But could it be said that the administration was using this international crisis to achieve one of its campaign goals? As Rahm Emanuel said during the early stages of the economic crisis that dominated President Obama's first days in office, "Rule one: Never let a crisis go to waste."

I didn't want to believe any of that. So, at least for the moment, I didn't.

The next two weeks were frenetic with activity, mostly behind the scenes. At the end of those two weeks though, a package arrived with a return address of a corporation in Washington, D.C., that I didn't recognize. A thick padded envelope. My secretary left it in my inbox and I let it sit there for most of the morning. Finally, before I was ready to go to lunch, I decided to open it. I'd had some training in explosive ordnance disposal when I was a SEAL, but I'd never been trained in letter bombs. The fact that I didn't recognize the company gave me some concern, but I really didn't think anyone was going to try and blow me up.

I ripped open the envelope, and still standing, pulled out an Iomega portable hard drive. It was three by five inches and three quarters of an inch thick. I turned it over. It was a two-terabyte hard drive. I then looked at the sticky note on the back under the technical information. Someone had typed on it, "For Jack Caskey's eyes only." Why would anyone go to the effort to type on a sticky note? Obviously to protect their identity. I looked at the corporate name again, and typed it into Google on my computer. There were no hits. There was no record of a company of that name. I typed the address into Google and looked at it. It was the address of the Belgian embassy. This was somebody's idea of a joke. Or perhaps not.

I took a USB wire out of my desk drawer, and hooked the hard drive up to the laptop on my desk. I opened the drive icon and saw that there were two files on the hard drive. One of them was in French and I didn't understand it, and the second was in English and had the name of the company that had supposedly chartered the Falcon7X to fly my clients from Peshawar to The Hague. I double-clicked on that file and there were hundreds of PDFs. I clicked on the first one. It was an English translation of a contract between the jet company and the charterer. Notably, the charterer was referred to as "the client." That was curious. I hit print and watched the multipage contract spit out of my printer on the other side of my desk. I went to the next PDF. There were several letters from various companies requesting to charter the Falcon 7X. Most were rejected, but letters without a return address from "the client" seemed to be agreed to.

I opened the next PDF. It seemed to be an accounting ledger. There were numerous ledgers in French, but superimposed on those entries were English translations. It was professionally done and easy to understand. Somebody had spent a lot of time working on the documents that were now in front of me. I printed the ledgers. I called my secretary to come into my office. She came in quickly. I deselected the hard drive, disconnected it from my computer, and handed it to her. "There are a bunch of documents on this hard drive. Most of them are in French, but there are duplicates in English. Please print all of the documents in English. Two copies. Then have this hard drive backed up onto another hard drive. Then I want you to put this hard drive in my safe deposit box at the bank. Do you understand?"

She looked at me with an ominous look. "Of course."

"Thanks."

I took the ledgers and the contract into the room with the attorneys that were helping me. Kristen was in there.

I said, "Hey guys, check these out." I laid the documents out on the table so that anybody could see them.

One of them asked, "What are they?"

"The contract for chartering the Falcon 7X to fly our clients from Peshawar to Holland."

Kristen picked it up and looked at it. She frowned. "It says that the charterer is simply 'the client.'"

"Exactly."

"Well who is that?"

"That's the question. No name, no address, and the signature is illegible."

She looked up at me with concern. "Where'd you get this?"

I looked back at her. "Look at the date on the contract."

She looked at it and looked at me, looked at it again. "What about it?"

"Effective date is three weeks before the shoot-down. Somebody knew all this was going to happen and chartered this aircraft for three weeks, then sent it to Peshawar before the bombing. That jet had been there, or around there, for a couple of weeks, waiting for the circumstances to develop. And now we have a contract proving that this was not only anticipated but it was by someone who doesn't want his identity known."

Kristen asked again, "Where'd you get this?"

"I got it in the mail today. On an external hard drive in an envelope from a company that doesn't exist. I checked out the company address and it's the Belgian embassy."

She wasn't buying it. "Were you expecting it?"

"Expecting what?"

"These documents."

"Kevin said he was going to ask a friend if he could talk to somebody if he could get them, but I really don't know what happened."

She said quietly, "They stole them."

"I just know I got them in the mail."

Her face flushed red. "Can we talk?" she asked as she walked past me outside into the reception area.

I followed her out. "What?"

She pointed at my office. "Into your office."

I walked into my office, waited till she came in and closed the door behind her. She started right in on me. "What in the hell are you doing?"

"Meaning?"

"You put Kevin up to this. He found somebody who does what he does, and they broke into the company and stole these documents. Is that what happened?"

"Maybe, but it may be that he found somebody inside the company who was more than eager to tell them what was going on. I don't know the answer."

"And you don't really care either, do you?"

"Sure I care."

"What I mean is, you don't care whether getting these documents was over the ethical line."

"What ethical line?"

"All ethical lines. Show me an ethical line over which this did not pass. Show me any jurisdiction in the world where it's okay to steal evidence from a private company."

"Show me anywhere in the world where you have to

defend yourself from criminal charges and lifetime imprisonment without the right to subpoena documents from someone who knows what happened."

She stopped. "You can't subpoena documents?"

"No. I can't just sign a subpoena and force people to turn over documents. Under Article 57, Paragraph 3, if I want documents, I, *we*, have to petition the pretrial court, which will consider it, after consulting with the prosecutor. It has to be "material." Well I sure know they're going to say how the defendants were transported and by whom is irrelevant at this point, and is not "material" to whether they committed war crimes. So we'd never get them. And it would show our hand."

"So that justifies it? Because they don't have the subpoena powers that you like, you break the law?"

"I didn't break any laws."

"You may have. You may have been part of a conspiracy to commit trespass and theft."

"I'm part of a conspiracy to get my clients out of jail. Guilty."

"You took an oath."

"This is warfare."

"No, it's not. It's law."

"It's warfare using human rights laws as the weapons. It's called lawfare. Go read *Unrestricted Warfare*. It's from China. Written in 1999 by two Chinese air force colonels, Qaio Liang and Wang Xiangsui. It tells you how to defeat technologically superior opponents. One of the tools you use is international human rights laws to attack those who are vulnerable to moral manipulation. That's us in spades."

"I can't believe what I'm hearing."

"Hey, if you don't want to be part of this team anymore, just say the word, Kristen."

She turned, walked out the door, and slammed it behind her.

# TWENTY

As I stood there trying to decide whether to pursue Kristen, the phone rang. I turned and walked to the desk and looked at the phone number. It was Chris. I picked up the receiver. "Where have you been?"

"Sitting around doing nothing. Where have you been?"

"Same. What the hell is going on? We're pulling back the battle group?"

"The president decided it was sending the wrong message."

"What wrong message was that? That we might actually take action?"

I could hear the annoyance in Chris's voice. "Save your political speeches for the press. You know how complicated these things can be. There are all kinds of competing interests at work here."

"Like what?"

"Like making sure the former president doesn't get indicted and that that indictment doesn't stay open."

"That's exactly why they did it! To make him pull the battle group back and now he's done it!"

"Maybe. But he's got to consider all these things."

"So what's the plan? Sew a human rights quilt and give it to the ICC as a token of our *respect*?"

"Your clients will get a trial, and there's no reason to believe it won't be fair."

"Oh please. You know this entire thing is rigged. No reason to believe it won't be fair? How about the fact that they got a midnight Kangaroo Court indictment and had a jet waiting to fly the defendants out of Pakistan even before the indictment came down? How about that?"

"We're here to help you, Jack. The entire Department of Justice is at your disposal. Whatever you need."

"I am using their briefs. They're doing good work. But they don't have witnesses. They don't have documents. They have a bunch of attorneys sitting in a building in Washington."

"I'm just telling you if you need any help, whatever you need. We'll do it."

"I need *witnesses*. I need you to order everybody on my witness list to be there. Whether I call them or not, I need authorization from you—from the White House—that they are to go."

"You said that it's likely that any witness who comes in support of your clients will be indicted."

"Right. To intimidate them and keep them from coming."

"Well, we'll do the best we can, Jack. And like I said, we're here to help."

"My two clients are being abandoned. Just like Uriah."

"Who?"

"Uriah. When King David was committing adultery with Bathsheba, he had Bathsheba's husband, Uriah, sent to the front lines. He told his generals when the battle started, they were to pull back and leave Uriah engaged. He was killed. That's what Obama is doing, and it's because he's committing adultery with the International Criminal Court."

"Great story. Thanks. I'm just telling you you may not have the whole picture. Don't assume you do. Defend your clients in trial. Do your absolute best to get them off. And we will help you any way we can. But you let *us* worry about the international political implications. You're way out of your league."

"No. *Obama* is the one who is out of his league. He should be the president of the United Nations, not the president of the United States."

"Call me again after you've taken your sedatives." Chris hung up.

I looked out my window and screamed, "Shit!" and slammed the phone down on its cradle.

I looked at my watch. It was 4:00 P.M. I picked up the phone and dialed Kristen's cell. Much to my amazement, she picked up. "What?"

"I think I just yelled at Chris and I think I probably said some harsh things. I accused the president of being an adulterer. I think I'm a little bit out there. I need to calm down. I'm going home. But I've got an idea. How about you let me take you to dinner? I think I owe you an apology anyway."

There was silence on the other end of the line. I thought I could hear her breathing but she might have left her phone in the street knowing that I was on it. Finally she said with some reluctance, "Where?"

"The Marine Room. You know the one down under the bridge."

"Seven o'clock."

I actually felt a little odd going to dinner. It caused me to look back over how I had been working with Kristen since the day she agreed to come work with me. I had demanded a lot of her, hadn't listened to her as much as I should have, and really hadn't given her much of a chance to understand my perspective. On second thought, I'd probably given her too much of a chance to understand my perspective and not listened to her. I got to the restaurant a little early and went to the bar. It was a beautiful modern bar that wasn't overly crowded. I found a high table with two high-back stools and ordered a beer. I texted Kristen that I was in the bar and within five minutes she walked in. I stood up from my stool and greeted her as she approached the table. I extended my hand and she shook it. She was unsmiling.

She sat down and I ordered her the martini I knew she liked. I said, "I didn't mean to go off."

"You're entitled to your opinions."

"Yes well, I need to explain myself a little bit. Over dinner I'll tell you about my conversation with Chris."

"He called."

"Yes."

I looked around to see if I recognized anyone else in the room. "I had to find out what the president was actually planning. Since he was pulling back the battle group, there had to be another plan, right? Turns out there isn't."

"So they're pulling back the battle group and they're going to do nothing?"

"Yep. We're on our own."

She sipped from her martini, crossed her legs, and thought. "I never really thought they would send troops into Europe and attack the prison anyway. Did you?"

"I don't know, I guess I held out hope they'd send a special ops team and do something fancy. But maybe they never really intended to. Maybe that was all just intended to intimidate the ICC, but to do what? Like they're going to let our clients go? I could see them trying to impose some plea bargain in exchange for freedom, or promise of the United States jailing them here for a period of time, which would be absolutely incomprehensible. So, I don't know where it was going. But wherever it was going, it's not going there anymore. It's all on us. It really pissed me off."

The hostess came and told us our dinner table was ready. We followed her to the corner by the river. It was beautiful, quiet, and I had to admit, romantic. I also had to admit that was part of my reason for suggesting the restaurant, although I had serious doubts that it was part of her reason for coming.

We looked at the menu and I quickly decided what I would order. I tend to order the same thing a lot. I watched her scan the menu, and when she put it down I said, "So I really did want to apologize for the way I said things back at my office. I needed to find a better way."

She looked at me with an intense look. "So what you're saying is that you apologize for the way you said things, not what you said."

"I don't know. I'd have to think about everything. I certainly know I meant it when I said it, but I think I was patronizing. I can be like that sometimes. I'm sorry."

"So what did Chris say?"

I related the conversation, leaving out nothing, including the inflection, the yelling, the anger, and the ending. She listened quietly as she ate her spinach salad. She finally said, "You told him that President Obama was committing adultery with the ICC?"

"He is. He's enamored by the same thing that most liberals are enamored with. That we're all part of the world community and if we could just be friends then everybody would get along fine. That's just a crock of shit. Yet people continually try to pacify the 'international community' at the expense of American interests. This is just the latest example. He's ready to sell our clients down the river into the devouring mouth of the 'international community,' which is personified in the International Criminal Court."

Kristen rolled her eyes and looked out the window. She finally looked back at me. "You are so full of it.

President Obama had no choice. First of all, there's no way he's going to break into a prison in Europe and pull out a couple of Americans, no matter what law was passed during the Bush administration. Second, the charges against our clients are unfair, and we should be able to get them off. I think he's relying on the system working properly"—she put up her hand indicating to me to not interrupt—"and third, what would you do if you were the president and they indicted your predecessor at the International Criminal Court, taking this to a whole different level? You would try and take the heat out of it, not inject *more* heat into it. Some stupid things you let die a natural death; you don't have to fight every fight. This was a symbolic gesture on the part of the ICC."

"Well it worked. It got Obama to back off and send the battle group home. It looks like we're retreating."

"That's where you came up with the whole Uriah thing. Where did you get that?"

"David and Bathsheba. Uriah was Bathsheba's husband."

"Right. But how do you have that in your head?"

"I thought everyone knew that story. It was just the right analogy."

"No, it's an open sore with you. It got your back up. It made you yell at Chris and me when you never would have done it otherwise. That story represents something to you. It's got your internal righteousness smeared all over it. You've told it before, I'd bet. What's it about?"

"Nothing in particular. I just feel undercut."

Kristen was taking a bite of fish, and looked up

when I said that. She put the fish down, put her hands in her lap, and studied my face.

I looked at her. "What?"

She said, "You've never told me why you left the navy. Why did you quit being a SEAL?"

I waved my hand at her dismissively. "Doesn't matter. Nothing to do with anything."

"Tell me."

I took another bite, took a drink from my beer, and said, "We have a lot of jobs as navy SEALs. A lot of people think we can do anything. Any special operation, any kidnapping of a high-value target, extracting people from dangerous situations. You name it, we do it. That's on top of all the maritime stuff we do, like the snipers who took out those pirates off the east coast of Africa. People think we can do it all, and to some extent that's true. We certainly think that we can do anything, and better than anyone else in the world could do it. We do everything they do, plus we do underwater ops, long-range insertion, jumping out of airplanes to boats in the middle of the ocean, anything."

"Yeah, I've heard. But I want to hear about you."

I played with my food as I thought about talking about what I didn't like to talk about. I felt close to Kristen, but also knew that she probably didn't feel very close to me. I began, "There were a lot of things. It just wasn't for me in the long term."

"Meaning?"

I could detect a little bit of glee in her voice. She was pleased with herself that I was going to tell her. It made me think about what Kevin had said. At the end of all this she was probably going to write a book and put us all on report. I had to watch myself.

"Well?"

I told her the story of that night in Baghdad. Capturing the jack of spades and then going to help a Marine squad that had been ambushed. "I didn't really think that much of it, until some reports started circulating that a bunch of civilians had gotten killed."

Kristen frowned. "That's not good. What happened?"

All the anger from the incident and the following months came flooding back yet again. The very thing I tried to avoid by not talking about it. "Well first, a civilian is a question mark, or was, in Iraq. Who are the civilians, who are the fighters, and how do you know one from the other? Is a fighter who has dropped his rifle a civilian or a former fighter or a prisoner? And what if he dropped it yesterday? What is he today? It was tough. But our rule was pretty simple. If the person has a weapon, they're in the game. The problem was, some of these bad guys, some of these assholes, would break into houses at gunpoint, and start firing at Americans. When we would return fire, the occupants of the house would get killed, either instead of the bad guys, or in addition to. It was a mess.

"And that's what happened here. A bunch of guys invaded houses along a street. I don't know if they knew the Marines were coming or just got lucky, but they opened fire on the Marines with AKs and were just relentless. The Marines did what they were supposed to do in an ambush and broke toward the houses firing their weapons. They started firing into the houses.

It was a serious firefight, and lots of bad guys were killed. But so were about fifteen people who were the occupants of the houses. The press got ahold of it and started calling it a massacre. They started showing pictures of all these old men and children who had been shot and claimed that the Americans shot them. That was true. They had been killed by American rounds. But that didn't really reflect the whole picture of what had happened. That didn't matter. Several of the Marines and two members of my team got charged with murder. And it was complete, total, and utter bullshit."

Kristen hesitated, "*If* what your guys told you happened is true."

I sat back and shook my head with a wry smile on my face. "See, you can't even listen to the story without challenging it. That's what pissed me off about the press, and frankly some of the people in the military, and that is a little bit of what pisses me off about you. Always ready to believe the worst about the Americans. Always ready to believe that American troops, including SEALs on my team, are murderers."

She looked down at her hands, and then back at me. "Sorry. I wasn't challenging anything. I was just doing what attorneys do. Defendants' stories exonerate them *if* what they say is true. That's what we always do. Sorry."

"I understand. I get it. That's what I do all the time; it just gripes me when they're talking about something I know about. I was there." I could *feel* that she wanted to say "Yes, but you weren't in the room when those civilians were shot. You don't *know*."

"So what came of it all?"

"Three of them were put on trial for murder, including one of my team members."

"What happened?"

"They were convicted. The UCMJ equivalent of manslaughter."

Her face showed surprise. She wasn't sure whether to keep probing or not. Finally she asked, "What do you think about what happened?"

"My guy did what he should have done. I've walked through the whole thing with him. He did exactly what he should have done. And in a court-martial of his 'peers' they said he was guilty of negligently killing civilians. I think the press wanted a scalp. And they got one."

"So you went to law school and you've been fighting the government ever since."

I looked at her with annoyance. "I guess that's one conclusion you could draw."

"Is it wrong?"

"I'm not really into psychoanalyzing myself."

"It explains why you got out, why you've been battling with the government instead of getting a high-paying job where you might actually own a house and it really explains why you care so much about this case."

"Don't forget I worked for the Department of Justice for a while. If I hated the government, I wouldn't have done that."

"You might have been, as you might say, just gathering intel on the government."

"Oh please."

"Well, we'll see. Our job of course is to win this trial."

"No doubt. I am getting those guys out."

"You mean off?"

"Right. Off."

"And how are you supposed to do that if the government has deemed them expendable?"

"We'll get them to cooperate. They'll give us a couple of witnesses. They can't completely pull back. The country wouldn't put up with it. The fact that Obama blinked, and bowed down before the altar of the ICC, will be noted. People will ridicule him for it. The right-wingers will be all over him for it. But he can survive that. But if the government completely withdraws support of us in the trial, they won't let him forget that ever."

"I guess we'll see."

The rest of the dinner was uneventful. I enjoyed her presence, I liked being around her, but at the same time she aggravated me. Maybe because she was like an external conscience, pointing things out about me that I didn't want to acknowledge. On the way home I called Kevin.

When President Obama withdrew the battle group, it was like a teacher had come onto the playground right before the fight was about to start. All the classmates had broken up the circle in disappointment. And like on the playground, all the people who had been intensely interested turned and walked back to class. They didn't linger to find out what happened to the two boys. Now that it looked like it was going to be just a trial, there was interest from the legal side of the press, and some moderate interest overall. But it wasn't the daily press reports and press conferences by congressmen that it was when the battle group was off the coast of Holland.

After ten or so days of preparing for trial eighteen hours a day, I received a note. I was looking through phone messages at my secretary's desk when the door to the street opened up and a man walked in wearing long bicycle pants, bicycle gloves, a bicycle helmet with a small mirror attached to it, and a black messenger bag over his shoulder. He was carrying his front bicycle wheel in his right hand. He put the wheel down, opened up his messenger bag, and took out an envelope. He handed it to my secretary.

"This is for John Caskey. Sign here." He pulled out a clipboard; put an X next to a spot. She looked at me and I nodded. She signed it and handed the clipboard back to the messenger, who put it back in his bag and turned around just as quickly as he had entered. She handed me the envelope. I opened the innocuous business eight-and-a-half-by-eleven and looked inside. There was a smaller envelope. The size of a greeting card. I opened the sealed envelope and pulled out a card. It was a birthday card. A simplistic Hallmark card. It had a picture of a birthday cake with a few candles on it and the words "Happy Birthday" in script across the bottom of the card. It was the kind you might get at a gas station. My secretary saw me looking at the card. She said, "It's not your birthday."

I responded while reading the card, "Nope."

"So, who thinks it's your birthday?"

I shook my head as I read. It wasn't addressed to anybody. It had no "Dear Jack," or any other "to" portion. It was unsigned. It was in a woman's handwriting. Flowery and cursive. It said, "Don't call me. Don't text me. Don't e-mail me. Don't refer to me. Come to your office in Holland. Come alone. Across the street, third floor." I turned the card over to see if there was more. There was a key taped to the back. I slipped in into my pocket, and said to my secretary, "Book me a business class seat to The Hague tonight."

# TWENTY-ONE

As I drove to Dulles, I called Kristen and told her where I was going. She of course wanted to know why. I said I had to get the office set up and talk to the prosecutor again about trial witnesses. She wasn't persuaded; she was perceptive, and knew I was up to something. She was right. But I didn't even know what I was up to.

When I got to The Hague, I grabbed my suitcase and took a cab straight to the new office address. Like Kevin said, it was directly across the street from the ICC building. It was a modern office building, about eight stories tall, red earthy color, with a lot of glass, part of a complex of similarly built buildings. I took the elevator to the third floor. The elevator opened onto a deserted floor. At least that's how it looked from the lobby on the third floor. It was an attractive area, but all the office doors were closed and there was no one to be seen.

I looked around for the door that my key might work in. I saw a door leading to offices that would have to overlook the ICC. I tried the key, and it opened. I walked in and closed the door behind me, putting the key back in my pocket. It was one huge room. It could be built out to any shape or design of offices you might want, but for now it was just an extremely large room with an electrical conduit sticking up from the floor and carpet marked from the last walls and carrels. When we had furniture brought in, it would be very nice. The room extended to the end of the building, and bent around the corner for some distance down the other side.

I walked to the window and looked out over the International Criminal Court building. It was even newer than the office building in which I stood. I looked at the serious security fencing that surrounded the ICC, and thought of the new courthouse they were building on the outskirts. Huge amounts of money everywhere. It was a big effort by a large number of countries to do a good thing, to put war criminals on trial. But like so many good ideas, it had been partially hijacked by those who wanted to use it for political purposes, particularly to challenge and limit the power of the United States. I had no problem with anyone trying to limit the power of the United States, that's what countries did. They tried to assert themselves and limit the power of others. International relations, short of war, was one long series of maneuvers and manipulations to improve the lot of your own country, sometimes at the expense of others. Ideally, to the benefit of both, or all, but not always.

As I stood looking over at the ICC, I suddenly heard somebody walking in the room around the corner, where I couldn't see. I felt exposed and looked for weapons and escape routes. The only way in was the double door I had used, and it was closed and locked behind me. I began walking toward the sound. As I reached the corner I saw him. It was Kevin. He had on his horn-rimmed glasses and his backward baseball cap. I was shocked. "What the hell are you doing here?"

He looked around me and out the windows and then back. "You got my note?"

"Obviously. How did you get in here?"

"Well, there's a lot of space in this building that's for rent. I took the space above you and next to you."

"I thought you said Europe wasn't your thing."

"This is personal. There's something I haven't told you. I did tell you that I was one of the teams in place to snag the people at the al Qaeda and Taliban meeting. So I'm pissed about that. But then when our boys got captured and dragged through the streets of Peshawar, I was sent to free them. They gave me what they thought was a location, and through some people who were willing to help me out, I found them. They were being held in a building right in the middle of a residential area in Peshawar. A place where they knew we would never be able to drop in from the air, but I don't think they expected us to simply drive up in front of the building and go in after them. And that's what we did. It was the biggest goat rope you've ever seen. We went in with a very minimal plan but enough to know how we were going to get out of there. We found all their equipment, their parachutes, and the survival radios. One of them had turned on his survival radio with the locator beacon that was transmitting silently. That's what allowed the satellite to pick it up, and give us the location. Unfortunately, they had already gone. They were on their way to the airport to get loaded onto that Falcon 7X and sent to Holland.

"One of my men was killed. Spike. He was sort of a punk rock fan. He'd have worn his hair spiked, but of course we didn't allow that, but he had some tattoos, was into death metal, kind of an unusual guy. But man was he good. And he got hit and died. So I've got an agenda here, Jack. I've got a real personal agenda."

I looked for other people. There wasn't anyone. "I want to hear all about that, but how did you get in here? The door was locked behind me."

He jerked his head toward the side of the room he had come from. "I'll show you." He turned the corner and walked to the end of the room where there was nothing but a blank wall. He went to the corner; put his hands carefully on the wall right at the corner and pushed. The wall gave way from the floor to the ceiling. I looked for panel marks and hinges and saw nothing. It was remarkable. He walked through the wall, and I followed. He closed it behind me. I looked around the room. There were perhaps eight men sitting at tables, at consoles, studying high-definition screens and otherwise looking extremely organized and mischievous. Some of them I recognized from Pakistan. I nodded and waved to them. They looked up and waved at me and went back to what they were doing. I looked around the rest of the room. While the room was much like mine, mostly an open space, it was full of electronics gear. I frowned as I put my hands on my hips and looked back at Kevin. "What in the hell is this?"

"I don't think you appreciate that those who are trying to put our boys away do not plan on losing."

"Oh, I'm fully aware of that."

"They want you to lie down, be part of the process, and lose."

I nodded.

He continued, "So I knew that they might have some friends, like whoever it is that owns that Falcon 7, who would try to find out what your plans were for defending the case and pass it on to the prosecutor. I'm not saying this is the ICC itself, but whoever sent that airplane has the kind of money that it would take to make sure in whatever way he could that you don't win. Including bugging your office, or making things more difficult for you. So we've got cameras in every room and in every corner of your offices, we've got monitoring devices for any transmitting devices, to see if there are any bugs, and we will be ready for whatever they bring. I've got another setup like this on top of you. We've got you covered. If anybody tries anything funny, we'll be there and have a chat with them."

He walked over to the small conference area, which had a microwave and coffeepot. He turned and said to me, "Coffee?"

I nodded. He gave me a mug of black coffee and we sat at the table. I frowned. "Who's paying for all this?"

"I am," Kevin said. "I've told you, this is personal. I've made good money in my various crazy escapades on behalf of Uncle Sam. And the private work I do is very well paying. I'm doing fine. This is my contribution to the cause."

"I appreciate it."

"So, since we've been here, I need you to understand that there's a lot going on in this little neighborhood. They clearly don't know we're here, and they're not looking for us. Up until just a couple weeks ago, they were looking for a battalion of Marines to walk over the hill and shoot them all in the head. They had a lot of assets down by the waterfront, and a lot of boat activity. I don't know if you've ever taken a look at the lay of this city, Jack, but this is a maritime place. Lots of canals, lots of boats, lots of ways to get in and out of here pretty easily. And they were looking for that. When we got here, they were still adding security. People you can't see. People I don't even recognize. These aren't ICC people. These are international security people."

"How do you know?"

"It's what I do."

"Right. So?"

"So when I see other security people, it gets my attention. I wonder what they're doing here. In this case, I pretty much know. They're trying to make sure nobody comes in and grabs the Americans."

I sipped from the coffee and sat back. "Looks like that risk is over. The battle group left. And the president told the special ops guys they couldn't hurt anybody, so that makes it pretty much impossible. We're stuck going through the trial."

"I don't know, I'm going to look around. See if there may be a chance to do something crazy."

"Meaning?"

"I don't know. I would just like to be able to affect this outcome. I'll just see how I might be able to contribute. So you let me know if I can do anything for you."

"Well one thing you were going to help me with was finding the owner of the Falcon jet. I got the hard drive—the documents—thank you very much—and I've looked through them. I assume you have too."

"Yeah."

"What do you think?"

"We tracked the lease to a corporation. But it's a shell and the listed owners are difficult to find. In fact, I think they don't exist."

I remembered what Chris said. "Well, before I left, Chris told me we could use the full capabilities of the Justice Department to help us. I think since they've abandoned the military option, they're trying to step up and give us whatever legal help they can."

"We don't need the Justice Department. We need the CIA. We need some spooks with bad attitudes to go find out what the hell is going on here. But you know what? I've got a feeling it isn't going to happen. Tell Chris to activate every badass in Europe. I'm just telling you that I would be willing to bet at the end of the day, they don't help. I just have a feeling."

"Why would they do that?"

"Because, if you haven't figured it out yet, they don't *want* to aggravate the Europeans. I don't think they want to find whoever set all this in motion. Because then they'd have to do something about that. And what is it they're going to say? That he did something illegal? What? What did he do that was illegal? Probably all he did was make sure that the prosecutor pursued charges that he thought were necessary. Hell, it could be George Soros, or somebody like that. Somebody who hated President Bush, somebody who hates what we're doing militarily, and would love nothing more than to see us get our comeuppance. Nothing illegal about it. So I'm still not so sure we're going to get a lot of help. I think we're going to have to take care of that ourselves."

I put my coffee cup down. "What are you talking about?"

"I keep telling you, Jack, this is personal."

"And?"

"Even if the CIA doesn't find this guy or decides not to do anything about it, I'm going to sure as hell try and find him and do something about it."

"Like what?"

Kevin got up and tried to pour another cup of coffee but the pot was empty. He talked to me as he made some more. "Well, this is where you and I come to a fork in the road. I'm here to work beside you, frankly, to look out for you. I'll be everywhere. I'll be on top of you on the floor up above, and I'll be here on the same floor. We're going to make sure nobody else is bugging you, eavesdropping, or doing something else they shouldn't be doing. So you can relax about that. But I've got to tell you, I don't trust your sidekick. I don't trust her, I don't trust her whole damn firm. They're just Soros clones. They're just Moveon.org trying to undermine our war efforts. So I don't want anything to do with them. I don't trust them. And if I come up with something clever, I don't *at all* put it past them to tell the wrong people at the wrong time, either before or after. Either to sabotage the plan, or to call the *New York Times* and tell them what happened after the fact, both of which would be a disaster. The other thing is, I've been asking around, frankly for a long time. I already knew about you, but I didn't know that much. You have sort of a reputation among the teams. Particularly the old-timers. You were the master of the unexpected plan, and were almost always successful. So if I'm going to think of something really smart and clever, I want your help."

"For you to grab my two guys?"

"Thinking about it. How's that strike you?"

"Good."

"Well keep your hot sidekick out of it and maybe we can do something here. I've been thinking a lot about how to do it."

I spent the next several days renting furniture, office equipment, telephones, and talking to Kristen on the phone. I didn't tell her anything about Kevin being there, I wasn't really sure what to say. And Kevin had been adamant that she was not to be included in whatever conversations he and I had. I felt strange about that. I had grown to trust Kristen even though we still disagreed about most things. I thought she was trustworthy and straight, but Kevin had a preconceived idea about certain groups of people, and just didn't trust them at all. It didn't matter what they said or did to try and persuade him otherwise. And if he was going to try something questionable, the last thing he needed was more people knowing about it, or even theoretically knowing about it.

As for me, the time had come to confront the prosecutor. I called and made an appointment, and his secretary said he would be more than happy to see me that afternoon.

I walked across the street to the ICC building, passed through security, and went up to his floor. I waited in the lobby for a moment, then was escorted to the conference room where I had met with him before. It was just two of us. Liam and me. He smiled, extended his hand and shook mine, and said, "Welcome back to The Hague, Mr. Caskey."

"Good afternoon, Mr. Brady. It's good to be back at The Hague. One of my favorite places."

Brady smiled. "We approach the trial, Mr. Caskey. We are only weeks away. Are you looking forward to it?"

"I'm looking forward to getting my clients off. The trial itself, no. Exoneration, yes."

Brady looked around the room and then at me with a frown. "Where is your friend?"

"Kristen?"

"Yes. She was what, your girlfriend?"

"She was my co-counsel. As you well know."

He shrugged. "That doesn't mean she can't be your girlfriend too. I think I saw you looking at her. I think you wish she was your girlfriend but she is not. Am I wrong?"

"You are wrong. You are wrong about a lot of things, that is just the latest."

"Really? And what else am I wrong about?"

"You're wrong about the entire way you've approached this. I'd love to ask you a few questions."

"I am not a witness. But you may ask me what you like about the trial and the procedure. I'm sure you feel a little bit out of your element."

"No, being in trial is *in* my element. It's what I do. The setting is a little different, but evidence is evidence and witnesses are witnesses. And thankfully, when the ICC was setting up its procedures, they provided for cross-examination. All I need is the ability to cross-examine whoever you call."

"And I have the same opportunity."

"Exactly. That's one of the things I wanted to ask you. I need an assurance from you that you won't indict witnesses I call for the defense."

Brady shook his head. "That I cannot do. How can I decide that someone is not subject to a war crimes charge? That is not up to me. That is up to the tribunal."

"So you charge somebody with war crimes, and any witness who shows up to support the accused is part of the conspiracy and almost certainly subject to charges himself. Is that how this works?"

"That can happen yes. But we do not compel them to testify."

"Of course you don't. Because they'd testify for the

other side." I shook my head and played with the cap on my pen. I looked at him intently. "Tell me about the Falcon jet."

He leaned forward. "Why don't you tell me? You were in Peshawar. You went to the airport, and you were responsible for the deaths of many men in the mountains. Perhaps I should charge *you* with a war crime. Killing people in a misguided attempt to defend other war criminals."

"Who owns the Falcon and how did it happen to be there? How did the International Criminal Court know all that was going to happen?"

"I just know that our operations group looked for a charter to fly them back here that night and were successful in finding one."

"Yes, of course. Because they fully expected there would be business jets with an eight-thousand-mile range available out of Peshawar on a moment's notice. Very reasonable expectation."

"If you would like to make this go easier on your clients, I would suggest that you recommend to your clients that they plead guilty. To one of the lesser war crimes with which they've been charged."

"I'm quite sure they would literally rather die then plead guilty to a war crime."

"Nevertheless, you should give them the opportunity so they do not regret it after they are convicted and spend two or three times the amount of time in prison that they would have spent had they not pled guilty."

"They're not going to spend any time in prison."

"Really? Why? Do you think your President Obama

is going to save them? Obviously not. He has decided to pull back the United States forces. I take it he would rather protect your former President Bush and the others."

"Yes, that was a nice touch. To indict everybody in sight from the previous administration to intimidate the current president."

"No, no. No intimidation intended. Those indictments have been in the works for years. The timing was fortuitous to encourage the United States to stop its saber rattling." He stood and extended his hand. "I don't think there is much more to say. I will see you at the trial."

"I look forward to it."


I was obligated to discuss the possibility of a plea bargain with my clients. That was a conversation I didn't want to have. There is nothing quite like suggesting, or even discussing, pleading guilty with a client who is innocent when he knows he's innocent and you know he's innocent. To even suggest that he agree to plead guilty to a crime he didn't commit causes even the most hardened person to erupt in anger and frustration.

I went straight to the prison to meet with my clients. I was ushered into the room where we had met before. They came in, dressed in their prison garb, unsmiling and concerned. They sat down, and we exchanged greetings. They looked thinner and less healthy. I asked, "Do they let you guys get exercise?"

Raw said, "We can walk around in the courtyard, and there's a workout room. It has machines for pretty much anything you want. You can't take them apart and you can't take the weights off or cables or anything. But you can do whatever you want."

"It looks like you're losing weight."

"I'm losing weight 'cause I'm losing patience. We've been in this shithouse for months and nothing's happening. I thought Obama was going to get us out of here. We were packed."

"Yeah. You heard what happened."

Raw replied, "Well, we heard what the news said. We didn't hear anything from you. The news said that Obama blinked. That when push came to shove, when he had the chance to come in here to get us with a battle group, Marines, special ops people, whatever, he got cold feet. All it took was this asshole Brady indicting Bush and Rumsfeld and everybody and he turned and ran like a scared rabbit. So he leaves us hanging. He's ready to just let us rot."

Since that was pretty much my thinking, I couldn't exactly push them away from it. "I don't know if it was quite like that. He has a lot of considerations that we don't see."

"Oh please," Raw said.

"I haven't been told the reason by President Obama, so maybe he still has something in mind. What I do know is we're starting trial in three weeks and we've got to get ready."

Raw asked, "So what exactly have you been doing? We haven't heard from you in weeks. We're sitting here wondering what the hell is going on, watching the news, surfing the Internet—yes they let us—and all we hear about is the fighting in the U.S. over whether we should go to prison or not. Apparently half the country thinks we should, which is very comforting. And then we're left with you, hired by the government, although supposedly by our wives, who isn't getting very much support according to the news reports. Looking for witnesses, prosecutors threatening to charge them just like they've charged us, and we're about to go to trial. So tell us how you're going to get us off?"

"Well, the first thing to keep in mind is that you aren't guilty. I always count on justice being done."

"Really? You have a lot of experience with justice being done in international war crimes trials?"

"I mean when rational people evaluate evidence fairly, they should come to the proper conclusion. That's all I'm saying."

Raw replied, "And you now think Brady is a rational person? He's after the United States, and we are the United States for his purposes right now."

"Don't get carried away, we're going to get you out of here."

They both looked up. "Out of here? Not off?"

"I just don't feel free to talk to you about everything I have in my mind right now. I don't trust them not to be recording us. Like you, I don't trust anybody in any direction. So I can't talk to you here freely. You should just be ready for anything."

Dunk asked, "What does that mean? How do we get ready?"

"You be ready to go to trial, you be ready to testify,

you be ready to go to jail, and you be ready for anything that could possibly happen between now and then. That's what I mean. Anything."

Dunk thought a while, paced the room, and then looked back at me. "When are our wives coming over?"

I nodded. "One week before the beginning of the trial, they'll be here. I'm getting the whole office set up right now, all the other attorneys, paralegals, IT folks, everybody will be here two weeks before the trial starts. Some before that. But your wives are coming over the week before."

He looked at me without saying anything. I knew what he meant. If I was implying what he thought I was implying, and we were going to try something dramatic, the last thing he wanted was to leave his wife behind. Believe me, I'd thought about that. I hadn't yet thought of what to do about it yet, but I'd thought about the problem.

# TWENTY-TWO

I went straight back to my office and knocked on the door to Kevin's room. He opened it and I walked in. "Can I talk to you?"

"Sure." He turned and took me back to a desk he had set up in the corner. I could see maps of The Hague strewn about, as well as various communications information which didn't make sense on its face.

I said, "What's your initial thinking?"

"It's a damned hard target. And if we do it without the government, we'll really be hanging it out. If we get caught they won't go to bat for us. They'll say we were stupid."

"So, we can't get caught."

"That's usually our intention."

"And we can't kill anybody."

"Which is what makes this even harder."

"Get the planning team together. Throw this map up onto the wall and let's start talking this through."

Kevin looked over my shoulder at whoever was standing behind me. I didn't turn around. I could see from Kevin's face that he wasn't sure what to do with me. He stood up and we went into another room that I hadn't seen before. I followed him.

There were maps taped all over the walls, and another set of computers with people working on them furiously. "What's this?"

"This was our planning room. This was where we were finalizing our plans."

"Were?"

"We kinda came to a dead end. We don't see how to do it without taking out about ten people. But shooting Europeans is just not something I'm ready to do. That's how you end up in prison forever."

I took off my jacket and put it on the chair. I turned to one of the men in the room, who was standing behind everyone else, and said, "Would you mind getting me a cup of coffee?"

"Not at all, sir." He turned and left the room.

I said to Kevin and the others, "Let's go through everything. Start to finish. Everything you've considered. I want to spend the next forty-eight hours with you on this. Then we'll see if we come up with something we can actually pull the trigger on."

I quit reading the newspapers, turned off the television, and stopped listening to the politicians, and concentrated for the final two weeks on preparing for trial and meeting with Kevin. The hardest part now that Kristen and the others had moved to The Hague was keeping my work with Kevin separate.

The other attorneys debated who should have which desk, who should be by the window, and who would have what assignment during trial. I didn't care, so I let Kristen make all those decisions. We finally settled in and started having meetings in our makeshift conference room. We agreed we would not comment to the press, wouldn't discuss anything with the prosecutor other than procedural issues, and would put all our efforts into protecting our clients.

One complicating factor was now that the wives of the two navy officers had arrived, they had nowhere to go. So they were at our office from dawn till the last person left every day. I gave them the job of reading every press report that had been issued since the day of the incident to see if there was any insight on witnesses we might want to talk to even at this late minute, or who might testify against me. That gave them plenty to do since the press had been unrelenting. It also helped them see the size and scope of the forces lined up against us, and the political machinations. Just concentrating on the trial and the evidence was refreshing and productive. Kristen, on the other hand, was neither.

She wanted to know why I had insisted on coming to The Hague by myself last time, and why I had insisted on meeting with the prosecutor by myself. And what I had in my mind that I wasn't willing to tell her about. She was sure there was something. I didn't tell her about my meeting with Kevin, or his presence just on the other side of the wall. What was the point? It would just get her aggravated.

We touched base with our witnesses, got our outlines polished, prepared our exhibits, and prepared for trial. The last weeks passed in what felt like a day. The press figured out where we were officed and camped out on the sidewalk. Some of them made their way up in through the elevators to our floor, even without keycards, but we didn't allow them in and didn't speak to any of them. What they mostly wanted was for me to criticize President Obama. I was certainly willing to do that, but not in the press. That wouldn't help anything.

As the weeks ended, the trial began.

The first day of trial, Kristen and I went early. The pretrial proceedings were scheduled to begin at 9:00 A.M. We went to the building at 7:30. The entire press corps was waiting. Cameras were everywhere, as well as reporters with microphones and recorders. Everybody wanted comments and we weren't giving any. We smiled and waved at them trying to look confident, and pushed our way into the building.

While waiting at the security line, I looked for other entrances and exits. I studied the ceiling, which appeared to be made of concrete. It gave me concern that the entire building was concrete-floored. The building was a fortress.

The number of people being let through security was small compared to the throng pushing for entrance, access, or pictures. There were guards everywhere. Kristen and I finally made it through to the other side of the metal detectors where we were wanded for one last look. We made it to the elevator and went to the court-room floor. As the doors opened again, I noticed four armed guards in the corridor next to the elevators, and two more at the entrance to the courtroom.

We walked down the hall, into the courtroom, and to the tables set up for counsel for the accused. As I have mentioned before, the courtroom looked like a high-tech combination of an operating room and a class-room. There were light-wood-colored tables or desks in very specific rows throughout the courtroom, and then the seats for those who were to observe the sur-gery. I placed my briefcase on the chair; our table didn't face the judges, it sat sideways in the somewhat long room. The judges' bench and the clerks' benches were to my left, the prosecutor's tables were across the room facing me, the witness tables were to my right, and be-hind the witnesses tables were the observers' glassed areas. There were two stories of seats for observers with glass walls in front of them. The best I could tell, the total seating for observers was maybe a hundred. They would be able to hear only through the ampli-fied sound with speakers in their rooms. There were flat screens in the corners for them to observe what-ever was presented as evidence by document or im-age.

Much to my surprise, we were the only ones in the courtroom other than one of the court clerks, who was preparing something on his computer.

Kristen and I placed our notebooks and materials on the desks in front of us and the door on the other side of the courtroom opened. Liam Brady walked in and gave us a perfunctory wave. I stood up and crossed the room. I said, "Good morning," as I extended my hand.

He turned and looked at me somewhat surprised. He took my hand and shook it. "Good morning. You seem in a chipper mood."

"Not really, just glad to be getting this underway so my clients can go home."

"Yes of course," he said, fighting back a smile. He started to walk away, then turned back to me. "To that end, I would suggest that you talk to Ms. Debra Craven."

I tried to think of someone by that name, but didn't recognize it. "Who is Ms. Craven?"

"She is from your American Justice Department or State Department. She has apparently been sent over here to negotiate a plea bargain on behalf of the United States government."

I was stunned. "What? The United States government isn't a defendant. They can't speak for my clients."

"I'm sure you're right. But you still may want to speak with her. Because apparently there is quite a discussion involving the position of your country with regard to the International Criminal Court, the indictments of the members of the previous administration, and your clients. I think you should speak with her."

"Believe me, I will. Do you have her number?"

"Sorry, no. Perhaps you should call some of your friends in Washington. They probably have her number. Didn't you work at the Department of Justice? They should know her. Don't you know people there who could help you find the person who's negotiating a sentence on behalf of your clients?" He turned away again and ignored me.

I walked back over to Kristen and told her what Brady had said. She looked at me in shock. "That's not possible. How could they negotiate a sentence without us being involved?"

"I think he has it in mind that it will be presented to us as a fait accompli. They will tell us take it or leave it, and then probably leave it to us to sell it to our clients. Some small insignificant jail term, then return to the United States on the quiet. But a guilty plea to something. They'll never go for it. Neither will I."

Kristen seemed knocked off her horse by the whole conversation. She asked, "What do we do?"

"We need to find this woman. I'll send a text to Chris. I'm sure he'll be able to track her down. I'll tell him to have her call me at lunch. We'll ask her to come over to our offices. I'm not going to have this entire defense sabotaged by the State Department."

We sat down and I noticed the gallery. The few people who were going to be allowed to watch the opening day of this critically important war crimes trial had begun making their way into the room on the other side of the thick glass. I looked and then I did a double take. The first person through the door was Kevin. He was wearing a European-looking suit with a striped shirt and a tie with a large knot that you only saw in London. He had no glasses on, and had his hair combed back. I barely recognized him. He was carrying a journalist's pad and looked very much the reporter. A dressed-up reporter. A sophisticated reporter. Someone working for the *Financial Times* or *Wall Street Journal*. How he was pulling this off was beyond me. I turned to Kristen and began looking through my outlines. The rest of the participants made their way into the courtroom at the same time the galleries filled, both at the level where I sat and the next level up, sort of the theater balcony. They all stared at Kristen and me, probably wondering how we could defend such horrible people. I hadn't paid that much attention to the European press, and didn't know how it was being represented. I did get the sense though that a lot of people were very happy that some Americans were finally going to get what they deserved.

After the gallery was seated, a door had opened in the wall behind the judges' bench and our two clients were ushered in. They were given the seats next to us, which also had monitors in front of them. They wore poorly fitting suits with ties.

They had neither their hands bound nor guards standing behind them. They were remarkably free given the circumstances, for which I was grateful. The security guards stood in the corner with their weapons and nightsticks. They did not look particularly formidable.

The three judges entered from a door behind their bench and walked to their seats. They stood stiffly as the clerk asked everyone to rise, and paused as the judges stood momentarily behind their seats. They were wearing their black robes with long blue collars and white cravats and looked very formal and serious. Judge Hauptmann told everyone to be seated, and we did.

After some administrative work, the judges were

ready to commence the trial. They called the court order and the presiding judge made specific announce-
ments about how the trial would be conducted, the order
of witnesses, the manner of cross-examination, and all
the trial procedural details that were written into the
rules. They wanted to make sure that the procedures
were clear to all the parties. They of course were. While
they were presenting the rules and procedural details,
Kristen was writing on a pad of paper to our two defendants what had happened in our conversation with
Brady this morning. As soon as they got to the part where
she wrote "plea bargain," Raw pushed her pad away in
disgust. He realized everyone in the gallery was watching him, and tried to control his emotions, but his eyes
burned as he looked across the room at Brady. Kristen
tried to find out if anybody had mentioned this to them
from any source at any time, but they had stopped communicating. They didn't want anything to do with the
topic. They crossed their arms and began to feel what I
had been feeling for months—that more forces were
against them than they had feared.

   After a few minutes the chief judge asked Brady for
his presentation of what the evidence would be. In an
American trial, we called it the opening statement. The
previous ICC war crimes trials that I had watched
showed great variance. Some prosecutors saw no particular need to even give an opening statement. But I
could tell that Liam Brady was not one of those. I had
never seen him dress with any flare whatsoever, yet he
seemed to have come into his own. His hair looked like
it had been specially cut and oiled and he seemed taller

and thinner than before. I was prepared to wager he'd put lifts in his shoes. Not that he was short, he just saw this as his chance to fulfill his destiny. I could feel it. I ran into these kinds of attorneys all the time. This was when the world was finally able to recognize their greatness.

Brady turned to address the court. He knew his audience. Three judges he probably knew by their first names. Three judges who were officed in the same building he was. No jury of peers of my clients, no jury of ordinary citizens, just judges, who, in my opinion, were often quicker to prejudge a defendant than ordinary people were. They'd seen it all before.

As Brady began his comments, I found myself paying no attention at all. Kristen was taking notes so furiously they had to be verbatim. I put down my pen, sat back, and checked out the room. I tried not to look at the ceiling but I was tempted. I examined the seams of the glass to see how thick it was and whether it was bulletproof. It looked to be very thick, two to three inches, and almost certainly impenetrable by any ordinary means. The walls also looked to be wood panel but over concrete. The room was almost certainly sealed concrete except for the entrances. There were four. The door behind me that Kristen and I had used and to which we had been directed by security. The door to my left that our clients had come through and which was an exclusive corridor for prisoners with no entrances and exits between the courtroom and the holding room. The door behind Brady, which was almost certainly the same as ours only on the other side of the courtroom. And the fourth door just on the other side of the judges through which they entered the courtroom. There were no entrances from the courtroom to the gallery area. If I was inclined to overwhelm the guards, which wouldn't be impossible, there would be nowhere to go except outside the door I had entered. It had a handle and could be opened from our side, but we would then simply be in the corridor among the security forces lining the hall and left to try and get down the stairway or the elevator. It would be foolish to try, at least without an extraordinary plan. But no such plan was occurring to me.

I drifted into Brady's comments and back out, thinking of innumerable things. That's not how you were supposed to go into the trial, but that's how I was going in. I felt completely freed in the defense because I thought the defense was futile. But I was going to give it my best; I just didn't need to hear his rambling. In the pieces that I was hearing, I learned that my clients were the tip of the iceberg in a long systematic series of war crimes. And while the mastermind of any given war crime was certainly accountable, so were the soldiers. The fact that they were just the pilots, just doing their job, just executing their orders, was the exact defense that had been tried and failed at Nuremberg when the United States put on war crimes trials against the Germans—along with the other Allies—with no treaty in place whatsoever. No International Criminal Court treaty, no Treaty of Rome, no debate on what constituted war crimes, no debates on the burden of proof or standards. All this was wildly inappropriate in an American court, but the judges looked almost disinterested.

Brady went on for an hour, listing each witness and the cumulative testimony. But what he said at the end caught my attention. He said that while some would, very few of the witnesses would need to be presented by videotape, that most of the witnesses would be live, including the most important witness of all. A member of Pakistani intelligence. He lowered his voice to gain attention. The very one who had told the American intelligence about the location of the meeting and that there were refugees there. He would come and tell the court that he warned the Americans that refugees were present at the building when he gave them the target information, but they decided to bomb it anyway. After Brady was done, he paused, surveyed the room, and sat down very pleased with himself.

It was my turn. The chief judge nodded to me. I stood and went to the lectern next to my table. I addressed the judges. I was as brief and direct as I could possibly be. I took less than fifteen minutes. My position was quite simple. I looked the chief judge directly in the eye and told him what I had told him in my motions. The court had neither the authority to accuse anyone from the United States of war crimes, nor the jurisdiction over my individual clients to accuse them of anything, let alone war crimes, nor the facts to support any such charge. I told them that the prosecutor would lose this case, and the International Criminal Court would lose face. It brought the entire area of human rights and war crimes into disrepute. It had put the court into a position of using international law for political manipulation. For what in the United States was called payback. It was being used as a means of communicating displeasure with American policy, even though that policy was the same as NATO's and was joined by other members of the International Criminal Court, including France, Germany, Italy, Great Britain, and notably, the Netherlands.

I then took the court into a direction they didn't expect. I told them that the actions taken by the prosecutor to convene a midnight Star Chamber to force through an indictment threw the entire process into doubt.

Brady objected several times to my statement, and the court sustained several of them. I knew I was out on the edge, but I didn't care. I was speaking to the world audience that was watching by television. And at the end, the evidence would support exoneration.

As Brady was about to call his first witness, the court noted the time and called for a two-hour lunch recess. They took our two clients into the holding cell to feed them lunch, and Kristen and I headed toward our office. The press was everywhere. As we came out of the ground-floor lobby to the outside of the building, it was a sea of people. It was impossible to get through. Several security guards walked beside us and pushed the crowd away. The television and print journalists yelled questions, for explanations of my statement, like whether I was trying to be the next William Kunstler. I found that amusing. Perhaps the most radical left-wing attorney in modern American history. I might be radical, but it had been a long time since I've been called left-wing. In fact, I don't think I ever had.

The security led us across the street to our building

and into the now guarded lobby. The landlord had retained his own security to keep people out of the building, which I appreciated. We went to the elevator and up to our office. I had forgotten to turn on my phone, and when I did it buzzed with a text message. Chris had sent me the phone number for Debra Craven. As we stepped into our office and its whirl of activity, I highlighted the number and dialed it.

I put my briefcase down on my desk next to my computer overlooking the International Criminal Court building and waited. A woman picked up after the third ring.

"Debra Craven."

"Jack Caskey. I think you know who I am."

"Of course."

"I was illuminated this morning by Liam Brady. He told me you had been talking to him about a plea bargain for my clients. True?"

She paused, clearly taken aback. "We have had many discussions with him over the past few months. He mentioned the possibility of a plea bargain. I didn't offer anything."

"Where are you right now? Physically. Where are you?"

"I'm at the U.S. consulate."

"Get your ass over here to my office right now. I'm directly across the street from the International Criminal Court. We're on the third floor." I hung up.

Kristen sat down at her desk next to me and turned in her swivel chair. "I wish you'd let me know what you were going to say in your opening statement before you said it."

"Sorry. I haven't kept you in the loop on a lot of things. I've just been going. I apologize. What did you think?"

"Well, if you wanted to stir things up, you did that. If you wanted to get our clients off, I'm not sure you helped at all. You inflamed everybody. You insulted the court, you insulted the signatories to the treaty, and you insulted the prosecutor. You pretty much just threw a Molotov cocktail into the whole thing. What's your plan?"

"My plan? My plan is to go at this as hard as I can. To cross-examine every witness that I have, just like I expect you to cross-examine all the witnesses that you have. I expect to fight back at every turn, object to every document, and watch the court come back with a conviction."

"Really? You think they'll convict them?"

"You think they're going to go through all this to find them not guilty? Not going to happen. I don't think there has ever been a war crimes trial that has found an accused not guilty. The accusation is the conviction."

"Well, then we just have to keep going. Because they're certainly not going to get off if we don't try. But I would very much like it, Jack, if you would not elbow me out of this whole thing."

I went on. "The first witnesses are some of the Pakistani villagers. In fact, the whole afternoon is going to be taken up by the first two people talking about the devastation, the death, the destruction, the dismemberment, the surprise, the horror . . . we'll have to go through it all. I may not ask them any questions."

I turned around and went through my outlines on my computer. Fifteen minutes later I got a call from the building. It was Craven. I told them to let her up. She came to our office door and knocked. One of the Covington and Burling associates opened the secured door. She walked in like she had been there a hundred times. She was very tall, over six feet. She had blond hair pulled back into a ponytail, and had a hard, humorless face and wore no lipstick on her thin lips. She wore a black suit and a high-collared white blouse. She carried a thin black briefcase and stopped to look around the room, finally seeing me and walking over as I stood up and walked around the desk. I shook her hand and gestured to my desk. She sat down. Everybody in the room could see and hear pretty much everything. While most tried to return to a semblance of work, many were trying to hear what was about to happen.

"Thank you for coming. I'm sorry I hung up on you, but it's kind of a crazy day."

"What can I do for you?" she asked coldly.

"Well, first you can tell me what you're doing here."

"I have been sent by the State Department to negotiate with the International Criminal Court in all regards."

"What is your position at State?"

"I'm the assistant to the deputy secretary for legal affairs. We are in charge of all things related to the International Criminal Court, international war tribunals, treaty negotiations regarding human rights, and the like."

"You work for Secretary of State Clinton."

"I guess you could say that."

"Okay. So why are you here now?"

"Because of the trial. Because of your clients."

"You don't represent them. We do."

"Generally true. But while you represent them individually as an attorney in this trial, I represent them—and *all* Americans—in treaty negotiations and discussions with the International Criminal Court. It's only peripherally about your clients."

"Again, why now? Why are you talking to the ICC now?"

"Well, Mr. Caskey, as you are quite well aware, there have been some very dramatic developments. Not the least of which is the indictment of our former president and several members of his cabinet. That is no light matter."

"It was a tool. To force Obama to withdraw the armed forces that were up here. You know that, he knows that. Everybody knows that."

"That may have indeed been one of their objectives, but it is not the only issue. Those indictments are still outstanding. Theoretically, President Bush—if he traveled to another country—could be arrested and sent to the International Criminal Court."

"Never gonna happen. Because then we *will* come and level the ICC."

"Don't be so sure."

"You're right. I'm not sure. We have rights under the American laws to get these two navy officers out of the prison. And President Obama had the forces in place to do it and he blinked. And the reason he blinked is because of these indictments. And now here you are bowing down before the court, kissing their rings, for the same thing. You've walked right into their game."

"I disagree with your characterization. We haven't walked into anything. We have chosen a course. You may not like it, but you also may not fully understand it."

I raised my voice. "Well then why don't you explain it to me? What is your plan?"

She hesitated. I could tell by her look that she knew I was going to be very unhappy. "We have reached a tentative agreement, whereby the International Criminal Court agrees to dismiss the indictments, and the United States agrees to sign on to the Treaty of Rome as it is currently drafted."

"You cannot be serious. What indictments?"

"All the indictments of President Bush and his cabinet members, members of the military from his administration, everyone."

"Including my clients?"

"Well, no. The discussion, where we left it yesterday, was that they could either go through trial, or they could plead guilty to a single charge from a single count. In fact, Mr. Brady said that you could choose, and they would then serve some token sentence of let's say sixty to ninety days, after which they would be released and returned to the United States."

I leaned back in my chair and put my hands behind my head. I stared at the ceiling and smiled. Kristen was sitting right next to me staring at Craven.

Kristen said, "They'll never plead guilty to anything. Have you even talked to them about this?"

"Of course not. I wanted to get the best terms I could before presenting it to them. To you."

I looked at her with my hands still up. "How can you even think of agreeing to that? How can you sign on to a treaty that has been rejected by each administration since and including President Clinton? How can you allow a court to manipulate you? It's stunning to me how you can be so completely clueless about what the hell is going on here. And now you're going to do *exactly* what is their best-case scenario? They get to watch President Obama back down from them before the entire world and send his powerful fleet home, to be followed by signing the treaty we despise, *and* they get a conviction of American servicemen for war crimes they never committed? And there you sit in the middle of it, acting like you've done something *good*? Well, you have screwed this all up so bad I don't know if we'll ever be able to extract ourselves. I'll tell my clients what you've told me, but I'll advise them against plea-bargaining to anything—"

"But you believe they're going to be convicted, don't you?"

"I do. I think they'll be convicted because this whole thing is a sham. The evidence probably doesn't even matter."

"And if they're convicted they could serve twenty or thirty or more years in prison."

"Theoretically."

"And that's okay with you?"

"No. It is most definitely not okay with me."

"Then how do you plan on avoiding it?"

"I plan on winning at trial. The odds of which are extremely low. And if we don't, then I plan on coming back here with several of my closest friends and blowing a hole the size of an ocean liner in that prison and carrying those two navy men out. And if I get arrested and spend twenty to thirty years in prison, so be it. Then I'll have some of my friends come and blow a hole to let *me* out."

"You and your friends are going to do this?"

"Yes, we absolutely sure as hell will. They have no idea who they're dealing with."

She laughed. "I had heard, Mr. Caskey, that you had some delusions. That you still had ill will toward the United States, and were something of a loose cannon. I would strongly advise you against doing anything stupid. I don't know who your friends are, but they certainly cannot overcome the strong security forces of the International Criminal Court. And I'd advise you on behalf of the United States government not even to try."

"Well, believe me. If I'm going to try anything 'stupid,' you'll be the last person to know. I will go back early this afternoon and tell my clients what you have said. I will let you know what their response is. Where can I find you?"

"You have my number. I'm watching the trial at the consulate on television. I think everybody in the world is watching the trial. I have to say so far, Mr. Caskey, you've looked more like a fire-breather than a careful attorney who is going to defeat this case based on the evidence."

"Thank you for your input, you've been most helpful." I turned away and Kristen took the hint. She got up and escorted Craven to the door.

Kristen sat down again next to me. "That is an amazing development."

"The usual United States government looking out for interests that don't reflect what the people really want. Have you seen the latest polls?"

"Yes. Obama's approval ratings have dropped to their lowest level since his election. They attribute it to his capitulation to the International Criminal Court."

"Yes and here we go. About to capitulate more. Can you imagine what would happen if I called Fox News and told them what Craven has just told me?"

"It would be a very bad day for President Obama. Do you want to do that to him? Sabotage this whole thing?"

I turned and leaned over to her in my chair. "I would love nothing better than to make this whole thing blow up in the face of whoever is making these decisions and quavering before the mighty International Criminal Court. What complete bullshit."

She looked into my eyes. "While you may *want* to do that, you're not *really* going to do that, are you?"

"No. I'm still not sure I have a full understanding of what's going on here. It's beyond unsettling when something like this happens the morning of trial. It makes you feel like the government is doing a whole bunch of things we don't know about that might affect things. Makes you feel like a puppet in a much bigger play. But

I have a lot of strings that I'm pulling too, that nobody else knows about. Including you. So I'm not sure I'm ready to blow up whatever it is they're trying to do."

She frowned. "Meaning what? What strings are you pulling?"

I looked at my watch. "Why don't you call over to the ICC security and tell them we need to meet with our clients fifteen minutes before the trial starts. Let's grab a quick sandwich, then we can head over there. After trial this afternoon, I'll fill you in. But you're not going to like it."

# TWENTY-THREE

The holding cell for war criminals was stark and barren. There were six security guards inside the room with us when we met at the table with our two clients. It was a large room and they were not close enough to overhear anything. Raw and Dunk were still in their ill-fitting suits. They sat on one side of the table and Kristen and I sat on the other. I filled them in on everything that had happened since I'd talked to Brady that morning, including what Kristen had referred to in her pad. They were outraged.

Raw said simply, "Never. I'd rather die."

I replied, "I'm not telling you you should. I'm not suggesting it or even recommending it. It's completely up to you. I just have to present it to you. It's my job."

"Where is this coming from? How do they think they can get us to plead guilty to anything? We didn't do anything wrong."

"There's going to be some ambiguity about who said

what, when, and what you knew. It shouldn't be enough to convict you, but with this court, who knows. I suppose anything could happen. The just and correct result is that you get off. But if you don't, you could be looking at life in prison, or maybe twenty to thirty years if you get a shorter sentence."

"Surely the United States would come and get us out if we got convicted."

"I don't know. Based on what Craven said, President Obama is getting very cozy with the International Criminal Court and the human rights community, and would prefer getting into bed with them than fighting them to get you off."

Raw leaned back and threw up his hands. "How do we win here? You keep telling us the trial is rigged, that they're going to string us up no matter what. What's your plan?"

I paused for a minute, and thought over all the things I'd said to them. I hadn't exactly been encouraging. "We have to trust that the truth will come out. We have some good witnesses who are prepared to testify for you. We have the air force intel officer who is going to tell the court that Pakistan told him that there *had* been refugees at the building but no longer were. He's going to say it was a clean target, and that you did your job. Everybody up the chain of command, some of whom will come here to testify—I think—will say exactly the same. They had a good target, good intelligence, and did exactly what they should have done. The fact the intelligence was bad isn't our fault; it's not your fault. It's the fault of those who gave us bad intelligence. But

I have to tell you, that guy, the person who talked to our targeteer, will probably come to testify, and he may say things differently than what our guy says. Unfortunately, there are no recordings, and no transcript."

The two naval officers looked at each other and then at the table. Finally, Dunk asked, "What's your best guess? You think we're going to be convicted?"

I looked at Kristen and back at them and said, "You shouldn't be, but I think it's a little bit more likely than not that you will. We'll appeal it, but you have to be ready for the possibility of a conviction."

Raw looked intently at me. "Are there any other . . . options?"

I looked at him just as intently and said, "No," in such a way that he knew I meant yes.

He looked at Kristen and realized she had no idea what message I was conveying and gave me a slight nod.

I said, "Sorry, we have to get ready for the afternoon's session. There won't be much to it, just more people talking about the devastation and being around when the bomb hit. It's a predictable start. Start with the disaster, start with the mayhem and the death, get everybody riled up, then go back and try and explain how it all happened. As I said, fairly predictable. We'll meet again tomorrow during the lunch break. I think that's the best time. They bring you here just before trial begins, and you leave right after. In those armored trucks. How many guys do they have in there with you?" I asked, apparently innocently.

Raw picked up on it. "Four guys inside the truck with us, and two in front, one driver and a guy riding shotgun. And usually three or four trucks that play sort of a shell game. We're in a different one each time and they shift around."

I nodded and stood up as I picked up my briefcase. "Must be stuffy in there."

"Very."

"Bunch of guys with machine guns and the like. And your hands are probably bound behind you."

"Exactly."

I nodded. "Thanks."

The afternoon went just as I had expected. More witnesses from Pakistan. What I hadn't expected was that Brady would pull out the pictures in the first day. He put up hundreds that were identified as accurate by several of the Pakistani witnesses. Pictures of devastation and death. I then first realized that there were members of the families of those killed at the site sitting in the courtroom. They were wearing Afghan clothing and sitting in the six seats across the room from us, directly next to the prosecutor, which were designated as seats for the "victims' representatives." Two of them looked like tribal chiefs and were staring at Raw and Dunk.

The afternoon was filled with three witnesses from Pakistan, and Kristen and I decided together, without any question, that cross-examination was not only unnecessary, but would be counterproductive. It would simply get them to repeat everything they had said. There was no dispute that a bomb had been dropped and that it had killed numerous people. There was no dispute that it had been dropped by a navy F/A-18F.

There was no dispute that Europeans were killed, that Afghans were killed, or that Pakistanis were killed. There was no dispute on the number killed. There was no dispute that it was an extremely violent event. The only real issue is why it had happened the way that it did. Cross-examining witnesses on the measure of the destruction would have no effect whatsoever. It also, by the time the third witness was done as we approached 5:00 P.M., had become numbing. There had been so much testimony and so many photographs of the devastation that you couldn't help but become hardened at least a little. To the judges' credit, they appeared unmoved by the evidence from the first graphic picture. Unmoved in an emotional sense. They certainly understood the implications of the evidence on the charges. By the middle of the third witness we were at the end of the day and the judges adjourned until the next morning.

Kristen followed me back to the office through the sea of what appeared now to be permanently stationed journalists, and over to our building. We went up to our offices, put down our briefcases and papers, and sat down heavily in our chairs, which were next to each other. The rest of the people working with us wanted a full report. They had watched it on television, but wanted any other commentary. Our two clients' wives were sitting at a table in a corner. They also approached. They had been there in the gallery for the entire day, but they too wanted to hear what we had to say. I knew we had to take the time to review the day's events, so I said, "Somebody get me a Stella out of the fridge, and let's do a quick review of what happened today." They all gathered around the area that we called the "kitchen" because there was a small refrigerator in that furthest corner as well as a small microwave and a toaster oven that people used to heat their croissants. When most people were in easy earshot and I had drunk some of my beer, I went over the day's events, the meeting with our clients—although without telling them much of the content—and that none of the evidence that went in was unexpected. Many wondered why we hadn't cross-examined the Pakistani witnesses, and what our plan was for the remainder of the witnesses. I explained my thinking to them the best I could, but I was impatient. I needed to get on with preparing for other things. After about forty-five minutes, I called it, and people returned to their desks. On the way back I whispered to Kristen that she needed to stay until everybody else had left. I decided it was time for her to understand exactly what was going on.

Most people had wrapped up their work by eight. A couple lingered until ten, then finally at eleven, the night of the first day of trial, Kristen and I were alone in the office. When the last person walked out the door, I pushed back my chair and stood up. I said to her, "Follow me."

She stood, adjusted her blouse and skirt waist, and walked behind me. "What's this about?"

"You'll see." I walked to the end of the office, turned the corner, and walked directly into the corner toward the middle of the building, where it simply looked like two unadorned walls coming together in the shadows.

Kristen looked around, looked up, looked at me and put her hands on her hips waiting. I pushed on the corner of the wall and the hidden door opened. She said, "What the hell?"

We stepped through into a darkened room full of computer screens. Kevin turned from his station, looked at us, and yelled, "Screens off!" Perhaps twenty computer screens immediately went blank, and the room was even darker than it was before. Kevin jumped up, ran behind us, slammed the corner door, and said, "Damn it, Jack! I told you she couldn't come in here. What the hell are you doing?"

Kristen said, "What is going on here?"

I said to Kevin, "She has to know. I'll explain."

Kevin threw the pencil in his hand back onto his desk and said, "That's it. I'm out of here. This is over."

He turned to the others and said, "All right guys, start gathering your stuff—"

"Hear me out, Kevin. Let's sit down."

He looked at me, still very angry. Still with his baseball cap on backward and with his glasses. He thought about it. He said loudly, "Stand fast. Let's hear him out."

He motioned to the table, sat there, and waited, seething.

I sat down with Kristen. She continued to look around in complete amazement. I said to Kevin, "Look, Kevin, if we're going to do something here, if we're going to get these guys out, we've got to go with them. We can't leave Kristen behind, or me behind, because then they'll put *us* in jail and somebody else will have to do it all again. She's part of my team. I trust her. She's not going to do anything stupid, and she has to know what's going on. I could also give her the chance of just going home now. If she sees where this is going and doesn't want to be a part of this, she can head home."

"And tell the *Washington Freaking Post*."

I looked at Kristen. "We're going to make a move to get our clients out of this trial. At some point we're going to grab them. We haven't finalized our plan yet, but we're working three options. All three options have problems, but we think we can pull it off. The hard part is doing it without killing anybody. But knowing that, if you want to go home, say you're sick or say you're sick of the trial or me, or we can't work together anymore, or whatever you want to say—you can feel free to pull out. I don't want you caught up in this if you don't want to be. I can finish this by myself. Especially if we're not going to finish the trial anyway."

I waited for her response. She looked baffled and angry. She ran her fingers through her hair and took a deep breath. "Let's start first with what is going on here. I take it you had all this set up while I wasn't here. Which explains why you didn't invite me to come over last time. What is it exactly that you guys have in mind?"

I jumped in before Kevin had a chance. "We don't know when or how we're going to do it, and we don't even know for sure that we're going to try; but we're going to have some plans in place in case we decide to. If the trial starts going our way, if the evidence starts falling in our direction and we think we have a strong likelihood of prevailing, then we'll wait. We'll do nothing. We'll let it go to the judges, and see if our guys can get off. But if it looks to us like our trial is doomed, and our clients will be spending the next few decades in prison, we're going to get them out."

"You can't do this. This is only legal if the *president* authorizes this. And even then, it's not legal here. If anybody gets caught, they'll be put in prison for years, or decades, in addition to our clients. And people could get hurt or even killed."

"That's all true, but we're going to do it. We just needed you to know. Because if we do it while you're here, we're going to have to evacuate you, or you'll get arrested and they'll question you and probably charge you with something."

She glared at me with a look that was a little too close to hatred. "And what about all of our friends and other attorneys who have been working with us? The paralegals? The secretaries? How are they going to get out?"

"They'll be questioned. But they won't know anything. They won't have anything to hold them."

She replied, "I could have been in the same situation. But now that you've brought me in here, you've made it so I have to choose. I have either to go home or be part of this. I can't claim ignorance anymore. And the last thing you'll want is for me to be testifying. So, what is it you want me to do, Jack?"

"I want you to stay here and be part of the trial and in the off chance it gets fair, maybe we'll win. Who knows, but we'll be ready in case we need to pull our clients out of here. We're going to have a plan, it's going to be pre-cise, and we're going to execute it. People might get hurt, you're right. But we will get out of here."

Kristen stood up, looked around, and shook her head. She walked through the concealed door and Kevin closed it behind her.

Kevin sat back, took off his baseball cap and put it on the desk. "Brilliant. Just brilliant. What were you thinking, Jack?"

"She wouldn't have gotten away as easily as the as-sociates will. She already knew about you, and some of what was going on. They would have assumed she was part of it. I had to get her to buy in."

"Yeah, dumbass, but now she'll do the very thing I *told* you she would do. She'll call the *Washington Post* or the *New York Times*. And if we do pull your guys out, she'll tell them about the whole plan, the setup, every-thing. Shit, Jack. You just poisoned it." He stared at me, then said, "I may leave you on your own to do your law-yer shit. 'Cause I can't do this with everything on the front page of the *New York Times*."

"I've been thinking about our alternatives. But I don't know what you can get."

Kevin looked at all the other people, who were lis-tening, and said to them, "You can get back to work." Their screens turned back on, they turned away, and the hum of the room that had been there when we ar-rived began again. Kevin stood up and poured himself a cup of coffee. He came back and sat down. "What are you thinking about?"

"What can you get?"

"Like what?"

"We're not going into the prison. Too hard a target. We've got to get them on their way to court, in the trucks, but they're armored. Could be big trouble, but we've got to leave that option open. Can you get RPGs, C-4, motorcycles, Dragon Skin, everything we need?"

Kevin nodded. "I can get anything."

"In a couple of days?"

"Yes."

"And if we go into the court itself, which I'm beginning to think is the way we need to do it, we may need to get out through the top. Can you get a Chinook?"

Kevin thought for a minute. "That's a little tougher, I don't know."

"Find out."

Kevin nodded. "By the way, I think I've got the identity of the owner of the Falcon."

"Who is he?"

"It's still a little bit cryptic, but we think it's a super-rich Belgian guy. He has a long history of speaking out against the war in Iraq and the war in Afghanistan, and was pushing everybody he could get to listen to him to indict Bush when he was president. Check this out."

Kevin spun around, wheeled over to his desk, and hit the space bar. The screen lit up and he opened a file from his desktop. "Here's his picture." He called up a picture of a gray-haired thin man wearing a suit and the picture was his photo as the CEO of a corporation whose name I couldn't pronounce. Kevin closed that and opened another which showed a photograph of him giving a speech in front of an industry group. He then showed him at Davos, Switzerland, listening to speeches by world leaders and shaking hands of numerous international celebrities.

I spoke, "Impressive guy. How'd he make his money?"

"Shipping. He owns the largest Belgian shipping company in Antwerp. That's where his company is headquartered. But he owns a bunch of companies. He has a huge estate outside Antwerp, owns a huge place on a Greek island and several other houses."

"He's the one who made all this happen?"

"Looks like it."

"What's his motivation?"

"Political leaning. Hangs out with George Soros, all the usual international suspects, drinks the Kool-Aid of all the anti-American rhetoric that's so common here, but has decided at some point to do something about it. Big supporter of the International Criminal Court. Attended some of the trials."

"But if he's really behind this, then he's responsible for killing several European medical people and numerous refugees. How could he do that?"

"I don't know. I'm sure there's justice in there somewhere from his perspective. It doesn't matter to me."

I stood up and prepared to go. "You know where to find this guy?"

"Yeah."

The outline of a plan was beginning to form in my mind. "While you're figuring out whether we can get close to him, see how hard it would be to get two Falcon 7s, on the QT. We may need them. With pilots we can trust."

"What for?"

"Transportation. And print out that guy's picture. I'm going to show it to Dunk and Raw. He may be the guy who was sitting in the back of their airplane."

The next day of the trial was much like the first. More witnesses from Pakistan, and then in the afternoon came the woman who had yelled at me in Pakistan. Elizabeth Vos. She looked different, but it was her. The same look, the same hair, but now dressed very professional. People in the gallery stood up. The judges gave her special attention. They had heard enough reports of the mayhem; they wanted to hear how this had *happened*. She introduced herself, and told of her background. She was Belgian, and a doctor, and had been trained at the University of Leuven. She had spent years working in refugee camps in Palestine, Africa, and Afghanistan. She made an excellent witness. She spoke excellent English, and was sympathetic and articulate.

She recounted the history of her refugee organization, and how they had gone from being primarily a medical group to caring for the refugees, including shelter, food, and clothing and even their "immigration status" as she called it.

She spoke of the other people who were on her staff, person by person; the ones who were killed. The French woman doctor, the German in charge of food, the Irishman who tried to work politically with the tribal chiefs, the Pakistani authorities, Afghan authorities, and those who were in the gray areas. She described several Pakistani employees who did the day-to-day work, those who did the wash and prepared the food and dug new toilets away from the village.

Then she described the refugees. Brady knew what he was doing. Before we had had the pictures of body parts lying all over the village, a hand here, a foot here. Now, he put those body parts on the people to whom they belonged. He had done DNA testing to identify whose hand or foot it was. He then put up a picture, a close-up of a hand or finger, and then put up a picture of the person from whom it had come, which Dr. Vos had in her possession. She had taken a photograph of every person who had come to her facility. These were incredibly well-done high-quality photographs of people that were candid or semi-candid. They were doing ordinary things such as mending a shirt or carrying water. She was especially good at photographing children, a very difficult task. She had a high-quality camera with very dense digital pictures that maintained their quality even in extraordinary size.

Brady put up a picture of a leg that was found a hundred yards from the building. It was a woman's leg with a worn shoe, leggings, and part of a skirt. If you stepped back from the picture it looked like it was simply a side view of some woman wearing a skirt. But then if you saw the entire picture, you could tell the leg had been blown off and was lying on the ground by itself. He told her that he would represent to her that this leg through DNA testing belonged to a woman named Laila Sababi. He asked for her to assume that was her name. She replied that she didn't need to assume it. She recognized the skirt. "That was Laila's skirt. I watched her repair it." Dr. Vos paused. "She wore it every day. It was the only one that she owned." She began to tear up thinking about this young Afghan women for whom she cared so deeply.

Dr. Vos began to describe the week before the bombing. Several new people had fled from a heated battle in the mountains of Afghanistan to cross the border, and several had arrived at the facility. She described their fear and hunger and in particular the three young children. What they liked and disliked. What they feared and the nightmares that woke them up every night since their arrival. Then she went on to describe the day of the bombing.

It had been the day for linen changes and each bed had been changed. All the sheets were taken out to be washed. They had been washed, dried, and brought back in. They were stacked in the corner for the next change. As they were stacking the linens, she had been told that one of the new children that had come to the facility had been accused of stealing by one of the village leaders. The evidence was thin, but many felt strongly he was guilty, including his parents. They wanted him to make reparation to the boy whose shoes they thought he had taken. Dr. Vos had gone to mediate the dispute that night. She had been negotiating an apology to the family deep into the evening when the bomb hit. She was sitting at the table with the family in their dining area. It was dimly lit by a lantern as they had no electricity.

She was about to conclude the meeting and head back to the building when she felt as much as heard an enormous WHUMPF from behind her. She'd never heard or felt anything like it. It was a physical blow. It knocked her forward and knocked the other people backward. No one fell, but each thought that something catastrophic had happened—a meteor or an instantaneous earthquake or a massive explosion. They ran outside the house and looked toward the direction of the noise. She tore down the hill toward the devastation, fighting back the panic and sobbing that tried to overwhelm her, nearly deaf from the explosion. As she got closer to the fire and debris, her spirit was crushed by what she saw. She knew it was a bomb, but didn't know where it had come from; a truck bomb, a car bomb, or some other source. She never thought for a minute that it was a bomb that had fallen out of the sky from an American navy fighter.

It wasn't until later when she was told what had happened that her anger burned against America and the so-called allied forces in the so-called continuing war on terrorism. The war that she hated, like all wars. She was a woman of peace. All she wanted was to make people's lives better. And her project, the one into which she had poured her life, was completely destroyed, along with all the people she was trying to help. She ran toward the fires but realized she could do nothing. She fell to her knees and sobbed.

It was a moving story. I was moved. She meant every word. No doubt in my mind. She said she was a woman of peace. I didn't doubt that either. The world needed people like her. She was making a measurable difference in the lives of the people she helped. Even if it was a small difference, it mattered to the people she helped.

So it was with some concern that I stood up to cross-examine her. Kristen looked up at me in surprise, wondering what I had in mind, knowing that if this went wrong, it would make things far worse. Better to just let her be a woman of peace, and talk about how hard it was on her and not to have her attack our clients.

"Good morning, Dr. Vos."

"Good morning." I was grateful the trial was in English, and all but two of the prosecution witnesses had spoken English. I looked around the courtroom, slowing things down, getting everyone's attention before I started.

"You were negotiating with the village leaders the night the bomb dropped. Correct?"

"Yes."

"You have some influence in the region, true?"

"I'm not sure what you mean by that. But I know most of the tribal leaders, and the women who know everything that is going on in the village. I don't know if I have any influence."

"Well, you didn't tell us the outcome of your negotiation on behalf of the boy who stole the shoes. You had achieved a resolution of that matter, had you not?"

"Yes, it had all been worked out."

"And while it may sound like a small matter, it was significant in the village, wasn't it?"

"Yes."

"Because the last thing they want is a refugee camp in the village that invites thieves in who steal from the local villagers, right?"

"Yes, there is truth to that."

"You are aware of the tension in the region, correct?"

"What do you mean?"

"Well there are two kinds of tensions right now. The tension between the ruling of the area by the Pakistani government and the tribal leaders, correct?"

"Yes, there is some question of allegiance and authority. It's been ongoing for years."

"Right. And the other is the tension between the growing forces of the Taliban and the tribal leaders. Correct?"

"Yes. There is Taliban influence."

"And an increasing presence of al Qaeda, which is exemplified by the increase in car bombs and suicide bombings ever since the new year, correct?"

"Yes, there has been an increased presence of what some call al Qaeda."

I was surprised a little bit by her answer. "Are you not familiar with al Qaeda? Do you call them something else?"

"No, al Qaeda is fine."

"And in fact it was because of al Qaeda's increased presence that you believed that the bomb that you felt was an al Qaeda bomb that had blown up your refugee facility initially, correct?"

"That was my initial thought." She nodded with sadness in her face.

"As someone who knew the area and knew the political tensions, you were personally aware that al Qaeda was operating in that area. Correct?"

"People said that. I didn't know personally, I didn't

meet any of them that identified themselves as al Qaeda, but that was on people's minds."

"And you absolutely knew that the Taliban was operating in the area. That they had leadership, structure,
and armed men throughout the area. Correct?"

"I don't know about throughout, but there is a Taliban presence and they are armed."

"And they're menacing. Correct?"

"I don't know what you mean by that. But you
certainly have to be aware of where they are and,
unless you are part of what they're doing, understand
the difficulties that might come from confronting
them."

"And you understand do you not, Dr. Vos, that the
reason that this building was bombed, this is the assertion by the prosecutor," I said and pointed to him, "was
that there was supposed to be a high-level meeting between leaders of al Qaeda and the Taliban that night.
You understand that?"

"I heard that in the press."

"It was true. Wasn't it? There was a meeting scheduled between al Qaeda and the Taliban to consolidate
power in your area. True?"

"There was no meeting that I was aware of."

I doubted she would know about it. Although if it was
inside her building I wondered how she wouldn't. I decided to take a flier. In law school and all trial training
courses you might ever take, they'll always tell you not to
take a flier. Don't ask a question you don't know the answer to. Well, I didn't care. "The night of the bombing

there were a couple of men in your facility that you didn't know. True?"

"There were two men I hadn't seen before who were from Afghanistan. They said they were looking for their families."

I couldn't believe her answer. "You don't know they were there looking for their families in actuality though, do you? That could have been a Taliban leader and an al Qaeda leader meeting at your facility exactly as the intelligence had indicated. Correct?"

"Oh, I don't think so."

"But you don't know. Do you?"

She paused. "I hadn't thought about it."

"So you don't know, do you?"

"I guess I don't."

# TWENTY-FOUR

I thought I had at least put it in the minds of the judges that it was possible that the intelligence the United States had received, and that Pakistan had apparently received, was actually good intelligence. That there had been a meeting between two "Afghans looking for their families" who were actually leaders of the Taliban and al Qaeda, who chose that place because no one would know them and they would be protected from attack. The safest place to hide from an American aerial attack is a hospital. What I had begun to doubt though was that she actually did not know who these people were. I couldn't imagine two men walking into her refugee building and having the ability to wander around and meet in private inside this facility. But leaving open that possibility was all I intended with her, and I thought I had accomplished it.

As we headed back to the office for lunch, Kristen still hadn't said much. She seemed to be engaged in what was going on. She didn't seem angry, but she was very cool. As we stood in the elevator on the way up to our offices during the lunch break, I asked her directly, "How are you doing?"

She hesitated, and then said, "Okay."

"Have you called the *New York Times* yet?"

"No. I'm still negotiating the fee."

"Good idea."

She turned directly toward me. "How exactly do you see this playing out, Jack? Let's say you succeed. That you and Kevin come up with some way to get our clients out of custody, and away, probably back to the United States uninjured, and that nobody is killed in the process. Assume that. Then what? What happens after that? Holland would go crazy, the whole European Union would come unglued, they would probably start demanding that you and Kevin and maybe me get extradited back to Holland for breaking some law or other, or ten, and then what?"

"No, it would be totally legal. And then there'd be a conflict of law. The United States would never extradite us back to Holland when we're doing something that is specifically authorized."

She shook her head vigorously. "No, you're missing the point. The Servicemembers' Protection Act only applies if it's authorized by the *president*. By definition, this isn't authorized."

The door opened and we stepped out onto our floor. There was no one around on the floor and we stopped. "We'll get the president to authorize it retroactively. They'll cover us once we accomplish our objective."

She frowned. "Really? And who has told you that would happen? Chris? Because if I recall, you're the one who was calling President Obama a 'pussy' for withdrawing all of our forces. So you're saying that he is going to withdraw the actual forces, then let you do this on your own, and then claim it was his idea all along? That's your plan?"

"Something like that."

"You better start thinking this through a little bit better, Jack. You've started thinking like a SEAL again, getting the mission done. The hell with the legal implications. That's not the way it works. You're a lawyer now. You're representing two clients in a war crimes trial that is being watched by the entire world. You can't go playing GI Joe and just hope it all works out."

"I know that, Kristen, but this is real. This isn't some hypothetical on a law school exam. These are two men who are about to spend their lives in prison based on a charge that is bogus."

We walked up to the door and I waited before opening it. I looked her in the eyes from maybe eight inches away. "So I need to know whether you're with me or not on this. You can play ignorant and play dumb, and maybe get left behind and take your own chances, but if you want to go back to the United States where nobody will touch you, you gotta let me know. Or if you're going to turn on us, and rat us out, you probably oughta let me know that too."

"So I get to get myself somehow pulled out of here, flown back to the United States, and never visit Europe again."

"I don't know. I don't know what the future holds. I can't predict that far ahead. I'm just telling you that something may happen here and I need to know where you stand. Kevin doesn't trust you, I do. But you're going to have to choose."

She looked down at the floor and waited. I left my hand on the door handle. She finally looked up at me. "I'm going to have to think about it."

I looked back at her hard. "Tomorrow. I have to have an answer by tomorrow."

"Why?"

"Because we're in our final planning stages. It could happen any day."

The remaining witnesses that day were more people from Dr. Vos's organization. Two had been in Afghanistan the night of the bombing, and one had been back in Geneva. There was nothing new or particularly insightful in their testimony, but the last event of the day was an announcement by Liam Brady that the next witness would be a gentleman from Pakistani intelligence. The one who had told American intelligence, those responsible for targeting the building, exactly what the status was. He would be the first witness tomorrow. None other than my good friend, Tariq Qazi, from Islamabad. That would be interesting. I had a few new questions for him.

After trial that day, Kristen worked for maybe a half hour at the office, then left. She was obviously consumed with trying to get out of the box I had put her in. The one thing I couldn't allow was for her to go to the press before we even had a chance to get our clients out. I knew I was taking a risk, but I didn't think she would do it.

I waited until everyone else was gone, and then met with Kevin.

He had found a pizzeria nearby and there were several open pizza boxes on the table. When I came through the door Kevin was stuffing more pizza into his mouth. He looked at me and nodded without saying anything. He finally swallowed and stood, saying, "Come on in."

I sat down across from him and grabbed a slice. He nodded as I wolfed it down. I was surprised at how hungry I was. I loosened my tie and took a deep breath. I sat back and put my feet up on one of the other chairs.

Kevin asked, "How's it going in the trial?"

I swallowed and said, "Like I expected. Some of the witnesses do better than I anticipated, but I guess in this environment you have to assume they've been incredibly well prepared. Mine will be too though. But don't worry about that. How are you doing?"

Kevin nodded as he ate more. "We own the night. The boys get here about nine o'clock and we do everything at night. That's why the windows are blacked out, it looks like it's just an empty office building floor but we're humming away."

"Are you planning all three contingencies?"

"Yeah. The more I plan them though, the more it seems to me there's only one choice."

"I'm coming to the same conclusion. The Chinook?"

"Yup. We can do motorcycles, we can do trucks, we

can do a lot of different things, but the Chinook is really the only answer at this point. But then we've got to get out of here."

"Can you line up the Falcon 7s?"

"Done. They're for the Ford Motor Company."

"Perfect." I thought of something that had been nagging at me. "This guy, the Belgian who started all this."

"Yeah."

"How did he do it? How could he have set all this up?"

"He's got to know people in Pakistan. He has to know someone at the ISI."

"Or more likely the ISI alerted him ahead of time so he could get the airplane and the court lined up," I said. "By the way, it looks like the meeting may have been real. Dr. Vos confirmed there were two men that she didn't know in her refugee facility the night the bombing happened. Two men supposedly looking for their children from Afghanistan. I'm thinking those were the Taliban guy and the al Qaeda guy. And they probably got vaporized. Looks to me like this whole strike was legitimate, except for the part about the refugees. That means he had to know about that too. The whole thing. The meeting, and the fact that the refugees were there."

"That's what it sounds like to me."

I drank and thought, then said, "That means our antiwar Belgian sacrificed a bunch of his European pals."

Kevin nodded. "Ice-cold, man."

"You think he could do that. Is he that type of a guy? I mean that's evil."

"A lot of evil out there, Jack. You know that."

"Sure. I expect to see al Qaeda behaving like barbarians. But I don't expect some big-time Belgian businessman to be blowing up fellow Europeans all in the hope of entrapping the United States in some war crimes trial. It just doesn't add up."

"Maybe the ISI didn't tell him everything. Maybe they used him."

"Either way, we can't just let this guy go. We've gotta take care of him."

Kevin looked at me intently. "What do you have in mind?"

"Have you tracked him? Do you know whether he has a PSD?"

"Personal security? I assume so, he's a big shot. Probably a billionaire. They've all got pretty high-quality bodyguards."

"Check them out. See if we can get him."

"I'll get some guys on it. You thinking about doing this at the same time? That's putting a whole new layer of complexity on top of what we're doing, brother."

"I know. But he may be an important piece of what I'm coming up with. Tomorrow night, you and I are going to sit down and diagram this out."

Kevin nodded enthusiastically. "About time."

"You sure you can get everything we need? Including all the nonlethals?"

"Yeah. That's no problem. I've got whatever we need. We've got stuff even the U.S. military doesn't have. I might need a couple of days for some of it to get here."

I started to leave, and then I stopped and turned

around. "Tomorrow's a big day. As I said, our good friend from Pakistani intelligence Qazi, is going to testify. Turns out *he* was the guy who talked to Curley. Wonder how he failed to mention that when we were there? You know some other people in Pakistan?"

Kevin nodded slowly.

"Call them. Let's get into Qazi's knickers. I should have thought of this a long time ago. We've got to get on it. Tell them what we're thinking about for our shipping friend."

"You got it."

I went back to the hotel, exhausted. I walked into my room, closed the door behind me, and quickly realized someone was sitting in the chair by the window. It was Kristen. I was surprised. I put my bag down and threw my suit coat on the bed. "How'd you get in here?"

"I used the key you gave me."

"I gave you a key?"

"Yeah. The day I got here you gave me a key to your room and said I could use it anytime I wanted. I think you had something in mind."

"Sorry. That was rude."

"It's about what I expected."

"So what's going on?"

She was wearing tight jeans and a loose-fitting sweater that looked particularly attractive. She had on blue flat shoes. She stood up. "I told you I'd get back to you on what my thinking was on all of this. I've got to tell you,

Jack, it's been eating me up. I can't be part of some big escape plan. Somebody's gonna get hurt, probably killed. I can't have that on my conscience."

I waited, but she said nothing else. I replied, "But you can handle watching this court put away our clients forever."

"There's only so much I can do about that. I can appear and represent them, but I can't control it. My conscience will be clear."

"So it's all about your conscience? Not about what's right or just, just whether you have a clear conscience."

"You think it's right to break into the International Criminal Court building and help prisoners escape?"

I looked at her directly. "Yes. Not only is it fine, it's authorized."

"Again, only if the *president* authorizes it. And even then, it's still illegal as hell in Holland, which is where we are currently standing."

"I get that. I'm prepared to run that risk. You're not, I get it."

"I'm sorry, Jack. I just can't do this. I'll go into court with you tomorrow if you'd like, and announce that I'm withdrawing."

I felt anger welling up inside of me. I had guessed wrong. I thought she was someone I could rely on, and would be a huge help. What a miscalculation. She had turned out to be far more trouble than she was worth. Now she was a problem. "No, that's the last thing we need. The whole world will think that you've seen evidence to make you think that our clients are guilty. We can't allow that. I think you should just get on an airplane and go somewhere and disappear."

She looked like she was about to cry.

"I'll tell them you weren't feeling well and had to go home. I'll try the rest of the case myself. But once we say that, the press will hound you. They'll be on your doorstep, they'll be at your office, they'll be at your parents' house and your friends' houses; they'll pursue you twenty-four/seven until you tell them what's going on, and of course you can't tell them. And when we say that you aren't feeling well, you can't go to work in New York every day acting like everything is fine. So, what's your plan?"

She seemed defeated. "My parents have a place in the Adirondacks. I could have my mother meet me there. We have a pretty long private driveway; you can't even see the cabin from the road. I'll have my mom come there with me, and I won't set foot off the property until the trial or—whatever—is over. She can go buy soup and Advil and tell everybody that she is taking care of me and that I'm going to be fine and that's all she'll say. She can pull that off."

I nodded. "They'll hound her too. You have to know. But if you stick by that, you might be okay. I only need a few days."

She crossed the room and stood directly in front of me. I could smell her perfume and started having thoughts that weren't appropriate. She said, "I also want you to rethink what you're planning. Not because of any legality, but because I don't want you to get hurt."

I looked at her carefully and thought that she actually meant it. "Suddenly you care?"

"I've always cared."

"You have a funny way of showing it."

"I don't show it in professional relationships. It doesn't help."

"Well maybe after all this, we can have an unprofessional relationship."

"Maybe so. Where do you think you'll end up? Back in D.C.? If you do what I think you're going to do, if you just show up in D.C. as a criminal defense lawyer again, Holland is going to try to extradite you. Do we have an extradition treaty with Holland?"

I nodded.

"You've already checked."

I nodded again.

"Then what's your plan? The U.S. might have to honor it if you don't get the president to buy in that this whole thing was his idea."

"I'm not sure yet. It sort of depends how this plays out. But don't change your cell number. You may hear from me from someplace unexpected someday."

She nodded. She went up on her toes and kissed me on the cheek. For some reason it irritated the hell out of me. It felt patronizing and dismissive. But I was in a pretty chippy mood at the moment, so I wasn't trusting my perceptions.

She walked around me and out of the room and the door closed behind her. Well shit. Isn't that just perfect, I thought. Now I'm by myself. Going to the heart of the trial, preparing our witnesses, cross-examining the crit-ical witnesses from the prosecution. At least my plan-ning sessions with Kevin could go on undisturbed. No more explanations, no more external conscience.

The next day it felt strange going to court by myself. The press noticed immediately and peppered me with questions as I crossed the street. They always did, but this time the questions were about Kristen. I told them that she had taken ill and wouldn't be in court. I didn't tell them she was on her way home. They'd figure it out later. She had sent me a text that she had gotten on the first flight out that morning, and was already gone. I had even lied to the other attorneys and told them that she was sick, that she had some condition she hadn't told me about, and that she had gone home to get it taken care of. They were immediately all very concerned and started texting her, assuming she was pregnant and I was responsible.

She didn't respond to any of them, which was a good sign. It sounded like she was going to do what she said she would. Although I was distracted, and thought a lot about the relationship I wanted to pick up with Kristen after this was all done, I had to refocus.

Today was to be Qazi's day. The very one who had told Major Curley about the target. This would be the turning point of the trial. If he testified as I expected, the blame would pour out against my clients. He was a slick operator with his fake Rolex. I wondered if he would wear it.

I greeted my clients, who looked angry and irritated,

even more than usual, and we sat. While there was some commotion in the courtroom, before we were in session, I put the printed picture of the Belgian shipping magnate in my notebook and went over to my clients. I bent over to talk to them quietly and opened my notebook slightly so they could see the picture. I whispered, "This the guy sitting in the back of your airplane when you were flown to Holland?"

They sat forward and looked at the picture. Dunk said, "I can't be sure, but it looks like him."

Raw said, "Definitely. That's him."

"You sure?"

He nodded, his eyes burning with the possibility of revenge.

I closed my notebook and took my seat. The judges looked particularly spry that morning, with their freshly pressed robes and stunning blue collars that hung down about eighteen inches in the middle of which was the ruffled white silk cravat. Very distinguished.

As the court grew quiet, Brady stood and called his next witness, Mr. Tariq Qazi. And in he came, looking more polished than he had when Kevin and I met with him in Islamabad. He had his hair cut. He was clean-shaven, and he wore a nice-fitting European suit. I wondered where he had gotten it. He was smaller than I remembered him, but looked supremely confident. He sat in the witness chair, moved the screen slightly, and looked at Brady. I could see his "Rolex." Phony asshole.

Brady began. "Would you state your name?"

"My name is Tariq Qazi."

"Where are you employed?"

"I am employed by the government of Pakistan."

"What do you do for them?"

"I work in the field of intelligence. Collecting information, checking its validity, and telling the government what I've learned."

Brady led him masterfully through his entire career in the Pakistani army, his intelligence training, his time in the ISI, to his current position. He asked questions that gave Mr. Qazi an aura of mystery. People are always intrigued by intelligence. The idea that there are people in the world who know incredibly important secrets that the rest of us don't get to know is irresistible. Those who are in that world know how to play on that mystique, and Brady was taking full advantage. Finally, Brady focused on the day in question.

He spoke softly, "Now, Mr. Qazi, on the day of this disaster when all of these people were killed in Pakistan, you were on duty and working in intelligence. Is that right?"

"Yes. I was assigned to be the liaison with the United States intelligence services, and particularly those involved in prosecuting the war in Afghanistan."

"And on that night, were you asked about a certain meeting that was to occur between members of al Qaeda and the Taliban in the mountains of Pakistan?"

"Yes, this was something we had been tracking for quite some time. We had learned that there were discussions between those two groups on coordination and particularly how they might coordinate their efforts to control the mountainous areas of western Pakistan." His accent seemed less Pakistani and more British than I had remembered.

"Was there in fact to be a meeting of men from those two organizations?"

"Organizations," I thought. What a cute way of referring to them.

"Yes. We had heard rumors. But we also had good intelligence that such a meeting was going to happen. We weren't sure when or where, which of course is typical for them. It's almost impossible to find out information about such meetings, but we had it from several sources that a meeting at the highest level was going to take place. And then we got information on the where and the when but only shortly before the meeting was to occur."

Brady leaned forward. "How did you receive that information?"

Qazi shook his head. "I cannot reveal this. It is difficult for me even to discuss what I knew—what our intelligence was—let alone how we got it. My country will not allow me to reveal our sources of intelligence. It would compromise those sources."

Brady nodded quickly and deeply. "I understand completely, Mr. Qazi. I'm not trying to intrude into your sources, but if you could give the members of the court some indication of the nature of those sources, they would then be able to better evaluate the information that you had."

Qazi appeared to be thinking. It then struck me that this entire thing was scripted. Every question that Brady was asking, Qazi knew was coming. Every pause, every head nod, every tickling, slow revelation was planned.

"I can say this," he finally said firmly. "They were human sources. People who we know who are in various positions to know certain things. That's as much as I can say."

Brady smiled. "That is perfectly adequate, Mr. Qazi. What did you learn that night?"

"We learned that the meeting was to take place that night in the village. We didn't know the time, but we had an approximate window of two hours when they would probably be there."

"What were those hours?"

"It would have been based on local time in the village, and that would have been between ten P.M. and twelve A.M."

"And where was this meeting to be?"

"That was the key question. Because if we knew exactly where it was going to be long enough ahead of time, we could have people there to grab them, arrest them. But that was the important piece of information. That was the most closely guarded secret."

"But at some point you learned where the meeting was to be held."

"Yes. We did."

"What did you learn?"

"That day, in the middle of the day, we got confirmation from one of our sources that the meeting was to be in that village."

"That was it?"

"Yes, but we asked for more information. We wanted

to know where. If there was a landmark, or a building or someone's home. We needed specifics. That village is not big, but it is not tiny. There are probably a thousand people who live there. And if it was in someone's house, and they were just two men, we would never find them. We might have found them if we were able to encircle the entire village, but if we did that, they would see us and never go to the meeting. It had to look empty of military force."

"So what was the plan that was developed?"

"It was multilayered. We had Pakistani forces on the way to the village, but they would probably not get there in time. There were local American special operations groups nearby, just across the border, which is very close, and they were also on their way. Then the Americans sent a drone to monitor from high altitude so it could not be seen. We pulled out everything we knew, all the information we had on that village, for possible locations of a meeting. We knew the names of the people that lived there, people with ties to the Taliban, even though they claimed they didn't, and tried to put it all together to determine where the meeting would be."

"And did you finally make that determination?"

"Yes. Actually we were told. We received another communication. And we were told it was at the refugee facility."

"Did you know what that meant?"

"Yes. We had been aware that the AMI organization had taken over a building in the middle of this village to handle Afghanistan refugees. Mostly those with medical conditions."

"And it was your understanding that the meeting was to occur at the refugee facility?"

"Yes. Exactly."

"Did that surprise you?"

"A little. Usually I would have expected these men to meet somewhere out where there is no public eye, where there is no one around except their own people."

"Why do you think it was different?"

"Two things I think. First, while they were getting together, they don't trust each other. They are competitors in one sense and they don't trust the security of the other. So to go somewhere say in a cave or a tent in the middle of the mountains, with each surrounded by the other's security or armed men, is not necessarily the place they would feel the safest. Sometimes, especially if their faces are not known, they like to meet in a public area. Where they leave their forces behind, and infiltrate a town or village, then meet, and then leave by themselves. It is actually easier for them to do that than to go in with a force of a hundred or fifty or twenty-five armed men. Also, the second thing, and sort of clever, is the idea of meeting in a refugee facility. That way if the Americans are watching, or someone else is watching and decides to attack them, they will have to kill a large number of innocent civilians at the same time and they know the Americans are reluctant to do that."

Brady went on. "What did you do with the information that you had?"

"I had a conversation with American intelligence. As I said."

"What did you tell them?"

"I told them just what I told you, that the meeting was on, that there was a window of probably two hours, and that it was at the building in the middle of the village. I gave them the exact latitude and longitude of the building so there would be no misunderstanding."

"Did you tell them that it was a refugee facility?"

I watched his face carefully. He replied quickly, "Yes. I did. I told them there were refugees there."

"Why did you tell them that?"

"For the obvious reason. They were planning on attacking the men in the meeting. They might have some special operations people nearby who might do something that would result in damage to the building or to the people inside the building, or they might bomb it. I was talking to one of their targeting men, and he could send a drone to do it, or an airplane, or anything. We, of course, discourage them from attacking anything inside Pakistan but that doesn't really make much of a difference. They do what they want to do. So I wanted to make sure they didn't bomb this place."

What a nice speech. Very moving. And as I looked at him, I didn't believe a word of it. I thought he was full of shit. But he was clearly selling it to the judges.

"You didn't call in an air strike on this building, did you?"

"No. Of course not. My hope was that there was some special operations people near enough to grab these two men once they emerged from the meeting."

Brady waited, then asked, "To make it clear, did you tell the Americans that the building where the meeting was to occur had refugees in it?"

"Yes I think I said that. Yes."

"Any doubt about that? Any possibility for misunderstanding?"

"I don't think so. My English is not of the same accent as America, but I've never had any trouble being understood."

"And after you heard of the bombing, what did you think?"

"I thought the report must be wrong. I thought some stray bomb had fallen off an airplane or it was a suicide bomber."

"And once you learned that the bomb had come from a United States Navy F/A-18 what did you think?"

"Again, I thought it must be a mistake. But then when I heard that it hit the refugee facility, right in the middle of the building, it sounded like it was intentional. They hit the building that they meant to hit, probably because the meeting was occurring there. And they killed the refugees and the workers there anyway because the targets made it worth the cost."

I stood up and objected. "Your Honors, this calls for pure speculation on his part. What he thought is not relevant to this case."

"Sustained," the chief judge said.

"Mr. Qazi, have you met with anybody from the United States about these matters?"

"Just one. I met with an American lawyer."

"Why did you meet with an American lawyer?"

"He came to Islamabad to ask me about what I had told the American targeting man."

"Who was that person that you met with?"

He looked at me, pointed, and said, "It was him."

Brady turned toward the judges. "I have no more questions."

# TWENTY-FIVE

This was it. This was their critical witness. Without him, they had no evidence or knowledge or that gotcha moment of the Americans having run over critical intelligence and doing exactly what they pleased. I'd been preparing his cross-examination since I saw his name on the witness list.

I stood. "Mr. Qazi, you're a member of the ISI, correct?"

"Yes, that is what it is called."

"And you're familiar with the history of the ISI, correct?"

"I don't know what you mean."

"Well, the ISI has been part of the Pakistani government for decades. Correct?"

"Yes."

"And back in the 1990s after the Russians were thrown out of Afghanistan, the ISI helped found and fund the Taliban. Correct?"

"I have heard that asserted before, but I know nothing of this."

"In fact, many people inside the ISI maintain very good ties with the Taliban, correct?"

"No. The Taliban is not a friend of Pakistan."

"You deny that there are people inside your organization that keep close ties with the Taliban. Is that your testimony?"

"Yes. I know nothing of this."

"All right. Well, let's discuss what this specific case is about. You were the one who was aware of the intelligence that a senior al Qaeda official and a Taliban official were going to meet on the night of the incident. Correct?"

"Yes. I had that information."

"And you believed that information. Correct?"

"Yes."

"And in fact, it was true. There was a meeting that was to be held that night between al Qaeda and the Taliban. Right?"

"That is what we believe."

"Controlling the western provinces of Pakistan is very difficult, isn't it?"

"What do you mean?"

"Well, there have been open battles between the Pakistani army and the Taliban for control. For example, in the Swat Valley. Right?"

"Yes. The Taliban has had a great deal of operational freedom, which is not acceptable inside Pakistan. It is a problem."

"And if al Qaeda worked with the Taliban to help them gain this control, or they shared control of the mountainous regions between, say, Islamabad and Afghanistan, that could almost create an entirely separate country that would be extremely difficult to stop. Correct?"

"I don't know about a separate country, but yes."

"A meeting between the Taliban and al Qaeda is not something that Pakistan would tolerate within its borders if it knew about the meeting. Right?"

"That is correct."

"So that night, you wanted that meeting to be stopped. Correct?"

"Yes."

"And you had intelligence that men were in fact meeting. Right?"

"That was our intelligence."

"And you said two men, didn't you?"

"Yes."

"Were you listening to the other testimony in this trial?"

Mr. Qazi frowned. "What do you mean?"

"Have you listened to the testimony of the other witnesses that have testified already in this trial?"

"No. Why would I?"

"Because the only person who has ever mentioned that there were two men who were meeting is Dr. Vos, of AMI, who was in charge of the refugee facility. Nobody else has said there were two men."

"I don't know what she said."

"Well, in fact, sir, isn't Dr. Vos your source? Isn't she the person from whom this human intelligence has been gathered?"

Brady looked up concerned. He had obviously never thought about it. And I saw a look of fear enter Qazi's eyes. I had hit a nerve.

"As I said before, I cannot discuss or even imply who our sources were."

"So you're not denying that she was your source."

"As I said, I cannot discuss sources at all."

I nodded. I thought about the implications. If in fact she was his source, she told him that al Qaeda and the Taliban were meeting at her facility. She had in effect called in a strike on her own place, and just "happened" to be out when the bombing occurred. That was probably coincidence. There was not a chance she put her own workers and refugees in harm's way for whatever political gain there might be. She was as much a victim as anybody. She probably thought they would track them, and capture them somewhere else, not drop a bomb on the entire building.

I continued, "And you decided to tell the Americans about the meeting. Correct?"

"Yes. We share with them intelligence of this kind. They have capabilities that we do not have, including special operations teams and the like. We have some of that, but not to the extent the Americans do."

"So your intention in telling them was so that they could send special operations teams to capture or kill those two men. Is that your testimony?"

"Yes."

"Then why were you talking to the American targeting center in Qatar? To the men who chose aerial targets for the air tasking order?"

"I simply spoke with the person they referred me to. I told them that our time was short and that we had to act immediately. They put me in touch with this man."

"Do you remember his name?"

"I do not."

"It was Major Curley. Does that sound correct?"

"Yes," he said, nodding.

"Well, you knew that he was an air force intelligence officer and targeteer. Right?"

"I'm not sure what his position is. What his job is. I knew he was in Qatar and working with the U.S. intelligence on how to conduct the war. That's what I knew."

"Well, wait a second, you knew he was with the United States Air Force, true?"

"No. I knew he was a major. I did not know his service."

"You had spoken to him before. Right?"

"I believe so."

"And it's your testimony that he never told you that he was a targeteer?"

"I have already said what I thought. I don't recall that word."

"Well, I will represent to you, sir, that he will testify later in this trial that his job is to select, authenticate, and confirm targets for the air tasking order—for the air forces in the Middle East, including the drones. You knew that, right?"

"No. I don't think so."

"Well, isn't it true, sir, that in the past you had informed him of intelligence targets within Pakistan's borders that were then targeted by drones?"

"No. Well perhaps I gave him intelligence, but I never suggested a drone attack inside our borders. We think those are not helpful."

"But as you said, you provided him intelligence and subsequent to your telling him about those targets, they were attacked by drones, and you knew that. Right?"

"I think so, yes."

"But this time you told him about the meeting that everyone had been waiting for. The meeting between al Qaeda and the Taliban. Didn't you?"

"Yes. I did tell him that the meeting was going to happen. And I told him when and where it was going to happen."

"How did you get this information?"

He frowned and shook his head. "I told you that I was not going to reveal intelligence sources. I cannot."

"But you were confident in your information. Right?"

"Yes."

"Then if your information was accurate, the meeting did take place, and it took place where you said. At the refugee facility. That means that al Qaeda and the Taliban representatives—whoever they may have been—were there when the bomb hit, right?"

He sat back as if he had not even considered that possibility. "Yes, I think that must be the case. They probably were there."

"And they were killed when the bomb struck. Right?"

"If my intelligence was correct and they were there when I was told they would be there, then yes. They were killed."

"And you have no problem with that."

I turned around and looked at everyone in the room. "I would assume no one would have any problem if the Taliban and al Qaeda representatives were killed. That's not a war crime, to kill the enemy. Right?"

"I think that's right."

"So the only thing that we're really here to talk about is how it was the building happened to be full of refugees and medical workers at the same time. Right?"

"Yes, I believe that's right."

"So the real question here is whether my clients—who are the ones charged—should have known that the refugee facility had people in it other than al Qaeda and the Taliban. Right?"

"I don't really know what the charges are here or who needed to know what. I'm just here to tell you what I know."

"Okay. Fair enough. Let's talk about what you know. You did not have any conversations with my clients, did you?"

"No. I did not."

"In fact, the only American that you had any conversation with about this issue at all was this targeting person in Qatar. Right?"

"That's right."

"Well, he's not here as a defendant. The defendants, the ones who have been charged with war crimes—for knowingly attacking civilians—are my clients. That's your understanding, right?"

"That's what I understand."

"And you're the one who claimed to know that the meeting was taking place and the location. Right?"

"Right."

"And you don't have any information that somebody else from Pakistani intelligence had a conversation with my clients on their aircraft radio, do you?"

"No."

"And you never did, did you?"

"No."

"Okay then. As I understand your testimony, you had a conversation with an American targeting officer to whom you gave some information that may or may not have been passed on to my clients. Correct?"

"I don't know what was passed on to anybody. I just know that I spoke with one American."

"Let's go over what you told him. You gave him the nature of the meeting, confirmed it, and the location. Right?"

"Yes that is correct."

"And how did you give it to him?"

"I gave him the latitude and longitude."

"Of the building. The building that was destroyed that had the refugees in it?"

"Yes."

"So you gave an American targeting officer the latitude and longitude where they actually dropped the bomb?"

"Yes."

"And did you—after the bombing occurred—confirm the latitude and longitude and confirm that was where the bomb landed. By looking at BDA—bomb damage assessment—photographs?"

"Yes. The bomb landed exactly on the latitude and longitude that I gave him."

"Because that's where the meeting was to take place, right?"

"Yes."

"So then the Americans didn't miss the target, they hid it dead-on. The only thing then left, is whether the two men in the F/A-18 that dropped the bomb knew that there were refugees there. Let's address that. Did you tell this American targeting officer that there were refugees at that facility?"

"Yes. I told him there were refugees there and that it was a problem."

"Now listen carefully, Mr. Qazi, this is critically important. Did you tell him that there were refugees present *then*? Or that there *had been* refugees present at that location?"

"I think I used the word are. I think I said there are refugees at that facility, which is a problem. He said that he understood, and that was the gist of the conversation."

"Are you sure you didn't say that there *were* refugees at that facility? As in past tense?"

"No. I said are."

"No doubt?"

"No doubt."

I slowed down, and looked around the courtroom. I looked through the bulletproof glass to the gallery. They were giving me, and Mr. Qazi, their complete attention. The clerks were looking at me, the family representatives were looking at me. I returned my gaze to Qazi. "I will represent to you, sir, that Major Curley will come here to testify. And he is going to say that when you and he spoke you told him that there *were* refugees at that facility, not that there are at that moment."

"Well that is not what I told him."

I held my hand up. I wasn't finished. "I also have told him, and he has agreed, to bring whatever tape recordings he may be able to find of that conversation he had with you." I stopped, and stared at Qazi. I could see a slight momentary panic in his eyes. "Based on that, sir, do you wish to change any of your testimony here today, which is under oath?"

"No sir. I have told you the truth."

"Well, would you agree with me that if in fact the court believes the targeting officer who is going to come here and testify contrary to what you just said, if they believe him instead of you, then this whole chain of events was your fault. Right?"

"I don't understand."

"Well, if you *meant* to tell the targeting officer that refugees were present at that moment, and yet you did *not* tell him that, then the reason that a bomb was dropped on the refugees was *your* fault and not his, and that would mean that perhaps you are the one who should be charged with war crimes, and not my clients. Correct?"

Liam Brady stood up quickly. "I object to this question, Your Honors. This is outside of acceptable questioning."

"I withdraw the question," I said as I sat down.

Judge Hauptmann asked me, "Do you have any further questions?"

I stood briefly. "No, Your Honor."

"You may be dismissed," he said to Qazi, who hurried away from the witness stand, looking like he needed to go check something.

It was a strange evening with Kristen gone. Predictably, everyone wanted to know what had happened. Most of them were her colleagues from her firm, and had received no communication from her at all. They found that not believable, unless she had been wheeled out to an ambulance and taken away. If she was alert enough to walk onto an airplane, she should have been alert enough to text one of them to say what was happening. I should have worked on my story more with the other attorneys, and especially with the press, who were in a frenzy. But I ended up saying the same thing all the time. I told everyone that she had taken ill and needed to return home. No one was buying it. The new prevailing theory among the C&B associates was that she had heard enough and knew that our clients were guilty, and she was done participating in a failed defense.

But her absence also gave me a freedom that I had not felt until that point to meet with Kevin and plan our options. I gave everybody the night off and went in to eat pizza with Kevin early. He was surprised to see me that soon.

I sat in a folding chair, loosened my tie, and started on a piece of pizza. I said, "Any luck talking to your Pakistani higher-ups? Because Qazi lied through his teeth and is the key to this whole thing. I saw it in his eyes, Kevin."

"What did you see?"

"He's full of shit. He did not tell Major Curley that there were refugees present that evening. He told him there *used* to be. I'm sure of it. When I told him that Curley was going to testify and bring whatever recordings of the conversations he could find, he went a little bit white. He's good though. He kept it from showing very clearly, but I saw it. I saw that momentary panic. He doesn't know if I was bluffing, but he knows his head is on the block if I'm not. He probably knows Pakistan asked the U.S. not to record the conversations, but he has no way of being sure we complied. If we walk in with a recording, and show that he said there *used* to be refugees there, but not now, he's a dead man. So you've got to get with your Pakistani guys. You have contacts, you said, have you talked to them?"

"Yeah, I'm talking to them on a daily basis. They're watching this carefully. They're hanging on every word. This whole thing pisses them off. They're still furious that the International Criminal Court is playing a jurisdictional game with them. Pakistan has intentionally not signed the treaty."

"So?"

Kevin continued. "So the higher-ups, those above Qazi, are still pissed that the ICC saw fit to come into their country and assert a war crime and jurisdiction over that war crime, which clearly occurred in Pakistan—not Afghanistan as they like to try to say—and basically claim jurisdiction that they don't have. Pakistan thinks this entire thing is illegal."

"No doubt. But again, so what?"

"So they're ready to help us if we decide to do what we've been thinking."

"They're in?" I asked with surprise.

"They're in. And I've already talked to them this afternoon. They've heard Qazi's testimony, and they watched his cross-examination. They think he's dirty. So now they've turned their scrutiny on him."

"You know there's one thing we've never asked."

"What's that?" Kevin asked.

"If Pakistan records *their* phone conversations with the American intelligence."

"I thought we did ask Qazi that when we were in Islamabad."

"Nope. But if we did he sure didn't answer us. Are your guys able to look at his files without him knowing?"

"Oh yeah."

"They may be able to help us out and we may be able to help them out a little bit. I think I've got the whole plan now."

"Which one?"

"The one we've been talking about. You have all the equipment you need? Because we're probably two days away."

"Two days?" Kevin sat forward quickly. "Seriously? I thought we were going at the end of the trial."

"No, that's what they'll be expecting. This guy has testified against us now. He looked pretty bad on cross-examination, but the court's going to believe him and they're not going to believe anything we say. I'm going to put one of my guys on, and I want him on the record, but after that, we've gotta go."

"Shit, Jack. I thought we had like two weeks."

"No, we've got two days."

"I'm not sure we can get it all done then. I've got some things we've got to put in place."

"Have you received them all?"

"Yeah, not here of course."

"Can you get all this done?"

"We've got to put a lot of stuff in place, most of it is outside. Their general security here isn't all that great, so we can do it. But shit, two nights."

"Maybe three, it depends on the witnesses. I'm not sure when they're going to rest, but we're going to start putting on our witnesses probably the day after tomorrow. I'm going to start with one of our aviators—not both, Raw would kill us—and then put on the major who talked to Qazi. We've got to at least set that up. But you've got to get ready."

He nodded and drummed the pencil on the table as he thought through the logistics. "I don't know, Jack. I don't know if we can do it."

"You have enough people?"

He nodded. "Yeah."

He looked at me with a frown. "You do realize that some people may get killed?"

"We've got to do it nonlethal. Have to."

"I know. It's not us I'm worried about. They're going to have security guys with real bullets. Have you seen them?"

"Of course, every day."

"Well, while they are not highly trained special ops guys, they look serious enough. I think if we try to pull something, they're definitely going to try and stop us."

"Well sure. But our job is to stop them before they try and stop us."

"Easier said than done. As you know. I've gotta get going if we just have a couple of days. We've got to get out there tonight and put some other stuff in place."

"You have to be ready to go, I need a yes or no."

"Which plan?"

"Entebbe."

"No shit?"

"No shit."

"We'll be ready."

# TWENTY-SIX

"Where's Kristen?" Lindsay asked, one of the quieter associates from Covington and Burling. She was very thin with long brown hair that she kept in a French braid most of the time. Sort of nondescript, never wore makeup, and didn't speak very often, but she impressed me as being intense and her work was first-rate.

"I told you. She wasn't feeling well." I had been surprised that several of the attorneys had returned to work later that evening and were there when I got back into the office. I could tell they wanted to know where I had been, but no one wanted to ask.

Lindsay replied, "We finally got a group e-mail saying that, but we're not buying it. Just as we're coming to the critical part of the trial, she leaves. And now she won't respond to anybody's e-mails or phone calls. She's dropped off the face of the earth. What's going on?"

"What's going on is we're about to start our part of

the trial and we've got to get our witnesses lined up. Kristen was the one who was arranging for Major Curley, but somebody else is going to have to step in and do that. Lindsay, will you give him a call?"

"Sure, but why can't Kristen do it? Where is she?"

"She went home. And if she's not responding, then I guess she doesn't want to talk about it. Maybe she isn't sick, I don't know. But if she won't answer us, then there's not much we can do, is there?"

"Okay," Lindsay said, clearly not convinced. "I'll call Major Curley, but when you feel like telling us what the straight story is we'd really like to know. Because she was sort of our focal point. We know we work for you, but she was the one who really worked us through a lot of this."

"I know. Believe me, it's a problem, and it's painfully obvious to everybody who is watching this trial that she is not here. But we've just got to go on. So can you help me out or not?"

"Of course. But I'm just telling you we're a bit off balance because Kristen left. It makes us wonder if we should leave."

"Why would you leave now?"

"Why did she leave now?" Christopher threw in from behind her.

I looked at him. He had not said a word to me since we had gotten to Holland. His was all written work and was brilliant. But he was a lifelong seething cauldron of discontent. You could tell by looking at him. He was someone who was probably bitter about whatever circumstance he found himself in. And now he had decided to speak.

"I told you she wasn't feeling well. And if you've e-mailed her and asked for more information and she hasn't given it to you, then I guess she doesn't want to. I don't really know what else there is to say. And if you want to leave, you can leave anytime you want. But I need you, and I want you to stay here, and I don't want anybody to get distracted by this. We need to finish this, and take it to the end. So anybody who is distracted, or is off balance permanently because of Kristen, as I've said, you can leave at any time. But please don't leave us hanging. If you're doing something that we're relying on for this trial, don't stop now. Finish what you started."

They looked around at each other. Lindsay looked at Christopher, they all looked at me, and nobody said anything. "Good. Lindsay, let me know as soon as you get in touch with Curley. Tell him we need him over here now. We need to prepare him for his testimony, which is probably in two days."

Lindsay nodded and said, "Actually, I opened his file and I see that Kristen talked to him three days ago."

"She didn't tell me about that," I said, surprised.

"Yeah, he says he's going to be traveling, and that he has decided not to come."

"What? Where do you see that?"

I walked over to her computer and watched as she accessed his witness file on our shared database. She opened it, and looked at the notes section. She clicked on the last note, which was Kristen's of her conversation with Curley. There it was, in black and white. He had decided not to testify. Why wouldn't Kristen have told me about that? Either she forgot about it, which I had a hard time believing since he was our critical witness, or she got distracted by the other thing she was worried about, or she intentionally didn't tell me. That would almost be sabotage. That just wasn't her. It just didn't ring true. Why would she sabotage our effort? Until yesterday she was deep in it and would have looked just as bad as me if our key witness had chosen not to come. I didn't get it. "Call him. Get him on the line." I looked at my watch. "Right now. Wherever he is in the United States it's not bedtime yet."

Lindsay looked at me and I said, "Call him right now."

She turned around to her desk, startled, and picked up the phone and dialed the number on the screen and put it on speakerphone. I could hear others start to slow their typing and research and memo drafting long enough to see whether this call was going to go through. We waited and finally it rang. It rang several times, then went to his voicemail. "Hang up and try it again."

She glanced at me and redialed. It rang again, but this time he picked up. "Yes?"

I nodded quickly to Lindsay, who said quickly, "Major Curley?"

"Yes. This is Major Curley."

"This is Lindsay in Holland. I work with Mr. Caskey and Kristen Chambers."

"What can I do for you?"

"Well you're on speakerphone, and Mr. Caskey wanted to talk to you. He's right here."

"Major Curley, good evening. How are you? I wanted to let you know that we need you over here to begin preparing for your testimony. It looks like you'll be going on in three days. So the sooner you can get over here, the better. If you need us to make your travel arrangements, we can do that. Just let me know how you want to do it."

There was nothing but silence on the other end of the line. I waited. I looked at Lindsay and the others. Finally I said, "Major, you still there?"

"Yes, I'm here."

"So, when can you get here?"

The major was clearly hesitant. "I ah . . . told Kristen that I wasn't coming. I thought she told you."

"Actually, no, she hadn't told me that. I saw that in your file when Lindsay called up your name to dial it so that we could start lining up people to get them ready, but she had not mentioned that to me. That made me think you had been thinking about it, but were still planning on coming. So you are coming, right?"

"I gotta tell you, Jack. I'm a little spooked. Watching this thing on television, and listening to the analysis, and the veiled threat the prosecutor made of indicting me along with everybody else in the chain of command, it got my attention. I have to admit it. So I don't see that I really am needed over there, I think I'm just gonna stay here. I really have a lot to do, and I don't have time to take off from work."

"I can get you off work with one phone call. Are you

really telling me that as a member of the military you don't have time to come to the defense of another member of the military who's been charged with bogus war crimes?"

"Yeah, saying I don't have the time isn't really accurate. I don't want to come, Jack. You told me I didn't have to."

"No, I didn't tell you that. I told you it was your duty, and you should get your ass over here."

The major was annoyed. "Well, you can say what you want but I'm not going to come. It's not mandatory that I come, it's not part of my job description, and I'm not coming."

"So that's it. That's your decision?"

"I'll think about it some more, but basically yes. Where's Kristen, is she there?"

"No, she went home. She wasn't feeling well."

"Is that what she told you? I think she just didn't like the way this was going, Jack. Can't say that I blame her. Take care." And he hung up.

I stared at the dead phone. After what seemed like a minute, I turned to the others in the room. Finally I said, "Our odds of successfully defending this case just went down dramatically."

The prosecutor took another day to put on the rest of his witnesses, and then it was our turn. My e-mails and voicemails to Curley had gone unanswered. My e-mail to Admiral Lewis however had been responded to immediately. He told me to tell him the time and place and he'd be there. I was surprised. He was probably more at risk than Curley of being sucked into the vortex of war crimes indictments.

The morning had come for us to put on our case. I had known from the day that I met them that the only one of my clients who would ever testify was Dunk. He was calm, rational, and articulate. Raw would have exploded and started cursing at the International Criminal Court and telling them how illegitimate they were and accusing the prosecutor of being a tool. Dunk understood the game.

I looked at the sky as I walked across the street to the International Criminal Court. It was gray with a hint of blue and a chill in the air. It was going to be a beautiful day, but I was not quite so optimistic about the testimony about to come. I thought Dunk would do a good job, but I thought Brady might give him some difficulty. We were about to find out.

I made it to the courtroom by myself and prepared for the direct examination of my client. The press was energized by the idea of Americans testifying. They wanted to hear how this had happened from the ones who had done it. They'd heard hints of it in my questioning, but they wanted the full answer.

The court was called into session, and Dunk and Raw were brought into the courtroom. They sat behind me in their usual seats, and the clerk then asked me the name of our first witness. I stood up and announced, "I would like to call Lieutenant William Duncan, United States Navy." Since Duncan had been sitting through the entire trial he knew the routine for witnesses and walked to the witness chair, took the oath, and sat down. The gallery was jammed as it was every day but there was a certain intensity in the air. People were there to watch the American on the witness stand.

I began the questioning. I went through the preliminaries, his name, his background, his current employment as a weapon systems officer, a WSO in F/A-18F aircraft, and his overall experience.

I continued. "Lieutenant Duncan, let's focus on the day of the events which have led to this trial. What was your position on that day?"

Duncan shifted. "It was my second flight of the day. It was a night mission patrolling over the eastern hills of Afghanistan, and dropping on a couple of predesignated targets."

"How were you told about those targets?"

"They were part of our briefing package, and were on the ATO, the air tasking order."

"Where did your flight originate?"

"From the USS *Ronald Reagan*."

"Were those other two targets preplanned, in which you had target packages? With photographs, latitudes and longitudes, precise information?"

"Yes. We had complete targeting packages for both of the other two targets."

"Did you have any trouble identifying them or hitting them?"

"No, it was no problem. We found them quickly, and were able to take them out."

"What kind of targets were they?"

"One was an antiaircraft gun that had recently been set up on the hillside. It was a ZPU-1."

"What kind of weapon is that?"

"It's really kind of an old piece of equipment. Probably designed at the end of World War II. Not particularly effective, but it's 14.5millimeter and has a range of about eight thousand meters."

"Were you able to identify and strike that target?"

"Yes, we had a direct hit, and video confirmation."

"What was the second target?"

"It was a tunnel we had found through intelligence. They had some kind of infrared tracking going on with a predator and they had pinpointed a tunnel entrance that they were using as a hideout near where the army's ground objective was going to be."

"Did you drop a bomb on that tunnel entrance?"

"Yes."

"Direct hit?"

"Yes."

"How can you be so accurate?"

"There are a lot of different ways to do it, from laser guidance to dropping a JDAM on a location, which is essentially a GPS-guided weapon that navigates itself through GPS satellites to a fixed latitude and longitude. They don't usually miss. The CEP on those is less than ten meters."

"What is a JDAM exactly?"

"It's just an iron bomb with a GPS guidance unit on the tail. Essentially a brain and fins. JDAM stands for Joint Direct Attack Munition. Ours was just an old

Mark 84, a two-thousand-pound bomb, with the guidance system. I said GPS-guided, but the newer ones, like this, have laser terminal guidance and are actually laser JDAMs."

"What's a CEP?"

"Circular error probability. It means if you put a stick in the exact spot where you want it to hit and put a rope on it, how long does a rope have to be to make sure that you'll hit within that circle fifty percent of the time. And that's what the CEP is. And our CEP is ten meters with that weapon. Thirteen, actually. But for us it's closer to three. And for us it's not fifty percent, it's ninety percent plus."

"Have you ever missed a target?"

"Well with iron gravity bombs you can miss pretty nicely. But in this arena we don't drop unguided bombs very often, if at all. I can't remember the last time I just dropped an iron bomb on a target. Ours are all either laser-guided or JDAMs for the most part."

"Okay, so the building in Pakistan was not one of your briefed targets."

"Right."

"Then how did you have an extra bomb? Don't you carry the number of bombs you have targets for?"

"No. You have a load-out based on targets and have extra weapons available in case additional targets become available that were not part of the brief."

"So you anticipate the possibility of having additional targets given to you in the air."

"Yes."

"Had that happened before?"

"Numerous times."

"Anything extraordinary about that? Does it make it sound or feel questionable to you?"

"Not at all. You have to be able to be responsive to things as they change or develop. If you find a Taliban stronghold that won't be there the next day you have to target it immediately."

"Okay then, so focusing on the night again here. The first two targets you said went routinely for you and your wingman?"

"Yes. No problems. We were just about ready to head back to the carrier."

"And what happened?"

"We were asked if we had time for an additional target."

"Did they tell you why?"

"They said that a Predator was going to be used, but that the Predator was winchester."

"Winchester?"

"Out of ammunition. Weapons."

"And did that give you any pause, any concern that you were going to be undertaking a mission that had originally perhaps been allocated to a Predator?"

"Not really. It's all one big system. Just a number of different ways of putting ordnance on target."

"So what happened next?"

"So we got the latitude and longitude, and I put it into my system. I noticed that the target was across the border."

"So if I understand you correctly, when you first received the information you were in Afghanistan, operating in Afghanistan."

"That's right."

"So you get this new target and then what?"

"Well, we're asked if we could do it—if we had enough fuel. I checked our fuel and saw that we had enough to hit the target and return to the carrier. I made sure that we could stay at a fairly high altitude, which was no problem. The target was in a mountainous area, so we were able to do it, and from high altitude. We can drop from high altitude anyway, but I didn't want to have to do a low cave run or something. We wouldn't have had the fuel."

"Were you told what the target was?"

"No."

"You get a latitude and a longitude?"

"They may have said a building, but I don't really remember. The question is what is the latitude and longitude and what is the weapon we're going to use."

"All right, so you turned and went across the border into Pakistan, is that right?"

"Yes."

"Have you ever had a mission into Pakistan before?"

"No, usually those targets are handled by Predators."

"Why is that?"

"I don't really know. You'd have to ask Pakistan, but it's my understanding that they don't like us attacking targets inside their borders."

"Do you mean that targets that are selected inside

Pakistan, whether for a Predator or for something else, are done without the approval of the country of Pakistan?"

"Well, I'm not really sure. I think there's what Pakistan says for public consumption and then there are the back-channel communications where they approve the very thing that they deny approving to the public."

Brady rose to his feet and objected as improper testimony. The judges sustained the objection.

"Well, regardless of what you know about Pakistan's approval of targets, is it your understanding at least that this target was approved by Pakistan?"

"I would assume so. I don't think we'd be attacking a target with a jet inside Pakistan without them approving it."

Brady rose again. "Your Honors, this question is pure speculation."

The chief judge said, "Sustained."

"Okay, Lieutenant Duncan, what happened next?"

"Well we had to confirm the target latitude and longitude with the images that the targeting group had. They therefore vectored the Predator—without any weapons—to the area and with its IR camera. It verified the building. The Predator also stayed in the area to laser-designate the target. The JDAM can take both types of guidance."

"So you flew directly to the target and then what?"

"Well after we had received confirmation, verification from the Predator, and clearance to fire and clearance to drop, we pickled our JDAM to the target, and turned to head back to the ship."

"You don't have to loiter in the area for laser guidance?"

"No, once we drop our job is done. The bomb is self-guided by GPS and terminally guided by laser if necessary. We don't need to be there."

"How far away from the target were you when you dropped?"

"I don't really remember. Probably about eight miles."

"So the people on the ground never saw you?"

"Not at the target site. Unlikely."

"This was dark, right?"

"Yes, it was about twenty-three hundred local time I think."

"So the bombing assignment, and run, was normal?"

"Yes, other than it being in Pakistan."

"Were you at any time told the nature of the target or that it was a refugee facility?"

People were on the edges of their seats listening for this answer.

"No, they never told us what the target was at all. Just that it was a building."

"Were you told who was in the building, or how many people were there?"

"No. Not at all."

"Would that have made any difference?"

He was surprised by the question. "You mean if they had said there were a bunch of refugees in there would I have still dropped on the building?"

"Exactly."

"No. No way."

"Why not?"

"Because you don't do that."

"What if they had said al Qaeda was meeting with the Taliban at the highest levels inside the building?"

"I don't know. And you still know there are refugees in the building?"

"Yes."

"Then it's a no-go."

"Even if you refuse, and they order you to?"

"I just wouldn't do it."

"So again, you were not told the nature of this target, or that there were civilians—particularly refugees—in the building?"

"No, never. We were never told that."

"So what happened after you dropped the bomb?"

"We turned away sharply, and headed toward the ship."

"And then?"

"And then I saw a bunch of light on my starboard side. I looked over there and saw there were missiles that had been fired. They're pretty clear—easy to see at night—and they were heading toward us."

"How many?"

"I don't know. Maybe a half dozen."

"What did you do?"

"We took evasive action. We do what we do when faced with a missile threat. We turned into it, dropped flares, changed altitude, all the things you do."

"And what happened?"

"Well, I don't know but one or more of the missiles guided to us through whatever it was we were doing and through our flares. Maybe we didn't have enough flares, I don't really know. But one or more of them went right up our tailpipe and blew the back half of the port engine off of the airplane, which resulted in another explosion, which took off pretty much the entire back end of the aircraft after the forward edge of the vertical stabilizer."

"Did you see that happen?"

"Yes, I was turned around in my seat watching."

"What'd you do next?"

"Well, you can't fly without the back half of the airplane, so I ejected."

"And when you eject does that automatically eject the pilot as well?"

"Yes, he goes out right behind me."

"And then what happened?"

"We landed in the middle of nowhere, all was well, we were uninjured, and we got on our radios to call for help to get some rescue helicopters down there."

"Did you talk to anybody?"

"Yeah."

"How far away were they?"

"A couple hundred miles. It was going to take them a couple hours to come get us. We were okay with that. We sort of hunkered down, hid our parachutes the best we could, and started walking away from our impact area. We didn't want to be near our parachutes if people started looking for us. Parachutes are easy to find, but people less so."

"And then what happened?"

"It seemed like in five minutes, we were surrounded by a hundred people with rifles. It looked like we landed right in the middle of somebody's pasture. And it all happened fast after that. They tied our hands behind us with ropes, blindfolded us with some smelly cloth, threw us into the back of a pickup truck, and drove us somewhere. There was a lot of yelling and pushing and screaming and they apparently turned us over to the local Taliban or al Qaeda—I'm not really sure who they were—and we got thrown in the back of another pickup truck. We drove for a couple hours on this bouncy dirt road just getting creamed, and then we heard a city. They pulled us out of the truck, tightened something around our necks, pulled off our blindfolds, and the next thing we knew we were being pulled through streets while bricks and stones and bottles and things were thrown at us. Probably what everybody saw on television that night."

"Were you in Peshawar?"

"Well, we didn't know that at the time. Everybody now says that we were. All the video of the event says that it was in Peshawar. I don't know where it was and I'm not sure how they know. But that's what everybody thinks."

"Then what?"

"Then they blindfolded us again and threw us into a van. Next thing we knew we were sitting in plush leather seats in a business jet. We took off without waiting even five minutes. I thought we'd been rescued, and were being flown somewhere safe, but then they took our blindfolds off and we were sitting in a Falcon jet. I don't know who was on the airplane. There was one Westerner, an old guy with gray hair, a distinguished-looking guy, and other than that there were guys who looked like security guys. Tough guys, and the pilots, of course. I'm not really sure."

"And where did you end up being flown to?"

"Right here. Holland."

"When did you first hear that you had been taken captive by the International Criminal Court?"

"When they walked us into the prison here. That was the first time we really knew what was going on."

"And what did you think when you heard you'd been charged with war crimes?"

"I thought that some political event was happening. Obviously, it had nothing to do with what we had done. We didn't even know the kind of target we were bombing."

"Again, if you had known this was a target full of refugees, would you have dropped your bomb?"

"Not a chance."

"No further questions."

Brady stood up like he'd been shot out of a cannon. He immediately started asking questions. "Lieutenant Duncan, you do not deny that you dropped a bomb on the building that was full of refugees in Pakistan. Correct?"

"I know I dropped a bomb on the target I was supposed to hit and I hit that target. I do not know that it was full of refugees, everybody says that it was but I don't have any personal knowledge of that."

"You dropped a bomb on the building in the small village in Pakistan that you were told to bomb. Right?"

"That's right."

"And after that at some point you learned that it was full of refugees and European medical assistance workers. Right?"

"Well, again, I don't know that. I know that you and others have said that, but I don't know that to be true."

Brady raised his voice more than he had at any point in the trial. "Are you saying that you deny that building was full of refugees?"

"I'm saying I don't know. I have no personal knowledge of that. I have not been to the place, I wasn't there after the bomb hit, I was being paraded through Peshawar and being pelted with stones so I did not have any opportunity to do a bomb damage assessment, which we would have done on the ship at which point I might have learned that. But I have not learned that, other than from what you and others have said. That's what I'm saying."

I was impressed by Duncan's resilience. He was not intimidated by Brady at all, and in fact was looking at him with a look that was just short of hatred. It was a very intense, but appropriately intense, look. Brady continued. "You agree that if you did know that the building was full of refugees and you dropped a bomb on it, that would constitute a war crime."

"Objection, it's speculation, and irrelevant." I said.

"Overruled," Judge Hauptmann replied. "It goes to his state of mind, which is relevant."

Dunk answered, "Well that's a hypothetical example that didn't happen so I don't know how to answer that. That's not what happened."

"But you are aware of war crimes, are you not? Are

you Americans not trained—extensively—to not commit war crimes, or are you saying you have no idea what war crimes are, and that you can do whatever you want?"

"No, that's not what I'm saying. I have a general idea of what war crimes are and understood to be. I don't know what you think war crimes are, and I don't really know what the International Criminal Court thinks war crimes are. They must not be the same as what the United States thinks, because our country refused to sign the treaty. So I don't really know how to answer that."

"You've been doing some research on the Internet while you've been confined in the prison I take it?"

"I've been reading the newspapers online, that's about it."

"What this is about sir, is that you killed sixty-five innocent people, and wounded thirty more. That's what this is about, do you understand that?"

"I understand that's what you claim. If everything I read is true, our bomb hit a facility that turned out to be a refugee facility. So that's what I understand this to be about. But it seems what it really is *about* is whether or not we did this intentionally. I am here to tell you that we did not kill any civilian intentionally. I simply hit the target that I was told to hit. It's just that simple."

"And you come in here claiming complete ignorance of the nature of that target, right?"

"Not complete. It was a building, and it was a target selected and approved by the targeting people for the allies, and, I believe, approved by Pakistan."

"You have no knowledge of whether this target was approved by Pakistan, do you?"

"As I said, I absolutely believe it was approved by Pakistan, as we would not drop a bomb on a target in Pakistan without their approval. They may claim to have not approved it, but that's not our policy. We would never go into a country and attack a target without the approval of that country."

"And you expect me to just accept that?"

"No sir. I don't expect you to accept anything I say. I'm just telling you what is. Whether you accept it or not doesn't matter to me."

There was a murmur in the courtroom and the judges looked concerned. Duncan was getting a little testy, but I actually liked it. This was the drama that everybody wanted, so they were going to get it. Brady was starting to get frustrated. Although I couldn't believe that he really expected a confession out of a naval weapons officer who did nothing wrong. Brady returned to his computer and hit a button. On the screen popped up one of the more grotesque figures of one of the people who had been obliterated by the bomb. He looked at Duncan. "Do you see this?"

"Yes. I've seen it before."

"You did this."

"That's what I understand."

"Are you proud of this?"

I would have objected, but the question was so obviously stupid I decided to let it go.

"No."

"Do you have an explanation for this?"

"The one I just gave. I was told to hit a target, and I hit it. It's just that simple. Apparently we got bad intelligence on the nature of the target. That's all I can imagine. I don't know for sure because I didn't get a chance to go back to my carrier and find out."

Brady wasn't going to stop. "You admit that you are responsible for dropping the bomb at least?"

"If those are in fact photos from the place where the bomb hit. I again don't know that personally, but I accept what you're saying."

"But you do not accept responsibility for their deaths?"

Dunk looked at me clearly perturbed but prepared to answer. "I take responsibility for dropping the bomb on the target I was given. So in a sense I am responsible for the bomb. But if what you're really asking me is am I responsible for intentionally killing civilians, the answer is absolutely not. I had no idea there were civilians at that location."

Brady asked, "Are you telling me they don't tell you the nature of the target? Just a 'building'?"

"It varies. Sometimes you'll hear that it's an antiaircraft facility, or a truck park, or something like that. But if it's a building, you're just told about the building. Sometimes we'll know what it is if we have time to brief it and look at the target package, but if it's just on the fly—where you're given a target in the air, you're just told to hit the target and that's it. That's what you do."

Brady was frustrated. "You would agree with me,

Mr. Duncan, that if you dropped a bomb on civilians intentionally, that would be a war crime for which you should be imprisoned?"

Another improper question, but I wasn't afraid of it. Duncan was winning. He answered, "Well, I don't really know what constitutes a war crime in your eyes, Mr. Brady. Because you seem to have charged me with a war crime for something that I didn't do. And whether that's really a war crime or not I don't know, but I sure know that you don't intentionally attack civilians, ever. And I would never do that."

"No further questions."

He had done so little damage to Duncan I couldn't believe it. I wasn't about to open new areas by questioning Duncan more. I stood up, "I have no further questions either, Your Honors."

The afternoon was remarkable in a lot of ways. First, for no reason that I could tell, and none that was expressed by the court, Judge Hauptmann adjourned for the afternoon. Brady looked as puzzled as I did. I was happy for the reprieve and not quite ready to put on the next witness, which was to be the admiral. He was prepped and ready to go so I had to call his aide and tell him he'd be on the next day.

But the biggest shock was who was waiting for me when I got back to the office. Standing at the office door was Debra Craven from the State Department. She looked nervous and uncomfortable. She was wearing a long gray coat and long gray slacks with very high heels. They made her taller than me, which, knowing her, was probably her intention. She looked down at me with her ice-cold contempt. I put down my briefcase and spoke to her abruptly. "What's up?"

"We need to talk."

"What about?"

"In private."

"Come into our briefing room. It's actually just a fancy word for a conference room. Sort of the only enclosed space we have here. The rest of it is pretty much out in the open, as you can see." I grabbed some coffee from the kitchen on the way, not offering her any, and walked into the conference room. I shut the door behind her. I sat on one side of the table and she sat on the other.

I started right in. I didn't have any time to waste. "So what's going on?"

"Two things. First, I got a call from the prosecutor."

"Brady?"

"No, his boss. The chief prosecutor."

"What did he want?"

"Apparently they don't think the trial is going as well as it should. I think that this idea that they have to prove intent is starting to haunt them. They know they can't prove intent, they can just show that these men dropped a bomb where they were told to, and the result was disastrous. In the minds of a lot of people, that's not a war crime. So they're hanging their hats on the charge of excessive killing of civilians."

"So are they prepared to drop the charges?"

"No. They think the statute, the treaty, is vague enough that if they can show recklessness, which they think they can, it will be good enough."

"The joy of a vaguely drafted treaty."

"Be that as it may, they've offered us a deal."

"I'm waiting."

"They want your two clients to plead guilty to one count, and they will try to get them released within six months."

I laughed out loud. "You've never done criminal law, have you?"

"Why?" she asked merely to perpetuate the conversation. She wasn't interested in why.

"Because that is a nondeal. A guilty plea in exchange for a promise to 'try'?"

"They couldn't guarantee anything yet. He thought that they might be able to soon, but it's complicated."

"Don't bother."

"Well, that's part of what I have to tell you about, Jack. This is sort of out of your hands."

"Meaning?"

"This comes from the DOJ and State. We're talking directly to the chief prosecutor. I've been *instructed* to make a deal. As soon as possible. We've got to stop this trial. It's embarrassing to have our officers sitting on the witness stand, especially Admiral Lewis tomorrow. We're making the country look stupid. This is about way more than just these two officers. So I've been told to try and make a deal on behalf of the United States with the chief prosecutor. And while I can't really promise it, I think we're going to be able to get them out after thirty days. That's the sort of winking agreement I have with the chief prosecutor."

A rage boiled inside me. The government was trying

to really stick it to us. I knew that they had quit supporting us, that was clear enough. But turning on us? Affirmatively undermining us? That was completely intolerable. But instead of blowing up like I *really* wanted to, it occurred to me that maybe I could use her to our advantage.

I nodded slowly. After a false pause of intolerable length, I spoke in a disappointed tone. "I guess that's the best we could hope for. It's probably realistic. I'm too close to this to want to plead, even if it's a minor charge. But if that's what you think we should do, then I guess I'll have to at least consider it. But you need to have those conversations soon. I know you have been, but tomorrow is a very important witness. Admiral Lewis will be on. We have to do everything we can to avoid that."

"Who goes after him?"

"Probably experts. We've got experts on military operations, communications. The former head of the RAF is going to testify about targeting and the difficulty of knowing for certain what it is you're hitting, a lot of ninja dust. But if the admiral testifies, it could be that Brady will indict him. The last thing we need is another American charged with a war crime."

She nodded enthusiastically. "I understand completely. I'll reopen discussions with him tonight, and see if we can't complete it by tomorrow."

"Make sure that the chief prosecutor understands that you and I have spoken and that you *think*—but can't guarantee—that I'm on board. You can imply that I feel boxed in, and don't think we can win this trial. If they think I'm caving, it will make them happy."

She sat back in the folding chair and adjusted her hair. She had a wry smile on her face as she said, "I have to tell you, Jack, I'm surprised. I thought you'd go off on me. I thought you'd start yelling at me, and telling me I was out of line, and that the United States had no business negotiating on behalf of your clients without you. But that's why I came here. I want to negotiate with your blessing. I want to do what's best for your clients, and I'm glad you see it my way."

"It's pretty much an irresistible plan. I mean thirty days in the can for all this? And make sure you ask if time served counts, by the way, and maybe we'll be able to get these guys out in a few days."

"That goes without saying. Well I'd better get going. I need to get on the phone. I really appreciate your cooperation and how you've handled this." She was almost unable to hide her glee, that at a pivotal moment in diplomatic history, *she* was going to come out as the one who made peace.

"Get on this right away. The fewer witnesses we put on, the fewer chances we have to embarrass ourselves."

She stood quickly. "I understand completely. I'll let you know as soon as I have anything to report. Give me your cell again."

I wrote the number down and gave it to her. She smiled, folded it, placed it in her purse, and extended her hand. I shook it, and she turned and left the office.

As soon as she was out the door, I went to the wall

in the far back corner and knocked on it loudly. I then pushed it open and closed it behind me. Kevin looked up with surprise. He looked at his watch. "What's up?"

"We've got to go to general quarters. DOJ and State are trying to sell our clients down the river. We've got to move this up. We go tomorrow."

Kevin grimaced. "Tomorrow? *Shit*. I thought we had at least a couple more days."

"No. You got the actor?"

"Yes. We're set, but I'll have to tell everyone. This is going to be tough."

"The actor has no idea what's going on, right?"

"Don't worry about that."

"All right. I want it as close to dark as I can get it. We'll go right at the end of the day. We just received word that the court is dark tomorrow morning as well. So I'll put the admiral on in the afternoon, and drag him out until about four o'clock. And that's when I want to strike. I want to bring the admiral with us."

"That wasn't part of the plan. He doesn't know anything about us. I don't want him sticking his nose in." Kevin rubbed his face in concern.

"If we leave him, they'll arrest him and indict him."

"I don't want him. It makes it look like he called the whole thing, and he hasn't lifted a damned finger."

I considered our options. "Maybe we can send him back to the U.S."

"I'd think hard about that before we do this."

"Okay. I'll think about it. Do you have the police radio frequencies set?"

"Yes. We've got them all. We have the internal frequencies too."

"What about the PSD on that asshole?"

"Yeah, he's got security, but they're nothing. It won't be a problem."

"You've got to get him tomorrow morning."

"I know. Don't worry about that. You just worry about being ready."

Suddenly behind me there was a loud knock on the walls that I had just passed through. No one knew about that door. I looked at Kevin, who looked at me. One of his men hit the lights, and several of them surrounded us and produced submachine guns from locations I couldn't even imagine. We had a building escape plan, but we didn't really expect to have to utilize it. The other men were quickly shutting down computers, and pulling out hard drives. I went to the door and opened it a crack. It was Kristen. I looked over her shoulder and around her, and saw no one else. I opened the door and pulled her in. Kevin threw up his hands and one of his men turned on the lights again.

"What the hell are you doing here? I thought you abandoned us," I said as I closed the door tightly behind her.

"I've got Curley."

"What?"

"I've got Major Curley. I got your message. Your text, whatever, that the major had reneged on his promise. I decided to go get him and bring him here."

Kevin looked at her skeptically, then at me, wondering if I knew what I was getting into. Things were going

484        *James W. Huston*

to be a lot easier with her not being here. But now that she was here, our plans had to accommodate her.

She sat down as the other men looked at her, all as skeptical about her and unhappy at her participation. They didn't give a shit about Major Curley or who testified, they were all about getting the two Americans out of Holland. Her showing up could only make it more complicated.

I said, "So that's it? You heard about Curley and decided to fix it?"

"Pretty much. Plus I really didn't want to spend the rest of my days wondering if I could have made a difference here."

I looked at Kevin with some concern and then looked back at her. "Is he ready to go? Because we may need to put him on tomorrow afternoon. We're dark in the morning, but I'm going to put him on first thing in the afternoon. What do you think?"

She nodded, glad to be back. "I went over his testimony with him the whole way over. I sat next to him on the flight, in coach I might add, and went over everything, start to finish. He's got the same weaknesses, the same problems, but he's ready."

"Okay. But you've also got to know one other thing."

"What's that?" she said, closing her eyes and rubbing her face with her hands.

"Tomorrow is the last day we're going to be here."

"What are you talking about?"

"You know that we've had some plans in play. Well, the time has come. The State Department and the Department of Justice have agreed amongst themselves to sell our clients down the river, and plead guilty for them—even though they don't want to—in exchange for a thirty-day jail sentence. They just want to get out of this thing. They're going to publicly accept guilt for our clients and the ICC is going to accept it. They've cut our legs out from under us so we need to move. Everything's in place, and this thing is happening tomorrow. Right after Major Curley testifies, we're out of here."

"What do you mean by out of here?"

"We're going to get our clients out."

"How?"

"Do you really want to know the details?"

"No."

"Look, I'm glad you came back. It was courageous and the right thing to do; but if you want to go back home tonight now that Curley is here, and avoid what's going to happen tomorrow, that might be smart. I'm not sure you want to be part of what we have in mind. In fact you might just get in the way."

Kristen sat back, deflated. Just when she thought she was coming back at the right time to do the right thing to help out in a way no one else could, she learned that she had walked right back into the craziness that had made her want to leave in the first place.

I asked her, "So what do you say? You did a good thing. You've brought Major Curley here. That's worth a lot. Coming back is a big statement, Kristen. And if you want to go home before the shit hits the fan, I will totally understand. Because the shit is *really* going to hit the fan. It's going to be something that will go down in history. And I can't guarantee it will be in a good way, either. We're going to do our best, but there are no guarantees."

She looked at me hard, trying to read my face. "Will it be dangerous?"

"We will minimize casualties, but the short answer is yes."

"And what will happen to me? If everything goes right, what happens to me?"

"You'll be home in the States."

"Do I have to do anything?"

"Just do what I say without arguing or questioning. And I *really* mean that."

"And when the *New York Times* comes and asks me for an interview, which I will give them, what do I tell them?"

"You tell them whatever you want. Tell them the truth, the complete truth. You can't violate any client confidences, but you can tell them about me. About whatever it is I tried to do and whether I'm still around. You can tell them about some of these guys—without names— that agreed to help for nothing, because they thought it was the right thing to do, and they were ashamed that their country hadn't taken the steps that it should have taken."

Kristen nodded. She seemed resigned. "I've got to be there for Curley's testimony. He's relying on me. If I don't show, he may not either. Even if you find him, and take him to the court, he may lose his confidence. So I'll be there until he's done. And I guess that means I'll be there when you do whatever it is you're going to do."

I was surprised. "Okay. Then tell Curley to be here

tomorrow morning at ten o'clock. We'll finish our preparation for him, and then we'll walk over to the court like normal. A regular old day. Me with my briefcase, you with your briefcase. You suddenly healed from your sickness, and Major Curley in tow. But then, Kristen, you're going to see stuff that will make you maybe wish you hadn't agreed to do this. But let me just tell you one thing. Do *exactly* what I tell you—or Kevin tells you—to do. Don't argue, don't debate, just do it. Do you agree?"

She hesitated, then said, "I agree. Let's go."

# TWENTY-SEVEN

After Kristen left, Kevin and I stayed up to finish the plan. It was audacious and required split-second timing. Part of that was difficult because some of the events had to occur in Antwerp, and we had little control over the timing. But that wasn't the critical part. The critical part was in The Hague, and that was down to the second. To do a proper op though, we needed to do a rehearsal. But we didn't have the time or the means. That made our likelihood of success much lower.

Kristen met me at the office with Major Curley at ten o'clock sharp. Things looked normal. The office was humming, all the attorneys were working diligently, and everything was in place. I knew that behind the wall, the wall that none of the other people but Kristen knew about, had been evacuated. They had been up all night moving everything out, putting everything else in place for the afternoon's events. When their location would finally discovered by the authorities during their investigation, they would find nothing. They could probably dig some DNA out of the carpet, but it wouldn't matter by then. Everything else would be long gone. We spent three hours preparing Curley over croissant sandwiches and coffee until he was ready to go. Admiral Lewis was also there for his preparation and we told him he was likely to go later in the afternoon. He was surprised by the major's proposed testimony, particularly the notation about RG. That caused the admiral to frown and made him wonder what he was doing there. I told him we would call him during the break and ask him to come over to the ICC building. One of the attorneys would escort him over there and he would wait in the witness room on the floor next to the courtroom. I wasn't going to tell him much more than that. The less he knew about what was about to happen, the better. Because he was going to get grilled. There was some chance he'd be arrested, even some chance he'd face the charges that our clients were currently facing. I considered telling him to go home. To tell him that we didn't need his testimony anymore and that he could go back to his ship. But if I told him that, he'd know something was up.

The day was cloudy and cool with a hint of rain. The more cloud cover, the more weather there was, the happier I would be, unless it made our operation impossible. But the weather forecast had been for just this, overcast with occasional sprinkles, but nothing terribly significant. The ceiling, the distance from the clouds to the ground, was a thousand feet. That was perfect. Made it fine for helicopter flying but not so much for fixed wing airplanes looking for helicopters.

As we approached the courtroom my iPhone buzzed. I looked at the text. It was from Kevin. It said, "Got him." I looked up just as the media noticed Kristen's return. They immediately started asking her questions, to which she responded that she was feeling much better, and was ready to continue in the trial. They saw an American major in uniform and switched their attention to him. They yelled out to him and asked him what he was going to testify to. He followed our instructions and did not respond. He waved at them and gave a weak smile showing a little of his nervousness.

We went straight to the courtroom, and called him to the witness stand after Judge Hauptmann called the court to order. He took the witness seat, was sworn in, and adjusted the computer screen in front of him. He looked distinguished in his air force dress blue uniform. His ribbons were brand-new—I could tell he had purchased new ones just for this event—and his shoes were newer than his ribbons. His appearance was impeccable. He had a fresh haircut, a close shave, and looked every bit the American military officer. To the rest of the world he looked confident, and as the first person to testify during the trial in uniform, he drew the attention of everyone. They thought that finally they were going to get to the bottom of what had happened. The audience was actually leaning forward behind him in the glassed-off area. Everyone anxiously awaited his testimony. I did too, but it was as much out of fear as hope.

He stated his name and I began his questioning. We covered his background, his training in the air force, his job as an intelligence officer at the CAOC, the Combined Air Operations Center. He noted that it was also called the AN/USQ-163 Falconer weapons system. Leave it to the air force to call a building full of people a "weapons system."

I asked him what his position was.

"I am in the ISR, the Intelligence, Surveillance Reconnaissance division. We do analysis, correlation, and fusion of intelligence and sources on various targets."

"Where is the CAOC located?"

"It's at Al Udeid Air Base, in Qatar."

"And—"

I was about to ask another question when Curley interjected, "It's the most advanced operations center in history."

I knew Brady would make him regret saying that. I changed the subject to his previous tours in the Middle East, and then what he was doing on the day of the bombing.

"I was on night duty. I worked from 2000 to 0800. Twelve-hour days."

"That's eight P.M. to eight A.M., right?"

"Yes, sir."

He had been doing his usual target review, target selection, and intelligence fusion work when the phone rang.

"Did it ring on your desk?"

"Not initially. It was sent to me by our sergeant who takes all the incoming calls to direct them to the correct person."

"And who was it?"

"It was a Pakistani intelligence officer."

"Military?"

"No, civilian."

"How did you know who it was?"

"I had spoken with him before."

"Did he tell you his name?"

"He had a nickname. Wazi."

"Had you spoken with him before?"

"Yes. Several times."

"Did you recognize his voice?"

"Yes, I did. Same guy."

"Approximately how many times had you spoken with him before?"

"I don't know, maybe half a dozen."

"So then what happened?" I asked.

"There had been some intelligence previously that a high-level meeting was to occur in the western part of Pakistan. There are rivalries and allegiances between various factions of al Qaeda and the Taliban, and we had been hearing rumblings for a couple of months that there was to be a high-level meeting to unite their forces to not only continue to destabilize Afghanistan, but to destabilize the government of Pakistan. This is what we thought was the beginning of the big play by the Taliban to essentially create an independent area in eastern Afghanistan and western Pakistan where they could operate freely. To set up what Afghanistan used to be.

An operating center for al Qaeda, and any other Islamic radicals who wanted to go there. So we'd been hearing about this possible meeting. Most of the time it was associated with Sirajuddin Haqqani. No details though, just the idea that there would be a meeting."

"Who is Sirajuddin Haqqani?"

"I'm not sure how much I can say, but he's a Pashtun leader of the Taliban who has an entire network operating out of southern and northern Waziristan, attacking coalition forces inside Afghanistan."

"Is he an important figure in the war?"

"Yes. Very."

"So it was thought he himself would be meeting with al Qaeda?"

"Yes."

"Okay, so what happened?"

"So that night, in the air tasking order we had several targets in eastern Afghanistan, and a couple of targets for Predators in the western mountains of Pakistan. Everything had gone according to plan and we were at the end of that cycle when suddenly we got the call from Pakistani intelligence that I was just talking about."

"Okay, this Wazi fellow."

"Yes."

"Why Wazi?"

"I think because he had expertise about Waziristan."

"By the way, did you see his testimony on television when you were back in the States?"

"Yes."

"Was that Wazi?"

"Yes. Same voice."

"Was he reliable?"

"Impeccable. He gave us access to fantastic Pakistani intelligence that had always turned out to be correct. So when I talked to him that night, I thought this was it. The big meeting."

"What did he say?"

"He told me that the meeting was on. This was obviously a critical piece of intelligence, and we had to do what we could. We had to either put ground forces on that spot, or drop on it."

"When you say ground forces, what do you mean?"

"Well, based on the information we'd been getting, that there was going to be a meeting, we had several special operations teams in the area. Generally inside Afghanistan, but this village wasn't far from the border."

"What was the name of the village?"

"It was Danday Saidji."

"Was the location significant?"

"Yes. It was just seven kilometers from Miranshah, which is not only the capital of North Waziristan and the Federally Administered Tribal Area, but it was where Haqqani was often thought to have his operational base."

"And how far from the border of Afghanistan is this village?"

"Miranshah is like ten miles, if that, and Danday Saidji is maybe two miles from the Afghan border."

"Easy to get to Afghanistan from there."

"Very. It's in a long valley, and a road runs right to the Afghan border. Our objective was to get one of those teams on the meeting if we could to capture the individuals. It was something of a long shot, and worst case if we couldn't get somebody there we'd simply drop a bomb on the meeting."

"Go on."

"Okay. So Wazi told us this meeting was to take place at this small village in a hut. A fairly large hut, and gave us the latitude and longitude. I typed that latitude and longitude into my database, and pulled up the image that we had of the village, a satellite image, that was not particularly current, but it was accurate. We could see the building very clearly. I asked him if it was a large flat building and he confirmed it. Then he said there used to be refugees in that building. That gave me a little bit of a concern."

I slowed. "Are you clear on what he said? Did he say *used* to be?"

"Yes. He said there were refugees there."

Ugh. "Were as in they were there at the time you were speaking?"

"No, that they had been there in the past. It used to be a refugee facility but was now empty."

I could tell he was pushing it. "Did he say that it was empty?"

"No, just that it had been a refugee facility in the past."

"You're sure he said in the past?"

"Yes."

"What did you do next?"

"I ran an emergency tasking order to set the building as a target."

"Without giving us too much detail about the process, tell us how you did that."

"I have to submit it up the chain of command based on the information that I have. I told the colonel in charge what I had learned, and based on that he authorized a strike on that latitude and longitude, on that building."

"Based on what you had told him?"

"Right."

"Did you tell him that the building had refugees in it, or used to have?"

"Well, no, because I didn't believe it did have refugees in it. I thought it was an empty building that was going to be used for a meeting between al Qaeda and the Taliban."

"Based on what this Pakistani intelligence officer said?"

"Yes. I never understood that there was anyone in that building other than the people there for the meeting."

"If you had known that there were refugees there, if you knew that there was a European medical organization that was running a refugee medical facility, and that the meeting for al Qaeda and the Taliban was still going to take place in that building, would you have recommended the strike?"

"No. No way. You don't do that. I would have passed on it as an aerial target. I would have recommended that the special operations team advance as far as they could, and try and get the people at the meeting going in or out. They were too far away to get there in time for the meeting itself, but they could try to do the best that they could. We could also monitor it with a Predator, and hit the vehicles going away from the meeting. But it was going to be two hours or more before we could get an armed Predator to the area; the Predator there was out of weapons."

"We discussed that the Pakistani intelligence officer with whom you spoke has already testified in this trial. Is what he said true?"

"Well, a lot of what he said was true. But the idea that he told me there were refugees in the building at the time is not the case. He did not tell me that."

"Are you sure? Is this possibly an issue of language where he said that refugees *are* there and you heard him to say *were* there?"

"I guess that's possible. I didn't misunderstand anything else he said. He speaks pretty clear English so I don't think so."

"You do understand that he testified that he told you clearly that the refugees were there at that time."

"I know that's what he testified to, but that's not what he told me."

"So to summarize, you took the information from the Pakistani intelligence officer, passed it up the chain of command through targeting, and assigned the target to the F-18 that was nearest. Is that about it?"

"Yes, sir. That's exactly what happened."

"Did anyone tell the F-18 crew that there were refugees at the target that you just assigned to them, or that there used to be, or that there even had been a mention of refugees?"

"No, not at all. They weren't told anything about that."

"No further questions."

I sat down and Brady stood up simultaneously. Major

Curley looked at Brady waiting for the onslaught. Brady spoke quickly. "You understand why we're here, do you not, sir?"

"Yes, sir."

"And you understand what you just said is in complete contradiction to the testimony of the Pakistani intelligence officer who has already testified here under oath."

"Yes. I understand that."

"So, if he's right, and you're wrong, then you were part of a war crime. Isn't that right?"

"Well, he's not right. He never told me that."

"Did you bring a recording to prove that? Because I understand that you Americans are very careful and would record any such important critical conversation."

"No, actually we don't record those kinds of conversations. So no, I didn't bring a recording."

"Really. And why is that? Because Mr. Caskey there told Mr. Qazi that he had asked you to bring whatever recordings existed. Was that just a bluff?"

"I don't really know what Mr. Caskey was doing. There's no recording."

Brady smelled blood. "Surely since you're memory is so good, you must have notes."

I shifted uneasily in my seat. Curley said nothing.

Brady pressed. "Did you make notes of that conversation when it occurred?"

"Yes I did."

You could almost hear the people behind the glass gasp.

"Where are they?"

"Right here." Curley said as he reached into his inside pocket and pulled out a copy of the sheet of notes that I had seen.

Brady asked, "May I see them?"

"Of course."

Brady crossed the courtroom and took the sheet of paper. He returned to his position and studied it. He looked up at Curley. "Why did you not mention during your direct testimony that these notes existed?"

"I don't know. I guess I wasn't asked."

Brady looked at me and looked back at Curley. He looked down at the notes. He knew he was on to something but he wasn't sure yet what it was. He read them again, looking at all the notations. "You confirm everything in these notes that you've testified to here at trial. But of course the critical question is whether the Pakistani officer told you there were refugees in the building. You'd agree that's the real question here, wouldn't you?"

"Well, I know it's a question for you, but it's not a question for me, because I know there weren't. There was no such statement made."

Brady looked down toward the bottom of the page. He looked up at Major Curley, his eyes full of mischief. "Who is RG?"

Curley shook his head. "I don't know anyone named RG."

"There is a reference here on the page to RG, what is that about?"

"Refugees."

Brady paused and stared at Curley. He waited for at

least thirty seconds, waiting for the tension to build and Curley to be as uncomfortable as possible for the next question. "This means that you spoke with the Pakistani intelligence officer about refugees during that fateful conversation, correct?"

"Yes."

"And he told you there were refugees at the building, didn't he?"

"No. He told me there *had* been."

Brady lowered his voice until it was barely audible. "If it was unimportant, if it meant nothing to the mission, then why did you make a note of it?"

"Because he said it."

"You didn't make a note of everything he said here, did you?"

"No, probably not."

"You made a note about refugees because it was still relevant. Correct?"

"No, it was just something he'd said. Something to make a note of."

"Isn't it true, Major Curley, that you don't actually remember whether Mr. Qazi said that refugees were at the facility on the night that he gave you the notice of the meeting? You don't know what he said, do you?"

"Yes, he told me that there had been refugees there."

"You don't remember that, do you? You're saying that now retrospectively because you understand the implications. Correct?"

"No."

"You would agree with me though, wouldn't you, that nowhere in your notes does it reflect that the refugees are *not* at the target. It lists the target, and says refugees. Correct?"

Major Curley hesitated. The hesitation was probably fatal. Finally, he said, "I agree that I didn't write 'were' or 'formerly' on the notes. I didn't need to."

"But you didn't, did you?"

"No."

"And the result of this strike that you authorized, that you ran up the chain of command, that you forwarded on the latitude and longitude for, that you knew that at least there had been refugees there, was the destruction of sixty-five innocent lives. Correct?"

"That seems to be the case."

"No further questions," Brady said triumphantly.

I looked at my watch. We were fifteen minutes away. I turned to Kristen and told her to text Lindsay at the office. I whispered, "Tell Lindsay to tell Admiral Lewis we won't need his testimony. And tell him that he needs to leave *now*."

She nodded and began a subtle texting on her Black-Berry. I stood up to rehabilitate Major Curley—and to stall.

Curley looked shaken and uncomfortable. I asked, "Major Curley, Mr. Brady has implied that you knew there were refugees at the place where you recommended a strike. Did you?"

"No, of course not."

"Then how did this happen?"

"Well, there's really only one way as I see it. The prosecutor seems to imply that I might have misunderstood the Pakistani intelligence officer. I didn't misunderstand him. There was no question about what he said. We were speaking English together just fine. He seems to think that I ordered a strike on innocent civilians, which is ridiculous. I think the only answer here is that we got bad intelligence. Either intentionally or accidentally."

"Bad intelligence meaning what?"

"We were told that it was a good target. So whoever told us that either knew that it wasn't, and wanted us to do it, or was also misinformed and didn't know that there were refugees at the location. But since he mentioned that they used to be there, that seems to imply to me that he knew about the target. So I think if I were looking for the cause of all this, I'd look to the gentleman who testified here earlier and told this court the opposite of what he told me."

"Thank you." I sat down.

Brady smiled slightly as he stood back up. "Sir, you would agree with me that however this strike was designed, whatever it was approved to do, it was not designed or approved to kill innocent civilians, was it?"

"No, it wasn't."

"Yet it did ultimately kill numerous civilians, true?"

"Apparently so."

"And you would agree with me, that those civilian deaths, because none were authorized, were excessive."

I winced. I hadn't briefed him on the implications of calling civilian deaths excessive. I hadn't reminded him that one of the war crimes with which Dunk and Raw were charged was excessive civilian deaths. When the ICC treaty was drafted, it probably was contemplated that that clause would apply to thousands if not hundreds of thousands of deaths, like Germany's bombing of London in World War II, or the bombing of Dresden or Tokyo or Hiroshima by the United States. But, like other things, the treaty did not define "excessive." There was no number tied to the charge, which left it as a matter of opinion on when civilian deaths were excessive. I think most people would think any civilian noncombatant death was excessive in some sense of the word. But civilian deaths are an inevitable outcome of war. Always have been. To make every civilian death excessive and a war crime was a problem. But I hadn't talked to Curley about it.

The major replied, "I think any civilian death is excessive. There shouldn't be any. We do our best to avoid all civilian deaths."

Brady wanted more. "So, Major, you would agree with me that this strike, the strike conducted by your two comrades in arms, Lieutenant Rawlings and Lieutenant Duncan, resulted in excessive civilian deaths. Isn't that right?"

"Yes. From my perspective, they were excessive. As I said, even one is too many."

Brady was quite content. "I have no further questions of this witness."

I looked at my watch. It was five minutes before 4:30, when all hell was going to break loose. I had to get in a couple questions. I stood. "Major, are you aware that there's a charge against Lieutenant Duncan and Lieutenant Rawlings for excessive civilian deaths?"

"Here?"

"Yes. As a war crime. One of the war crimes defined

by the treaty by which this court is bound is excessive civilian deaths. Are you aware of that?"

"No. I had no idea."

"As I thought. So when Mr. Brady, the prosecutor," I said, pointing to him across the room, "asked you whether these deaths from this bombing were excessive, you meant only in the sense that no civilians should be killed. Not that they had committed a war crime, is that correct?"

"Absolutely. I have no idea about any war crimes charges."

"Thank you very much." I sat down as the major was excused from the witness stand. I needed another witness. I needed four more minutes. "Your Honors, I call Lieutenant Rawlings to the stand."

Rawlings looked up at me in surprise. I had told him he wasn't going to testify. I hadn't prepared him as a witness at all. The last thing I wanted was for him to be on the witness stand testifying, and then, worse, subject to cross-examination. I knew he would get angry and say a lot of regrettable things. But if things went as I expected, he wasn't going to have to say much of anything. He took the stand, gave his name, and watched everyone in the room and the audience shift. They also thought he was never going to testify and were now shocked that he had taken the stand. He waited anxiously. I asked him his name, and he replied a little too enthusiastically.

"Lieutenant Doug Rawlings, United States Navy. Fighter pilot."

"Sir, you were the pilot of the F/A-18 involved in the bombing in question. Is that correct?"

"Yes, sir, that is absolutely correct."

"Did you intentionally bomb civilians or refugees?"

"No. Absolutely not. That's completely ridiculous."

My digital watch hit 4:30, and I knew what was happening outside.

At that instant, a motorcade pulled up in front of the International Criminal Court building. The second vehicle was a large black Mercedes limousine with Dutch flags flying from the two front fenders. Four other vehicles accompanied it, two black Mercedes sedans, and two large Mercedes SUVs. From the car in front stepped four men dressed in suits with earpieces who were clearly a security detail.

The doors opened from the two vehicles behind the limousine and more men got out, several from the Dutch army, a couple in ceremonial military uniforms, and a few more suited, Secret Service–type security guards. They looked around the entrance to the court for any threats, and one of the men in the ceremonial uniforms put on his cap, joined with one of the other uniformed guards, and one of the men in a suit, and walked to the entrance. The three opened the doors and went into the lobby. The security officers inside the court were immediately alerted as it was clear that these three men were armed. Before the security guards could say anything, one of the men in the uniforms said in Dutch, "Any security threats you're aware of right now?"

"Who are you?" the guard asks. "No one comes in here armed."

"We are security for Her Highness, Queen Beatrix of the Netherlands. She is here to observe the final half hour of today's proceedings on the third floor. If we're all clear in here, she'll be coming in now."

The guard looked wide-eyed. "We had no warning that she was coming. She may not enter."

The honor guard said with contempt, "*No one* gets notice the queen is coming. Not since the attempt on her life at Apeldoorn on Queen's Day in 2009. That maniac had a map of her motorcade route in the car he used to kill five people. Queen Beatrix *never* announces where she's going. You know that." He spoke into a microphone on his uniform and outside, the doors of the limousine opened. Out stepped Queen Beatrix and three more guards. She was wearing a navy blue suit with a beautiful and attractive hat. She had a matching purse on her right arm and navy blue pumps that complemented her outfit. She looked very distinguished and pleased to be there. One of the guards was dressed in the most elaborate ceremonial uniform one could imagine. He even had a sword. He put on his officers cap and extended his arm. Queen Beatrix took it and they walked up the few steps to the lobby level of the International Criminal Court. As he opened the door, the other ceremonial guard yelled out in loud Dutch and then English, "Her Royal Highness, Queen Beatrix of the Netherlands!"

Everyone in the lobby from the administrators to the

security force was baffled. They looked around at each other. Some bowed, some stared, all felt uneasy and out of place. Suddenly, over their radios and into their ears crackled a stern Dutch voice. Queen Beatrix will be attending the final session of the day of the International Criminal Court trial of the two Americans. You will clear her through. Everyone stood at attention as the lead ceremonial guard escorted the queen through the security. Several men dressed in Dutch army uniforms hurried into the lobby with helmets, body armor, and Belgian assault rifles. They were wearing Dragon Skin body armor. They walked right though the security check, setting off the metal detector, which began a continuous, noisy protest. They army men acknowledged the ICC guards, like fellow security officers, and lined the sides of the lobby. The International Criminal Court security stood frozen. One of the army officers went to the head of the ICC security at the security station and told him that they would be going up with the queen and leave with her when she exited. He asked whether there were any security concerns that the ICC was currently aware of, and the ICC security person shook his head. He grabbed his radio and started transmitting. Exactly as expected.

The ceremonial guard and the queen crossed the lobby and waited for the elevator. The door opened and they and four others walked into the elevator and pressed the button for the third floor. The doors closed in front of them. As the doors closed, some of the other members of the queen's security team went up the stairs to the left of the elevator, while still others broke into a run to head down to the other end of the hall to walk up the other stairway.

After they had all disappeared into the two stairwells, the ICC security force suddenly activated. The officer in charge of the unit still talking on his radio trying to find out what was happening with the queen was getting nowhere. He had seen enough to have serious concerns. He drew his weapon and motioned to two of his men to follow him. He entered the stairwell but the ones who went in before him, the Dutch army men, were ready for him. Three waited behind the door for the security forces who were sure to pursue. And pursue they did. They burst through the door and ran up the stairs. The Dutch army men shot them in the back with shotguns loaded with rubber slugs. The slugs smashed into each of the security guards with the force of a sledgehammer, but hit body armor, as expected. The force knocked each of them to the ground and the army men were on them. They grabbed them from behind and slammed them into the stairs. They pulled their hands behind them and bound them with steel zip ties. No one coming along with a knife would be able to free them. It would take bolt cutters. They bound their feet in the same manner, taped their mouths, then took out syringes and injected them with sedatives. They dragged them underneath the stairwell and left them there. They returned to the entrance to the stairwell, and jammed several steel doorstops under the door, and rigged a booby trap to the back of the door that would set off two flash-bang grenades if the door was opened.

They turned and ran up the stairs to the second floor where they placed similar doorstops with a small sledge-hammer. It would take an extraordinary amount of force or a lot of explosives to open one of the metal doors against the steel doorstops.

Next, they dashed up to the third floor and several men entered through the door. The others ran the rest of the way up the stairs and disabled the doors all the way to the top. They then headed back down toward the third floor.

The queen and her ceremonial escort—Kevin—stepped onto the third floor and walked directly to the attorney entrance to the courtroom. The radio chatter for the ICC security group was reaching a fever pitch.

But Kevin's men, dressed in army uniforms, suits, and ceremonial garb, were not only on the frequency, they were creating half the transmissions. One voice in partic-ular who claimed to have knowledge of the queen's visit was trying to calm the ICC security detail. Soon calls began going out to the leader of the security in the lobby, who was lying unconscious under the stairwell. He was not responding and others were beginning to panic. Fi-nally, one of the guards called for an emergency lock-down and reinforcements. At that exact moment, the queen entered the courtroom.

As the door opened and Kevin walked in with Queen Beatrix right behind him, Kevin said in a loud authori-tative voice in English, with a slight German or Dutch accent, "All rise for Her Majesty, Queen Beatrix of the Netherlands." She walked further into the room and Kevin removed his hat and announced to the judges that the queen would take a seat in the corner of the court-room and did not mean to disrupt the proceedings.

Judge Hauptmann looked shocked and said, "This is irregular. We've had no notice that the queen was coming. While we appreciate her presence, she must be on the other side of the glass with the observers."

The guards for the court stationed in the courtroom looked around nervously and fingered their weapons. Beatrix's guards, dressed in the army uniforms with the Dragon Skin body armor, walked over and stood next to each of the security guards and nodded, as if to give them comfort that they were on the same side, ready for whatever might come.

But Judge Hauptmann seemed more uncomfortable even than the security guards. Kevin pointed to a chair that was available at one of the journalist's desks, grabbed it, and placed it in the corner by the wall and motioned for the queen to have a seat. She made her way over to the chair and was about to sit, indicating to the others in the room that they also might sit at this point, but Judge Hauptmann wasn't having any of it. He smelled something was wrong. He said, "Your Majesty, while we appreciate your presence in our courtroom, it is unauthorized and you must leave immediately. If you are intent on watching the proceedings, you must go to the observers' area on the other side of the glass. No one is allowed in the courtroom other than the participants and the witnesses."

Suddenly, Raw stepped out of his witness chair, ran to Kevin's side, pulled out the ceremonial dagger that was on his waist, and grabbed the queen around the neck. Her hat flew off as he put her in a headlock and placed the dagger at her throat. He screamed, "You will take me out of here now!"

The ICC guards readied their weapons and pointed them at him, but the men standing next to them immediately grabbed the rifles, and jerked them out of their hands. They beat the guards down with the butts of their rifles and quickly put the steal zip ties around their hands and ankles and tape over their mouths. They took their weapons and threw them over their other shoulders. One of Kevin's men then ran to Kristen, and held a gun to her head. He yelled at her, "Let's go!"

Dunk, Raw, Kristen and I, Kevin and the queen, and the rest of the security men that were with him left the courtroom while everyone stared at us in complete disbelief both inside the courtroom and through the glass. As we exited the courtroom, several additional ICC guards ran down the hallway. Before they could even raise their weapons to fire, the men dressed in the army uniforms pointed their exotic-looking weapons at them and began firing in automatic fire. But they were not firing bullets. They were sophisticated paintball guns that had large reservoirs of small, hard paintballs in reservoirs on their backs. But the balls were full of intense pepper spray. Each of the guards was hit with ten or more of the pepper balls, which exploded on their chests and covered their faces with the impossibly hot pepper spray. They grabbed their faces, turned away, and fell to the ground.

While we ran to the stairwell at the end of the hall, the men with the pepper spray guns and goggles ran toward the downed men and slammed them into the floor. They grabbed their hands and put the metal zip ties on them as well as their ankles and took their weapons.

Kevin's communications experts in a remote location began transmitting on all the police bands and the ICC security frequencies that Queen Beatrix had been kidnapped inside the building of the ICC and was being held hostage. Reinforcements were on their way from the police and the army. Coordination was imperative.

The communications experts' next transmission was a fake Reuters news bulletin: "Byline: The Hague, Netherlands. Queen Beatrix of the Netherlands had decided to visit the ongoing war crimes trial at the International Criminal Court and visited the courtroom late this afternoon, unannounced. But rather than being a celebration of international law and an observation opportunity for the beloved Queen, one of the accused Americans jumped up and grabbed a weapon from one of her guards and has kidnapped the Queen. He forced her security detail to escort him out into the stairwell where she is currently being held. Her current status is unknown."

As soon as we got into the hallway, the man who had threatened Kristen of course put his handgun away and told her that he was sorry for that, but that was just for the cameras. She was free to do whatever she wanted. I looked at her and said, "We've got to get out of here, to the stairwell."

Those with the paintball guns followed us into the stairwell, and we began rushing up past the doors that had been blocked by the men who had started into the stairwell after Kevin from the lobby.

We ran up past the fourth floor and were approaching the door to the fifth-floor hallway when a guard on the other side of the door, frustrated with his inability to access the stairway, had begun firing his weapon through the door. Bullets burst through it and ricocheted around the concrete wall lining the stairway. One of Kevin's men took a Belgian assault rifle and fired back through the door, making sure to keep the bullets aimed at the floor on the other side. As the shooting from the other side stopped, probably due to surprise, the rest of us raced by the door and up to the next level. We continued to go up the stairs, as fast as we could. Kristen was a little slow in her heels and skirt, but keeping up.

The radio traffic was now continuous. The ICC was on the radio with local police and the army. Confusion was everywhere. In the middle of it all, Kevin's communications men continued to transmit false information and contradict information that others said that was accurate.

As we passed the eighth floor the queen had run out of energy. As an actress who usually played matronly roles in small dinner theaters around Amsterdam, she was not accustomed, particularly at her age, to race up ten flights of stairs. Kevin had anticipated this and the man who had been designated to carry her picked her up and threw her over his shoulder. We continued to race up the stairs with more ease than I had expected.

We could hear voices below us as some of the ICC security guards had broken through one of the doors and were racing up the stairs behind us. A timed transmission went out that the Dutch army would be sending reinforcements to protect the queen and would be coming in from the top of the building via a Chinook helicopter. As we passed the tenth floor, one of Kevin's men pulled several flash-bang grenades out of his pack. He threw them down the stairwell as the men behind us approached more closely. By the time they went off we were approaching the twelfth floor, but the light and explosion were still painfully loud. They went off a couple of seconds apart and anyone coming up into that would be forced to stop. We went on. As we approached the top of the stairwell, I was getting winded but heard the Chinook approaching.

The men monitoring the radios told us the police had called their own helicopter and several other police special operations or SWAT teams were approaching the building. We waited inside the door as guards from the ICC continued to try and come up the stairwell. We stood in front of the door to the roof directly in front of us, and waited. The queen looked confused. She asked in English, "Are you sure this is going like it's supposed to?"

"Perfectly. This is fantastic, you're doing an excellent job."

She smiled gently, but with uncertainty. "Well, good."

We could hear the Chinook. The massive blades, forward and aft, were beating the air down onto the building as the helicopter approached to land. Kevin got the call on the radio that he was waiting for from the

Chinook, and yelled at us, "Everybody get ready, we're going right to the helicopter." About that time, we heard several men running up the stairs two flights below us. Kevin pointed and two of his men pulled out sting grenades, hand grenades that looked like regular hand grenades but contained hard rubber pellets rather than steel shrapnel. They pulled the pins and dropped them down the stairway three to five seconds apart. They then followed with handfuls of flash-bang grenades. They started going off and the noise was deafening. On Kevin's signal, we threw the door open and headed for the Chinook. It was painted in Dutch army colors. It was hovering three feet above the building, with the aft ramp down waiting for us. There was a line hanging down and a man waiting to pull us up once we got our leg on the ramp.

Three men stopped after we all exited the door, slammed the roof access door behind us, and spiked it shut with their sledgehammer. One took out a large Kevlar blanket from a backpack and pinned it against the door. He drove spikes through its large steel eyelets onto the concrete structure around the door. The men who had closed the other roof access door on the other side of the building had done the same. They ran to the Chinook when we did, and appropriately, the queen was the first to board. The one who had been carrying her put her down, and then with one bounce lifted her up into the Chinook, where she was grabbed by another man and led forward into the massive vibrating helicopter.

It was nearly dark, and the helicopter's lights were

off. I looked to see if there was any other threat on the roof and saw nothing.

Kristen was next, helped up the ramp by two strong men who each took one arm and tossed her up onto the ramp. She hurried forward and the others followed up the ramp, the army men, the ceremonial guards, and the Secret Service types. Kevin and I were the last two. I yelled at him, "You got everybody?"

He nodded and pointed to the ramp. We jumped up and were pulled into the helicopter. The ramp closed behind us and the helicopter lifted up slightly over the building. I could see bullets flying through the access door to the roof and being stopped by the Kevlar blanket.

Kevin's communications specialists transmitted on all the radio frequencies: "The queen has been rescued, and she is aboard the army Chinook. She is being evacuated from the roof, and flown to army headquarters for safekeeping. Hold your fire, do not fire on the helicopter."

The critical moment had arrived. As we lifted off from the building, several security reinforcements and SWAT vans approached from different directions. The guards who were unable to get out of the door to the roof of the building had emerged from the bottom of the building out onto the street with their weapons. They pointed them at the helicopter when they heard the relay that the queen was aboard the helicopter. They weren't absolutely sure it wasn't her, and they hesitated.

The trucks and SWAT vans approached to reinforce the security catastrophe that had befallen the Inter-

national Criminal Court. But Kevin's men had anticipated every possible approach route. They had set up
miniature video cameras at the top corner of a nondescript building on each approach, and had set up a trap
for each of the trucks. The first one was a standard army
truck full of armed troops. It raced down one of the narrow streets. Kevin's communications specialist, who
was sitting in a building not too far away in an office
where he would never be found, watched the video
screen as the truck approached. As it got to within
thirty yards of his trap point, he triggered the Z-Net
device, which pulled a net across the street that lay flat
in front of the approaching truck. They noticed it and
slowed but were not concerned. Even if it were a spike
strip as they expected, their tires were solid rubber and
it would have no effect.

But what they didn't know was that it was a special
kind of strip. It had spikes all right, but as the truck
rolled over it, the spikes embedded themselves into the
tires and pulled the net up around the tire and into the
axle. It froze the front wheels, forcing the armored car
to come to a screeching halt in fifty feet. The driver
gunned it, but could not force the truck to move in any
direction. He shifted into reverse and backed up, same
result. He wasn't going anywhere. The soldiers jumped
out of the back of the truck and ran toward the court,
but they were still a half mile away and could play no
part in what was unfolding.

Two other trucks met an identical fate on different
approaches with such narrow roads that not only were
the trucks stopped dead, but they blocked the road for

any other traffic. Reinforcements could not make it to
the courthouse as the Chinook beat its way into the air
and turned toward the sea. The guards who had hesitated
finally decided that they had been tricked, and looked up
as the Chinook flew overhead. They began firing. The
communications specialist sitting in the office was ready
for that. He triggered the sniper on the roof across the
building—our old building—at the soldiers looking up.
The hypersonic sound antenna—which did for sound
what the laser did for light, channeling it in a very narrow
beam—took the sound of sniper fire directly through the
cacophony and to their ears. They were positive they
heard a sniper fire directly behind them. Small pre-
planted explosives went off on the walls behind them
leading them to believe the sniper had missed and hit the
wall. They turned and faced the sniper's location and
saw repeated flashes on the rooftop. They could see a
figure lying prone on the roof firing at them. But it wasn't
anyone, it was a dummy—a mannequin dressed in black
clothing with a wooden rifle and a light that simulated
the flash of a muzzle next to a hypersonic speaker aimed
at them.

At the same time, another speaker that was placed at
the top of a light pole nearby began generating the
sound of multiple explosions and gunfire directly at the
front of the ICC building. The security guards dived
for cover and looked for the location of the explosions
and the assault.

All up and down the roads, from numerous speakers
on top of light poles, sounds of explosions and gunfire
echoed throughout the buildings. There were screams

of wounded men and calls for help in Dutch, English, and French, rocket-propelled grenade firings and explosions followed by broken glass and falling debris. All simulated, and all just on the speakers aimed at the approaching soldiers and security guards to cause mass confusion.

Because all we needed was sixty seconds. In that time the Chinook got air underneath and dropped down from the top of the high roof of the International Criminal Court as it headed toward the sea. The pilot flew as low as he could, lights off, in the now twilight sky, and made a beeline for the ocean only two miles away. We flew over one group of soldiers who fired at the Chinook but vainly. By that time, we were gaining speed. The guards still had not broken onto the roof and we were long gone, well out of range of any of their small arms. Now we had to worry about whether they had called the air force.

We flew low over the city. The helicopter had a nose-down attitude and was flying as fast as it could. Seconds later, we broke free of the coast of Holland and were over the North Sea as it became part of the English Channel.

I looked around in the helicopter and could see from what little light there was that everyone was sitting on the canvas troop-carrying seats strapped in as we had been instructed. We didn't know what was coming, and had to be ready for anything. Men manned guns in the two forward hatches.

Now that we were over the ocean, we descended so low that we could taste the salt spray in our mouths. I undid my belt and sat up to look out the hatch. The man at the gun nodded at me indicating it was okay. I looked out and saw that we could not have been more than twenty feet off the water. I put my mouth up to his helmet and yelled, "How high are we?"

He smiled, and posed the question to the pilot on the headset. He got the answer and smiled more. He said, "Depends on which part of the aircraft you're talking about, but generally ten feet."

"We're flying ten feet off the water?"

"Yes, sir. That's how you evade detection."

I didn't know how good the Dutch radar was, but they had to believe we were headed for an American carrier or ship somewhere out on the North Sea that they had not tracked, or a merchant ship. That would have been a good plan, but it wasn't our plan. We were going to make a very unexpected move.

We continued flying west, into the darkening sky. It was almost completely dark now, but not quite. There was no moon, which was much to our liking. Our pilots were flying on night vision goggles, and our lights were off. We were low enough that we could hit anything that we didn't see, but one of the benefits of flying over the ocean is the absence of power lines and unexpected hills or trees. I asked the gunner, "Anybody following us?"

He nodded. "There was a police helicopter that tried, but we left it in the dust. We're by ourselves now."

I nodded toward the pilots: "They think we are being tracked?"

"They don't think so."

I sat back in my seat, next to Kristen. It was very loud, and we had been handed canvas headsets with ear protection to help dampen the sound. You could still make yourself heard though. I leaned over to Kristen and said, "Are you doing okay?"

"Yes. I am still in shock."

"You will be for a while. And then you'll really be in shock when you get back to the United States and everybody is going to be looking for you."

"Me? You're not coming back?"

"No, we're going in two different directions."

"Perfect!" she yelled. "So I get left holding the bag? I came back for this?"

"It will be something you can tell your grandkids about."

She shook her head and leaned back and closed her eyes. "This was the very thing I was trying to avoid."

"Nobody got killed."

"You don't know that."

"Yes I do."

After flying for twenty minutes out into the ocean, we turned due south, and headed toward the English Channel. Still flying incredibly low, and without lights, the danger now seemed commonplace. Either we would hit the ocean and all die instantly, or we would reach our destination. But Kevin's pilots were among the best in the world, formerly, as he told me, with a 160th SOAR, the Special Operations Aviation Regiment, from Fort Campbell, Kentucky. They were the ones who flew the American Special Forces on their missions. But a few of them had gotten out of the army, and now worked for Kevin.

After flying south for several minutes, we turned back east and headed in toward Belgium. We flew low and fast and entered Belgian airspace before they even had a chance to know we were there. We flew over the water and the broad Westerschelde estuary, which fed into the Scheldt River. We banked and curved around the narrowing river until we were in the outskirts of Antwerp, headed to the international airport. Our pilot banked our dark helicopter through the city until he saw what we wanted to see—a business jet approaching a landing. The airport was known for its short runway—only five thousand feet—and could not accommodate larger aircraft. The pilots were hopeful a smaller plane would be on approach and it was. They pulled up immediately to fall just behind the business jet, and they followed the jet in toward the runway. The radar would be unlikely to pick up the difference between the jet and the helicopter as the helicopter's Identification Friend or Foe was off. Unless the radar operator had his radar on raw data, he would never see the helicopter. The jet approached and landed and as we came up the threshold behind it, we banked right and headed for the transient operations building where our two Falcon 7X jets were waiting.

We came to a stop and settled onto the tarmac. The pilots kept the engines running while we all fled down the aft ramp. As soon as we were off the helicopter, they gunned the helicopter, and flew back the way we had come without talking to the tower. A complete and utter flight violation for any airport, but they knew what they were doing and they knew nobody could stop them.

Each of the Falcons had one engine turning, waiting for its passengers. Out of the building came two men escorting an elderly gentleman. He had his hands behind him, and I was sure he was handcuffed. We stood on the tarmac with everyone looking around for police or other interference. Nothing yet.

Raw and Dunk looked like they were in the middle of a movie set. They didn't know whether they were free or about to get put in prison for some new charge. The two men approached us and Kevin grabbed the older man. He dragged them over to where Dunk and Raw were. He asked them, "This him?"

Dunk looked at Raw, who looked back at him, and they both looked at the old man.

Dunk yelled over the jet noise, "What are you talking about?" He looked around again.

"Is this the guy who was in the airplane when you flew to Holland from Pakistan?"

Raw exclaimed, "Shit! That's him! You son of a bitch!" He looked like he was about to hit the old man.

The old man looked confused and stunned by the developments. He said in English, "Who are you?"

Raw responded, "We're the sons of bitches you set up and flew back to The Hague for war crimes trials."

"How did you get away from there?"

"Maybe one day you'll be able to read the papers about that," I said, "but not for a while. Let's go."

Everybody was standing around not sure what to do.

I began yelling instructions. "Dunk, Raw, you go to that Falcon over there. Kristen, you go with them, back to the States. The Falcon can make it nonstop, and will be landing at a private airport, then disappearing."

I turned to our queen. "Madam, thank you for your assistance. You are now free to return to your home in Amsterdam. There is a limousine waiting for you on the other side of this building. The driver has your check, plus a very healthy bonus. You were fantastic."

The two men who had escorted the older man put their arms out and she took them and they walked her back to the operations center.

Kristen looked stunned. "You're really not coming with us?"

"No. I've got some unfinished business. Kevin and I and this fine man will be heading in a different direction."

"What are you going to do to him?"

"I'm not going to do anything to him." I said loudly, "All right, everybody that's going with Kristen needs to get on that aircraft, the rest of you come with me."

Kevin said to several of his men, "You guys get the vehicles. You know where to go, and we'll be in touch."

I looked and saw a police car, with its blue lights flashing, racing down the exterior road by the airport. I yelled, "Let's go! Let's get out of here."

Kristen shouted, "Where are you going?"

"You'll see."

"The States?"

"No."

"When will I see you again?"

"I don't know. May be a while. Depends on how all this ends."

We raced for our two Falcons, and the doors were brought up behind us. They began taxiing at the same time, without even asking the opinion of the tower operator. They could see it was clear, and headed down the taxiway to take off on runway 11. We went first. Our pilot positioned our Falcon 7X on the runway. He watched the police car as it turned onto the taxiway and raced to where we were sitting. We watched from our side window and felt the airplane go to full power. Our pilot released the brakes and the Falcon charged down the runway eager to get airborne. After what seemed like only seconds, the nose of the airplane came up and it leapt off the ground and raced into the sky.

The police car was a good indication that our location was now known. They knew where we were, and they knew we had switched into these two Falcons.

But we had filed a flight plan for this airplane as a charter from Ford Motor Company. The flight plan said we were heading to London. As we cleared the airfield climbing through five thousand feet, Departure Control came on the radio and told the pilots that the police had come to the tower and asked us to return to the airport. The pilots, Kevin's pilots, had told them we were on a charter, and did not have time to return to the airport. The controller then insisted that we return at the command of the Belgian police. Again, we politely declined and passed through ten thousand feet. The pilot switched radio frequencies and I moved to the back of the plane with Kevin and our prisoner, Mr. Picqué.

He was furious. His hands were still handcuffed behind him even though he was belted into the plush leather seat of this fabulous business jet that was climbing away from the ground at six hundred miles per hour. It was rewarding to see him with his silver hair mussed and his two-thousand-dollar suit rumpled, his hands handcuffed behind him, and a glare on his face surrounded by the plush interior of this Falcon 7X, the same background for the humiliation my clients were forced to endure through his planning and money.

As Kevin was about to ask him something he spoke first in barely accented English. "You'll never get away with this," he said to Kevin first, then looked at me.

Kevin replied, "With what?"

"With kidnapping me and holding me hostage."

Kevin shook his head vigorously. "No, no, we're not going to hold you hostage, we're going to free you very soon. You'll see."

"Then you'll be arrested and imprisoned for kidnapping."

Kevin disagreed. "I don't think so. First they'll have to catch me, which they're not going to do. Second, this will be seen as part of an extremely large international incident, which you started. And right now I'd say you're the one who didn't get away with it. You think you're so damned clever, manipulating everybody, pulling all your strings, prepositioning your Falcon 7X to take our men to The Hague. Well, that didn't work out so well, did it?"

"You'll never get away with this."

"I heard you say that. But I'd just like to know who you were working with inside the ISI. Was it Tariq

Qazi? Because I think it was. And I think you and he are going to have a little more trouble than we are. I could be wrong about that, but I don't think so."

"You'll never get your men out of the International Criminal Court. They will be convicted, just like they deserve to be."

I looked surprised and leaned forward toward him across the aisle. "I guess you didn't see them at the airport. Didn't you notice them identifying you as the one who personally escorted them on the jet from Pakistan to Holland? They were there. They got on that other Falcon. They're on their way to the United States. They're far over the ocean headed toward home at this point."

He looked horrified. "How? How did they get out of the court's custody?"

I put my hands out. "Of course, you wouldn't know. You may not believe this, but Queen Beatrix of the Netherlands had finally seen enough. She came and personally intervened with the court—appeared in person—and escorted them out of the court freeing them."

He was completely confused. "Queen Beatrix? She has no authority to do that. She's a misguided old woman."

"Well she's younger than you and I don't think she's that misguided. In any case, I'm sure you will see the footage of her appearing in court on their behalf. Did you not see her at the airport as well? She came with us to see the Americans off. I'm surprised that you didn't notice her or the American aviators that you took such great pains to capture."

"You better turn this airplane around. Where are you taking me?"

I unbuckled and walked up to the front of the airplane and stuck my head into the cockpit. The two pilots looked at me and nodded as they leveled off at 38,000 feet. One of them handed me a headset, which I put on. On the wire was a button to activate the microphone to allow me to speak to them without yelling. I said, "How's it going?"

"Well, we're lighting up every controller in Europe. They definitely know who we are, and they think we have the two pilots on board. They think we're trying to escape with them. They're not really sure which Falcon has them, but they're trying to pursue us both."

"Pursue us how?"

"They've been spending the last ten minutes trying to persuade us to turn around. We have of course politely declined. So they are sending interceptors. Most likely from Germany; Belgium and Holland are behind us. They'll probably send somebody up from southern Germany. Probably German F-16s."

"What do you make of that?"

"We'll just have to see. If they're serious about this, they should be here in about ten minutes."

I had anticipated such a move; the question was what steps they would take. Would they really shoot down a business jet full of civilians even if they were fleeing the jurisdiction? Good question. But I wasn't quite done. "Let me know if you see or hear anything from them."

I went to the back and opened up the small refrigerator toward the front and pulled out two beers. I took the caps off and handed one to Kevin. I indicated to his other men, who took up all the remaining seats, that they were welcome to help themselves. They did. They took off their helmets and Dragon Skin and ceremonial uniforms and Secret Service suits. They made themselves comfortable and began snacking on the food and beer in the refrigerator.

I sat down next to Kevin and across from Picqué. I said to Kevin, "Pilots say they're threatening to send F-16s up to stop us."

Kevin nodded and said, "As expected. You gonna talk to them?"

"Yeah." I looked over at Picqué. "How'd you do it? How did you know when the Predators would be out of weapons? How did you know that an F-18 would take the assignment and how did you get ahold of the shoulder-fired missiles to take down an American jet? How did you pull that off?"

"Go to hell."

"Aren't you proud of it? Aren't you amazed and pleased that you pulled it off? I just want to know how you did it."

He turned and looked out his window into the darkness and refused to respond.

"That's okay; we have it essentially figured out. And you'll have plenty of time to decide whether you want to talk about it."

He jerked his head back around to glare at me again.

"What do you mean plenty of time? Plenty of time where? To do what?"

"You'll see."

Suddenly over his shoulder I saw the lights of an airplane very close to our own. I looked at Kevin, "Here we go." I moved back up to the front between the pilots and put the headset back on. I hit the intercom, "This them?"

"Yeah. Two F-16s, one on each side. They're really coming on strong. They're transmitting on guard frequency."

"What did they say?"

"That we must turn back and land immediately. That we are to follow them to an airfield, where they will take custody of the two American fliers, return them to the International Criminal Court, and take custody of everybody else on this airplane to be charged with multiple criminal charges."

Suddenly the radio crackled and I heard the pilot's voice in the lead F-16, "Falcon 7, you are directed to immediately turn back and land. If you do not, we will shoot you down."

I put my hand out in front of the two pilots indicating I would respond. I depressed the ICS button the internal communication system, talk to the pilots first. "Am I hooked into the radio? If I hit radio transmit on my headset here will they hear me?"

The pilot in command nodded.

I pressed transmit. "Good evening, gentlemen, what squadron are you with?"

The pilot that I thought was in the aircraft to the left

that was now mere feet from our Falcon was the one I thought was responding, although I couldn't be sure. I could see the glow of his instruments on his visor and oxygen mask. He said in a heavy German accent, "My squadron does not matter. You must turn around and land immediately."

I knew that everything I said was being recorded and would be broadcast worldwide within hours. I wondered what kind of a storm this was going to create internationally, and which way international opinion would fall. But more important to me was which way American opinion would fall. I wasn't sure. I said, "Sorry, we can't. We have an appointment that we cannot miss."

"You have the two Americans from the International Criminal Court aboard and they must be returned to The Hague."

"No, actually we do not have them. They are in the other Falcon that is now far out over the ocean in international airspace. You'll have to go talk to them about that. They are not aboard this aircraft."

"If you do not land immediately, we will have to shoot you down."

"Now, you're not really going to do that and we both know that."

"I have orders to shoot you down unless you turn around."

"That's very unfortunate."

"What are your intentions?" the pilot insisted. His tone seemed to be darkening as his mind began considering that he might be required to shoot down a civilian business jet with many people aboard.

I waved my hands in front of the pilots that I would not be responding to this transmission and that they should not either.

"Falcon 7, come in. Will you be turning around?"

I again shook my head.

We waited. About three minutes passed with the two F-16s bobbing up and down next to us at 38,000 feet. I felt a tap on my back and turned around. It was Kevin. He said, "What's going on?"

"They're about to shoot us down."

"Think they'll actually do it? Think they actually have the order?"

"I don't know. Europeans are pretty hesitant to take a life, any life, regardless of how badly you've behaved. So it's hard for me to imagine they're just going to whack us right now, right out of the sky. But I think we have to assume that they might."

"I agree. Let me know if I can do anything."

Kevin went back and sat across from Picqué, who had now been handcuffed to the seat.

Another two minutes passed, with several transmissions from the German pilot and no response from us. Finally, he pulled back to the left and behind us. The airplane on the right banked away from us to the right and behind us. Our chief pilot said to me over the intercom, "They're taking up shooting position."

"Okay."

"You going to say anything?"

"When they give us our final warning."

"How do you know they're going to do that?"

"It would be impolite not to."

I thought about our position for a minute and asked the pilot, "Do we have a radar detector on board? Can we tell when his fire control radar has locked us up?"

"No."

"Okay then. We wait."

After what seemed an eternity, I heard the German voice again. "Falcon Seven, you have ten seconds to turn back, after which I have been ordered to shoot."

I pressed the transmit button. "I should caution you that Mr. Christian Picqué is aboard. Perhaps you read in the news that he had been abducted in Antwerp. Well, he is aboard our airplane. He is the one who set this entire series of events in motion, and set up our American pilots and flew them to the International Criminal Court. He is aboard. If you shoot us down, you will be killing one of the leading citizens of Belgium."

"How do we know he's aboard?"

"I'll let you talk to him. But there's something else you should consider. If you shoot us down, then you will be the next war criminal. You would be subject to immediate arrest because Germany has signed the Treaty of Rome subjecting itself to International Criminal Court jurisdiction. You would have intentionally killed civilians, myself included, but also Mr. Picqué of Antwerp, Belgium, which is a war crime. You would be responsible for the charge my clients were charged with, excessive killing of civilians. Because as we established at the International Criminal Court, killing one civilian is excessive."

My transmission was met with silence. I could visualize the F-16 sitting some distance behind us, half a mile perhaps, with its radar locked on to our business jet and his missile ready to fire, but now hesitating. Surely he was transmitting to his ground control to see if the authorization still stood with this new information.

After a long pause, his voice returned. "How do we know that he is on that airplane?"

"Hold on."

I turned to Kevin, pointed to Picqué, and motioned for him to bring him forward. Kevin understood and unlocked his handcuffs, grabbed his arm, and pulled him forward. The cabin was tall enough for a six-foot-tall man to stand upright without touching the ceiling, but Picqué was probably six feet three. He bent over and his tie hung down from his neck like a leash, and he came forward toward the cabin. I motioned for the copilot to give me his headset, which he did. I took off my own and handed it to Picqué, who put it on. I put on the copilot's headset. I pointed to the copilot to transmit, and said, "He's on, you may speak with him."

Picqué looked at me and yelled, "I won't talk to them. I won't help you!"

I yelled back, "You'd better, because if they shoot us down, you're going with us."

The German pilot said to him, "Mr. Christian Picqué, are you on that airplane? We need to know whether you have been taken on that airplane against your will."

"Yes," he yelled. "I was kidnapped this morning on my way to a meeting. I was held inside the back of a van and then I was forcibly taken onto this airplane."

I nodded, ripped the headset off his head, and handed the copilot's headset back to him. I put a headset back on my own head. I indicated for Kevin to take him back to his seat. The German officer asked, "Are you being harmed? What is your physical condition?"

I answered, "He's fine. He went back to his seat. He's a little tired."

"You must let him go."

"I certainly plan to do just that. But now you have to decide whether you're going to kill him or let us proceed."

There was no response. I waited on the headset for two or three minutes. Still nothing. I took the headset off, and went to the back of the aircraft. I tried to look out the windows but saw only darkness. I couldn't see directly behind the Falcon. I went back up to the pilots, put the headset back on, and asked, "Is there some way to know whether they're still behind us?"

"Not unless we look."

"How would we do that?"

"I'd have to bank the airplane."

"Do it."

The pilot turned the yoke gradually into a twenty-degree left bank and kept turning until he had turned ninety degrees. He then said, "Hold on," and turned the wings up to almost seventy degrees angle of bank, and pulled hard back on the yoke. He looked up through the top of the front windscreen to see if there was any sign of an airplane. I could feel the aircraft buffeting as it fought to stay at the same altitude in the thin air in which we found ourselves. He then turned the yoke hard back the other way, seventy degrees angle of bank to the right and pulled hard, and again looked up to see what he could find. He leveled the wings, and returned to the original heading. "They're gone."

"Then on we go."

# TWENTY-EIGHT

The rest of the flight was uneventful. There was a lot of discussion between our pilots and the various controllers who handed us off from one area to the other, as our purpose had spread throughout the world, particularly the aviation world. We were now a special case and were closely followed by everybody. Everybody that is until we crossed the border of Afghanistan into Pakistan.

We began our descent with a very helpful and apparently pleased controller. He gave us a straight-in ground-controlled approach. We descended over the beautiful mountains of western Pakistan into a sunny crystal-clear morning. The pilot lowered the landing gear, we slowed, flared just above the runway, and settled onto the pavement at Peshawar with quick screeches from the tires. We stopped and taxied over to the very same building where Kevin and I had stopped with his men on our trip to Pakistan. We came to a stop and the lineman put chocks around our starboard wheels. The pilots shut down the engines and lowered the access door. I stood up with Kevin. I said, "Here we go."

Kevin agreed. "Yup, we're about to find out whether we have pulled this off, or whether we are in deep shit."

He looked at Picqué. "Stand up." He unhooked his handcuff from the seat and handcuffed his hands behind him. The other men and the pilots left the plane before we did, then we went down the stairs. There were six or eight Pakistanis waiting for us, some in uniform.

Kevin shook hands with one of the Pakistani officers. Kevin said, "Thanks for meeting us."

"My pleasure. I will take custody."

Kevin handed Picqué over to him. Picqué looked shocked. "What is the meaning of this?"

"Sir. You are under arrest. You are under arrest for conspiracy to commit murder—of sixty-five innocent civilians—and for conspiracy to kidnap two Americans who were on Pakistani soil and take them to the International Criminal Court without referral or authorization from this country. If there was an issue to be dealt with, it was our issue, not yours. We have not signed the International Criminal Court treaty and do not acknowledge its jurisdiction on our soil. For reasons just like this. We now know that you were working with Mr. Qazi, to create this entire event."

The officer looked at Kevin and me. "We've already arrested Qazi. We were watching his testimony. He said that we do not record our communications. That was untrue. It made me sure that we should review those tapes. I have done so. He told your American major that there used to be refugees at that facility, not that there are. He gave him intentionally false information so that they would drop a bomb on that building killing the innocent Afghanis and Europeans. He has shamed us before the whole world. We of course have now reviewed all his files and communications. It is clear that he was working with Tehrik-i-Taliban. They have long had support of people inside the ISI, but we have not been able to confirm it. Now we can. And not only was money received from a Swiss account, but also from Saudi Arabia.

"We have tried to eradicate these people from our service, but it is a continuing effort. This has nearly wrecked us but we think we have found those responsible." He returned his gaze to Picqué. "So you, sir, will be on trial here. You are the one who committed a war crime, on our soil, and you will be tried for murder. Thankfully, Mr. Qazi has agreed to cooperate in exchange for a promise from us not to employ the death penalty. We are also getting other good intelligence from him. He has been very cooperative."

Picqué shook his head vigorously. "I have no idea what you're talking about. I have done nothing."

"Do you think that we don't know that you were here inside that Falcon 7 waiting for the Americans? Do you think we don't have security cameras around our airport? That we did not see you going in and out of the airplane making cell phone calls? Please sir, give us some respect."

He turned to Kevin. "How can we be of further service to you?"

Kevin put his hands on his hips and took a deep breath. "Well, I think I'm going to have to be here for a while. I don't think I can go back to the United States, and I certainly can't go back to Europe for a long time. Not until they've either given up looking for us or forgotten about our little adventure in Holland. But I have a feeling that may never happen. So maybe I can help you here fight this war on this new front in the western mountains of Pakistan."

The Pakistani officer beamed. "Your help would be most welcome."

"Thanks for your help." Kevin shook his hand and the Pakistani men left with Picqué in tow.

"Let's go," Kevin said to his men as we proceeded through the small private aviation terminal and out into the parking lot where we had been months before. I saw several trucks parked there that I knew had to be with Kevin's men. I recognized some of the men now approaching us.

Kevin turned to me as the other men shook hands, quietly congratulating each other on a job well done. "And what about you?"

"That's the big question, isn't it?" I said looking around. "I can't go anywhere. You're in trouble, but I'm a pariah. If I set foot in the United States or Europe I'll be in prison inside of an hour."

"You're always welcome here," he said. "You're the best planner there's ever been. We'll get you back in shape, get you back on some firearms, and before you know it you'll be right back at it. Let's go," he said as we walked toward one of the trucks.

We got in the back seat of one of the Toyota pickups and drove out of the parking lot with several other trucks and cars. I put my head back on the headrest and closed my eyes. I was exhausted. I thought we might get out of the ICC, but I really wasn't sure we'd pull off the entire plan. I felt my pocket buzz as I ripped my tie off my neck. I pulled my iPhone out and looked at it. Chris Marshall. "Well, well," I said.

"You son of a bitch," he said. "I can't believe you pulled that off. What audacity."

"I didn't know if we'd make it. And thanks for all your nonhelp."

"You've set off a firestorm, Jack. The whole world is going crazy. You better lie low."

"Yeah, I'm going to disappear."

"What's your plan?"

"I'm joining up with Kevin. We're going to do some work in the mountains of Pakistan. I'm going to vanish. You can take over my shitty apartment and take over the lease on my fancy office."

"You should come back to the United States. You're being hailed as a hero by half the country."

"And accused of war crimes by the other half, no doubt."

"Something like that."

"I wish the government had believed in us enough to help out. We hung our asses out there and you just watched. You should have gotten the president on board. I needed your help."

He paused. I waited, wondering what was causing him to pause. "You really think that Kevin calling you early on in the case was just a coincidence?"

I opened my eyes and sat up. "What?"

"You really think that Kevin just showed up out of the blue?"

"You told him to call me?"

"You really think he could come up with a Chinook painted with Dutch colors and Dragon Skin body armor and the most sophisticated nonlethal weapons in the entire world? You think he makes that kind of money?"

"Yeah, I thought he did."

"Good. He was supposed to make you think that."

I looked at Kevin sitting next to me, who was looking out the window. He was pretending not to listen. I said to Chris, "You were behind this the whole time?"

"You're the best planner the teams have ever had, Jack. Everybody knows that. I knew if we linked you up with Kevin you'd come up with a solution. But we had to make you angry enough to actually do it. Had to make you feel abandoned. I sure didn't see this solution coming, it was brilliant. And I also wasn't sure you were going to pull it off."

"And if we hadn't, we wouldn't be having this call."

"Plausible deniability. That's where I live."

"Shit, Chris. You did this on your own?"

"Nope. No way I was going to be the next Ollie North, left to twist slowly in the breeze. People knew."

"Who?"

"Doesn't matter."

"So now what?"

"You know where all this started?"

"No."

"When Humam Khalil Abu Mulal al-Balawi blew himself up on the Agency base in Afghanistan, in December 2009. At FOB Chapman, killing a bunch of very good people. Near Salerno, the base you used to know."

"Sure."

"Had to be working with the ISI."

"And?"

"So we're been drilling down for a long time, trying to find out who his source was. It looks like Qazi was their guy inside the ISI. And you got him. So whatever you want, my friend, just say the word."

I said nothing.

He went on. "Everybody is going crazy here. People are shooting off fireworks. The Europeans are apoplectic. They're accusing *us* of having done this. Can you believe that? But of course we're denying it."

"But you sort of did do it. Indirectly."

"True enough."

"And what about the president? If you get him to sign on to this, then we can claim it was all authorized under the Servicemembers' Protection Act. I can come home and start my life over again."

"I'm working on it. He knows all about it, and he knows if he signs on, he'll have a very angry Europe to deal with, but fortunately you didn't kill anybody. Shit Jack, the *queen*?" He laughed. "How did you come up with that?"

"I figured just enough people have forgotten about Entebbe that it might work. All we needed was a couple minutes of confusion." I took a deep breath and closed my eyes. "So what do you think Obama will do?"

"He has to figure out the political angle."

"Well, until then I'll be in the hills. I don't think I was really cut out to be a lawyer anyway. I didn't realize how much I needed the action. It's who I really am. Makes me feel alive again. I refuse to just get older, get a belly, and grow my hair longer."

"I hear you. I'll call you as soon as it's safe for you to come back."

"Don't worry about me. I won't be anywhere where there's cell phone service. Later."

I hung up, and texted Kristen. "Wait for me. When it's time, I'll come find you." I hit send, pulled out the SIM card, and tossed my phone into the wilderness of Pakistan.

# AUTHOR'S NOTE

When I read a book like this one of the questions that linger in my mind is how much of it is real? Real as in possible. Which laws, procedures, and the like are actually in place? This book is based on a real possibility. The International Criminal Court, founded by the Treaty of Rome, does assert jurisdiction over countries who are not signatories to the treaty. It is true that President Clinton signed the treaty, but then instructed the Senate not to ratify it unless revisions were made that covered the concerns the United States had with the treaty. Those revisions never happened, so President Bush withdrew even the signature of the United States. And because of the possibility of the ICC asserting jurisdiction over Americans in action overseas, Congress passed and President Bush signed the American Servicemembers' Protection Act. The act is still on the books.

For those of you versed in the procedural technicalities of the ICC, I admit taking some editorial license to streamline the story. So don't be too concerned about my descriptions of what the prosecutor wears (I know they actually wear robes), their evidentiary rules, the unlikely assertion of jurisdiction in this story (Afghanistan versus Pakistan), and the like. More importantly, all the listed charges are real and could be brought by a prosecutor of the ICC. Notably in late 2009 the chief prosecutor of the ICC, Luis Moreno-Ocampo, said publicly that he was investigating the conduct of the war in Afghanistan and Iraq, and was examining the conduct of Americans (and others). And as to a European court indicting American leaders for war crimes, it has already happened. In late 2009, Judge Baltasar Garzón of Spain, the very one who prosecuted Chile's Augusto Pinochet, has continued his investigation and charges against former President George W. Bush, former Attorney General Alberto Gonzales, John Yoo (author of the so-called torture memos), Douglas Feith, then deputy defense secretary, Pentagon lawyer William Haynes II, former assistant attorney general Jay Bybee, and David Addington, a former chief of staff to Vice President Dick Cheney. Judge Garzón continued his investigation in spite of a request by the attorney general of Spain to abandon it.

In Belgium, under its statute of universal jurisdiction, cases charging war crimes were filed against President George W. Bush, Dick Cheney, Colin Powell, Norman Schwarzkopf, and Tommy Franks. Those cases were forced to be dropped in 2003 when the law was limited to cases where a Belgian citizen was involved.

Many of the characters in this book are, obviously,

real people, like President Obama and Attorney General Eric Holder. None of what they are doing in this book of course is real; it is a work of fiction. The idea was to put the story into a setting that would give it more authenticity.

# ACKNOWLEDGMENTS

I would like to thank my editor, Marc Resnick at St. Martin's, for his excellent work in helping me with this book. He is a craftsman. I'd also like to thank my long-time agent, David Gernert, for his infallible guidance.

I'd like to thank my wife, Dianna, for her continuing support of my writing. I'd be lost without her.

I would also like thank my daughter, Shannon, to whom this book is dedicated, for her help in editing the manuscript.

James W. Huston
May 2010
San Diego, California